L...

discov...

...swald is ...

...r *Benfro*. Currently, *Dream...* ...eturned on or h... *The Golden Cage* are all available as Penguin ...ooks. ... ...so the author of ...he Detective Inspector McLean series of crime novels ... er the name James Oswald.

...n his spare time James runs a 350-acre livestock farm in ...orth-east Fife, where he raises pedigree Highland cattle and ...w Zealand Romney sheep.

www.jamesoswald.co.uk
Twitter @SirBenfro

The Rose Cord

J D OSWALD

PENGUIN BOOKS

PENGUIN BOOKS

Published by the Penguin Group
Penguin Books Ltd, 80 Strand, London WC2R ORL, England
Penguin Group (USA) Inc., 375 Hudson Street, New York, New York 10014, USA
Penguin Group (Canada), 90 Eglinton Avenue East, Suite 700, Toronto, Ontario, Canada M4P 2Y3
(a division of Pearson Penguin Canada Inc.)
Penguin Ireland, 25 St Stephen's Green, Dublin 2, Ireland (a division of Penguin Books Ltd)
Penguin Group (Australia), 707 Collins Street, Melbourne, Victoria 3008, Australia
(a division of Pearson Australia Group Pty Ltd)
Penguin Books India Pvt Ltd, 11 Community Centre, Panchsheel Park, New Delhi – 110 017, India
Penguin Group (NZ), 67 Apollo Drive, Rosedale, Auckland 0632, New Zealand
(a division of Pearson New Zealand Ltd)
Penguin Books (South Africa) (Pty) Ltd, Block D, Rosebank Office Park,
181 Jan Smuts Avenue, Parktown North, Gauteng 2193, South Africa

Penguin Books Ltd, Registered Offices: 80 Strand, London WC2R ORL, England

www.penguin.com

First published by DevilDog Publishing 2012
Published in Penguin Books 2013
This edition published 2014
001

Set in 12.5/14.75 pt Garamond MT Std
Typeset by Jouve (UK), Milton Keynes
Printed in Great Britain by Clays Ltd, St Ives plc

ISBN: 978-1-405-91769-8

www.greenpenguin.co.uk

Penguin Books is committed to a sustainable
future for our business, our readers and our planet.
This book is made from Forest Stewardship
Council™ certified paper.

For Barbara

*Who first pointed out that 'Sir Benfro' was
a great name for a dragon*

I

In the early years of the Order of the High Ffrydd the slaughter of dragons was continuous. Charged by the word of King Brynceri, inquisitors and warrior priests spread out through the forest of the Ffrydd in search of their prey. Few dragons put up a fight, most accepting death as if they had been expecting it.

But with time the zeal of the order for its task began to wane. Inquisitor Hardy cast his magic upon the Calling Road, setting it to lure what few dragons were left to the monastery, and the order turned to its more familiar role of protecting the realm from foreign invasion. Of those dragons that had not yet been slain some strayed upon the road and were killed. The rest remained in their simple villages, waiting.

It is one thing to take up arms against a monster that steals your sheep and sets fire to your farmstead, but once the raids ended, so the people of the Hendry found there were more important things to do than hunt dragons. Years turned into decades, decades into centuries, and now there are many who truly believe that dragons are nothing but a myth. As they will never see such a creature in their lives, this belief does them no harm.

There are others who know the truth, who understand the real power of these lumbering, flightless beasts. They do not breathe fire, they pose no threat to the kingdom, but they are creatures of the earth who have an innate understanding of magic. And the seat of this magic is their jewels. For in the brain of every living dragon can be found such gems as are beyond description, and to possess one is to be wealthy beyond compare.

Father Charmoise, *Dragons' Tales*

Twigs and branches whipped at Benfro's scales as he ran through the forest. He had no idea where he was, where he was going. There was only fleeing and blind panic. A prickly sensation shivered over his whole body, pulsing and reaching for him with waves of fear as Inquisitor Melyn and his warrior priests extended their search behind him. It felt like an invisible force was reaching out to grab him, and each time it came close he could feel his muscles tense.

A root snagged at his foot and he tumbled head first down a gully. Benfro felt his wings twisting and snagging on bushes as the world rolled around him. Then, with a dizzying splash, he was face down in icy clear water.

The cold shocked some sense into him even as it drove all the air out of his lungs. He sat up in the fast-moving stream, spluttering and gasping but no longer out of control. He could still feel the questing aura of fear, but it was a weak thing, distant. He didn't know how he could be sure, didn't understand how he could feel Melyn at all, but he knew the man was searching in the wrong direction, getting further away with each passing moment.

Slowly Benfro dragged himself out of the water and on to a low silty beach that had formed in the lee of a fallen trunk. With his back to the tree he felt slightly more secure, though tremors of fear still shook him from time to time. He wanted to gather his thoughts, to try and make some sense of what had happened, but all he could see was that blazing blade crashing down. The sudden slump of his mother's body as the life leaped from it.

And there it was. His mother was dead. But she couldn't be dead. She would never have left him like that, so suddenly. She would never have bowed down to anyone, least of all a puny man, and let him chop her head off. Did she love him so little that she could leave him like that?

No, that was unfair. Guilt flushed through him at the traitorous thought. She had done everything in her power to save him, even if that meant sacrificing herself. And what had he done in return? He had run, scared and mindless, creating such a ruckus in his passing that the whole troop had come bounding after him. He had been lucky – he had evaded them for now – but it could all too easily have ended with him dead. Or worse, captured. Then his mother would have died in vain.

His mother was dead.

Benfro thrust his head into his hands, rubbing his scaly palms hard against his eyes. He wanted to scream, to sob, to cry, anything. Surely there was some emotional response in him. But he could do nothing. Nothing except watch as, over and over again, his mother's head fell lifeless to the ground.

He had abandoned her. He had to go back. His mother was wise, a skilled healer. He had learned only a tiny fraction of her craft. Maybe it had all been a ruse. Some near-magic trick to get the men off her back. She would be whole and hearty and waiting for him to come home. She would laugh at him in that loving way and explain how she had beaten them once more. And she would have a hot stew of venison bubbling away on the hearth, with thick crusty chunks of forest bread to help it down.

Benfro's stomach grumbled and he realized that he hadn't eaten since morning. The sky overhead had the dull purple twinge of twilight about it and already a gloom was settling in between the trees. But how could he think of food at a time like this? How could he be so callous?

And what if his mother needed him? What if the magic she had woven required his help to complete? He had to get back to her, had to make her whole again before she really did die.

Benfro picked himself up and clambered to the top of the bank, sensing as he did that the questing presence of the inquisitor was gone. No more the soft pulses of fear, no more the prickling in his skin. Evening birds had begun their noisy chorus, and the first nocturnal animals were scurrying about in the brush. If there were men in the forest now, they were a long way off.

It took less time than he expected to get back to the clearing. For all that his panicked fleeing felt like it had taken hours, he had travelled only a short distance from home. His senses, those inexplicable feelings he had never noticed before, told him that there were no men around, but still he approached the house with care, his hearts fluttering with a mixture of desperate hope and fatal realism.

The house stood in the darkening night, a familiar shape surrounded by familiar sounds and smells. Fourteen years, his life, had been spent in this clearing. Yet as he approached, even before he could see the spot of his mother's execution, Benfro knew that there was something wrong. As he edged round the corner of the house, feeling the comforting rough surface of its walls, he saw the one thing he knew would be there and yet hoped beyond hope would not.

His mother was dead.

Her body lay slumped on the blood-slicked ground.

Her head was nowhere to be seen.

Errol knelt in the small apse off the main worshipping hall that was reserved for novitiates. In front of him the rough stone altar was adorned with candles, flickering in the cold draught that always whistled around the older parts of the monastery. They cast shadows on the uneven mottled surface of the walls and ceiling which moved in small leaps and bounds like wild animals in the depths of the forest. Distracted for a moment, he remembered happy times in his childhood when he would sit in the trees and wait and watch. It was something old Father Drebble had taught him – that if he waited long enough, the animals would come to him. But he was not here to dwell on the past, he reminded himself. He was here to pray.

'I pledge my loyalty to thee, O Shepherd, and to my queen, Beulah of the House of Balwen, and to this most holy Order of the High Ffrydd. I humbly beg thee to give me your wisdom to guide me in my studies and your discipline to resist the myriad temptations laid in my path by the Wolf. I thank you for gifting me the opportunity to serve in thy name and promise always to do thy will in all things.'

Errol savoured the words and the sentiments behind them, revelling in the power and purpose of them and the pledge he made daily. This morning the apse was empty save for himself, and he was able to take some time over his meditations. When he felt ready to face the day, he rose, bowing his head once. Stepping forward, he pinched out the wick of his candle, snuffing the flame that he had lit after his prayers the night before. His candle was large; only a few hours passed between each lighting and extinguishing. Not all the novitiates were as conscientious as he was, and their candles were almost burned to the base. If a novitiate did not graduate to the priesthood before his candle melted completely, he would be cast out of the order. To be candled was the greatest of shames, and Errol had no intention of falling from grace that way. He would work hard and learn all he could learn. He would graduate with honour and serve the inquisitor's will, the Shepherd's will, in whatever way was seen fit. His loyalty was without question – had he not pledged as much even at his choosing?

'No, no, no, no!'

A sharp pain cracked Errol's hands and he looked down to see a raw red welt across them. For a moment he was confused, but then the image of the apse in the worshipping hall faded away, to be replaced by the familiar surroundings of the library archives. Andro sat across a

6

small table from him, glaring. The old man held a thin length of cane in one hand.

'I . . . I was there,' Errol said, trying to shake the disorientation from his mind. 'It was real enough, wasn't it?'

'Oh yes. Very convincing. I particularly liked the bit where you let your mind wander briefly to your childhood. Just the sort of thing a real novitiate would do. But you went too far, Errol. You started trying to justify your loyalty. No one's questioning it, not directly. Melyn won't come up to you and say, "Are you loyal to me?" He's going to look for signs that suggest you aren't.'

'It's too hard,' Errol said. 'I can't keep everything together at once. And that's without Melyn charging around inside my head. Ow!'

'Inquisitor Melyn,' Andro said. 'Or the inquisitor, or His Grace. He may be your enemy Errol, but he's also the head of this order and as such your superior. You will give him respect at all times.'

'Sorry, Quaister.' Errol bowed his head. 'I forget myself.'

'Exactly, Errol,' Andro said. 'You forget yourself. And you must not do that. Never. Your only hope is eternal vigilance. You've got to immerse yourself totally. Be the person who is unquestioning in his loyalty to the order.'

'But I hate the order.'

'No, you only hate what it's become. Remember that. If it helps, imagine that you're loyal to what the order used to stand for – knowledge and learning, the protection of the realm. Now I want you to start again, only this time I'm not going to tell you when I start trying to pry into your thoughts. You should be able to sense me and block me.

Melyn will expect you to block him too. But he won't expect you to succeed for any length of time.'

Errol settled himself down into his chair once more, laid his hands on the tabletop and closed his eyes, building the image of the perfect novitiate in his mind. A sharp rap on the knuckles startled him out of concentration.

'Eyes open this time,' Andro said.

The bulk of Morgwm's prone body lay exactly where it had fallen. Dark blood stained the ground around it, lending an iron tang to the air that reminded Benfro sickeningly of the end of the hunt, when a young hind or stag would be strung up and bled. For once he cursed his keen eyes which could pick up the slightest detail even in the quickening gloom. The ground around his mother's body was trampled where dozens of feet had milled around. The vegetable patch was ruined, the cabbage leaves all torn, potatoes smashed off at the haulm before they could ever have reached a decent size. The swing chair where he had spent many a warm evening listening to his mother's herb lore lay on its side now, shattered beyond repair. And someone had kicked in the door to the house. His eyes darted from this to that, never once settling on the one thing he didn't want to see.

He found his mother's head some distance from her body. A deep runnel in the ground showed where it had been dragged. His hearts leaden, Benfro steeled himself to approach. Any hope that his mother might have been alive, any triumph over the evil terror that had so suddenly swept into his life, had long since disappeared. He had to accept that his mother was dead. She would not be coming back. And now there was an important ceremony to be performed.

Benfro had touched his mother a thousand times before, hugged her, kissed her, held on to her and sobbed into her shoulder as only a son could. Yet it was the hardest thing he ever did to stoop down to pick up her severed head. And as he came close, he saw something that made him first pause, then leap away to retch dry empty heavings into the vegetable patch. For the once proud and beautiful features of Morgwm the Green had been split lengthwise between her eyes, exposing a raw ruddy mess of brain and bone within.

If Benfro had been angry before, it had been tempered by fear. Now his rage was pure and unbridled. Bad enough that these men should kill his mother, but to mutilate her after her death was beyond his comprehension. What manner of beasts could do that? And why? In his fury he lashed out at the vegetables, finishing the job of destruction begun by his tormentors before collapsing in a heap. The tears that had so long eluded him came thick and fast then, great sobs of pain and grief, anger, despair and hatred.

It was a long time before he could bring himself to go back to his mother's mutilated remains. Night had fallen completely by the time he managed to place her head in some semblance of the right position beside her neck. The sticky blood on his hands felt like a curse, and yet he couldn't bring himself to wash it off.

Inside the house the last embers were still glowing in the hearth. For a fleeting instant he felt a flush of guilt, knowing the trouble he would be in for letting the fire burn so low. Then reality came back to him again. His mother was beyond caring about such matters now.

The men had been through the house, turning things upside down as if just for the hell of it. Pots lay broken on the floor, wet and dry contents mingled to a sticky pulp that smelled sour and sweet with the pungent odour of drying herbs. Benfro did his best to ignore it, heading instead for the storeroom at the back.

By the time he had finished covering the prone body with Delyn oil, the moon had breached the treetops, full and fat. Its pockmarked face formed the shadow of a dragon with wings outstretched: great Rasalene, the father of them all. Except that Benfro knew no dragon could have wings that large. His own thin flappings were more of an embarrassment than anything else, a vestigial remnant of some earlier wild creature. Like the lore, the dragon in the moon was a pitiful, pathetic children's tale to his current state of mind. But there was one part of being a dragon that could not be denied.

Finally he went back into the storeroom and fetched the tiny blackwood box, sliding the close-fitting lid from it with trembling fingers. The powder within was darker than the night, as if it absorbed whatever light came its way. It smelled like nothing he had ever come across before, at once alien and exotic and frightening.

Benfro took a pinch between his finger and thumb, feeling its soft coolness almost numb his whole arm. His hearts were racing now, his mind a churning turmoil of grief and excitement and fear. He looked up at the moon-lit night sky, seeing the thousand thousand pinprick lights of the stars, and then with what he hoped was a flourish, he cast the powder over his mother's body.

It was late, the night sky outside pocked with stars where it showed through the low clouds that covered the city. Beulah sat in her stateroom, an empty wine glass in one hand as she stared out the window, thinking. She had tried to contact Melyn earlier in the day, but he was neither at Emmass Fawr nor close enough to Candlehall that she could trace him. She missed his wise counsel and thought, not for the first time, that she relied far too heavily on him. Not that she couldn't make decisions for herself. And this was a big decision, so perhaps it was better to take it in small steps.

As she walked out of her room, two guards snapped to attention and began to follow her down the corridor, maintaining a discreet distance and trying to keep their movements quiet in the silent palace. Beulah ignored them for as long as she could, before turning on them with a fierce fury in her stare.

'By the Shepherd, must you follow me everywhere?' she shouted, knowing that they had been ordered to do just that, and if they failed in their duty they would most likely be flayed alive. 'Oh very well then. Come with me.'

She turned again, stalking down the corridor towards the guest wing. When she reached the door she had been looking for she stopped.

'Now you can stand guard. Make sure no one enters until I am finished in here.'

The two guards saluted and stationed themselves either side of the door.

'Or leaves, for that matter,' Beulah said with a wry smile before opening the door and stepping inside.

The room was dark, only starlight picking out the vague shapes of the furniture. Quietly Beulah stepped around a low couch and two plump armchairs, approaching the great bed that dominated the far wall. By the time she reached its edge, her eyes had adjusted to the darkness. She stood for long minutes, watching the sleeping figure of Merrl, heir to the duchy of Abervenn.

He wore no nightclothes and the sheets covered only half of his body. His chest was broad, the muscles in his arms and shoulders well developed. His ginger-blond hair draped across his face, which was boyish and relaxed in sleep. Beulah sniffed the air, noting the gentle aroma of bathing oils. He was clean and biddable; he would do.

Silently, gently, she climbed on to the bed, reached out and stroked the light golden hairs on Merrl's chest, felt the tension in his stomach muscles and the powerful tautness of his ribs. He woke slowly, which was how she had planned it. Beulah could feel the colour of his thoughts deepen and coalesce as he slowly swam up out of the depths of sleep and into the dream state. Here he was at his most suggestible; here she could mould him to her will. It was just a question of finding the place she already occupied in his mind, finding the image he held of her, and reinforcing it with suggestions of love, loyalty and total commitment.

It was almost too easy. Beulah found that she was already at the centre of Merrl's thoughts and feelings. For an instant she was flattered to be the recipient of so much attention. But its flavour was wrong – this was not slavish devotion. Beulah knew what that tasted like; she dined on it daily from the masses who thronged her halls. No, this was a different thing altogether, something closer to the way her own thoughts had been: dominated by images of her rotting father in the weeks and months before he had finally died. Before she had finally killed him.

Merrl didn't love her; he wanted her dead.

Beulah probed deeper, her hands still caressing the firm body she now straddled. A tumble of images flickered past her: shadowy figures in cloaks with deep hoods standing around a fire in the darkness; an impossibly old man, yet still vital and brooding, undeniably Llanwennog – King Ballah; a young woman, still a girl in many ways, her face unmistakable despite her foreign garb – Iolwen; a dagger concealed in the sleeve of an elegant evening coat. The meaning was quite clear: Merrl was part of a plan to assassinate her and put her sister on the throne.

Beulah sighed. It was predictable, to be expected in many ways, but she had hoped for more from Merrl and the House of Abervenn. She knew that producing an heir was essential, however much the thought of pregnancy and childbirth disgusted her. There were other potential suitors, but none brought the huge financial benefits of a union with Abervenn. Then again perhaps she didn't need to worry about that any more.

She leaned in close to Merrl, her silk gown brushing against his chest as she whispered quietly in his ear, 'Wake, my love. Wake.'

Slowly Merrl's eyelids began to flicker. His body tensed beneath her as he sensed her presence; his hands reached out to feel her soft skin. Then he opened his eyes and gazed dreamily into her face. For a split second he was all contentment and hazy joy as she pushed herself against him, feeling his drowsy pleasure. Then his whole body stiffened, his stare widened in alarm and surprise.

'My queen . . . Beulah . . .' he started to say. She pushed him back against the pillows, silencing him with a single finger to the lips.

'This could have been yours,' she said, sitting up on his stomach and caressing his cheek lazily with one hand. 'You could have ruled by my side. In time a child of Abervenn would have sat on the Obsidian Throne. That won't happen now.'

It was a small blade of light, short like a huntsman's knife, but its blaze chased all shadow from the room. Merrl's struggle was futile and short-lived, his head swiftly parted from his neck. A bloom of warm red spread over the white sheet and sprayed across her face and arms, ruining her gown as, still riding his thoughts, Beulah felt the astonished life leach out of her would-be assassin.

2

In the most ancient days, when dragons were little more than base creatures hunting in packs through the forest, when meat was eaten raw and bloody, when pleasure was taken where it might be found with no thought for consequences or responsibilities, when petty rivalries might lead to murder and none think it of any great import; in those days of pain and anger and ignorance the living flame was considered just another weapon to be used. A dragon might breathe fire simply for the warmth of it, or to defend against the attack, aggressive or amorous, of another.

When the tree gave wisdom to the first of our kind, he looked upon the antics of his brothers with disgust, considering them no better than the wolves that roamed the land in murderous packs. He saw the nature of the land, knew the power that ran through it, and determined to be better. He learned to create with herbs and oils what once had been belched from uncouth lips, and this great knowledge has been passed down through generations of healers. With time, dragons have lost the ability to breathe fire, as they have lost the desire to kill one another for sport.

And so it is that the most important duty of any healer comes after they have finally failed in their calling, as all must fail eventually. For no other may conjure the fire of reckoning.

Healer Trefnog, The Apothecarium

Flames leaped up as the powder came into contact with the resinous oil. They caught readily, fire spreading over the prostrate form and turning it into a great pyre. Close as he was, the flame was not too hot. Not like the wood fire that heated the house. Many was the time Benfro had burned his fingers and, on one memorable occasion, his tail in that. This conflagration was more intense, and yet it seemed to him a friend, welcoming. On a mad impulse he put a hand into the flames. He could see how they consumed his mother's body, but they left him untouched, only tickling his scaly skin.

'Ah Benfro, you should never have had to see this day.' The voice was in his head, all around him, and with the sound of it his hearts leaped in his chest.

'Mother!' he cried. 'Mother, where are you?'

'I am here, Benfro,' the voice said. 'But I am incomplete.'

Benfro looked this way and that, staring at the edges of the clearing and over to the house. A desperate hope flooded him: his mother wasn't dead, she had simply cast some powerful trick that had fooled the men.

'If only it were so, young one,' the voice said, and it seemed to him that there was something not right about it. He knew his mother's voice like he knew nothing else.

It was the first sound he had ever heard. This voice was like Morgwm's, but there was something missing, some depth or warmth he couldn't quite identify.

'I knew as soon as Melyn appeared that my time was finished,' the voice continued. 'The only thing of any importance was to protect you. I could have fought, yes. But I would have lost. At least this way I had time to lay a hiding spell on you.'

'A hiding spell?' Benfro was still clinging to his hope, but a part of him knew it was futile.

'I couldn't let them find you,' the voice said. 'Nothing else mattered. The spell protects you from them; it dampens the fear they cast around and cloaks your thoughts from their senses. But it won't last for ever, Benfro. Already I can feel myself ebbing away. When I'm gone, they'll be able to track you down.'

'Gone?' Benfro asked. 'Gone where? Don't go.'

'Dearest Benfro, I can't stop myself. Melyn has taken a great part of me, and the further he carries it away, the less I know myself. I won't be able to protect you for much longer. You must flee here. Go to Corwen. He will teach you all the things I never had time to.'

'Corwen? Who's Corwen?'

'The dragon who taught me, who taught your father. He is wiser than either of us ever were.' The voice was fainter now, receding as if his mother were slowly walking away.

'Where will I find him?' Benfro asked, feeling the cold chill of night close around him as the flames flickered lower.

'North, beyond the Deepening Pools. Through the

Graith Fawr and across the great forest of the Ffrydd. Keep north and Corwen will bring you to him.'

'But what of the others?' Benfro asked. 'What of Sir Frynwy and Ynys Môn? Can't Meirionydd help?' But there came no answer. The voice was silent, the image in the flames long gone. Like an echo of an idea, it was almost as if Benfro had dreamed the whole thing. But he clung to the memory of that voice. It had been real and it had been his mother. It had been his mother and she was dead.

Cold wind whipped at his feet, swirling the ashen remains of Morgwm the Green. It was as if he were waking from a dream. The grief and the terror, the almost vertiginous feeling of being alone swamped him as the warmth ebbed away. Still that voice echoed in his head, and with a last desperate hope he dropped to his knees and plunged his hands into the ashes.

It was finer than any dust, enveloping him in a cold smoke that was at once peaceful and very sad. Soon he was covered from head to foot in white powder, and each individual mote seemed to be a different memory of his mother. Her smile, the tone of her voice when he was being scolded, the shimmer of her scales as she moved about the kitchen, her frustrated anger, slow to rise and quickly dissipated: all these and more flooded through him as if he was reliving the sum of his fourteen years in as many minutes.

He was so wrapped up in the memories, mingling images of his mother with dreams of great winged dragons soaring through the night sky, that Benfro had the stone in his hand for long minutes before he realized what he had found. It was small, no bigger than a pebble from the stream that burbled around the edge of the clearing. In the half-light of coming dawn it was cold and white, the dust of his mother's ashes dropping from it unnaturally. But it was the feeling that emanated from the tiny jewel that entranced him so.

It was as if his mother were in the next room, singing softly to herself. He could hear her voice but not make out the words. He could feel her presence close by, that reassuring knowledge that no harm would come while she watched over him. He could almost smell her, that familiar taste in the air that was as much a part of his life as his snout. And yet she was always, frustratingly, just out of reach.

Benfro couldn't say how long he knelt there, in his mother's ashes, clutching on to her last legacy. He was at once happy and plunged into the deepest pits of despair. Tears fell freely from his eyes and his breath came in great ragged sobs as slowly the darkness of the clearing lifted. Only when a cool morning breeze picked up the ashes and began to spread them thinly over the ground did he begin to wake from his stupor.

Inside the house the hearth was cold; what grey light filtered in showed a scene he could no longer recognize as home. Everything was broken, trampled, thick with the taint of men. Benfro had few possessions, but those special things he had been given for his birthday he gathered together. The heavy leather bag his mother had used for her herb gathering and to take medicines and poultices to the villagers still hung from a brass hook on the back of the storeroom door, miraculously untouched. It was much sturdier than the collection bag he had woven from fibrous leaves, and had many small pockets expertly sewn into it. Lifting it down, he slipped it over his shoulder, turned his back on the ruination and left the cottage for the last time.

Outside the moon was gone, and to the east he could see the faintest glow of the rising sun, red like the advance of a violent storm. And then he realized that the dawn light was flickering. Too late he remembered what also lay to the east. The village.

As they stepped out of the woods and back into the clearing Melyn felt a shiver course through him like someone had walked on his grave. Many of the novitiates and warrior priests in his small troop felt it too; he could see the shudder pass through their ranks like a ripple on a pond. Even dour Captain Osgal unconsciously made the sign of the crook with his right hand. At the back of the line, flanked by her four nervous guards, the dragon threw back her head and wailed at the sky.

'Halt.' Melyn backed his voice with a mental command. As one the entire troop came to a stop. Even the dragon he had spared ceased her moaning. He looked across the trampled earth to the empty cottage.

'What is it, Inquisitor?' Osgal asked.

'I don't know,' Melyn said, heading for the cottage and the remains of the beast he had slain. 'But something just happened here. Bring the dragon. I want to see how she reacts.'

She was a pathetic figure, limp-winged and pulled in on herself. Even so, her existence filled Melyn with a deep loathing. He longed to kill her, to part her head from her shoulders like he had the other one, but he knew that she was more valuable alive. For now at least.

'What was it that made you cry out, sweet Frecknock?' He spoke her native tongue and she raised her head sharply at the insult, the first sign of rebellion he had seen in her since her capture; the first sign of life.

'It felt like the passing of an old soul, the ending of a great magic,' Frecknock replied in his language, her words stilted and awkward-sounding, her mastery of Saesneg less than complete.

'An old soul? What do you mean?' Melyn asked.

'It's not death. Rather a presence. Someone there but not there. It was as if someone I hadn't seen for many years was there, by my side. Then, all of a sudden, she was gone. It felt like Morgwm.'

Something in the dragon's voice made Melyn look up. She was staring not at him but at a large heap of white ash that lay in front of the cottage. Something had disturbed it, spreading the pile around at one end. There was no sign of the mutilated corpse he had been expecting.

'Where is she?' Melyn asked, his anger rising. 'She was dead. Where's she gone?'

'She's been reckoned,' Frecknock said with what might have been a note of triumph in her voice. 'It must have been Benfro. Poor useless squirt, to reckon his own mother. And she must have been holding on to some great spell right until the end. No wonder I felt it.'

Melyn dredged his memory of dragon lore. He knew something of their reverence for the reckoning. What was it? A burning ceremony where the body was cremated and the soul freed to roam the afterlife? Something like that. Whatever the ceremony, it meant the young dragon could not be far away. He cast his mind out over the surrounding area, feeling for anything that might be a frightened mind. There was nothing. But what if he was not frightened any more? What if he never had been? Mind-fear was a potent weapon when used against a man, but this Benfro had already proved resilient to it.

'How could he have escaped us?' Melyn barked.

'He had his mother's protection,' Frecknock said. 'Even in death, she shielded him.'

'But he won't go far, will he?' Melyn said. 'He won't stray from what he knows.'

'What do you mean?' Frecknock asked.

'This reckoning,' Melyn said, ignoring the question. 'It means a lot to you, doesn't it?'

'It is our way,' Frecknock said. 'We can find no peace in death without it.'

'Thank you,' Melyn said, turning away from the bemused dragon. With a practised leap he swung himself back up into the saddle and spoke to the troop.

'Back to the village, lads, double-quick time. I've a hunch that's where we'll find our young Benfro.'

Benfro picked his way through the remains of the village, trying hard not to breathe in the tarry smoke that rose from the ruined houses. It was a small place; no more than four dozen dragons lived there. Most were older than Benfro could imagine, great lumbering beasts living out their lives in companionable misery. But it was home.

The houses, such as they were, sat back from the track which wound its way through the forest from the south, speared through the great clearing where the ford ran through the river and then plunged east to places Benfro had only ever heard of in stories: Beteltown and the Norne Kingdoms beyond the High Ffrydd, Llanwennog and darkest Mawddwy. To the south lay the Hendry, low country and the lands of men.

Benfro's legs grew heavier at the thought of them: that creeping, paralysing numbness spread through his bones. The warmth and loving sadness he had carried with him since his mother's reckoning flickered and died, a chill wind whipping the ash from his scales and hide. It was more and more difficult to move. He wanted only to stand and wait for the inevitable to happen. If he just stopped, then soon it would be over.

A crashing noise of falling timbers broke through his misery and Benfro shook his head, trying to push the heavy weight of fear from his shoulders. To his surprise it worked. The more he moved, the less he felt trapped and helpless, the less inevitable was his capture and death. The fear still hung around him like flies on a warm day, but it was a frustrated unfocused thing born of anger. He could almost see the burning eyes of the inquisitor searching out over the forest for him, but he knew he could hide from that gaze. He wasn't powerless after all, and he took solace in that small victory, treading lightly through the destruction with a new sense of hope that was as misplaced as it was short-lived.

He found the elder dragons in the great hall. It had been an important building, the focus of village life. Some of Benfro's earliest and happiest memories were of the vast kitchens at the back, where he had found a steady supply of food, some graciously given, most inexpertly thieved. He had sat for many hours at the white-scrubbed table, watching the intricacies of meal preparation and all the while pestering with his endless kitlingish questions whoever's turn it was to prepare the food. All the dragons of the village took their meals in the great hall, meeting twice a day at dawn and dusk to discuss their mundane lives and to listen to the tales of old, when dragons, not men, had ruled the world. If ever there were a symbol of the permanence of dragon culture, the great hall had been it.

And now it lay in ruins.

The roof had collapsed and the massive oak frame lay twisted and black, although even the fire that had cracked the great foundation stones had not been able to get those timbers to burn properly. The glass windows were smashed; the lathe-and-plaster infill scorched and blackened where it had not fallen out entirely. From the midst of the mess, the last of the oily black smoke rose with an inevitable steadiness, lading the air with a heavy, sickening smell of roasted meat.

Pushing aside charred timbers still hot to the touch, Benfro elbowed his way into the building. Slate from the roof lay everywhere, smashed and scorched. The smaller beams had burned merrily and were all but gone now. Their sooty remains lay strewn across scale and hide like a kitling's finger drawings. He could not be sure whether fear had held the old dragons in their seats as they burned or whether they had unanimously decided to die with dignity. Benfro wanted to think the latter was the case, but he couldn't be sure. Not from looking at them.

They sat around the great table, each in the place they had habitually taken. Benfro could recognize them only by their individual bulk: great Sir Frynwy slumped at the head of the table, flanked by the smaller form of Meirionydd; there Ynys Byr, his frail hands covering his eyes at the end; there dark Ynys Môn, defiantly upright, staring straight ahead with eyes whitened by the heat. The others all sat in various contorted shapes, some crushed by the falling ceiling, some almost unscathed but for the look of terrified determination on their faces.

Benfro lowered his head in respect for his extended family. He could feel a rage growing in him then, a righteous fury that demanded release. And yet he was powerless against an enemy that could force these dragons to sit still while they burned to death, an enemy that could conjure a blade of light so sharp it could cleave a head from a neck in one swift arc.

Suddenly the terror was upon him once more. It was difficult to move, his arms and legs refusing at first to answer his call. Looking around at the assorted dead dragons, he felt the panic begin to rise and swamp him. Then he caught those staring white eyes of Sir Frynwy. They cut through him with an accusing glare. This was not how the great Palisander would have reacted to such a threat. The warring brothers Gog and Magog had split the world over who should win the hand of Ammorgwm the Fair. They would not have stood motionless, helpless while a powerful enemy crept up on them.

Benfro could almost hear the old dragon's voice. 'Fight

them,' it seemed to say. 'Live up to your birthright.' He struggled, feeling his legs as things of stone. Slowly, painfully, he managed to inch one foot forward. Then the other. It was like wading through river mud, but with each tiny step it became easier. The panic began to subside, replaced by an angry grasping, as if someone were digging talons into his skull and dragging it back. Shaking his head, Benfro pushed past the charred remains of the dead and through into the great kitchen.

The fire had not burned so much here and the roof still held. At the far end of the room the back door opened out on to the orchard and beyond that the forest. Benfro made his way as quickly as he could towards it. He knew he shouldn't have come to the village. Head north, into the great forest, his mother had told him – if that had been his mother he had heard in the heat of her pyre. It didn't really matter now. There was nothing for him here any more, and at least heading north would take him away from the realms of men. A new life awaited him far from these horrifying deeds, and the beginning of that path was just a few tens of paces distant.

Melyn sat on his horse in the middle of the village, watching impatiently as the novitiates and warrior priests went from house to charred smoking house in search of the young dragon. One by one they returned to the green, their heads shaking. Only the big hall, where all the old dragons had gathered to die, was unchecked. Smoke still poured from the ruins of the roof, and he could feel the heat radiating from the blackened stone.

'You two,' he said to the nearest novitiates, 'go and

check the hall. It's just possible he's stupid enough to be in there.'

He watched as the two young men, hardly more than boys really, crossed the trampled grass and approached the burning building. Then, settling himself into his saddle, Melyn closed his eyes and slipped into the aethereal.

The colours almost knocked him cold. He was used to the world appearing flat and drab when viewed with the mind's eye. Here everything seemed to flow and pulse with life. The trees surrounding the village towered over him like great sentinels, leaning inwards as if to grab him and rip him limb from limb. The houses, burned and wrecked in real life, stood tall and proud as if nothing had touched them. The life shapes of the novitiates and warrior priests were pale and insubstantial things and even his own projection was a mere shadowy glimmer of the body form he normally conjured. For the first time in many years Melyn felt a frisson of fear not of his own making.

It was a skilful working, he had to admit. But the more he probed it, the more he understood that it was as dead as the dragons who had no doubt woven it, the last dying remnants of the glamour that had protected their village from discovery. He had seen through that and now he pushed aside the unease like the slave it was, shifting his focus to the burning hall.

The fire raged as if here in the aethereal it still feasted on the spirits of the dead. The building held its shape memory, flickering and insubstantial among the flames, and the two figures of the novitiates hovered anxiously around the edge, not daring to get too close.

Melyn soared over the pyre, taking in every last detail,

looking for signs of life hiding among the destruction and death. All he could see was flame, billowing up walls, bursting out of windows, feeding greedily on the wasted corpses of the dragons he had slain. With a savage glee tinged with disappointment at not finding the hatchling, he slipped back into himself and opened his eyes.

'There's nothing alive in there, Your Grace,' one of the novitiates said. Melyn recognized him as Clun, Errol's stepbrother. The boy had filled out in the months since his choosing: he was a fit young man now. Perhaps ready to be tested.

'You checked the whole building?'

'What we could get into,' Clun replied. 'There are parts where the roof has collapsed and it's still burning. I tried to sense out any life, but I couldn't feel anything.'

'You have the sight?' Melyn asked. 'Quaister Ffermwyr has told me nothing of this.'

'We haven't begun our formal training yet, Your Grace,' Clun said, dropping his gaze to his feet. 'It's something my stepbrother and I found out about in an old book. We tried it before our choosing. I hope I've not done something forbidden.'

'Far from it, Clun. It's a rare gift you have. I only wish more of my novitiates showed the same initiative. I'll have Ffermwyr begin your instruction as soon as you return to the monastery. But for now, since you seem to show more ambition and drive than your fellows, I've a task for you. Take three novitiates and escort the dragon to Candlehall. You will present her to the queen.'

Clun's face lit up with excited enthusiasm, the boy showing through the young man's face. He dropped to

28

one knee and said, 'Your Grace, you do me a great honour. I'll not fail you.' Then he leaped up like the ground beneath him was on fire and bounded off to round up his team. Melyn watched them gather their belongings together, collect up the bedraggled form of Frecknock and usher her at speed out of the clearing.

'Was that wise?' Captain Osgal asked. 'None of them is experienced enough to deal with a dragon should it decide to be uncooperative.'

'She won't,' Melyn said. 'Her spirit's broken. And besides, what sort of a test of his leadership potential would it be if it was easy?'

'What of the other one?' Osgal asked. How are we going to track it down in these woods?

'We won't,' Melyn said. 'He's been hidden from us by magic, and I don't have the time to try and sort that out right now. But it will wear off soon enough. We'll make best speed back to Emmass Fawr. I need to ride the Calling Road and rework its glamours. I know enough now about this Benfro to make it irresistible to him. Trust me, Osgal; he'll come to us.'

3

Magog, Son of the Summer Moon, was drained by the great magic he had wrought in splitting the world in two, and he mourned for Ammorgwm, lost in the great battle between him and his hated brother. And so it was that he set off for his secret retreat to rest.

He had not been gone long, however, before a new threat to his power became apparent. The men who lived and warred in the Hendry below the Ffrydd began to expand their influence into the great forest. Not the simple men of old; these new warriors were fanatical and ruthless. And more yet, they understood the subtle arts, wielding them with the same grim determination as they did any other weapon. When dragons tried to intervene in the war, they were soon cut down, their jewels hacked from their bleeding heads and taken off as trophies for the king.

Magog rallied his followers against this new threat, but what the men lacked in strength and size they made up in numbers. Long-lived, dragons bred slowly and kept their numbers in strict harmony with the earth. Men multiplied in short years, each generation increasing their numbers more.

The battles raged for years until even proud Magog was forced to admit that the dragons were losing. In an attempt at diplomacy he arranged to meet the king of the men so that some accord might be agreed between them. The day before the meeting the great mage retreated to the place of his hatching to rest and prepare himself. This place he had protected with powerful glamours so that none could find it who had not been invited there. Yet even these magics proved insufficient, for Magog did not meet the king. No dragon has seen him since, and as the years pass by so the deeds of Gog and Magog have passed into myth and legend.

Sir Frynwy, *Tales of the Ffrydd*

The further he travelled from the clearing of his childhood life, the denser the forest became. Benfro thought he had explored far from his home, thought he had ranged through the woods all about the village and the single track that wound its way from somewhere distant to somewhere even further away. In truth three days' walking took him past the last recognizable tree. Soon he wasn't even sure what some of the varieties were. Oak and beech he knew, and huge cedars that spread their needles out in vast dark circles, but here the trees grew straight up into a black canopy too far above to make out. Their trunks were tens of feet thick and spread out at the base with huge root-arches, some forming bowls big enough for him to hide in, should he wish.

Somewhere overhead, Benfro knew, the sun was past its zenith and headed into the western sky to set. That would give him his direction, but at the forest floor it was cool and dark. Occasional strips of light broke through the canopy, their tracks marked by hardy ferns climbing up thick-ribbed trunks, but they were no help in pointing the way. It was many hours since he had crossed the last clearing, a swathe cut through the forest by a massive oak, top-heavy and dead. Even that had been too small a patch of sky to get any feel for the position of the sun. Now he walked on instinct, hoping he wasn't going around in circles.

Hunger was Benfro's constant companion. It sat heavy in his stomach like some bloated bag of gas. He would have tried eating the leaves of any number of plants he came across, but every time he tried to recall one of his mother's lessons, he saw the blazing arc of light swing down in its unstoppable sweep. When he saw any small animals he might have tried to catch, it was only their fleeing backsides disappearing into holes or rustling the thick underbrush around patches of light. He had tried to hunt, but that brought him the memory of past trips with Ynys Môn. The image of his extended family, all dead, was never far from his mind, and whenever it came to the front, walking was the only way to keep from breaking down entirely.

Hunting in this deep wood was not an option anyway. Mostly in the forest floor murk there was nothing but endless hours of thick leaf mould and foot-tripping roots, deadening silence and the occasional bright, squawking flash of some disturbed bird.

Night was well set in when Benfro came across a clearing. He was quite far into it before he realized that the air had a different texture, the silence an echo of gently stirring breeze. It awoke him like a slap in the face and he understood he had been walking half asleep, his mind switched off to dull the horror. He stopped, breathing deeply the cool air. It was sweet compared to the stagnant fug that he had been travelling through for countless hours, and he took a curious pleasure just drinking it in with great gulps, as if he had been holding his breath for too long. Slowly the fog lifted from his mind and he began to take in his surroundings.

The clearing was at least as big as the one that held the village, although there was no obvious sign of any habitation in it. Underfoot lay a carpet of meadow grass pocked with clumps of thicker vegetation difficult to identify in the darkness. The ground sloped away from him down to where a small stream pooled around a great black rock that rose in a jagged point to the sky. As if drawn to it by a curious magnetism, Benfro found himself wandering down the slope towards the pool. Overhead, the waning moon climbed into the night sky, its silvery glow lighting the scene with eerie monochrome clarity.

Close to the water the shadows took on a terrible blackness. The rock pointed up at the stars, as if it were an accusing finger cursing the heavens for the fate of the world. Still, Benfro was drawn to the stream's edge. Pooling around the base of the rock, the water was still and deep and dark, a mirror image of the sky so perfect that it seemed a shame to break it. He knelt on the sandy beach that rimmed the pool and stared down into the night, transfixed by the peace of the place and the weary mix-ture of grief and fear in his hearts.

'What's this?' A voice spoke, clear and strong. 'A dragon should not be so sad.'

Benfro whirled round, losing his footing in his hunger-weakened state. Tripping on his own tail, he fell backwards into the pool with a splash that sent flocks of roosting pigeons clattering up into the darkness from their perches on the towering rock.

'Not very graceful,' the voice said. 'But each to his own.'

'Who's there? Who are you?' Benfro stood up, aware of how heavy his body felt, how sore his feet were even on the soft wet sand.

'No, no, no, that's not how it works.' The voice had a mad mischievous humour in its tone. 'I was here first. I've been here the longer. You tell me who you are and then I might think about telling you about me.'

Benfro waded out of the water, walked around the rock, peered up its obsidian flanks. He might as well have looked for a black stone underground for all the light the moon was casting on the scene.

'Where are you?' He sniffed the faint breeze in the hope of catching a telltale odour. At least he could not smell men, which was some solace.

'Nah, nah. You first. Tell me your name, little dragon.'

Benfro reached up to the rock, looking for a handhold. It was rough and pocked with holes made slimy with pigeon dung. Gritting his teeth, he hauled himself up the steep climb to the top.

'Where are you going? You won't find me up there,' the voice said, a delighted chuckle giving the lie to its words.

Benfro ignored it and continued his task. It was not too difficult a climb for one who had spent his childhood scrabbling up trees. Nevertheless he was out of breath when he reached the top. It was a small flat area, just big enough for his adolescent frame. A fully grown dragon most likely would have ended up taking a quick dive into the pool below. He looked down at the water's surface, perhaps forty feet beneath him, and gasped.

The whole pool was shaped like a dragon's eye staring up at him. The black sky reflected off the water was a shining star-pocked iris, the waning moon a piercing glow of intelligence lurking within. Even the sandy beach contrived to look like the folds of a lower lid.

'Good, isn't it?' the voice said, louder now. It was right by Benfro's side, and he foolishly spun round. He was smaller than an adult dragon, but still plenty big enough to fall off the narrow platform. Especially as the previous occupants had left a considerable amount of greasy droppings underfoot.

'Oops', said the voice, glee obvious in that one simple word.

For an insane moment Benfro teetered on the brink, arms whirling. Even his wings stretched out in a creaking painful reflex spasm, for all the good they would do him. But hunger had robbed him of more than just strength, and it was with a curious weary resignation that he allowed himself to plummet towards the staring pool.

'You have failed your order. You've failed your country. And worst, you've failed me.'

Queen Beulah of the Speckled Face sat upon the

Obsidian Throne in her massive hall and scowled at the two guards prostrated in front of her. From their attire they were Candles, Seneschal Padraig's men. He stood beside them, his face a mask but for his eyes, which stared transfixed like a rabbit's before a hawk.

'Your Majesty, is it fair to blame these men when the betrayal came from . . .'

Beulah's stare was enough to silence the seneschal.

'I need to make an example, Padraig,' she said. 'If not these men, who were supposed to guard me, then who? Would you like to have your neck stretched?'

Padraig shifted nervously on his feet, his composure leaking away under her unblinking gaze. Beulah knew that he favoured closer ties with Llanwennog, peaceful dialogue over war. But he had been as surprised by the plot as anyone. His hold on power was fast slipping away, his influence a pale shadow of what it had been under her father's ineffectual rule. She knew she had won her battle with him; perhaps it was time to throw him a bone.

'You're right, of course, Seneschal,' she said, noting with satisfaction the look of confusion her change of tack threw across his face. 'These men were following orders. It was Merrl and his cronies who started this. Merrl won't be troubling us any more, but I need to know how deep this canker runs. I expect your order to turn all its energies to the task. And we'll have no more talk of peace with Tynhelyg. This plot came straight from Ballah, despite anything his embassy might say to the contrary.'

'Of course, my queen,' Padraig said, bowing his defeat.

'I want all Llanwennog emissaries out of the city by

nightfall,' Beulah said, 'and out of the country by Suldith at the latest.'

Padraig's face dropped further still, but he didn't argue. Bowing his acquiescence, he dismissed the prostrated guards. They scuttled away to the great entrance doors, and as they exited a single stooped figure stepped through. Duke Angor of Abervenn looked like he had ridden all the way from his castle without stopping. He limped up towards the throne, falling to his knees in a cloud of dust.

'My queen, I came as soon as I heard,' he said. 'Is it true? Is my son really dead?'

'Didn't you see his head on the traitors' gate?'

'Traitor? What?' the old man blustered, his pale face reddening as he rose to his feet.

'No one told you?' Beulah asked, lounging in the throne as best she could, putting on an air of indifference as she brushed the edges of the duke's confused thoughts for signs of complicity.

'Tell me what?' the duke asked, turning to Padraig. 'Seneschal, what's going on here?'

'Young Merrl was part of a plot to assassinate our good Queen Beulah and place young Iolwen on the throne,' Padraig said. 'He nearly succeeded too.'

'But this is preposterous,' Angor said, blustering. 'Merrl would never . . . No son of Abervenn would ever . . .'

'But he did,' Beulah said, and in the front of the duke's mind she could see a meeting – indistinct faces, purses of money changing hands. 'Tell me, Angor,' she continued. 'How much have you made this last year in your trading with Llanwennog?'

'I . . . I wouldn't know,' Angor said. 'I don't have much

to do with the day-to-day running of things. I'd have to ask my major domo.'

'But ten thousand gold flocks would be a fair estimate?' Beulah saw the figure in the old man's head, an image of a great pile of wealth spread out on a wooden table in front of him.

'Abervenn contributes handsomely to the royal treasuries,' the duke said. His posture was changing; for an old man he gathered his wits quickly, Beulah could see. His eyes darted from side to side, searching for guards, no doubt. At the moment there were none in the great hall, Beulah had seen to that.

'And would it continue to do so, if the throne were subservient to Tynhelyg?' she asked. 'Or would it switch its allegiance more openly to Ballah and his clutch of little princes?'

'My queen . . . these accusations . . .' Beulah noticed how with each word Angor took a step closer to the great throne. She hadn't seen him step up on to the dais, but now he was no more than a couple of paces away. He held up his left hand in supplication, making strange distracting motions in the air with his outstretched fingers like a cheap conjuror. But Beulah knew the first rule of false magic and ignored the diversion. She saw in his mind exactly what he planned and watched in appreciation at his skill as he palmed a thin blade with his right hand.

'I don't think we need to pretend any more, Angor,' she said. 'You never wanted war with Llanwennog; that would disrupt your lucrative trade. You'd much rather see the kingdoms united. Well, I'd like to see that as well, but under my rule.'

'You'll destroy us all. I'm doing the kingdom a favour,' the duke said. His words weren't even finished before he sprung into the air with surprising agility, stiletto ready to plunge. Padraig let out a frightened yelp of alarm, but Beulah simply smiled. She conjured a blade of light with a lazy thought, swinging it in an arc faster than a blink, back and forth with a thrill at the power she wielded. Momentum carried the duke forward still, but he landed on the floor at her feet in several wet pieces.

'Your Majesty,' the seneschal said after a long silence.

'Oh come now, Padraig. Don't tell me you've never seen someone wield a blade of light before.'

'But, my queen. You're –'

'A woman, Padraig? I know you've taken a vow of chastity, but I assume you know something of the difference between the sexes?'

'But it's not permitted. It's not –'

'Nonsense,' Beulah said. 'It's no more than bigotry and superstition that prevents women learning magic. I am queen; I will do as I please.'

'Of course, Your Majesty,' Padraig said, his eyes fixed on the glimmering blade. Beulah extinguished the light, feeling a heady surge of power as she absorbed it back into her self.

'Now, a proclamation. From this moment forth all Abervenn lands are forfeit to the crown, as is the title that goes with them. Find me Melyn; I need him to dispatch a trusted captain to oversee the dukedom until I've rooted out this subversion.'

'Your Majesty, I thought you could communicate with the inquisitor at will,' Padraig said.

39

'And yet you complain about the blade?' Beulah laughed. 'It's true I can contact Melyn, but I need to know where he is first. Otherwise I'll just waste too much time trying to find him. The last I heard he'd gone off on some dragon hunt. Send word to Emmass Fawr that I must talk with him urgently. I need to find out what's going on in Llanwennog.'

'I'll send someone immediately,' Padraig said, bowing.

'Good.' Beulah slumped back into the throne. 'And get someone in to clean up this mess.'

It seemed to take longer than it should have done for him to hit the surface of the water. Benfro had spent many a happy afternoon diving off rocks into the river, chasing and occasionally catching fish; he knew instinctively how fast he should plummet. Perhaps it was the darkness making distance seem shorter than it really was. The muscles between his shoulders at the roots of his wings felt heavy and strained, wind tugging at the folds of skin as if he might have actually flown. When he hit the water, it was not a triumphant pool-emptying eruption so much as an almost graceful controlled entry. Still, he had fallen a long way, and the force of his impact knocked most of the wind out of his lungs. The water parted for him, then closed in over his head and sucked him down deep.

Surprisingly warm, the dark pool embraced Benfro like his mother. He was weightless after what seemed like an eternity of aches and pains. The grief and fear fled his mind and left him with a glow of contentment. All he wanted to do was drift slowly to the bottom and the sleeping friend who waited there for him. So he couldn't breathe. Well, breathing was overrated really. Much better to just relax, settle into the depths with his new friend. Soon they could be together for ever.

Down and down he drifted, calm and relaxed. There was something he ought to be doing, he was sure, but it couldn't be that important or he would be able to remember. So he just settled, the silty bottom of the pool easing aside to accept the bulk of his battered, drained body.

In the murk he could see strange ghostly shapes spread out around him. They looked like sticks reaching out of the sand. Strangely symmetrical fingers strung with gently swaying fronds of weed. Closer, a rock caught his eye, such was the perfection of its whiteness. It was domed at one end, tapering to a thick truncated tube at the other. Black spots of pondweed on its surface looked like eye sockets, nostrils, perhaps an earhole and a jagged, violent crack where someone had taken a heavy axe to a sleeping skull, rolling the murdered body into the welcome embrace of the pool. With a gasp that sent the last few precious bubbles of air spiralling up from his nostrils, Benfro realized that he was looking at the skeleton of a long-dead dragon, discarded like some twisted rag doll on the bed of the pool. And deep within the broken skull a single small shining jewel glowed a bitter red. He lurched back awkwardly and half breathed, half gulped with surprise, suddenly all too aware that he was completely immersed in water.

Benfro's stomach churned. The pain rolled up through his throat; he tasted bile at the back of his mouth. He couldn't breathe. A dreadful weariness pulled at him. His mind started to dull again; thoughts so hard to force through the jelly that was setting all around him. All he could see was a pale light, far away and murky. It was a misshaped disc blotched with darker grey, the image of a dragon with improbably large outstretched wings. The moon. He had to reach for the moon.

The image was turning fuzzy, hard to focus on through the thick, warm, enveloping goo that surrounded him. Yet somewhere Benfro could feel a rhythmic pulsing ache. Was it his hearts? Could they beat so slowly? No, something else surged against his back, pushing him forward, up towards the light. Away from his new friend.

It cried to him, pleading for him to come back, digging talons of love and want deep into his soul. But it was a cruel, selfish want, Benfro knew then. It was a heartless lonely thing that wanted only to possess him. He concentrated instead on the pulsing rhythm, each beat dimming his sight but bringing him closer to the moon.

He struggled to focus on the steady beat that rippled along his body. All he could feel was the water sliding over his scales and the dreadful lonely longing that wanted to pull him back down to its despair, a companion in misery for all eternity below.

With a last effort that he was almost unaware of making, he burst from the surface of the pool like an osprey. His wings, which had propelled his bulk through the thick water, grabbed at the too-thin air, dragging him almost fully clear before his strength failed entirely. Still, they carried him far enough to crash into the shallows, sending a huge wave of water up the sandy beach. Crouched on all fours, it was all he could do to lift his head above the ripples, but somehow he managed it. He coughed up what seemed like gallons of water, retching with the effort of clearing his lungs. Then, finally, he could breathe in great gulps of night air.

He sat, eventually, in the cooling stream, just breathing deep breaths and occasionally turning to cough and retch out more water from his lungs and stomach. For a long while it was quiet, only the gentle night breeze stirring the grass and bushes close to the water. As his mind cleared and he recalled his dreamlike experience under the water, Benfro was not really surprised to hear the voice come back to him.

'I'm impressed,' it said, sounding a little less like a petulant kitling, a little more scary. 'It's a long time since I've been impressed.'

'How long?' Benfro asked. 'How long have you been down there – here – wherever you are?'

'I don't know. Days are just days when you're dead.'

'Who are you?' Benfro asked. 'What are you?'

'Why should I tell you? You've given me nothing.'

'You tried to kill me. I think you owe me an explanation at least.' Benfro shivered, only partly in fear. The water was cold now, sapping what little heat his empty body could muster. Slowly, painfully, he began to inch forward towards the beach. Each movement was an incredible effort of will and brought with it only increasing weight as he hauled himself on to dry land. The gentle night breeze had stiffened now, its chill tendrils plucking at his wet scales and skin.

'True.' The voice seemed oblivious to his plight. 'But

'I'm still not going to tell you my name. A name is a powerful thing. If I give you that you could just give it to anyone you meet.'

'So?' Benfro asked. 'What if I did? How many dragons have come this way since you died? How many men?'

'Men?' the voice said. 'What would I care of men? Other than for a nice meal of an evening. Oh yes, time was I could eat a dozen young maidens and still be hungry. Ah me, those were the days.'

Confused and weary beyond his comprehension, a sudden mad thought flitted through Benfro's mind then. 'Are you Corwen?' he asked. Silence greeted his question and for a moment he thought he had been hallucinating, had dreamed the whole episode. Then the voice came back with a spiteful little cackle.

'Corwen? Hah! What kind of a name is that? Come, little dragon child, you can do better than that if you're going to play guessing games. Try something a bit grander. Try Palisander of the Spreading Span, or Llys Frôn the Munificent.'

Benfro recognized the names from Sir Frynwy's tales. They were the bedrock of all dragon mythology. 'You must be the great Gog, Son of the Winter Moon, then,' he said, picking the first name from one of the stories that came to his mind.

The water in the pool started to glow red, a darkening of the star-pocked night blackness above that grew from dull blood through the angry heat of burning coals to the full-blooded rage of a forest fire. The water boiled, first great bubbles, rising and bursting singly, then smaller eruptions spreading over the pool's surface like a sudden shower of rain. Steam billowed into the cold night air as a heaving foam erupted. Violent orange light flooded over the slopes that climbed away to the distant trees, picking out the accusing rock in sharp relief. Benfro could feel the heat emanating from the pool even as he scrabbled away from the edge as fast as his weary legs and arms would take him. He backed up into the night, realizing too late that his path was blocked by thick undergrowth and he could go no further. Had he looked round he might have found an escape route but he could not take his eyes from the sight in front of him, could scarcely move for fear.

The water rose up out of the pool in a glowing red column. It piled up higher and higher until it towered over the rock, swaying slightly. From his ringside seat Benfro could see great salmon writhing around in the boiling water, their eyes turned instantly white with the heat. Water splashed into the vacant pool from the stream, gushing up in great gouts of steam as it hit the bone-dry bottom and the red-hot bones of the long-dead dragon. Its skull was a blaze of fire, the jewel within an evil crimson.

'You dare utter that name here?' the voice screeched, a terrible sound that filled Benfro's head, chased away any thoughts he might have had. The column of water spread out now, taking on the shape of a huge dragon, wings outspread as it dived on its prey. Dived on Benfro, who could do nothing but watch in helpless terror.

Then, as suddenly as it had started, the great edifice collapsed. For an instant Benfro thought he could see thick veins of fire pulsing through the ground to focus on the pool. But as soon as he noticed them, they were snuffed out, gone as if they were no more substantial than an after-image from staring too long at the sun. Tons of scalding water plunged back into the pool. It fell with a crash that rang around the clearing for long seconds, fading finally to leave the echo of a mournful wail, a last desperate cry of rage and frustration and fear and surprise.

4

An unreckoned jewel is a terrible thing. Quite apart from the tragedy of any dragon dying alone and so far from others of his kind that no healer can be informed of his demise, a dragon's jewel not cleansed and set by the living flame will slowly melt away as its essence leaches back into the Grym. Jewels thus left still hunger for experience, but with time the good nature of the dragon is gone; only his base desires are left, and with them a desperate, mad craving for survival. Unreckoned jewels glow red with a thirst to know everything, and should you inadvertently touch one that has lain for more than a few years, it will latch itself on to you with a power few know how to break. Unchecked, such a jewel will slowly inveigle the corrupted character and personality of its dead owner into your self. This process is insidious and often unnoticeable until it is too late to rectify. In time you will cease to be, and an evil shadow of the dragon whose jewel you have touched will live again in you.

The only sure way to reverse this process, or at least halt it, is to conjure up the living flame and reckon the jewel. Such should as a matter of course be done with all haste when a fallen dragon is found, but in those rare cases where there is nothing left of the body, or where the jewels have been removed to a distance and the remains left unmapped to rot, then reckoning will not work. For the living flame must have both body and jewel to set the two together. There are mages who profess a knowledge of how to untie the binding between an unreckoned jewel and the dragon it is trying to usurp, but they are few and spread far in all the realms of Gwlad.

Healer Trefnog, The Apothecarium

Errol didn't see the inquisitor ride into the main court-yard with his troop of novitiates and warrior priests. He was tucked away in his room, deep in the library archives with Andro, practising the art of thinking deception. It wasn't until word came down that his presence was required in Melyn's study that he realized his time had come.

'You can do it, Errol. Believe me,' Andro said. 'Just stay focused; don't let your mind wander.'

Put like that, it sounds easy, Errol thought as he hurried through the cold stone buildings ever upward to the tall building where the inquisitor's private rooms were situated. The truth of it was far more complicated, and he spent the time reinforcing the view of the world that he had constructed until he almost completely believed the lie.

'Come,' Melyn said the moment Errol knocked on the black oak door. He entered and found the inquisitor slouched in a low-slung leather chair, a goblet of wine in his hand.

'Errol, it's good to see you,' he said in perfect Llanwennog.

'I'm glad you've returned unharmed,' Errol replied in the same tongue. It was not the test he had been expecting, but then he remembered their last meeting, when the inquisitor had bid him learn the language of the enemy so he could become a spy.

'Have a drink, lad.' The inquisitor pointed to where a jug stood beside an empty goblet on the table. Errol poured a small measure of wine and took an even smaller sip.

'How was your hunt, Your Grace?' he asked, again in Llanwennog. 'And how is my stepbrother, Clun?'

'So you know about that,' Melyn said, fixing Errol with his yellow stare. Errol felt the itching in his brain that told him the inquisitor was trying to probe his mind. Concealing his disgust with all his will, he tried to imagine a lust for the kill, a burning desire to destroy all dragons.

'It's been the talk of the monastery since you left,' Errol said. 'They say you went to fight an army of dragons.'

Melyn laughed, and the itching in Errol's brain fell away slightly. 'Not an army, that's for sure. More a ragtag collection of decrepit remnants. I did them a favour dispatching them all. As for young Clun, I've sent him on an errand to Candlehall. We captured one of the beasts, younger than all the rest. He's taking it to the palace to present to the queen.'

For a moment Errol's concentration wavered. He remembered the night he had somehow travelled across the great forest and seen the dragon Melyn had gone to hunt. Had she died, or was she even now being dragged along the road to the Neuadd for an even worse fate?

'You're interested in dragons?' the inquisitor asked, and the itching in Errol's brain started again. From nowhere he knew he conjured up an image of a tall man wielding a blade of pure white light, swinging it through the thick neck of a recumbent dragon, parting its head from its body with a single blow.

'I recently came across a manuscript written in their language,' he said, trying to convince his mind that the disturbing image was one he applauded rather than abhorred. 'Quaister Andro said he'd teach me how to read it.'

'Perhaps, when you've finished your other studies,' the inquisitor said. 'But for now I want you to continue practising your Llanwennog. It's good, but not good enough to fool a native for very long. You might pass for a borderer in the north, a northerner at the border, but in Tynhelyg you'll just sound out of place.'

'Do you want me to go to Tynhelyg?' Errol asked.

'Not today, no.' The inquisitor chuckled again. He drained his goblet and held it out. Errol quickly refilled it. He bowed, not daring to hope that the interview was over so soon. 'Is there anything else you need me for, Your Grace?'

Melyn was about to say something, but a knock at the door interrupted him.

'Come,' he barked. Captain Osgal entered, stared hard at Errol and then bowed to the inquisitor.

'A messenger has just arrived from Candlehall, Your Grace. Queen Beulah wishes to speak with you as soon as possible.'

Melyn let out a sigh, then stood up and put the full goblet down on the table beside the jug.

'Very well.' He turned to Errol. 'Go now, boy. But remember what I've said. I'll be testing you regularly so you'd better work hard.'

Errol bowed, not daring to say a word, then turned and made to leave. As he was stepping through the door, a heavy hand caught his shoulder. The captain bundled him out into the corridor and pulled the door shut behind him.

'Don't you think you've got it easy just because the old man likes you,' he said. 'I'll be watching you from now on. One step out of line and you'll be out of the order. Got me?'

Errol nodded, still not daring to speak. A small part of him wondered how he might provoke the captain into carrying out his threat, but he knew the inquisitor would never allow him to leave. At least not alive.

'Well don't just stand there. Get back to your books.' Osgal clouted Errol over the head so hard and fast his knees buckled. No need to be told twice, he ducked his head and ran.

The sun was high overhead when Benfro woke. He lay still for some time, staring at the slowly moving clouds and trying to work out where he was. Every part of his body ached. A deep pain throbbed in his head as if he had been drinking some of his mother's more potent potions. For a moment he wondered how much trouble he was in with her, sleeping out like this. Then the memories came flooding back and he had to move just to overcome the helplessness.

He sat up, woozy and unstable, and gazed at the sight in front of him. A tall rock stood at one end of a still, calm pool, which was edged on his side with a sandy beach. It was just like the strangely realistic vision he had dreamed during the night. It had been a dream, of course. Nothing like that could really have happened.

Then he saw the fish.

They lay there, dead, on the beach, in the grass and draped over the short scrubby bushes that pocked the clearing. Some had been pecked at by birds; a lone crow was tugging at one nearby, trying to drag away a fish five times its weight and in the main succeeding. Where it was going to take it to, Benfro couldn't think. It wasn't important. The dream was important. Except that it hadn't been a dream.

Slowly he stood up, feeling oddly unbalanced, willing the ground to stop swaying. After a few minutes it complied and he stepped forward to the water's edge. A slight current ran through the pool, keeping the water fresh and clean. Benfro knelt and splashed a cold cupped handful over his face. Nothing stirred in the black depths and no voice spoke to him. Only his reflection looked back, a thin haggard thing that he almost didn't recognize. How long had he gone without food? A couple of days at most. Surely that wasn't long enough to have had such a profound effect. A sudden fairy-tale thought flitted across his mind. What if he had stumbled into the clutches of some evil spirit and was trapped in a night that lasted a thousand years?

The nearest dead fish to Benfro was a large salmon, easily as long as his arm. Such a beast would have been a splendid trophy back in the village, a testament to his skills as a hunter. Reaching out, he hauled it closer, noting as he did that there was no smell of rotting. No more than a dozen hours had passed since it had died, so he had not been sleeping for days. Its eyes were white, and he remembered the water boiling as it took on the dragon form. Carefully, he slit its belly with a sharp talon, removed the entrails, gills and head. The flesh was pink and firm, but cooked rather than raw. It wouldn't have bothered him either way. Grateful for food wherever it came from, he ripped chunks from the body and shoved them into his face.

Nothing could have tasted better. Even gulping down great lumps with indecent haste, Benfro was aware of the sweetness and succulence of the meat. Still, his stomach lurched and groaned at the sudden introduction of food. He took a long drink of the pool water and settled down to a more measured devouring of the fish.

Belly full and with the warm sun at its zenith, Benfro could feel the tugs of weariness pulling at him again. He was stiff and sore from the previous night's exertions and needed to stretch. His wings in particular felt heavy and ponderous. He had never really noticed them before, in the same way that he had never really noticed his hands. His wings were there. They had always been there. And if they had changed at any time in his life it had been such a slow change that he was unaware of it. But now his wings felt different.

For a start, they felt. Even folded, he could sense the rippling heat of the sun on them, the gentle tickling of the midday breeze. The muscles in his back were bunched and solid, as if they had grown while he slept. He tried to flex them, stretch them back into the smooth shape he remembered, but instead of the familiar shrug which should have folded the thin vestigial flaps against his side, Benfro found himself spreading them.

It was like suddenly discovering he had a second pair of arms. And they were so much bigger than he could believe. Benfro stood tall and stretched wide. He looked left and right, marvelling at the sight. Surely these were not his wings. His were pathetic. These were magnificent great things. Tiny scales of green and gold fringed their leading edges, spreading back in ever larger patterns. He could feel the tips, like fingers he could use to grab the wind and twist it to his every whim. These were the stuff of his dreams.

For a moment he felt he could leap into the sky, catch the air on these massive sails that flowed from his body. Then the crushing weight of skin and bone dragged him earthwards. The middle of his back burned with an agony of muscles stretched beyond their capacity. He collapsed into a huddle, his wings folding themselves back tight to his body in a reflex action.

The pain was excruciating, like someone was stabbing him with hot knives, over and over again. It dimmed his sight, brought tiny sparks of flying light to his vision. He knew with a deadly certainty that he was going to pass out.

Melyn looked at the scrap of parchment in his hand. It was small, designed to roll up and fit around a messenger bird's leg, and the report on it was written in a tiny hand in a coded language. It had taken him two hours just to decipher the message, which bothered him. And try as he might, he couldn't think past the problem it contained. He felt tired and unfocused, as if the trip to the dragon village had been more like a summer's campaign. Even drawing power from the lines no longer energized as once it had. There was no denying it: he felt old.

The stone under his knees was cold and hard, the single candle flickering in the permanent draught that whistled through his private chapel. Only the glittering of the flame in the tiny polished gem set in its ring of gold in front of him held any warmth. Trying to quiet his frazzled mind, the inquisitor began to recite the words of the Shepherd's Prayer, taking comfort from the simple catechism.

'Who is my comfort through life? The Shepherd and him alone. Who shows us the true path and protects us from the corrupting Wolf?' As the familiar words soothed his mind, so Melyn began to relax, slipping at last into a state of grace where he might communicate with his maker. It had been long months since last the Shepherd had spoken to him; there was much he would have liked to discuss, but he knew that his god would reveal himself only when his servant was deemed worthy.

'Fear not on that account, my faithful inquisitor.' Melyn shuddered inwardly as he heard the familiar voice. His aches and pains disappeared; his body felt at once renewed.

'You are concerned by the betrothal of Princess Iolwen to Prince Dafydd of the House of Ballah,' the voice of the Shepherd said. 'And you worry about the factions that plot the assassination of Queen Beulah so that her younger sister might take the Obsidian Throne.'

Melyn knelt in reverent silence, bathing in the presence of his lord and the sure knowledge that, at this moment in time, he was worthy.

'Princess Iolwen will marry a man of the Hendry,' the voice continued. 'But you must take steps to remain in control of the situation. Send a spy to Tynhelyg. Someone who can enter the royal apartments. Someone who can blend in, speak to her, dissuade the prince if necessary.'

'And what of the queen? I fear for her safety,' Melyn said.

'Is your faith become so weak you no longer trust me to safeguard the throne?' The voice was mocking, but the inquisitor still felt the surge of guilt. He would scourge himself for his lapse.

'You have already done what I intended you to do to protect Queen Beulah,' the voice said. 'The gift you have sent her will prove more valuable than even you realize.'

'The dragon?' Melyn asked, but he could feel the departure of the Shepherd as a lonely emptiness in the room, a seeping cold that was almost fear, his joy had been so intense. Always his god left him so: burning with a desire to carve the world in his image, but also hollow and empty that the Shepherd no longer filled him with his presence.

Slowly, but with greater ease than when he had knelt, Melyn rose. He made the sign of the crook, bowing his head once more to the altar, then pinched out the candle, lifted the reliquary and placed the ringed finger back in its leather box. By the time he reached the door, his mind was once more calm and collected. He knew what needed to be done. As ever, the loyal Captain Osgal stood guard.

'We must put a spy into the Llanwennog royal

household. I need someone to put Princess Iolwen off the idea of marrying Prince Dafydd. Or, failing that, to arrange a little accident for the prince.'

'How are you going to get someone that close?' Osgal asked.

'Duke Dondal's sympathetic to the House of Balwen,' Melyn said. 'For enough of Queen Beulah's gold, he'll introduce one of ours as a page to the court at Tynhelyg.'

'A page? That would mean someone young,' Osgal said, a look of distaste crossing his face. Seeing it reminded Melyn of Osgal as he had been years ago, when first chosen for the novitiate. Melyn had favoured him then and now it seemed the captain harboured jealousy in his heart. It was of no matter. Either Osgal accepted that he was no longer the inquisitor's favourite, or he would find himself posted a long way from home.

'Fetch the boy Ramsbottom to my quarters,' Melyn said. 'I have a task for him.'

Benfro dreamed of the dragon that called himself Magog, Son of the Summer Moon. He knew it was a dream this time and not some fantastical reality. The dragon was alive for one thing, not a collection of bones washed clean by uncounted years of running water. He was a huge beast, Magog. Far bigger than any dragon Benfro had ever met before. And far grander. His hide was as dark as the night and his scales were a polished black so shiny that they reflected moon-white. He was standing in the clearing next to the rock and staring into the sky. Reaching up, he could put one massive hand on the top of the rock where Benfro had precariously stood the night before, such was his size. But it was his wings that were the most magnificent thing about him. Unfurled, they were each as big as the house of Morgwm the Green. The scales along their edges were in turn tar-black and white as chalk. In the middle of each they patterned to form a perfect image of the full moon, its own dragon wings outstretched. And surely these were the wings of the dragon who lived in the moon.

Benfro watched in awe as the great beast folded his wings, looked once more up into the sky and then settled down beside the rock to sleep. No sooner had he fallen into the rhythmic breathing of rest, or so it seemed, than a great wind buffeted the clearing, ripping at the bushes and flattening the grass. In his dream Benfro looked around from the security of his resting place. He was much smaller than the bush in which he hid and well able to avoid being seen by the creature that flew down towards him. Still he was gripped with a fear far greater even than the inquisitor could induce.

At first he thought it was a crow, or perhaps one of the kites that occasionally soared above the village, mewling at the sky. But it was far too large to be such a bird. Its head was easily as big as he was and its eyes glowed with an evil intelligence. It landed only a few paces away from Magog, shaking the ground on contact. Still the great dragon slept on, unaware of the stench that filled the air. Benfro gagged as the curious beast stepped forward with an odd chicken-like gait. Its legs seemed ill constructed and were covered in a thick black coat of glossy hair like that of a boar. Its feet were bizarrely misshapen, with great fleshy claws, blunt and curled as if arthritic with age.

Benfro knew what was going to happen next. Still he was not prepared for the sudden, unprovoked brutality of the attack. One moment the bird was standing over the sleeping dragon, just looking at it with that quizzical manner crows have when they find something just recently dead to eat. The next it had seized a huge rock in its foot, more like a hand Benfro realized, and dashed it down on Magog's head.

There was no recovering from that blow. Even a dragon as large and obviously bone-headed as Magog stood no chance. His skull broke with the first blow, bright red blood gushing out of the wound. The bird creature dropped its rock on the sand and heaved against the quivering corpse, rolling it into the water and pushing it out until it cleared the shallows. It stood, knee deep and watching as the uncomplaining form of Magog slipped slowly under the surface. Great bubbles rose in a slow procession, bursting like dropped eggs in the reddened water. After what seemed like for ever, they stopped and the bird stalked out of the river. It strode up the beach, gathering speed with each stride. Benfro was convinced it had seen him, was running to kill him, the only witness to the murder. But it passed him at a gallop, desperately flapping its great wings and leaping into the air then falling back to earth.

It took a long time, running, bounding into the air, then crashing earthwards to try again. Each leap took it higher, kept it aloft longer. Each landing was lighter, a little spurt of dust in the increasing distance, until finally, just short of the trees and avoiding a painful collision, the creature was aloft. It banked, screeching, and headed back for the rock and the pool, slowly fighting its way higher and higher into the sky. From his hiding place Benfro looked up at its passing and for a moment felt terror bite into him again as he realized how exposed he was from above. But the creature did not see him, even though it circled the pool for a few moments before heading off towards the setting sun.

Almost at the same instant as the creature disappeared from Benfro's vision, the bubbles started to rise once more in the pool. Slowly at first, the surface boiled and churned, the water lifting into a vast dome that parted to reveal the great dragon.

Its head was smashed in, blood and brain dripping from the ruined side of its skull. Still there was a fire in its one good eye, and it fixed Benfro with an uncompromising stare.

'You have bested me, little dragon,' Magog said. 'Or maybe my anger has finally devoured me. Either way, I owe you a debt of gratitude. I cannot count the days I have lain here, unknown, forgotten, powerless. You have woken me and you have shown me the simple truth I could not bring myself to face.'

Benfro wanted to ask what this was, but in his dream state he could only watch, listen, absorb. He was powerless to act.

'You've shown me that I'm truly dead, little dragon,' Magog answered as if he had heard the question. 'You'd think one so wise and powerful as I would know something like that when it happened, but in my arrogance I could not accept it. So I've lain at the bottom of this pool these countless years, trapped by my anger and hatred, by my own proud sense of injustice. For what could be less fair than the mightiest of dragons laid low while he slept by a mindless carrion beast?'

The great ruined dragon was sinking now, the pool slowly reclaiming its prize. In his dream Benfro was full of questions. If this truly was the Magog of legend then what of the other great dragons? What of the tales of fabulous courage and daring, of love and hate, trust and betrayal? All the stories he had clung to as a kitling, the dragon myths that Sir Frynwy had taken so much delight in telling, if these were somehow based in truth then perhaps there was some reason to go on living.

There might be some way in which he could avenge his mother's murder.

'You're too full of questions, little dragon,' Magog went on. 'And I've no time left to me in this place. I've already given you a great gift, although it's one that no true dragon should need to receive. Perhaps, even after all these years, there may be some small thing of use in my memory. But that you will have to find for yourself. Now tell me ere I go: what is your name?'

Benfro thought the answer before he remembered that he had struggled so hard the night before to keep that information secret. He was still not sure why, but it was the only thing of his he could protect, the only thing that was now his alone.

'Benfro,' Magog said, the name sounding absurdly grand. 'You need not worry that I will use it against you, friend. I am bound for a place where none will be able to wrest it from me, save if they are themselves dead. And it is a noble name for a noble beast. You will do great things, Sir Benfro. Of that I am sure.'

Benfro watched, a mixture of horror and pity, frustration and relief flooding through him, as the great Magog, dead for thousands of years, sank beneath the waters of the pool for the last time. There was no drama, no great surging tide, no struggle against the inevitable. It was almost as if the dragon turned to mist, faded to a sudden soft pulse of light that shot away from the river's edge so swiftly that it was as if he had never been there, leaving Benfro with the after-image of a web spun wide over the land.

He woke up, lying propped against the bush and staring out over the pool to the clearing and wood beyond. The scene was so exactly like his dream, the transfer from sleep to waking so subtle, that Benfro could not be sure it had been a dream after all.

Without thinking he hauled himself up from the bush and headed for the water's edge. His newly enlarged wings still ached at their base, but the muscle spasms had subsided into a dull ache that would hopefully ease in time. He paid it no heed as he waded out to where the sandy beach dropped into the depths below. Then, taking a deep breath, he plunged into the pool.

5

The conjuring of the blade of light is not to be undertaken casually. The light is a focus of all the energy of the land. In effect you are stealing a little bit of life from everything around you and concentrating it into one small space. To contain this force and mould it to your will requires both a rigid mental discipline and a perfect and intimate knowledge of your self. The wielder of such a blade must have both total control over his aura and complete confidence in that control. If he falters or hesitates for even an instant then the caged power will be unleashed. At the least this will result in a nasty burn. At worst the conflagration will consume anything within a twenty-yard radius. For this reason, the conjuring of such blades is forbidden to all novitiates under the age of fifteen and may otherwise only be attempted in the presence of a warrior priest until such time as the order considers your training complete. Breaking this rule will certainly result in expulsion from the order and may well end in death.

Father Castlemilk, *An Introduction to the Order of the High Ffrydd*

Beulah sat on the Obsidian Throne, her mind slipping back and forth between the aethereal and the real. She had noticed before that the great hall of the Neuadd appeared different in the dream state, but this was a distraction. Since Merrl's death and the seizing of Abervenn lands she had lost some of her taste for palace intrigue. The plot had been so easy to discover and overcome she felt almost insulted by it.

When the noise came, it took a few moments for Beulah to realize that it was in the aethereal and not the real. It gave her a strangely disjointed feeling as she hung somewhere between the two, but it was the most interesting thing to happen in hours, so she slipped out of herself and went off to investigate.

The walls of the Neuadd slid past her as she headed towards the source of the sound, and flickering by on the periphery of her vision she thought she could see flying dragons in the jumble of colours. But it was too late to investigate that, for as she floated out into the sunlit space of the quadrangle she could see the real thing walking towards her.

In an instant Beulah had conjured her blade of light, if anything brighter here than in the real plane. She dropped silently to the flagstone path that led up to the great oak doors, ready to do battle, and then stopped.

This wasn't the dragon she had seen before, with great wings and an arrogant air. Neither was it so much walking as shuffling. It was hobbled, with chains around its legs linked together somewhere beneath its dull belly, and it was being led towards her by a young man.

Beulah wasn't quite sure how she had missed him

before, although it was most unusual for people to appear as recognisable images in the aethereal. As she stared, she realized that the man was accompanied by three others, all ill defined in much the same way as the majority of her people. They were little more than pale shapes, but their leader was fully formed, quite strikingly handsome. And familiar too, though she couldn't immediately place him. It was obvious that he was no adept, for he couldn't see her, but he was heading for the Neuadd and he brought with him a dragon. Slipping back into her body upon the throne, she opened her eyes.

'Let them enter. Open the doors,' she said to the guards, pitching her voice so that it would carry across the hall. They looked around at her, bemused for a couple of seconds, and then scurried to open the doors as a dull thud hammered on the ancient wood.

He was younger than his aethereal presence, Beulah noticed at first, as if he were more mature than his years. It was difficult to tell if he was as handsome, since he was covered from head to toe in the mud of the road. To her surprise he wore the cloak and insignia of a novitiate of the Order of the High Ffrydd, not a full warrior priest. His companions wore the same, and for an instant she feared that something terrible had happened to the inquisitor. Had this dragon slain Melyn, then fallen upon the troop, only to be defeated at the last by this ragbag of novitiates? As they approached, their captive chained and head down, she let out a tiny laugh at the idiocy of the idea.

Full twenty paces from the dais upon which the throne sat, the curious group stopped at an unspoken command from the young man. As one they knelt.

'My queen, I bring this dragon, a gift from His Grace Inquisitor Melyn,' the young man said, and with his voice she recognized him.

'Bring it here for me to see, Clun Defaid,' she said, enjoying the look of startled alarm that crossed his features at the use of his name. He rallied well, she noticed, ordering the other novitiates to bring the creature forward.

'Her name is Frecknock, Your Majesty.' Clun tugged hard on the chain around the beast's neck and forced it to crouch. Beulah approached it with a mixture of excitement and trepidation. In all her life she had never seen a dragon except the one that had flown over the city in the aethereal. After that magnificently winged and iridescent animal, this mud-spattered thing was a bit of a disappointment. Its wings were far too small to support its weight in the air and its scales, even cleaned up, would be nothing better than a uniform slate-grey.

'Look at me, Frecknock,' Beulah said. The dragon raised its head in a slow uncertain motion. Its eyes seemed too heavy to roll up, fascinated with the polished floor. Finally it managed to match her gaze.

'What would you have me do with you?' Beulah asked.

'Whatever you will, Your Majesty,' the dragon said. Its voice was deep, resonant in the great hall as if the acoustics of the place had been designed for it. Yet it was unmistakably feminine. 'I am yours to command.'

'Really?' Beulah asked. 'How splendid. Roll over on your back and stick your legs in the air.'

She had hoped that maybe the creature would have protested, but it didn't. Without even a sigh, a shrug or anything which might have been taken as a sign of rebellion, it did as it was told. A dog would have been more fun, Beulah thought.

'What use are you to me, dragon?' she asked. 'I've decreed that all your kind be exterminated. Why should I keep you alive in my court?'

'I can keep watch over you, Your Majesty,' Frecknock said. 'I can sense any threat long before it comes close enough to harm you.'

'How? And how can I trust you?' Beulah asked.

'Trust has to be earned,' the dragon replied. 'As to how, I've some natural ability at what you call magic. I can sense the thoughts and feelings of your kind from a considerable distance. The guard now approaching, for instance, intends to do you harm.'

Beulah looked up just in time to see one of the guards from the door approaching at a run. He held a small crossbow pointing straight at her. 'For King Ballah and Llanwennog,' he shouted, pulling the trigger even as Beulah conjured her blade of fire.

It was dark and cold as Benfro struck out with steady strokes towards the bottom. Lungs filled with huge gulps of air this time, he had to fight hard to overcome his natural buoyancy, and, as the sunlight overhead weakened through the dark brown waters, he began to wonder if he would be able to find what he was seeking. Still he swam, down and down with nothing but the distorted sounds of his own movements for company.

A few fronds of tangling weed rose up to greet him as he neared the bottom. Even with his keen eyes, it was all he could do but make out vague shapes, looming and frightening in the hidden world. Then something appeared, a glowing curved spear. It caught the small light that made it this far. A rib.

Benfro's mind filled with panic as he approached. Either the cold confining darkness made a mockery of size or Magog had been a true behemoth among dragons. It was almost a sign of disrespect, but he reached out and grabbed the bone, using it to pull himself down and what he hoped was forward. He had a map in his head, a memory of the previous night when the whole area had been lit by some unearthly light, and now in the darkness he felt his way towards the fractured skull.

His lungs were beginning to hurt as he finally saw the ghostly glowing outline. It was huge, half embedded in the silt, the broken crack a black hole. Hurried now, Benfro shoved himself forward to a point where he could look inside. His hearts dropped when he saw nothing within. He reached a hand, a forearm, a whole arm into the skull, feeling almost sullied, or was it he who was doing the sullying? There was nothing but mud, fine and cold in his taloned fingers. No jewels left of the great Magog. No memories from that age when dragons had ruled the world.

And then he saw it, a glow so faint that he couldn't be sure it wasn't his eyes playing tricks on him, his brain starved of air lighting sparks in his vision. A dull red glow a few yards away from the fractured skull. With the last of his strength Benfro pushed himself towards it. The water resisted him, wanted to lift him skywards as if it took exception to his presence in its midst. He kicked hard against it, years of practice helping him toward his goal.

Now his eyes really were playing tricks, flashes and trills of light skeeting across his sight. But he knew where the glow had been. He could gauge his passage through the water. His outstretched hand reached the spot, clamped hard around mud and the small stone that nestled inside. With a swish of his tail and a kick of his legs, Benfro changed direction, pushing himself towards the surface.

He burst from the water with such force that this time he actually took off. He managed to take a deep breath of sweet, fresh air before gravity brought him crashing back down with a splash that stung his belly and nearly knocked the clasped jewel from his hand. The silt had all but washed away, leaving nothing more than a tiny pebble. Yet he clung to it as if his life depended on it. With weary muscles he struck out for the far side of the pool, away from the beach and the way he had come. The bank was steeper here, but easy enough to climb. He dragged himself out and flopped on to the grass, spreadeagled to let the warm late afternoon sun dry his scales.

After long moments of panting to get his breath back, Benfro finally lifted the tiny jewel to his eyes. It was palest pink, quite unlike the fiery dark red that had lit the pool the night before. It had about it a faint aura of magnificence, but he could not be sure whether this was due to his dream rather than any magical power. He was about to put it in his bag, retrieved from the bush where he had spent the night, but when he opened the side pocket to drop this last remnant of Magog inside, it felt wrong. The single white stone already lying there almost screamed in his mind, flooding him with a memory of scolding. Puzzled, he closed the pocket and slipped the tiny pink gem into the main compartment of the bag where it could lie alongside his few possessions.

The afternoon was fast turning to evening when he finally felt ready to leave the clearing. He had eaten more fish and toyed briefly with the idea of wrapping some in leaves for the journey. After a day in the hot sun it was beginning to turn, not enough to trouble his digestion, but it would soon start to smell, so instead he settled on gorging himself as best he could. He would try his hand again at hunting if he had not found Corwen in a day or two.

The sun was setting into the treetops when Benfro finally crossed the clearing and stepped into the forest. He had spent less than a day in the place, but it felt to him like weeks had passed. As he crossed from open space to dark cool woods it was almost as if he had stepped through a hole in time. His whole body tingled with static, and his newly sensitive wings trembled. For a second that was eternity he was in two places at once. Everything was split neatly down the middle of some dimension he could not grasp, and he stood in the void between the two halves. He could feel the gaze of the universe glaring down on him, more withering than a desert sun, more terrible than the mind-fear of the inquisitor. He was a naked creature, exposed to the endless now. And then his striding foot fell on forest loam. The contact was an anchor, dragging him back to the world he was meant to be in with a jolt that caught his breath, tumbled him to the ground.

Picking himself up, Benfro turned to take one last look at the final resting place of Magog, Son of the Summer Moon, but it wasn't there. Only endless trees met his gaze, tall as a thousand years.

Time seemed to slow down. Beulah watched the quarrel as it left the bow and headed straight for her. She knew that she could not dodge it or cut it from the air. Then the motion snapped back to real time, catching up with itself in a blur. She felt something heavy smash into her and she fell to the floor, pinned down by an enormous weight.

She took a few moments to realize that she was neither dead nor injured. The weight across her front was Clun, who had thrown himself in the path of the attack. He wasn't moving, but he groaned painfully as she heaved his bulk off her. The bolt stuck out of his back an inch from his shoulder blade.

The dragon still lay on its back, but now two of the novitiates were with it. The third was giving chase to the guard.

'Stop him!' Beulah yelled, stepping off the dais. At the same time as she realized that her blade of light had gone, she heard the dragon utter something in a tongue that hurt her ears, and by the open doors the would-be assassin dropped to the floor as if he had run into a wall.

The dragon rolled over on its side and clambered awkwardly to its chained feet. It bowed to Beulah and held out a long clawed hand.

'Your blade,' it said, and Beulah felt the returning sensation as the light sprang once more from her hand. 'Such a concentration of the Grym is a dangerous weapon, especially when released without the proper control.'

'I know that.' Beulah was unnerved by the calmness of the beast. 'Many novitiates have lost hands, arms or more trying to master the blade of light. You have my thanks, dragon, and your life. For now.'

She walked over towards the open doors, where her failed assassin was sitting in a semi-conscious daze. With a flick of the wrist, she beheaded him, then reabsorbed the power from her blade before turning to the very pale novitiate who had pursued the traitor.

'You. Run for help,' she said and with a whimper the boy complied. At the doors two guards lay unmoving in small pools of their own blood where the assassin's knife had done its work and, lying on the dais at the feet of the Obsidian Throne, Clun had passed out. The dragon, Frecknock, crouched in the midst of the carnage, hunkered down as if she was trying to look small.

Benfro's wings chafed. Every time he took a step they rubbed his back and sides. He could feel the blisters at the roots of his scales, a hundred tiny pricks of pain to accompany each jarring footfall. The muscles in his back had gone beyond aching, bunched up into a knot so tight not even a knife could cut through them. His hands were raw with brushing aside endless low branches, and the bag, with its weight of memories, hung heavy around his neck. In short he was miserable.

The rains had come on the second day of his march through the seemingly endless woods. He had woken to a dripping dampness and an empty stomach, although the fishy belches that had repeated on him for so much of the previous forty-eight hours had abated. It had taken a grim determination to get going that morning, gauge the position of the rising sun and try to set a northward course. Now he trudged through the incessant trees, his mind blank, his eyes blind to anything but the endless unyielding forest.

Quite how long he had been walking along the road, Benfro could not have said. The realization crept into his consciousness like the dawn, slow but ultimately impossible to ignore. Perhaps it was the light, filtering through the cloud that settled like a thin mist to the ground. Or maybe it was the smooth worn grass underfoot, no roots to trip him up, the pain in his back and sides slowly fading to a dull ache that could almost be ignored. Whatever it was, he suddenly found himself standing on the road and couldn't for the life of him recall reaching it.

The road was wide, presumably cleared many years before. It stretched, arrow straight, in either direction, although the mist made it hard for Benfro to tell how far. Neither did he know what those directions were. The sky was a greyish-white thick cloud refracting the sun and effectively cloaking its position. The trees to either side were close-packed narrow-trunked pines that speared up like two walls. Thin, spidery undergrowth eked out a precarious existence at their edge. They would provide no cover should someone else happen along the road, and he felt a frisson of fear as he realized that he was trapped.

The track rose gently in one direction, and Benfro was reasonably certain that was the way he had been walking. He knew from home that the men lived downhill, in the rich green valleys of the Hendry so often described to him by Ynys Môn. Perhaps that subconscious knowledge had directed his feet. In his current predicament uphill was the best decision he could make.

It seemed to go on for miles. Certainly hours passed as he walked the green road. His footfalls were dulled by the grass, any other sounds masked by the mist until it seemed like he had strayed into another land, an in-between reality. His stomach began to rumble as the day fell towards evening, the grey of the sky darkening like a threat of storm.

Night fell with the briefest of twilights as Benfro was making his way up a series of switchbacks. The trees still clung to the hillside in regiments, only sheer cliffs breaking their ranks. In the rarefied atmosphere they were shorter but still tightly packed, an impenetrable barrier that herded the young dragon ever onwards, ever upwards. He climbed wearily through the darkness, unwilling to rest on the road lest someone, some men, discover him while he slept. Some time in the night the cloud finally blew through and the moon climbed into the sky. Still he trudged on, mind blank of anything but the need to keep moving.

At some uncounted hour Benfro stopped climbing. Darkness hemmed him in on all sides. The road now took him in a great arc first one way then another, following a ridge as it snaked along. The rocky course narrowed to only a dozen feet or so, the sky so big it felt like he walked in the heavens. The horizon stretched far, a jagged edge of deeper black with occasional white-tipped peaks circling his vision like some improbable protective wall. And off in the distance there was a glow, always just beyond the next twist in the ridge, always a nagging fear in the empty pit of his stomach, the fear that he was being pursued, always the compelling need to keep moving, never rest.

And then finally he saw it, at the tip of a ridge whose near-vertical sides plunged into total blackness below. Silhouetted against the first glow of the dawn was a building from his worst nightmare. Vast, even at a distance of many miles, it was hewn from the same stone as the mountain it so totally dominated. Hundreds of tiny windows pocked its flanks, climbed its towers, and behind each a light glowed. It was a place he had been before, if only in his dreams.

Emmass Fawr, the home of Inquisitor Melyn and his warrior priests.

The ridge dipped around the next corner, dropping into a small plateau. Benfro hurried down towards it, searching frantically for a place to hide. As he approached, cautious at every sound, he caught an all-too-familiar odour on the breeze. Instantly he froze as the fear swept into him. There were men close by. But it was only their smell, not the paralysing mind-fear of the inquisitor. Benfro hoped they were unaware of his approach.

Carefully, as silently as he could manage on the now rock-strewn road, he crept across the plateau. There was a palpable sense of freedom, a lightening in his shoulders at the sight of flat ground to either side of the path. Benfro stepped on to the short wiry grass that struggled to grow at this altitude, heading for the plateau edge, hoping against all the odds that there might be a way down back into the forest.

The pre-dawn light had confused his sense of scale. The little scrubby bushes he had imagined from a distance were in fact large and ancient trees, their bark gnarled and their limbs twisted as if by some dread torture. Their cracked and mottled trunks afforded little in the way of a hiding place, and all the while dawn's thin glow was seeping into the world, painting faded colours over everything.

The edge of the plateau, when at last he reached it, was as vertical as the cliffs which climbed up to the vast building above. Shadowed from the rising sun, the valley below was a mottled dark mass of patterns that could have been a tree canopy. In the half-light it was almost impossible to gauge the distance down, but it was far enough to rule out jumping as an option. His hearts sank almost as deep as the drop. In the dark mass of Emmass Fawr smoke was rising from dozens of chimneys now, which meant that its inhabitants, the warrior priests, were awake. Soon they would be out and about, and if Benfro knew only one thing, it was that he didn't want to be around to see them.

He walked along the cliff edge, peering down into the gloom to try and make out a ledge. There was something down there, faint even to his keen eyesight, but it was further along, always just out of sight, always looking like he would be able to make it out if he moved just a little further. And then, suddenly, he felt something nudge his tail.

Benfro whirled around, almost falling backwards into the void as he saw what had touched him. It was a man, or at least a man-kit. Much smaller than the inquisitor and quite a bit shorter than the other warrior priests he had seen. He was dressed in a rough sacking material, rudely fashioned into trousers and a smock top. His hair was untamed and his face was smeared in mud. He had a long thin whipping stick in one hand and he was using it to prod Benfro's tail.

'What're you?' the boy asked in that curious tongue he had heard Gideon use with his mother. The meaning was clear from the expression on the boy's face. Benfro was surprised at how high-pitched and squeaky his voice sounded. Nothing like the sinister deep growl of the inquisitor. There was no aura of fear about him, no questing sense of malice. Instead he had an insatiable curiosity in his gaze.

'You after my sheep?' he asked again, and Benfro noticed for the first time that a small flock of white creatures had gathered to see what was going on. They were shorter even than the boy, with spindly black legs and a heavy coat of fibrous-looking wool. He could see no intelligence whatsoever in them as they tore at the meagre grass.

'Gonna tell my da' 'bout you,' the boy said, then turned and fled towards the arch that rose over the road closer to the monastery. Now that he looked closely, Benfro could see a number of rude huts clustered close to the road and sheltered by the monastery's great stone wall. Wisps of smoke were rising from the roofs of some of them, climbing straight up in the still morning air. The boy moved with some speed and was soon at the nearest of the huts. Benfro saw a brief flicker of light as he darted inside and then another a few seconds later as someone poked a head out. He could just make out the sound of shouting over the distance, and then the boy reappeared, running under the arch and up the road to the great stone building.

Benfro looked around in panic. It would take the boy only moments to reach his destination. A troop of warrior priests would be after him before he could even make the top of the ridge.

The road carried on up to the monastery, that much he had seen from farther away and remembered from his dream flight. But just beyond the arch it split, a narrow track heading down towards the forest, following a gorge that cut steeply into the cliff. Benfro's hearts leaped. There was a way he might evade the warriors yet. All he needed to do was pass through the arch, down the hundred yards or so of open road to the junction and then carry on down to the forest below. But fear held him where he crouched. He didn't want to expose himself to the castle's faceless stone stare, preferring the false security of the low wall between him and the warrior priests.

In the end the decision was made for him. Glancing back along the road, he saw two things that popped the bubble of his quiet euphoria. First the sheep had gathered around him in a silent circle. Some lay on the grass, others stood chewing silently. They were all staring at him as if he were the most interesting thing they had ever seen. Second and distant even to his keen eyes, he could make out a column of dust rising into the bright morning air. Someone was coming up the road, and judging by the cloud they were creating it was either a dragon the size of Magog or a full troop of warrior priests.

His mind made up, Benfro scrabbled over the wall. It was high enough to stop sheep from wandering, but nothing to his greater bulk and agility. The ledge on the other side was narrow, but widened nearer the road, the cliff giving way to a steep slope that led down to the narrow track. There were a few bushes and scrubby trees here too, Benfro noted as he picked a careful path down. The deeper into the gorge he went, the thicker and taller they became, sheltered from the worst of the elements. Soon he felt a lessening in fear as the wiry green vegetation spread around him, options for hiding opening up with every step. As the light from the rising sun shortened the mountain shadow over the distant trees, he began to relax and almost to enjoy the morning. Despite the lack of food, he was not hungry, and it even felt like the pain in his back was gone, his wings no longer sore against his sides. He was almost carefree trotting down to the track to whatever might await him.

Errol was in his dormitory going through his pack and checking off everything he needed when Carstairs, one of the younger novitiates, burst in through the door.

'Errol, come quickly,' the boy said. He was part of the new year's intake and less dismissive of Errol since he was much the same age.

'What's up?'

'Down in Ruthin's grove,' Carstairs said, gulping great breaths down as he did. 'There's a dragon. It came up the Calling Road.'

Errol leaped to his feet, dropping his pack on his bed before sprinting out of the door. He raced up stairs, along corridors and through open halls become familiar with the time he had spent in the monastery. Behind him his companion struggled to keep up, still acclimatizing to the thin air and the labyrinth. At the great courtyard entrance they both stopped. It was a hive of activity as novitiates, warrior priests and quaisters milled around.

'I can't go out,' Carstairs said, pointing towards the dark-tunnelled entrance passage. 'I've not achieved the first level.'

'I'll tell you all about it,' Errol said, noting the boy's obvious disappointment. It had been only a week since he himself had been granted leave to go out of the monastery, so it was with a distinct thrill that he crossed the threshold.

Beyond the monastery walls the early morning light was beginning to lift the night's mist. Errol followed a mass of people along the path and into the narrow gorge. Thorn bushes and whins crowded in on either side as they hurried down, narrowing the available space until everyone was backed up, immobile. Errol ducked under a scrubby tree, scraped past some thorns and scrambled part way up the side of the gully until he could see over the heads of everyone else.

At its base the gully opened up into a flat space, not much bigger than the archery practice yard back in the monastery. The far edge seemed to drop away abruptly, revealing a dark green vista overlooking the endless forest of the Ffrydd. A small stream trickled through the bushes, collecting in a still pool that must have emptied over the edge. Beside it a stone plinth had been carved right on the lip of the cliff, and for an instant Errol thought it was a statue of a dragon that stood looking out over the distant trees.

Then the statue moved.

Errol had seen a live dragon only once before, and he wasn't sure how real that experience had been. Sir Radnor had appeared to him as a magnificent mythical beast, but from what little he had learned of the Ffrydd dragons, he knew that they were simple, crude creatures. They were bigger than a large horse, it was true, but they were timid and bent, impossibly old. Their wings were small flaps of skin that most manuscripts said were used to regulate their body temperature and had never been intended for flight. They were opportunistic hunters and scavengers, thieving from flocks and herds, which was why men had taken to hunting them in the first place.

Much that he had read was at odds with what Sir Radnor had told him, and yet the female dragon he had seen in his strange trance had been a weedy, pathetic thing. The creature that stood on the plinth was much more like a dragon should be.

He was big, much the biggest living animal Errol had ever seen. He stood tall and proud, his legs as thick as tree trunks, his tail like some vast tropical snake coiled around his heavy-clawed feet. His scales were bright, reflecting the morning light in a shimmer of greens and blues, but it was his wings that were most magnificent, even hanging limp at his sides. They were huge, mottled with a pattern that would only reveal itself when they were stretched fully to take the air.

Slowly, as if only just noticing that there were people around him, the dragon turned. Errol was transfixed by the creature's face, its eyes, its long elegant nose and tufted ears. He was certain that they had met before. At the bottom of the gully the inquisitor strode purposefully towards the plinth, shouting angry words, blade of light held high, but the dragon paid him no heed. He was staring straight at Errol.

Why did you come here, of all places? Errol thought, and fancied that on some level he was communicating with the intruder. He knew the answer. He'd felt the pull of the Calling Road himself. If the inquisitor had strengthened it, then it was remarkable this dragon hadn't walked mindlessly straight to the monastery gate. Now Melyn would fight it, and it would die. Already he could feel the numbing mind-fear swamping the whole terrace, freezing many of the less adept warrior priests as it held the dragon tight. There wouldn't even be a fight. The inquisitor would strike at a helpless foe.

The wrongness of it all filled Errol with a cold rage. Sir Radnor had been his friend and teacher. He couldn't stand and watch as one of his kind was cut down, but what could he do?

The inquisitor was close now, coaxing the dragon with words of compulsion, urging it to come down, to submit to his will. With a start Errol realized that he could hear the words perfectly despite his distance from the scene. He could feel the glamour tugging at him too. And he shared the dragon's fear, exhaustion, confusion and grief. Improbable images tumbled through his mind with one repeating itself time and time again in an endless loop of horror: Inquisitor Melyn swinging his blade through the neck of a supine dragon. Morgwm the Green, he knew her. Mother.

'Who are you?' Errol asked, forming the words silently

with his lips as he tried to project them across the empty space to the tottering dragon.

'Benfro,' came back the reply, heavy with a weariness it was difficult to comprehend.

'You have wings, Benfro,' Errol thought, seeing an image of a magnificent dragon rising from a pool of water, launching itself into the air on great sails of skin and bone.

'I have wings,' Benfro replied, but his mind was almost dead with exhaustion, his thoughts so sluggish they could barely form in the maelstrom that was his memory.

'So use them,' Errol thought, seeing through Benfro's eyes the cliff edge and the drop to the forest far below. 'Jump.'

And to his surprise and delight, the dragon did.

6

An unguarded mind is an open book just waiting to be directed. Catch your opponent unaware and you can mould his every action to your own will. A skilled warrior will use his enemy to fight on his behalf, or lure an invading army into a trap without him ever realizing. Until it is too late.

As with all such magics, the key to success in this manipulation is mental discipline. If you cannot control your own thoughts, how can you hope to control those of someone else, let alone his actions? Meditation exercises can help to build up this discipline, but to truly succeed every moment of your life, both waking and asleep, must become a meditation. You must meditate while carrying out your daily chores, meditate while taking your lessons in swordcraft, meditate while making your sacrifice to the Shepherd, meditate while reading this book. Only when you can live your life in perfect control can you hope to take the next step towards becoming a true warrior priest.

In the course of your studies with the order you will find yourself under constant attack, tested by your classmates, by novitiates more senior to you and by the quaisters and warrior priests who call this monastery their home. You will find yourself doing things that you did not intend to do, drawn to places you never intended to go. If you even realize that this is happening to you, then you will have taken the first, most difficult step in your education. Very few who embark on this journey will make it even that far.

Father Castlemilk, *An Introduction to the Order of the High Ffrydd*

Benfro had never known fear of heights. He recalled how some of the old dragons had become agitated when he climbed tall trees or played near the bluffs that flanked the south side of the village. Meirionydd in particular would not go anywhere near the edge and had scolded him severely whenever she had caught him peering down at the treetops. Now, as he plummeted with increasing speed, he began to understand why.

The wind whipped at his face and hands, pulling his leather bag around his neck and threatening to spill its precious cargo over the rapidly approaching tree canopy. He twisted and turned in the air, head over heels. Everything was moving at great speed, and yet somehow time seemed to slow. He could feel the wave of hatred and fury from the warrior priests above, diminishing all the while. The fear grabbed at him like a huge pair of hands, as if the inquisitor were trying to defy gravity and pull him back, but Benfro knew it was not real and struggled to fight it off. Like taking a heavy weight from his shoulders, it faded away leaving him weightless as he fell.

Twisting and turning, he felt the aches and pains of the

past days come back, bringing new ones with them. His stomach was an empty pit, churning with acid fire. His legs cramped as if he had been running all his life, and his sides burned raw with the chafing of his wings.

His wings.

The thought hit his mind with the force of his inevitable impact with the forest floor. He had wings. True they were more of a hindrance than a help, so weighty they had knotted the muscles in his back beyond pain. But if he could inch them open just a fraction to slow his descent, he might even survive this fall. He tried to stretch them open, concentrating on the lumpen mass between his shoulders and flexing. For some reason his arms spread wide, grasping the air, the wind whistling through his outstretched talons. His tumbling increased in speed with his panic and he rolled over in an arc that spun the scenery round his vision: first the trees, then the rocky cliff face, cracked and scarred and pocked with tiny brave outcrops of vegetation. Then the sky whirled past him, the sun just beginning to reach over the wildly moving horizon.

Another turn and the trees were much closer now. He could make out their tops, not the soft welcoming embrace of a great spreading oak or beech, but the sharp stake-like jaggedness of row upon row of firs. They were short too, stout canes scratching for life on the rubble and scree that rose out of the plain to lap at the edge of the ridge. There would be no slow crashing through the branches, each break taking a little from the fall, no winded landing in a thousand-year leaf-litter loam.

Benfro struggled against his tumbling, trying at least to straighten himself out. Quite why, he wasn't sure. He didn't particularly want to watch the hurtling ground as it rose to meet him, but somehow it felt right that he should be that way around. His panic began to subside, replaced with a resignation, an acceptance of his fate. Instinctively he reached out to the air and steadied himself for the impact.

It came quicker than he expected. Pain ripped through him like a landslide. His head and arms were thrown forward; the stout leather strap on his bag whip-cracked against his neck and shoulders. For a moment everything went black with the abrupt deceleration. And then suddenly he was being hauled back, pulled away from the ground on a hoist attached to a burning pin sunk into the flesh of his back.

Opening his eyes, Benfro saw the treetops rushing past at great speed. They were so close he could almost reach out and touch them as they slipped by. Yet they remained steadily distant. The wind pulled hard at his face now, stripping tears from his eyes. He sneaked a look to one side, fearful that the air would pull his head from his neck, and saw a sight so magical he would never tire of seeing it again.

His wings were unfolded to their utmost extent. He had not realized how big they had become, but they stretched away from him now fully twenty feet. They cupped the air. He could think of no better way of describing it. It was like his dreams only more visceral, more real. And, like his dreams, all he had to do was think about it and he could bank slightly, turn this way and that, rise away from the trees or descend until he dared not get any closer.

Unlike his dreams, each change of direction was accompanied by a twisting of the white-hot point that was their fulcrum, a pain so intense that it painted spots of light in his vision. He held still as best he could, staring straight ahead and trying not to feel the weariness that was beginning to seep through him.

The forest followed the land, dropping away from the ridge and the mountains. It was this slow fall that Benfro followed as he glided away from the monastery. He covered the ground with incredible speed, the forest below him now an impenetrable mass of leaves. The scrubby firs had given way to taller, more majestic pines, and these in turn were replaced by thick deciduous growth. The trees undulated over valleys that would have taken weeks to cross on foot, and yet they were seemingly endless.

In the farthest distance more mountains rose to pierce the blue sky with their white caps. For a moment Benfro feared he had turned full circle and was heading back towards his enemies. The rigid lock of his wings and the straight-line rushing of the trees below assured him that this was unlikely. And he could see his shadow arcing across the canopy ahead of him and to the left, a great winged beast, which meant the sun was still at his back and he was headed north-west. But the pain was fast becoming unbearable, little jabs of fire spreading from his shoulders along the wing edges, senses coming from parts of his body that had never felt before.

Benfro remembered a game he used to play when he was bored. Simple enough in its rules, he would hang by his arms from a branch, holding his full weight off the ground, and count. The longest he had managed was a hundred and seventeen seconds and he had felt the pain burn in his muscles then as it did now. More particularly, he remembered how his hands had simply stopped obeying his command to stay clenched around the branch, how they had relaxed of their own accord, leaving him feeling as weak as a spider's web in a storm. The burning in his back and the new ache in his wings were beginning to take on the same quality that he recalled from his arms just before they could hold his weight no more. He could ignore the pain for quite a long time, focus past it, but there was no getting away from the fact that very soon his wings were going to crumple. And still there was nowhere to land, no gap in the solid green mass that spread beneath him.

It was closer now, the canopy. He could make out the shapes of individual trees, larger boughs poking up from the verdant sea that rushed past with dizzying speed. He wanted to push away from it, keep clear of the branches that whipped at his scaly belly and threatened to snag the heavy, dragging weight of his tail. But he seemed to have lost control of the air now, the trees reaching out to him with a magnetic embrace. He knew with a horrible certainty that his long glide was coming to an end.

The first branches caught his taloned feet, snagged and then released. With a last great effort, he tried to stop his forward motion, rear up as he had seen birds do when they came in to land. But there was no strength left in him. The next time he crashed into the canopy it was all he could do to fold his wings, to try to get them as close to his sides as possible before they were snagged and ripped in his inevitable descent. One tree domed up larger than its immediate neighbours and he ploughed into its leafy embrace with bone-breaking speed.

'Bring me young Ramsbottom and pick out a handful of men to ride before dawn. You'll be going to Tynewydd.'

Melyn watched as Captain Osgal bowed his assent and left the room without a word. There was no doubt the captain hated the boy, the angry glare in his eyes as his name was mentioned was enough, even if his mind wasn't an open book on the subject. In ordinary times Melyn would have admonished Osgal for his lack of mental discipline, but these weren't ordinary times.

Once more he saw the sight of the dragon perched on the stone dais in Ruthin's Grove, teetering on the edge as if held there by fear. Melyn had been so sure he had the beast then. He'd even allowed himself a little smile of victory, knowing that the powerful magics he'd woven on the Calling Road had succeeded where a half-hundred warrior priests scouring the forest had failed. As he'd always predicted, the beast had come to him, even if it had taken a few weeks longer than he had anticipated.

But then it had all gone wrong. Seeing the dragon fall had been a disappointment; he would have liked to have captured it alive, questioned it, broken it before he cracked open its skull. But if he had to recover its mangled body from the bottom of the cliff, then so be it.

What he had never expected it to do was fly.

In his weaker moments Melyn could allow himself to think that the beast had simply been lucky, that it had been gliding and caught an updraught strong enough to support its bulk. But he knew he was fooling himself. There was no mistaking those wings, fully ten times the size of any he had seen before. At the speed it had been travelling the creature would be halfway across the Ffrydd in a few hours, a journey that would take his men many weeks, even if he could spare them.

Melyn burned with the need to track down the dragon and kill it, but he knew he would have to wait. The assassination attempt on the queen had changed everything. Now he had to work to keep his anger in check, to concentrate on Beulah's plans and how best to put them into action.

A knock at the door broke through his musings. Captain Osgal entered on his command, followed by Errol. The boy was still wearing a leather arm guard from archery practice and looked slightly flustered.

'You wanted to see me, Your Grace,' he said, bowing.

'Yes, Errol. Come in. Sit down,' Melyn said. 'Stay, Osgal,' he added as the captain made to leave. 'You're a part of this mission too.'

'Mission?' Errol asked, and Melyn could feel his excitement rising. He skimmed over the boy's thoughts, picking images at random. Perhaps unsurprisingly the dragon's flight was never far from the front, but there were other thoughts too: an insatiable thirst for knowledge, a determination to complete the tasks set for him and a desire to be the top novitiate in his year's intake. None of the old uncertainties loomed large any more; time and the discipline of the order had pushed them far to the back of his mind.

'An opportunity has presented itself to put a spy deep

in King Ballah's court,' Melyn said, catching Errol's eyes in his gaze. 'Specifically, we need a young lad who looks and speaks like a native. Can I trust you, Errol Ramsbottom?'

'What must I do?' Errol asked, and Melyn could see in his mind a resolve to do the best he possibly could for the order and Queen Beulah. He could see the false memories and ideals now woven so completely into the boy's psyche as to be real. Melyn had never doubted that his control over the boy would be complete, but it was gratifying nonetheless to see his work bear such useful fruit.

Darkness enveloped Benfro as thousands of tiny twigs snapped and scraped him from head to tip of tail. Larger twigs cracked and jabbed at his scales. At least he had hit the treetop chest on, where his scales were thickest. He tried to cover his head as best he could while the swaying branches caught him, bent and gave. The noise was terrible, as if the very wood were screaming in outrage at his sudden violent arrival. Still he was powerless to do anything but fall, bounce, tumble and break. An unseen hand grabbed at the bag slung around his neck, jerking it so hard he thought it would snap his neck. Instead the branch broke, releasing its loot. Benfro grasped the precious bag under one armpit, reaching out with his other hand to try and grab a passing branch. It stung on contact, burning his palm as it rubbed through, bending almost back on itself before it broke. A thicker branch caught him square on the chest, driving the wind from his lungs and tipping him head over heels so that the next jarring crash was to his back. Pain upon pain greeted every new impact, but he was slowing. He reached out one more time to grab at a branch and this time held on even though it ripped at his torn flesh. The full weight of his momentum transferred to his arm, threatening to wrench it from its socket. Desperate, he flailed his other hand out, grabbed for the branch, held.

Leaves spiralled down into the darkness, their passage lit briefly by sunlight spearing through the great gash in the canopy. Benfro watched them as he desperately tried to catch up with the whirl of events. Somewhere in the back of his mind he could hear a voice counting: 'Thirty-one, thirty-two, thirty-three.' He shook his head, trying to get rid of the ringing in his ears and the stars clouding his sight. The branch he was clinging to dipped and swayed alarmingly so he stopped moving.

'Forty-two, forty-three, forty-four.' The voice was measured in its beat, implacable, almost hypnotic. Benfro hung from the branch just listening to it and staring down into the darkness.

'Fifty, fifty-one.' The murk below began to resolve itself into vague detail as his eyes became accustomed to the darkness and the spots in his vision began to fade. He could not make out the ground, only branches reaching out like great wooden limbs, spindly and malformed in the forest gloom, searching for a small spot where they might thrust a leaf or two into the light. Somewhere a trunk must have risen from the ground, but where it was Benfro couldn't see.

'Sixty-four, sixty-five.' He tried to shuffle his hands along the branch in what he hoped was the right direction. It dipped and wobbled alarmingly, creaks and cracks barking out to be muffled by the surrounding silence. His arms ached with the strain and the ripped palm of his hand hurt with every move. Still he was unsure whether he was going the right way or not, such was the darkness.

'Eighty-one, eighty-two.' The branch seemed to be getting thicker, which was good in a way, as it meant he was inching towards the trunk. Benfro knew he could clamber down to the ground if he could just get his footing and rest a while. On the other hand, the thicker branch was more difficult to grasp, and he lacked the strength to haul himself up over it. Pausing to think was not an option, the ache in his arms reaching breaking point. Instead he dug his claws into the soft bark, trying to ignore the pain as they took his weight.

'Ninety-nine, one hundred, one hundred and one.' Was that a deeper black in the gloom? Benfro could not be sure. It felt like he was getting close to some massive form: the air seemed stiller, the sound of his laboured breathing more damped. As gently as he could, he felt out with his feet, still clinging to the branch for dear life even though he knew his arms would not last much longer. His claws felt like they were being pulled out by some torturer, and he focused on that pain in the absurd hope that his muscles would not notice their plight. One foot brushed against what felt like a wall, rough and unyielding. It rose vertically to his left, a great nothingness, so close and yet invisible. There was no obvious sign of any other branches within his reach.

'One hundred and fifteen, one hundred and sixteen.' Benfro knew it was too late. He would fall now. Heedless of his efforts, his traitorous hands slowly loosened their grip, claws scratching through the soft bark like it was butter. His leaden arms could do nothing.

As he fell, a small measure of triumph lit the otherwise miserable resignation to his fate that flooded through him. He had held on for one hundred and twenty-five seconds, a new record. He didn't have long to enjoy his success as within seconds of letting go something slammed into him with such force it jarred his spine, cracked his legs and twisted his tail up in an agonizing wrench. Momentum tipped him forward, and in the dazed darkness a faceful of dirt rose to meet him.

'Lie still now. You don't want to open the wound up again.'

Beulah pushed the semi-conscious Clun back into the soft mattress of his bed with a firm but gentle hand. He had not woken properly since the attempt on her life, which was perhaps for the best. According to the surgeons, whatever poison the assassin had used to tip his crossbow bolt should have killed him. It would certainly have been fatal to the slighter queen, and only Clun's unconscious state had kept the toxins from spreading quickly through his bloodstream.

Now it seemed the worst was over. He would survive, but he was going to take a long time healing. Beulah wasn't quite sure why she had decided to nurse him herself. Perhaps it was his selfless act of sacrifice for her, or maybe she was intrigued by his clearly defined aethereal self-image. Undoubtedly he was a fine specimen of manhood, though she knew all too well how Padraig would react to her forming any kind of liaison with a commoner.

On the other hand, she could make him Duke of Aber-venn if she wanted to. After all she was queen.

'He shouldn't have that. Not here,' Clun said in a mumbling, indistinct voice that wiped the smile off Beulah's face. His eyes were still closed in sleep, but his muscles clenched against each other as if he were fighting some invisible foe.

'Hush now. Sleep,' Beulah said, wiping the beads of sweat off his forehead with a cool damp rag.

'But she's the queen. He mustn't bring . . . NO!' With a great lunge, Clun sat upright, his eyes wide open, his breath coming in ragged gasps. Beulah flinched back from his large hands, but the apparition he grappled with was not her. Slowly the terror in his eyes faded to be replaced with confusion. He dropped his hands to the bedclothes, took in the room, the wide bed and expensive furniture, the tall windows with their silk brocade pelmets and heavy curtains open to show the sunlight in the courtyard, and finally his eyes came to rest on her.

It was cruel to laugh at his reaction, but Beulah couldn't help herself. At first he scrabbled out of the bed, backing away from her in terror. Then he realized that he was wearing no clothes and a deep flush covered his whole body as he grabbed at the sheets to cover himself. And finally the poison-induced weakness overcame his adrenaline rush and he collapsed to the floor.

It was as well that the noise brought two ladies-in-waiting to the room. Beulah was too busy laughing to notice that the crossbow bolt wound had reopened and Clun was busy bleeding on to the floor. She retreated to the couch beside the window while the women hauled him back into the bed and re-dressed his shoulder. All the while he protested weakly that he shouldn't be there, that he should be sent back to Emmass Fawr for his training, but he was no match for the two matrons and finally lapsed back into the pillows, defeated.

Beulah waited for her servants to leave, then crossed once more to the bed. Clun had his eyes shut and his face was pale, but his breathing gave away that he was not asleep.

'You don't need to fear me,' Beulah said. 'And you really must rest.'

'It's wrong for me to lie here in the presence of my queen, Your Majesty,' Clun said, opening his eyes but refusing to meet her gaze.

'You took a poisoned bolt that was meant for me,' Beulah said, settling herself once more into the chair beside the bed and taking up the moist cloth. 'I think I can let you off, just this once.'

She reached out and wiped the sweat from his forehead again. At her touch he flinched and tried to pull away.

'Am I so awful that you can't bear even my touch?' she asked. Finally he looked at her.

'Your Majesty, no. Of course not. I . . . It's just that . . . well . . .'

'You don't think I should honour the man who saved my life by tending his wounds? Is that it?'

'Yes, no. I don't know,' Clun said. 'Your Majesty, it's not right. I'm just a commoner, a novitiate. Not even a warrior priest.'

'I'm not asking you to marry me,' Beulah said, noting with satisfaction the flush of embarrassment this brought.

'And don't call me "Your Majesty". It's too formal. In here, in private, you can call me Beulah.'

This was obviously a step too far for the young man. He turned his head away, wincing in pain as he stretched the wound.

'My lady,' he said. 'I can't.'

'Even if I order you to?' Beulah said, teasing. 'No, "my lady" is fine. I like that actually. Yes, Clun, you will call me "my lady" from now on, whatever the protocol of the occasion demands. And now you must get some rest. Heal. Don't worry about your position in the order. I won't let Melyn bully you.'

Errol shoved his few possessions into a small canvas bag and pulled the cord tight before throwing it over his shoulder. He took a last look around the dormitory, then stepped out into the corridor.

'Were you going to leave without saying goodbye?'

'I thought if I hurried, I could catch you in the library before Osgal marches us off to Llanwennog,' Errol said to his old tutor.

Andro smiled. 'Either you really mean that or I've taught you too well how to lie,' he said. 'But if I know anything about Osgal, it's that he'll punish you severely for holding him up. Come. I'll walk you to the courtyard.'

They fell into step, Errol noticing that he had to slow himself down to match the old librarian's speed. For a long while they walked in silence through the dark halls.

'You mustn't think that you can always fool the inquisitor just because you've done it this once,' Andro said finally.

'Did I really?' Errol asked. 'Fool him, that is.'

'He's distracted at the moment. Losing the dragon has angered him more than even he'll admit. But there's more to it than that. We're preparing for war with Llanwennog, and they're doing much the same. Melyn's hand has been forced by this assassination attempt. He needs you to be loyal and ready. That's why you've fooled him this time.'

Errol felt a moment's annoyance. He'd worked hard to master the skills Andro had taught him. Some credit would have been nice.

'Ah, Errol, even now you betray yourself,' Andro said. 'I can sense your frustration and I'm not even trying. You've got to keep a tight control on your thoughts at all times. Especially when you're among the Llanwennogs. What will you do when you're presented to King Ballah?'

'Ballah? But I thought –'

'That you'd be allowed to serve Princess Iolwen without first being presented to the king?'

Errol was about to say more, but they stepped out into the courtyard and an angry voice cut through his thoughts.

'You're late, Ramsbottom,' Captain Osgal said. He was already mounted, as were the other members of the troop that would escort him to Llanwennog. Hastily, Errol tied his bag to the saddle of his own horse, then hauled himself up on to the beast. He felt uneasy; riding was a new skill and not one at which he had practised much.

'I wanted to have a few last words with Errol,' Andro said to the captain. 'This is a dangerous mission he's embarking on, and he needs to practise the skills I've taught him.'

Osgal looked at the old librarian with a stony face,

nodding and grunting the most non-committal acceptance of his explanation. He threw Errol the reins he had
been holding.

'Well, you're here now,' he said. 'May we leave, Master
Librarian?'

Without waiting for an answer, he kicked his horse into
a trot. The rest of the troop fell in behind him and Errol's
horse lurched forward to keep up. He had a brief glimpse
of Andro's worried face, heard the old man say, 'Good
luck, Errol,' but he was concentrating too hard on staying
in the saddle to do much more than nod a reply. There
was a strange tingling feeling in his skin as they passed
through the magical wards that protected the gates, and
then they were on the Calling Road, heading for the great
arch.

It was a cold morning, dawn still about an hour off.
There was enough light to wash away all but the brightest
morning stars, but not enough that they could push the
horses into a gallop. Errol was grateful for the reprieve,
giving him time to get his balance. Even so, he knew that
he would be sore long before they stopped for the day.
Ahead, Osgal muttered something to one of the other
warrior priests, then allowed his horse to drop back until
he was alongside Errol.

'We're out of the monastery now, boy,' he said in a low
growl. 'That means you're my responsibility. The inquisitor might think you've got what it takes for this mission,
but me, I'm not so sure. You're trouble. I just know it.'

'I only want what's best for the order,' Errol said. The
blow came from nowhere, almost unseating him. Only as

his vision cleared did he see Osgal take up his reins. He hadn't seen him drop them.

'Speak only when I tell you to,' the captain hissed. He raised a fist, dark in the half-light, and squeezed it. Errol felt a pressure build in his chest as if the captain were squashing his heart. It was a brief thing, but frightening nonetheless.

'I'll be watching you, Ramsbottom,' Osgal said. 'And if I even suspect you're up to no good . . .' He flexed his hand once more, sending a bolt of pain through Errol's body. Without another word, he spurred his horse to the head of the troop.

7

Of all the myths attributed to dragons, none is more potent and yet also more plainly ludicrous than that of the mother tree. Said to be the source of all life, this legendary creature, or plant, resides in the midst of a great forest. Taller and wider than any tree, it yet remains invisible unless it wishes to be seen. It is said that in times of great need the tree will appear, or send one of its minions to give aid. It is also said that it can exist out of time and that to eat of its fruit is to be given the gift of second sight.

Plainly this myth is founded in the simple credulity of the forest dragons. Always on the hunt for food and scratching the most basic of existences, they have not the wit to improve themselves, instead making bearable their misery by inventing tales of better times to come. That such false hopes light their simple dreary lives is a mark of their true base nature. And yet do we not ourselves cling to similar fancies? For is it that different to cross oneself before entering a house recently visited by the Shepherd? Do we not still have a secret fear of prophecy and an unacknowledged wish to be touched by good fate?

Father Charmoise, Dragons' Tales

For long seconds Benfro just lay still: not moving, not breathing as the world settled itself down around him. He could feel soft loam in his hands, moist and spongy. Every part of his body ached, even his teeth, but he was not falling any more. He took a short breath through his nostrils, his lungs still loath to work properly. The air was warm, humid and scented with the rich fug of leaf mould. The forest at first seemed silent, but as he lay motionless Benfro started to notice sounds: the rustling of small animals scurrying about their business on the black forest floor, the twittering of birds flitting about the branches of the canopy overhead, the occasional grunt or roar of something larger and farther away. Slowly the sounds of the wild filtered back as the forest accepted this new intruder into its dark embrace.

As he lay panting in an effort to get the wind back into his lungs, Benfro started to make out shapes in the murkiness about him. Far from being black, the forest floor was a mass of delicate patterns painted green by the great canopy overhead. Something moved ahead of him, hopping through the leaf litter and rubbery-leaved plants that clustered around the clear area where he lay. It inched closer, no doubt curious to discover what this new thing was that had dropped into its world.

Closer still and Benfro could make out the shape of a squirrel. It was bigger than any he had ever seen, its bushy tail as big as his head. It came so near that he could almost have reached out and grabbed it, were not his arms still refusing to work. It would have made a tasty morsel.

Panic flitted across his mind then as he thought the fall

might have paralysed him. He longed to flex his hands, stretch his legs, but all he could do was lie there, stunned and motionless as the squirrel sniffed at his nose.

'Dragon,' it said in a tiny squeaky voice, then turned tail and fled. Benfro watched its departure and waited to see what happened next. Slowly the ache in his hands and arms lessened to the point where he could move. He pulled the leather bag out from underneath him and checked the small pocket for his mother's jewel.

The moment he touched it, he felt safe. His mother was just there, beyond the fringe of leaves, out of sight but watching. No harm could come as long as she was there to protect him. And yet there was a frustration mingling with his relief. She was so close, so calm. He could almost smell her on the still forest air, sense the pattern of her thoughts, hear the soft regular swish of her breathing. Closing his eyes, Benfro tried to imagine her smile and the play of sunlight on the tiny patterned scales on her face. All he could see was a single blade of pure white light arcing through the air, howling a silent scream as it went.

Shocked, he dropped the jewel back into its pocket, guilt mixing with grief and impotent fury. He couldn't afford to lie here waiting to be caught. He had to get up, move on, find Corwen.

His legs did work, he discovered, but not well. Nothing was broken, of that he was sure, but he was covered in great bruises where he had smashed into countless branches on his way down. They restricted his movements, not so much with pain but with a simple refusal to move. Still he managed to stagger through the sparse undergrowth to a root bowl in the nearest tree trunk.

Water had pooled here and he drank deeply before slumping against the wood.

The effort of moving just a few feet had exhausted him, the trauma of his fall and flight even more so. The deep wood was a comforting place, warm and unthreatening. It soothed away some of his earlier panic. The men were far away. He knew they would come after him, especially Inquisitor Melyn, but it would take them a month to cover the distance he had soared in a couple of hours. At least for now he was safe and possibly even closer to his goal than he could have hoped. Lulled by the gentle business of the forest sounds, Benfro drifted off into a deep sleep.

Something nibbling at his feet woke him. It stopped as he wiggled his talons, backing off a few paces into the murk. As his eyes shook off their sleep fug he could make out the speckled white spots of a fawn, quite small, eyeing him with great liquid orbs. It bobbed its head, turned and fled into the undergrowth.

Benfro didn't know how long he had slept, but looking up he could see spears of light striking through the canopy. Their angle made him think it was evening and their distance from him made him gasp. How could he have fallen so far without killing himself? The tree whose root he was leaning against was far bigger than anything he had encountered before. The trunk was as wide as the great hall back in the village, and it stretched up as straight as an arrow. Thin, weedy branches sprung from its top but nothing grew in the lower hundred feet or more except one bare branch perhaps twenty feet off the ground. A couple of branches hung by a thread where they had been snapped, fresh white wood flesh showing where Benfro had made his journey to the forest floor. He tried to gauge the distance from these to the branch that had finally stopped his fall, then on to the ground. How had he managed to catch hold of it? It was enough that he had done. Without that last stop he would surely have been killed.

It was dark on the forest floor, but not completely so. Somehow the evening light managed to penetrate the canopy, giving the undergrowth a brief period of energy. And what undergrowth! There were plants Benfro had never even imagined, let alone seen. Great shrubs with leaves as big as doorways that drooped and split as they neared the ground; thin wiry creepers like ropes that climbed into the trees; spiky flowers clinging to the rough lower bark, their petals formed into great cups that dribbled steady streams of water to the ground. Everything was moist, even the air, filling his ears with the sound of dripping, overlaid on the background cacophony as the countless creatures of the daytime gave way to their noisy nocturnal cousins.

Something was rattling the bushes not far from where Benfro sat. He watched, fascinated by the busy motion. He was too weary to be afraid, could not even bring himself to get up and investigate. Overhead, the light was fading as evening gave way to night. He would just sit here, rest. In the morning he would feel better; then he could look for something to eat and work out how he was going to find his way to Corwen.

The bushes gave a final startled rattle and a large squirrel popped into view. Benfro assumed it was the same one he had seen before, but in truth he could not be certain. It scuttled across the small bare patch of loam that surrounded the massive tree towards the mounded crater where he had landed, stopping when it saw the space empty. It scratched at its head with a small claw, looking this way and that as if astonished that something so large could be not there any more. Then it sniffed the air, circling until it was facing in Benfro's direction. It hopped through the leaf mould towards where he sat in the darkest shadows, pausing hesitantly, unwilling to commit itself to the darkness.

'Dragon?' it said in its curious piping voice. 'You there?'

Benfro revised his earlier opinion about it making a tasty snack. There wasn't enough meat on the creature to be worth the effort. And besides, he felt it would be somehow wrong to eat something that could talk. He had never before met a squirrel that could do this, but at that moment he wasn't too concerned. The beast seemed to be friendly, and he hadn't talked to anyone friendly in far too long.

'I'm here,' he said quietly.

'You walk?' the squirrel asked. Benfro considered the question. Yes, he probably could walk if he put his mind to it. But he would really rather stay put.

'Yes, I guess so.'

'Then follow.' The squirrel hopped off towards the greenery that fringed the space around the base of the tree. It stopped at the edge, glanced back to see whether its command was being obeyed, shrugged when it saw it wasn't. 'Follow, quick,' it said. 'Before darkness comes.'

'Wake up, boy! Ah, by the Shepherd!'

Errol heard the words a split second before something

hit him hard, knocking the wind out of him and throwing dusty gravel in his face. In his confusion it took him several seconds of retching and gasping to realize that he had fallen asleep in the saddle.

'Pick yourself up, you useless excuse for a novitiate.'

He looked up from the ground to where Captain Osgal sat on his horse, holding the reins of Errol's own mount. The captain's face was dark and angry, but that was nothing new. This was the fourth time Errol had fallen off his horse today. Or was it the fifth?

They were somewhere in the Dinas Dwyrain mountains, several days' ride east of Emmass Fawr. As Osgal constantly reminded him, they would be a good deal closer to their destination if only he could ride like the warrior priest he pretended to be. But try as he might, Errol couldn't keep up with the pace the captain set.

The first day had been hell, any joy at being away from the inquisitor soon lost to the constant chafing of his saddle and the ache in muscles he'd never known he possessed. Getting back on to his horse in the pre-dawn glow of the second day had been agony. Things had only worsened since then.

At least now, away from the well maintained Calling Road, they were forced to move at a walk most of the day, but Errol was so tired that the slower motion soon lulled him off to sleep. He suspected that some of the others in the troop slept in the saddle too, but they had developed the ability to wake up before they fell off.

Taking the reins from the captain, Errol hauled himself back on to his horse. At least the stables had furnished him with a patient old mare. Even so, he wished they had given him something a little closer to the ground. To add to his aching muscles he was bruised from head to toe, and his travelling cloak was tattered and torn.

'Right. Move out. We've another hour of light left and I want to cover as much ground as possible,' Osgal said, and once more they set off along the narrow mountain path.

An hour was optimistic. Errol could already see stars pricking the sky, and the folds of the mountains were dark shadows concealing all manner of terrible secrets. The uneven path climbed round ragged shoulders towards a yet-unseen pass, and the higher they went, the colder the wind that whipped through the holes in his cloak, the deeper the snow that lay in the gullies, waiting for more to come.

Without thinking Errol reached out to the lines for some warmth, and as he did so they swam into his vision like a thousand, thousand promises. He felt their tug, heard the ghost echoes of conversations, remembered the smells of childhood. There was something enormously comforting about their permanence and the way they called to him. They took away the pain in his arms and legs, soothed the aches and wrapped him in a comforting blanket of warmth. All too soon he could feel the tiredness dragging at his eyelids, and yet as they fell closed he could still see the scene all around him.

If anything, it was clearer.

The mountains were picked out against the night sky as if the sun were shining directly on them, yet he knew it had long since set. The dark shadows were still there, but at the same time he could see every rock and runnel, every scrubby bush and half-tree clinging to the poor soil. Every rabbit, mountain fox and nesting bird stood out sharp in his vision, even though they were so far distant he couldn't possibly have seen them.

Then he noticed the rest of the troop. They were still there, riding their horses, but they were indistinct. It was as if they were only basic representations of men. The horses they rode were clearly horses, but they seemed to have lost their harnesses. Looking around, he saw Captain Osgal's great beast holding itself tall and proud. It was even larger than usual, dwarfing the ill defined ghost-like form that sat on its back. And yet, even though it felt like Errol was looking at the captain through a heavy gauze and from a great distance, he was sure that it was Osgal.

Finally, Errol looked down at his own horse. She plodded along the line-scintillated path, dependable and steady. She had about her an aura of contentment and health, but she wore no reins, even though he could feel them in his hands.

His hands.

They weren't indistinct, like those of the other riders. His body was as he would expect it to look, complete with tatty travelling cloak and heavy cotton trousers, but his hands were somehow different. They glowed for a start, colours swirling in thick patterns around the edges of his fingers. He lifted them up to his face, the better to study them, aware somewhere that he had dropped his reins. It was as if a second thick skin of light clothed him, and as he looked closer, so he saw that it continued up his arms, over his body, down his legs.

Looking around at the captain again, Errol now saw a similar light clinging to Osgal, but it was a thin thing, little more than a flush on his featureless face. The other riders had it too, in greater or lesser amounts, but none of them as thick and vibrant as Errol's.

The more he studied it, the more he could feel the swirling patterns as an extension of his skin, like another sense. He shuffled in his saddle, feeling the light swirl around him like an envelope of warm water. And as he moved in it, so it changed shape, swelling and tightening around him to take on a different form, a more natural form, but one that pulled him backwards with an indefinable weight spreading from the middle of his back.

Looking over his shoulder, he saw for the briefest instant what looked like wings of light, then with a sickening sense of vertigo he slid off his horse.

'By the Wolf! There he goes again,' Errol heard Osgal say just before the ground knocked all sense out of him.

Benfro had thought he was in the middle of impenetrable forest, but he hadn't followed the curious squirrel for more than five minutes – just time to push his way through a thick swathe of rhododendron bushes – before they stepped out into a vast clearing. The ground rose slightly from the edge of the trees, culminating in a point perhaps three hundred yards away, although it was difficult to gauge distance accurately in the failing light. Rising from the top of this small hill and dominating the whole clearing was the biggest tree Benfro had ever seen.

'Come, come,' the squirrel said in its high-pitched chirpy voice. 'Mother see you now.'

The great tree rose up into the sky, its leaves reaching out two hundred yards in all directions from a trunk a half a hundred thick at its base. The canopy should have shaded the ground beneath it, but in the strange light he could see everything with equal ease. The squirrel reached the point of the tree's furthest reach and a supple branch dipped down to the ground as if to welcome it. The joy that swept over Benfro as it jumped into the leaves and disappeared almost brought him to his knees. It was a great wave of emotion, the blissful welcoming of a loved one returned. He was bathing in its reflected splendour when the voice spoke quietly in his head.

'It's many years since a dragon last visited these woods,' it said not unkindly. 'Even more since one came from the sky.'

Benfro didn't know what to say. He just stood, gawping, his senses overwhelmed.

'Who are you?' he said eventually, realizing as he did quite how rude it sounded.

'Have I been forgotten? Has it been so long?' The voice carried a note of great sadness in it.

'I'm sorry.' Benfro looked around, still uncertain where the voice was coming from. 'I meant no disrespect. My name is Benfro. Did you send the squirrel to fetch me here?'

'My little Malkin? No, I didn't send him. He's a great wanderer and a mischievous meddler in other creatures' affairs. He tells me that you crashed into the forest and were obviously in need. He was right to bring you to me. I've no quarrel with dragons any more. Your kind are always welcome to my shelter.'

'You're the tree.' Benfro finally understood.

'Not just any tree,' the voice replied, the merest hint of petulance in its voice. 'I am the world tree, the mother of all.'

Benfro stared up at the giant before him. Standing at the fringe of its reach, he couldn't see the top, only an endless wall of leaves towering over him. Where before he had thought it an improbably sized oak, he now saw leaves, flowers and fruit from a dozen or more different species. And those were just the ones he recognized. There were beech nuts, apple and cherry blossom, great fat pears dangling from low branches and enormous hairy chestnut casings fully as big as his fist. The foliage varied from almost black spines as long as his tail to great wide leaves fluttering gently in the night breeze.

The closer he looked, the more he could see. Thousands of birds slept in its branches, heads tucked under wings or just staring blankly ahead. Dormice, squirrels and curious long-armed creatures with thin agile tails leaped, scurried and generally busied themselves foraging. Occasionally they would meet something larger, usually resulting in a sharply truncated chirrup of surprise. Benfro found himself walking under the great lower branches, drawn by his curiosity ever closer to the great trunk that speared up ahead of him like a great wooden barrier.

'You're weary,' the voice of the tree said. 'And I suspect hungry too.' Now that he knew where it was coming from, he realized the voice sounded very much like his mother's. Not so much in the sounds – it was after all appearing in his head, not coming through his ears. It was more the inflections, the choice of words, the concern. It soothed him like a warm blanket on a chill night, smothering the tiny voice of fear and wariness that lurked in the depths of his mind. It was too calm, too comforting, too safe to be afraid here. No harm could possibly come to him.

'I haven't eaten in several days,' he said as he reached the great trunk, stretched out a hand and touched its massive bulk.

'Then come, enter my home. Let me provide for you. And in return you can tell me what brings you here.'

Benfro could not have sworn the opening wasn't there before, though neither did he remember not seeing it. Nor had he seen it open, but it stood before him, as natural as any cleft in an ancient tree might be. It was easily big enough for him to walk through and it led into the heart of the tree. As if someone had lit a candle around the corner of a long corridor, flickering light beckoned him in. Hesitant, he stood at the entrance in a quandary. Everything felt right, peaceful, welcoming, yet he couldn't help remembering the things he had stumbled upon, the dangers that lurked in the most innocuous of places.

'Caution is an admirable trait,' the tree said in its soothing voice. 'But I assure you I mean no harm.' As it said the words, an odour wafted from the passage so sweet it weakened Benfro's knees. It was stewed apples smothered in honey. It was chestnuts roasting on an open fire. It was the sweet tang of lemons and the expensive musk of spices he could only associate with great feast days. His stomach lurched and groaned at the promise of such delicacies, taking over the reasoning from his brain and relaying orders direct to his legs. He was several paces down the passageway before he even realized he had moved. The flickering light in the distance grew with each pace, and before long he reached the point where he had thought the corridor turned. He stopped, steeling himself to step around the corner, and gasped at what he saw.

He had entered a vast space, bigger by far than the village hall he had once considered the biggest thing it was possible to build. Grown out of the centre of the massive trunk, it rose up in a great arc, a dome of heartwood eaten away by millennia of insects and decay. Strange fungus sprouted from the walls in huge fans of luminescent flesh. They cast a green pallor over the whole which combined with the rich moist aroma, the heady scent of compost and the spicy smell of the wood to give an almost drowsy feel to the place. It was warm, and the soft floor deadened sound so that all Benfro could hear was the slow rhythm of his breathing and the regular *thumpity-thump* of his hearts.

In the middle of the great hall, apparently growing from the floor, a large table was laid with a feast. Wooden bowls were filled to brimming with fruit and nuts; platters spread with salad leaves and spicy herbs. Some plates steamed, their contents mysterious but promising much by their lush aromas. Benfro walked politely to the table, although he really wanted to run, grab, shove as much food into his face as he could without suffocating. Table manners had always been of supreme importance to the dragons of the village and, even starving, he couldn't bring himself to be impolite.

A large bench ranged along one side of the table, just the right height for Benfro to sit comfortably without damaging his bruised tail. At the table's head sat a single chair, far too small for any dragon. It was ornately carved of a wood so dark it was almost black. He stared at it, wondering what manner of creature could possibly sit in such a seat, for while it was undoubtedly a chair, it had no space at the back for a tail, and its high sides would have crushed even the smallest of vestigial wings. With a terrible lurching in his empty stomach, Benfro realized the chair was designed almost perfectly for a man to sit in. And then she appeared, shimmering into existence in front of his eyes.

She was a curious creature, far smaller than Benfro would have expected, yet tall and long-limbed where the men he had seen had been stocky and muscled. Her skin was almost white and smooth as the surface of an egg. She had long hair of palest gold which grew only from the top of her head but flowed down to her waist, tumbling over the back and sides of the chair. Her clothes were a fabric of rich green, embroidered with a motif that looked like ivy growing over her body. Her face was thin with eyes like a cat's, more green and gold than yellow. Her ears poked through her fine hair, slender and rising to pointed tips. She smiled at his open-mouthed stare, her thin red lips parting to reveal smooth, perfect teeth, white as polished old bone. Raising an arm, also encased in green, she motioned with the flat of her hand to the food spread out on the table, her long fingers curving almost back on themselves and revealing elegantly manicured talons that nevertheless spoke of razor sharpness.

'Eat, Benfro, eat,' she said. 'You look starved near to death.'

Not wanting to cause offence, Benfro sat himself at the

bench and reached for a plate of steaming white vegetables, speared one with a claw and popped it into his mouth. The taste exploded in him, wiping away all sense of decorum. For a full hour he fed, mouthful upon mouthful, stopping only to drink from a huge flagon of water, cold as ice and strangely, pleasantly sweet. He ate until he could feel his belly scales parting under the strain, and yet the table seemed just as full as when he had started. All the while the pale figure watched him silently, an indulgent smile on her face. Finally he could eat no more and a comfortable weariness began to settle on him.

'That's better,' the tree said. 'You had me worried for a while. I thought you had no aura left.'

'No what?' Benfro asked, trying hard not to belch aloud.

'No aura, Benfro. No spark of life. No glow. You were so drawn in on yourself I thought you might be lost. It's amazing what a little food can do to restore vitality.'

'Well, thank you for that most generous meal.' An embarrassed heat spread around Benfro's neck and behind his ears as he remembered his manners. He was starting to feel bloated now, stretched to a point not far from pain.

'It was nothing, really,' the tree said. 'These are the gifts of the green, nature's bounty. I merely pass them on. Now, young dragon, it's time for you to tell me your tale.'

Benfro recalled they had a bargain. And while he wanted nothing more than to find a comfortable corner in which to sleep for a thousand years, he was aware of his obligation. He knew also that sleeping so soon after eating, however right it felt, would only leave him feeling worse when he woke. Better by far to try and stay awake until the tightness around his waist subsided.

So he told his tale, beginning from the moment he had first become aware of the true danger the warrior priests posed to him and his kind. He stopped many times to slake his thirst at the flagon, which yet remained brimful however much he drank. His voice did not echo in the great hall, and there were times when he found it hard to describe what had happened, but he ploughed on as best he could right up to the point where he had stood in the clearing, gazing up at the magnificent tree. All through his tale the tiny figure watched him without interruption. She leaned forward, head resting on her hands, hanging on his every word. When finally he fell silent it was as if the whole world had been holding its breath.

'What a splendid story, Sir Benfro, indeed.' The tree clapped her hands together. He was struck by the way she used the honorific, the title that Father Gideon had mis-used, that his mother had given him, that Magog had so casually assumed of him. It sounded right, as if he was truly an adult now and worthy of the name.

'But you're exhausted,' the tree continued. 'You must rest now. You'll be safe here under my protection.' She waved a hand and the table disappeared, revealing a patch of soft ground covered with fresh leaves. When Benfro stood, his bench vanished too, as did the chair, leaving the strange creature that was the tree standing. Something about her struck a chord deep in his memory, as if he had seen her before, though he knew that was impossible. Her stance was like that of men and yet she couldn't have been more different.

'Once more I must thank you for your hospitality,' he said. 'But I can't help wondering . . . You are the tree, yet you have taken on this form. Why?'

She fixed him with a stare that was almost stern, a frown wrinkling the skin above her eyes for a moment before smoothing in what Benfro guessed was a decision made. In front of his eyes she changed, not so much melting as becoming different. It was at once slow and impossibly fast, so that Benfro felt he had watched her grow throughout a lifetime and yet for only a fraction of a second. Now in front of him stood a dragon, magnificent and huge. The villagers, even his mother, seemed plain by comparison with this creature, which was so beautiful he could feel the strength going from his knees even as he gazed upon her.

'I could have taken this form.' The tree now spoke with the pure deep tones and intonation of a dragon of the highest breeding. 'But I though it would only confuse you. None such as this has walked this land in many, many years.'

'Ammorgwm.' Benfro spoke the word as barely a whisper, but a flicker of a smile spread across the broad face looking down at him.

'That was a name I took, once upon a time.' The smile faded as she shrank back into the form she had taken before, her voice now coloured with a sadness like autumn leaves. 'But it caused only grief and pain. Something you'll understand in time, I've no doubt; you're linked to that story by your parentage. Now I take this form when dealing with the world outside. It was an idea I had a long, long time ago. The last of this race withdrew from Gwlad aeons ago, though once they graced the land with their beauty and intelligence. And I find the form comfortable. Do you like it?'

'Yes,' Benfro said more out of politeness than truth, though he didn't find it objectionable either.

'Good,' the tree said, and around the vast room the fungi started to fade to darkness. 'Sleep now, Sir Benfro. We will speak again.'

The blackness wasn't total. A faint luminescence still hovered in the air, somehow closer than the distant walls. For a moment the tree stood there, her white skin glowing in the dark, then she too faded away to nothing. Suddenly weary beyond caring, Benfro settled himself down into the bed of leaves. They were soft and warm and gave off a sweet lavender aroma as he turned, once, twice, to find a comfortable position.

He was asleep before the third.

8

One particular tale of the mother tree is perhaps worth repeating, since it helps to illuminate the otherwise rather dull mind of the average dragon. It is said that if one seeks the tree, and if the tree thinks the seeker worthy, then it will appear and welcome him in. It will provide sustenance, knowledge and whatever it is that the seeker truly desires. In return it will ask only for a story.

Many dragons claim to have set out in search of the mother tree, yet in all my travels among the villages and settlements of their slow kind have I encountered only one who claimed to have actually succeeded in their quest. An elderly creature styling itself Sir Crempog, he told of months spent wandering through the great forest of the Ffrydd, following tracks only animals knew and scavenging what food he could in that terrible place. Delirious with thirst and weak from too long without food, the young Crempog finally stumbled upon a clearing at the centre of which stood his great tree. Water flowed around its roots and fruit of all varieties hung from its lower branches, easy for him to reach. He fed well, his health almost magically restored in moments, and as he fed the tree told him all about the world beyond the forest: of the oceans and mountains and plains of wind-rippled grass, of great cities and halls of stone, of creatures older even than dragons and men. Then, when the tree asked him for his tale, he told it of his journey before settling down to sleep.

Waking on the morrow, the dragon found himself alone in a clearing in the forest, with no sight of the great tree to be seen. A track passed beside him and he had the choice of two ways to go. He had no way of knowing which direction led home and which wandered off into the rest of the world. A part of him longed to explore, for the tree had shown him many splendid things in his dreams. And yet he yearned more for the security and certainty of his village and the small nest of sad creatures he called family. So he set off, and the path took him home in less than two days' walking.

Father Charmoise, *Dragons' Tales*

Try as he might, Errol couldn't regain the strange sight over the rest of the journey. With the passing of days he tried, but his strength was building all the time and he no longer nodded off in the saddle quite so often. His riding improved too, and he quickly developed the ability to wake up and correct his seat before falling off.

Their route took them through the high country, the sparsely inhabited borderlands in the Dwyrain mountains, which divide the Twin Kingdoms from Llanwennog. For days they rode along the increasingly snow-capped ridge tops, skirting the actual border as if looking for a suitable place to plunge down into the enemy's lair. Now, finally, they reached a wide valley that cut a great semicircle through the mountains. At its centre a massive cone of rock thrust up from the flat valley floor, and clustered around this like insects attracted by some decaying carcass lay the town of Tynewydd.

Once they had dropped out of the mountains on to the high plain, the road widened and Osgal picked up their speed. Errol had to concentrate on staying in the saddle as he cantered and then galloped to keep up. At first he was scared by the speed, tense at the thought of falling off and the injuries he might sustain. But with each passing mile, so his confidence grew. And, as he relaxed, he began to feel the rhythm of his horse's movements, settling into them rather than fighting against them.

'Better,' Osgal shouted as he dropped back along the line of the troop, inspecting each of his men in turn. 'Maybe we'll make a rider out of you after all.' It was the barest compliment, but Errol accepted it nonetheless. It was the first time he could remember the captain saying anything to him that wasn't a criticism or a threat.

After about an hour they reached a ford over the river that had followed them down from the mountains. Osgal called a halt.

'Set up camp here,' he said to his warrior priests. 'I'll take the boy into town on my own. If I'm not back by the end of the week, head back to Emmass Fawr and tell Melyn I'm sorry for failing him.'

'Is that likely?' Errol asked. 'Is there that much danger?'

'Silence, boy!' Osgal cuffed him across the back of his

head. 'You will speak only when spoken to. And you will speak in Llanwennog. Or did you think they'd be happy to talk to you in Saesneg in Tynewydd?'

Errol kept his mouth shut, chastened. He had been lulled into a sense of security, riding with a troop of warrior priests into the wild lands. Now he was nearing the first stage of his goal, he remembered the true nature of what he had to do and what was at stake should he fail.

'Come on then, boy.' Osgal slipped into heavily accented Llanwennog. 'Let's get this over with.'

By mid-afternoon they had almost reached their destination. The great spire of rock seemed to shrink rather than grow as they approached it, dwarfed by the wall of rock that formed the far side of the valley. Errol could see that stone buildings had been hacked into its side, culminating in a stubby tower at its peak. A solid-looking wall circled the town, not quite containing all the buildings, and for the first time in many days he saw people milling around.

They slowed to a trot as they approached the gates to the town, then to a walk as they entered its shaded streets. Errol had expected there to be guards, had thought he would hear Llanwennog spoken by everyone around him. As it was, most of the people looked no different to the captain riding alongside him. And what snippets of conversation he heard were a mixture of both languages and a few words he didn't recognize at all.

They climbed slowly through the narrow streets of Tynewydd until finally they reached a wide courtyard. Ahead of them the spire of rock rose into the sky, and Errol could see now that it had been formed into a strong castle. Some time in the past this area had been rich and worth defending, but with the passage of years it had lost much of its importance and the wealth with which to maintain such an impressive fortress. At least that was what he surmised as they approached it, for it was a ramshackle, run-down place.

The gates were wide open but guarded. At their approach two soldiers stepped together, raising spears to block their path.

'State your business,' one of them said.

'I'm here to see –' Osgal began to say, but he was interrupted by a voice from the battlements above his head.

'Ah, Osgal, you're here,' a grey-haired man said in fluent Saesneg. 'Let them pass,' he added to the guards, switching to their native language.

They dismounted and led their horses into the castle, where the grey-haired man waited for them. Osgal bowed his head slightly to the man.

'Your Grace, may I be presenting to you Errol Ramsbottom,' he said in his imperfect Llanwennog. Then he turned to Errol. 'This is His Grace, Duke Dondal of Tynewydd. He is being your master now.'

Errol bowed but said nothing. The duke scarcely looked at him. Osgal unclipped two heavy saddlebags from his horse and a couple of stable hands appeared to take the beasts away.

'Give the captain's horse some feed,' Dondal said to the first of the two boys. They weren't that much younger than he was, Errol suspected. 'But don't bother with stabling it; he won't be staying long.' Then he turned away, heading across the courtyard to a large open doorway, motioning for them to follow.

Inside was dark, a hall lit by small narrow windows high in the front wall, its back hewn from the rock. The air was cold, with a damp musty smell of caves that put Errol in mind of some of the lower levels of Emmass Fawr. For some reason he recalled the mortuary and the strange hurried post-mortem of Princess Lleyn.

A long table of dark oak sat beside an empty fireplace, and Duke Dondal slumped into the seat at its head.

'You have something for me, Osgal?' The duke motioned with a hand encrusted with jewelled rings, still paying Errol no attention. The captain opened the first bag and emptied a pile of gold coins on to the table.

'The other one's got the same in it.' Osgal switched to Saesneg with what might have been a sneer in his voice. 'How soon before you set off to Tynhelyg?'

'Oh that'll be months yet.' Dondal casually picked up one of the coins. 'The boy's got to settle in here first, learn his new craft. People have to accept him as part of my retinue. But don't worry; I've the perfect cover for him.'

Osgal stared at Dondal, and in the half-light Errol fancied he could see the anger boiling off the captain like steam on a winter's morning. He stood, fuming, for some seconds, a poor imitation of the inquisitor.

'Was there anything else, Captain?'

'No, Your Grace.'

'Then I suspect you'll be wanting to get back to your monastery.' He pulled a sheaf of papers from the depths of his robe and handed it to the captain. 'Give this to Melyn, would you.'

If Osgal bowed, Errol couldn't see it. The captain

glared once at him, said, 'Remember what I told you,' then stalked out of the room.

'Such a coarse fellow. I find Padraig's emissaries so much easier to get on with. And they can at least speak properly.' He turned finally to Errol. 'And what about you, boy? Can you convince me?'

'Convince you of what, Your Grace?' Errol asked in his best Llanwennog.

'Well, at least you've got the accent reasonably well. Come here.'

Errol stepped forward, bowing once more. The duke grabbed him by the cheeks, pulling his head up and looking at him like he might judge a ram at a country fair.

'You're Llanwennog, that's for sure. Who was your father, Errol?'

'I don't know, Your Grace. My mother wouldn't speak of him, except to say he'd been killed in a tavern brawl months before I was born.'

'Did she say where she met him?'

'No, sir,' Errol said. 'Although I know she worked for a while at Ystumtuen.'

'Ah, yes.' Dondal let go of Errol's face. 'That might explain it.'

'Explain what, please, Your Grace?' Errol asked, immediately regretting his forwardness. The duke looked at him with a quizzical expression, not annoyed as much as surprised that someone would even think of asking him such a question.

'You have royal blood in you, Errol Ramsbottom. Not much, it's true. But it's there for anyone with eyes to see.'

*

Benfro stood on the green in front of the great hall, back in the village. It was as he remembered it from the day the old dragons had died. It *was* the day they had died, he thought. Only it was earlier somehow. Everything was still intact, unbroken.

Then they came, the warrior priests. They marched up the lane on foot, the inquisitor at their head on a horse. As if performing some dreadful dance, groups split off, one by one, into the houses. Their discipline was intimidating, their complete silence terrifying.

Some of the dragons resisted. Others, heads bowed, accepted with a modicum of grace the fate they had so long feared. None seemed surprised that this time had come. Only Meirionydd fought, lashing out at the nearest men with her talons and screaming such language as he had never heard before. Spells boiled the air around her, pushing back the warrior priests for an instant. He willed her to succeed, to kill one and then all of the dreadful creatures, but all too soon she was stopped. He could not see what held her, some invisible force that she struggled against with all her might even when they put her eyes out. Eventually she could scarcely stand. Blood was running down her sides and one arm was clearly broken. When she finally collapsed, the warrior she had first attacked stepped up to her, pissed on her head and then cut off her wings with a swiftly conjured blade of light. Only then would they allow Ynys Môn and Sir Maesyfed to pick her up and carry her limp body along with the others.

All were herded on to the green near to where Benfro stood, motionless and disregarded. Those that resisted were beaten with invisible blows that raised ugly scars, snapped scales and bones. Eventually, when the warriors had taken their pleasure, the cowed dragons were lined up in front of the hall in front of their chief tormentor, the inquisitor.

'Where is the hatchling?' he asked, his voice loaded with barely controlled rage. There was a moment's silence as the old dragons merely glared at their tormentors. And then a familiar voice came from the back.

'His name is Benfro. He's the bastard of that witch Morgwm and some great oaf calling himself Trefaldwyn.'

'Who speaks?' the inquisitor asked. 'Come forward and show yourself.'

He knew who was going to edge herself through the pathetic huddle. Frecknock. He had never understood why she disliked him. Could it just be that, until he came along, she was the youngest? Was it just petty jealousy that made her betray her own kind to these monsters? Vanity that had killed them all?

She stood in front of the inquisitor with her head held high. There were no marks on her hide so she had not resisted when they had come for her but gone meekly.

'Your name?'

'I am Frecknock, Your Grace.'

'Ah, sweet Frecknock, we meet at last,' the inquisitor said, his voice slipping into the unctuous tones of Sir Felyn as he spoke in Draigiaith. 'See, I am a man of my word.'

'You!' Frecknock wailed, and for an instant Benfro almost pitied her. She seemed to deflate in front of his eyes as, finally, the true cost of her folly dawned on her.

'Frecknock, what have you done? What have we forced you to?'

Benfro looked around for whoever it was had spoken, seeing Meirionydd, blinded and battered, trying to hold herself up with some semblance of dignity. He raged to see her so helpless, defeated yet defiant. It boiled in him like his stomach was a bed of coals. And yet he was powerless, invisible, not even there.

'Kill them,' the inquisitor said. 'Kill them all. Let the forest creatures pick the meat from their bones. We'll return for their jewels at our pleasure.' He turned his back on the dragons and made his way up the track towards the forest, where more warrior priests waited with the horses.

'Your Grace,' one of the younger men said, 'with respect, is it wise to kill all of them? A tame one would be a magnificent gift for our new queen. The young female might easily be broken and house-trained.'

'Why is it, Clun,' the inquisitor asked, 'that whenever someone prefaces a comment with the words "with respect", I just know they have anything but respect in mind?'

'Sir, I only meant,' the young lad stuttered, but he was cut short by the inquisitor's guttural laugh.

'Don't panic, boy. You're right of course. If a few more of you showed such backbone and intelligence I'd feel a deal more confident you might make it through the induction. Keep the young female; the others are no use to us. Kill them.'

Benfro watched helplessly as Frecknock was forced to

lie beside the inquisitor's nervous horse. The others meanwhile were being herded ever closer to the great hall. Suddenly they all stopped, turned as a mass to stare at their executioners. For a second he thought they might make a stand there. Fight. Sir Frynwy elbowed himself to the front. He stood tall and proud, chest out and fluttering his drab old wings like two pieces of chamois leather well past their best.

'We all of us made a choice, countless years ago,' he said. 'Every one of us could have roamed the world, alone and powerful. Yet we chose to live in gentle companionship here, no harm to anyone. Now we make another choice, all of us. You can kill us, true. You have that power over us. But we will not go to slaughter fearful, like cattle. We embrace our deaths with courage and dignity. Come, friends. Follow me.' And with a last contemptuous sneer at the inquisitor, he whirled round and led them all up the small stone steps and into the hall.

'Fine words, dragon.' The inquisitor waved an arm lazily across the scene. 'But you will still die.'

The warriors took up position around the building and Benfro watched as the inquisitor waved his hand once more. A ball of fire appeared from nowhere, hovering lightly over his outstretched palm. With a flick of the wrist, he sent it crashing through one of the great windows, closely followed by another and another. It wasn't long before the hall was a wall of flame. Yet no sound rose from the conflagration except the roar of the blaze, the popping of timbers and the crash of stone when the roof at last gave way.

When he was finally satisfied that no one was going to

escape, the inquisitor wheeled his horse round, turned his back on the pyre and shrugged his shoulders in an annoyed way, as if the catharsis he so craved had eluded him once more.

'Fall in,' he said. 'We've got a hatchling to find. He'll be frightened and helpless, so I want you all to tune in to his fear.'

Benfro watched as the warrior priests gathered together like a colony of disturbed ants. A smaller band appeared, leading a group of very nervous-looking horses and a couple of wagons. Soon all of the men were mounted. Frecknock was chained to the back of the last wagon without any complaint. Her face was a mask, unreadable. At a silent command, the column moved out of the village, the inquisitor casting treacherous flames into each house as they passed it. Invisible, Benfro could only stand and stare as the village that had been his home burned to the ground.

As he stood in the ruins of everything he had ever loved, the sky split open above him, torn like a sheet of paper. Huge taloned claws pulled the sides of the rent wide and a face poked through the gap, looking down on the scene with a malicious, hungry gleam in its eyes. It was a familiar face, draconian, though he could not remember where he had seen it before. He thought at first it had come to wreak havoc on the warrior priests, take revenge for the ill done to its kind. Instead it reached out for the burning hall, dragged the smoking timbers from the collapsed roof with a single taloned finger and then reached into the fiery mass.

It grabbed one of the seated dragons within, wrapping the still body in its fist and lifting the charred, smoking corpse to its mouth before swallowing it whole. It seemed to grow as it did this, not so much in size as in clarity. Powerless to do anything, Benfro could only watch as, one by one, the dead bodies of his friends were consumed. With each swallow the dragon in the sky solidified, its body gaining coherence to the point where it could begin to clamber through the tear in the sky and stretch its massive wings.

'Magog,' Benfro whispered to himself.

The dragon only screamed, a bestial noise that echoed through the forest. Surely the warriors would hear it, come running. But they didn't. And Benfro knew that they were long gone, his dream moved forward days or even weeks. For that was what it was, he now knew. A dream. Something had forced him to witness the terrible suffering and death of his friends and now it was eating their memory. Furious, he ran into the great hall, now no more than a weed-overgrown tumble of soot-blackened masonry and charred beams.

The sight that greeted him was if anything worse than the reality he had experienced so many weeks earlier. The dragons were dead, but they were not proudly, defiantly sitting in their places. They cowered, burned and twisted, under the table, in the lee of the windows, anywhere that might hide them from the dread creature overhead. And with a sickening lurch in his stomach Benfro realized that even in death they were terrified of the great dragon in the sky. As he stared at the carnage with incomprehension, he saw its massive hand reach down again, feeling about blindly in the mess of the hall and wrapping itself around the blackened form of Ynys Môn.

Instinct took over then. With a roar of anger that had all the power of his frustration and fear of the warrior priests behind it, Benfro launched himself towards the great hand. He felt a rage so hot it boiled in his blood, turned his stomach to fire. And then the flame erupted from him.

It was like the reckoning fire. It leaped from body to body, ignoring the wooden table and charred beams. As they were engulfed, the dead villagers seemed to straighten up, no longer cowering. And then the flame reached Ynys Môn, who was struggling mightily against the hand of Magog. With a cry of surprise and pain, the great dragon released its quarry and the hand withdrew. Looking up, Benfro could see only the sky, cloudy and darkening.

Movement dragged his eyes back to the great hall. All the dragons were again seated, determined and upright in their places. The flame played around them, not so much devouring their bodies as slowly, gently, fading them from solid to nothing. Benfro thought he should have been sad. Certainly he felt anguish and shame at having breathed fire, even in a dream. But the feeling of joy emanating from the dead wiped that shame away.

'I'm sorry for ever doubting you, Benfro.' The words were Sir Frynwy's, but surely the old dragon was too far gone to be speaking to him? 'You've set us free now and our spirits can mingle here for all time.'

'What . . . what did I do?' Benfro asked, confused and happy and sad all at the same time.

'We were dead yet unreckoned. Our memories were leaching away with the passing months. You've changed that.' The old dragon's voice was fading fast now.

'What do you mean? I don't understand.' Benfro longed for answers, but even as he asked the question the last flickering light of his fire guttered out on the breeze. The villagers were gone.

'No, boy! Hold it properly.'

The words were backed up with a sharp slap to the back of his head so that Errol almost dropped the soup bowl he was carrying to the table. Duke Dondal glared at him as if he was an imbecile but then allowed him to get on with his duties without further criticism. Errol carried bowls to all the other guests at the high table, bowing politely to each in turn. It wasn't what he had expected to do as a page, but it was better than living in constant fear of Melyn.

'Tell me, Dondal, where did you find this boy?' One of the guests asked, blithely ignoring Errol himself.

'Ah, well there's a tale,' Dondal said. 'You remember my brother Edgar? Used to spend all of his time up in the mountains hunting. Well, it seems he wasn't always hunting animals; caught himself a few wenches up there as well. This young fellow turned up a few weeks ago with a signet ring he claims Edgar gave to his mother as a token. More likely found it lying around and thought he'd take his chances, but he's got the family likeness.'

'Edgar,' the guest said. 'He died in the border wars a few years back, didn't he? Fought alongside Prince Dafydd.'

'Yes.' Dondal's voice went quiet. A silence fell on the room for a few moments, and Errol was painfully aware that all eyes were on him now.

'He's darker than his father,' one of the guests said after a while. 'I guess Edgar had a taste for the wild ones.'

If anything the silence was deeper, as if everyone had taken in a deep breath. Errol felt the air turn cold and he wished he could sink through the floor or turn invisible, but he knew this exposure was essential if he was to be accepted into Llanwennog society.

'Hah! He certainly did.' Dondal roared with laughter. The moment had passed and with it the attention. Errol slunk off to the end of the room, taking his position in the shadows behind the huge chair at the head of the table.

Not a day had passed since Errol had arrived in this backwater town, somewhere along the mountainous border between Llanwennog and the Twin Kingdoms, when he hadn't thought about running off. Freed from the glamours that bound him to Emmass Fawr, he could easily have slipped away in the night, had he not been so hopelessly out of his depth he couldn't even think about what to do. His duties as a page were so arduous that he had scarcely any free time to begin planning an escape, and besides he was far too busy learning his new role and trying not to give his true identity away.

He had lost count of the days and weeks he had been at Tynewydd. In the main he was confined to the castle, given endless tasks to perform, though once or twice he had been out on lavish hunting parties with the duke. It was two days now since the last one had returned, and the guests were still making the most of Dondal's hospitality. But deep snow had finally made it to the mountain passes and the season for hunting was closed. Soon it would be time for the duke to make his biannual trek to Tynhelyg to pay his tithes. As a gesture of loyalty to the throne, Errol would be presented as a page, to serve young Prince Dafydd and his newly betrothed Princess Iolwen. At least when he embarked on the trip to the capital he would be further still from Emmass Fawr and the inquisitor. And away from Dondal he might have more time to himself, time to learn about this new country and how to survive in it.

'I said wine, boy!' The duke's harsh words interrupted Errol's musings. Adopting his most subservient attitude, he took up a heavy pewter jug filled with dark mountain wine and hurried to do his latest master's bidding.

Benfro sat up and stretched his neck, trying to iron out the kinks that folded themselves from the top of his scalp right down to the tip of his tail. His legs and arms were stiff, his joints unwilling to bend the way nature intended. It felt as if he had lain motionless for months.

The first thing that he noticed was that he wasn't inside the great tree any more; he was lying in a patch of dry grass under a leafy canopy beside a sluggish stream. The sun had risen some time earlier, warming the air and stirring the gentlest of breezes. A light dew still clung to the ground in the shade.

Confused, he stood up, seeing for the first time two bags propped against the nearest tree trunk. The first was his bag, his mother's bag, which he had taken from the ruined cottage. The second was woven from thick grass, with sturdy handles made from braided hemp. Opening it, he found a selection of vegetables, fruit and some nuts. Enough to last him at least a week, longer if he were able to hunt or fish. It was, he thought, a gift from the mother tree. He remembered her strange appearance, the food she had given him and the story she had asked for in return. Her kindness and peace felt like something from the distant past; another crueller memory had pushed her to the back of his mind.

His dream came back to him in an agonizing series of disjointed images. It jumbled into his memory, blurring the boundaries of what was real and what was imagined. He had dreamed before, countless times, yet always come the morning he had known where dream ended and reality began. Now he wasn't so sure. The tumble of emotions: elation on seeing the village whole, horror on seeing it destroyed, terror on seeing the great form of Magog, guilt and shame as he breathed fire like some feral throwback to a time when dragons were naught but great lumbering beasts – all these were real to him. They sharpened the focus of his recent experience, swinging him rapidly back and forth between happiness and hopelessness, hot and cold like Ebrill showers on a sunny day, the shadows of scurrying clouds.

He recalled the image of Magog in the clouds, devouring the villagers one by one. Worried, he picked up his leather bag, rummaged around in it until he found the last remnant of Magog and plucked out the tiny pink fragment. It sparkled in the morning light, a pale crimson that radiated menace. His vision blurred as he stared at it. Were there really tiny tendrils of red light swirling around the gem like smoke, like thorny creepers growing around his fingers, gripping them tight so that he might never let go? How else had the terrible form of Magog invaded his dream?

With a determined effort of will, Benfro drew back his arm and threw the jewel as far away from him as he possibly could. It arced through the air, a tiny missile that whistled as it flew, further and further, until it came to a rest in the long grass, hidden from view.

'What Benfro do?' The little figure of the squirrel Malkin dropped from the branches of the nearest tree, its hands clutched around a large acorn.

'Getting rid of bad company.' Benfro slung one bag over his shoulder and bent down to pick up the other. He was pleased to see the squirrel and was about to ask it about the tree, but suddenly the world dimmed around him. His head spun and the ground swayed alarmingly as if there were some great tremor underground, some massive earth-bound beast turning in its grave. He fell forward first to his knees, then on to all fours, half-expecting the trees to come crashing down around his ears. On the ground he felt a little better – at least the swaying of the blades of grass was in time with the gentle breeze.

'Benfro all right?' Malkin asked.

He looked sideways at the little squirrel, its face a mask of apprehension as it sprang through the grass to his side. Its surefooted movements seemed to anchor him, and he was able to get a grip on the swinging trees and curious upward-flowing river.

'Fine,' he said after a while 'Just a little light-headed. I must have bent down too quickly.'

Slowly this time, he pushed himself up on to his haunches, resting the weight of his body on the thick stem of his tail. Things still felt unreal, his head fuzzy as if he had held his breath underwater until his vision started to swim away from him. He focused on the diamond patterns that blurred everything, trying to see through them, but a wave of nausea rolled over him and he toppled back to the ground.

He was on all fours, staring down at the long grass around the base of one of the trees. His first coherent thought was that this was not where he had fallen. The next was that Malkin could not possibly have moved him, given that he must have weighed close on five hundred times as much as his companion. Flopping over on to his back, he saw the squirrel eyeing him nervously from a few yards away. A long track through the grass led in a straight line away from where he was. With a sinking feeling he realized what direction he had come. Slowly, reluctantly, he lifted his right hand. It was clenched around something, and it took a positive effort of will to open his fingers, palm up to reveal what he knew was there. It gleamed a pale red and weighed more than its tiny size suggested. Magog's jewel.

'Benfro better now?' Malkin asked.

'I don't know, Malkin,' he said, still slightly breathless. 'What happened?'

'Benfro fall over,' the squirrel said. 'Lie very still for a long time. Then start to crawl to tree. Get here.' It indicated the place where he lay. 'Wake up.'

Explanation over, it hunched down beside Benfro and stared at him as if his head were about to explode or he was going to turn into some strange beast with too many arms. He found the squirrel disturbing but was nevertheless grateful for some company while he regained his strength.

'I think,' Benfro said after a few minutes' companionable silence. 'I think that I need to keep this close.' He held up the jewel to the light. It glittered in the sunshine and he imagined he could hear the sound of shattering glass in the far distance. 'But not too close.'

'Benfro put in food bag,' Malkin said. 'With nuts and berries and fruit.'

'Food bag?' Benfro asked. And then he remembered. 'Where's the tree? Where am I?'

'Mother come, mother go,' Malkin said. 'Mother say dragon need to rest a while. Dragon sleep. Now dragon awake, ready to find friends. Mother leave food to help on journey.'

Benfro looked across to the spot from where he had crawled, and sure enough there were the two bags lying beside his sleeping place. Wearily, he hauled himself to his feet, noting that his balance seemed perfectly fine now. Mouthing a silent thanks to the mother tree, he wrapped the crimson jewel in some leaves plucked from a nearby shrub and placed it right at the bottom of the food bag. Then he turned to look at his surroundings again.

It was not the clearing he had entered the night before, but a much smaller one, more of a thinning of the trees where a small river meandered through them. A hard-packed path forded the water in a babble of rapids over rocks, and downstream a deep pool moved sluggishly in the morning sunshine. There were bound to be fish in there, he thought.

He waded carefully out into the stream having first placed the food bag with its concealed gem deep inside as close to the edge as he dared. He didn't want to stray too far from the jewel in case it decided to incapacitate him again. The water was cold, fresh from the mountains and brown with upland peat. The pool was deep enough to dive and he plunged underneath the surface, striking for the bottom. Huge silver trout streaked past him as he pulled himself down to the silt and great swaying fronds of weed. He sat, holding his breath, keeping himself still until the fish calmed down, all the while letting a thin trickle of bubbles rise from his mouth. Soon, far sooner than he expected, the fish circled around him, curiosity overcoming their fear. In a flash he lunged, mouth agape, fangs catching a startled fin. He pushed up from the river-bed, swirling great clouds of brown, and rose to the surface like a cork.

The fishing was good, and Benfro soon had six fat trout laid out on the bank, cleaned, headed, tailed and filleted. He ate two of the succulent slabs and wrapped the rest for the journey. All the while the effects of his earlier mishap wore off. His strength returned and the nagging headache ebbed away so that by the time the mid-morning sun had dried his back he was ready to set out.

'Malkin come too.' The squirrel broke the fascinated beady-eyed silence with which it had watched him all the while. Benfro looked down at the small creature and realized that he was glad of the company, however strange it might be.

'Do you want to sit up here?' he asked as he shouldered the bags. The little squirrel scampered on to his out-stretched hand and up his arm, settling itself on his shoulder with a grasping of tiny claws in his thick hide.

'Malkin see better from up here. Travel faster,' it said. 'Which way?'

Benfro thought a while. He had no idea really, but he had been sleeping on one side of the river and had no memory of crossing it before. Enthusiastic for the first time since he could remember, he set off through the ford.

9

Gog, Son of the Winter Moon, built his palace in the low country, high on a rocky hill that rose out of a meandering bow in the great River Abheinn. Candlehall he called it, and his throne room was the Neuadd, lit with windows of coloured glass that depicted the stories of legend: great Rasalene himself and the courting of fair Arhelion. All about this massive hall he raised buildings, courtyards and galleries so that the whole was like a small city. His hospitality was legend and at times it seemed that all dragonkind flocked to that place.

Magog, Son of the Summer Moon, was more restrained in his domain. Ever the more contemplative of the two brothers, he preferred the isolation of a sharp spur rising out of the centre of the great forest. Here he built Cenobus, a simple but grand palace, and underneath it, carved into the cold stone, he placed the repository of all his vast knowledge. Bards, warriors and those that would be mages came to this place in the hope of learning at the feet of the master, but few showed enough promise to catch his eye. Still it was a place of learning, for just to be in the presence of such power was an education in itself, and only the mountain retreat of Maddau the Wise rivalled it in this respect.

Sir Frynwy, *Tales of the Ffrydd*

Duke Dondal's city residence was as run-down as his castle in the mountains, but it sat cheek by jowl with the sprawling palace complex, testament to how his family had once been both rich and important at the royal court.

From their first approach through the great southern gate right up to the courtyard of the house Errol stuck close to his patron, terrified he would get lost in the maze of alleys, vennels and closes. There was nowhere he could get a bearing from, no open vista and no instantly recognisable building he could use as a reference point. Tynhelyg was a chaotic mess of noise and smells, people, animals, machinery all jostling together in too little space. For a boy whose life had always been defined by trees and fields, it was an overwhelming and unsettling place.

From what he had read, Errol knew Tynhelyg was built on seven low hills, with five tributaries flowing into the great River Hafren, which bounded three sides of the palace complex. The older houses of the nobles clustered around the defensive wall that formed the fourth side. He recalled seeing a picture of the place in one of Andro's books before he left Emmass Fawr, but now he was here he couldn't begin to guess where the artist had stood to compose the image. There was no room within the encompassing walls to escape the crush of people and buildings.

They had ridden as far as the gates, but there the duke had insisted on dismounting and walking to his town house. Whether this was another way of introducing him to Llanwennog society or just one of Dondal's long list of eccentricities, Errol couldn't be sure. If he wanted people to believe Errol a simpleton from the back country, then it had certainly worked. Several times on their long journey the duke had reached out and snapped his jaws shut with a low chuckle.

Now they were inside and for a moment at least Errol could relax a little.

'So what do you think of our great city, eh Errol?' Dondal asked. 'Better than Candlehall, wouldn't you say?'

'I've never been to Candlehall, sir,' Errol said truthfully.

'Come now, lad, there's no need for subterfuge here. Nothing to be ashamed of having travelled Gwlad, seen a bit.'

'No, sir, honestly. I've never been to Candlehall. This city's very impressive though.'

Dondal looked as if he had been insulted by Errol's lack of worldliness. He was about to say something when a light tap on the door interrupted them. A smartly liveried young man entered the room on Dondal's barked command. He was not one of the duke's servants, of that much Errol was sure. Most of them were surly elderly men, and their uniforms were, in the main, older and more threadbare even than them.

'Your Grace, I have a message from His Majesty King Ballah.' The man gave the slightest of bows. He had a permanent sneer on his face, his nose wrinkled as if the room smelled of something he'd rather not have stepped in, and he looked at Errol, dressed in his page's clothes, as if he were the source of that smell.

'Well, what is it, man?' the duke demanded.

'His Majesty hopes you have had a pleasant journey and requests that you join him at your earliest convenience.' The messenger turned and left without another word.

'Time was I'd have skewered him where he stood,' Dondal said, his face purpling with anger. He fumed for a moment and then let out a great sigh. 'But my influence in the court isn't what it once was, and King Ballah doesn't much like it when you kill his messengers, however rude they are.'

'How did he know you were here? The king, that is?' Errol asked.

'Oh, nothing happens within ten leagues of Tynhelyg that Ballah doesn't hear of. Part of the reason I walked here was to give his spies time to report. I knew he'd want to see me as soon as I arrived. Oh well, I guess we'd better get it over and done with.'

'What, now? But we've not had time to change. Or eat.'

'Exactly. Keeps us on our toes, don't you think? Come on.'

They left the house by a back door, walking down a narrow alleyway towered over by buildings that must have been eight storeys high. After two or three turns they arrived at a closed and guarded gate. Dondal reached into his pocket and produced something which Errol couldn't see, after which the guard stepped aside. The duke stooped to the door and fumbled at the lock.

Errol assumed that he must have shown a key. 'Here, let me,' he said, reaching out to help. Before he had even finished speaking the guard had him in headlock and a sharp blade was at his throat.

Away from the river the trees soon closed in together, their canopies merging almost completely. And yet the path was still easily followed, its hard-packed surface suggesting it was well used, even though Benfro had not seen another traveller since he had flown from Emmass Fawr.

He chatted with Malkin as they worked their way slowly up the side of the valley, reaching the top of a shallow ridge by mid-afternoon. The squirrel was not a great fount of wisdom. Its answers, when they came, were usually more questions, so that by the time they stopped for lunch Benfro had learned nothing more of the strange creature than that it had decided, apparently on a whim, to be his travelling companion, and even less about the great tree. It was nice to have company though. It helped to keep the despair away.

The path turned to follow the ridge as it climbed towards a dusty rock peak that occasionally showed through the thinning canopy. The afternoon sun, beating down from directly overhead, soon became oppressive, and Benfro cursed himself for not drinking more while he had the chance. He had no means of carrying water and had been relying on the occasional rills that babbled through the wood, tumbling over the path or diving underneath it to rise, sparkling and spring-like, on the other side. No brooks rose on the ridge now, not even the tiniest of founts welling up from between the ancient scattered rocks.

On his shoulder Malkin had fallen silent, and a glance to the side showed Benfro that the squirrel had gone to sleep, rocking back and forth with the rhythmic motion of his steps. It seemed to be quite secure, perched as it was, and he reflected that it had most likely been awake all night while he had been stuck in his dream. For all he knew it was more of a nocturnal animal anyway, glad of somewhere safe to sleep during the hot day.

The forest gave way gradually to scrubby bushes and boulders strewn as if some giant child had been playing marbles in the sand when it was called away by an irate mother. Some of the rocks were small, no larger than a fist, while others towered over Benfro as big as a house. The track worked its way around these, twisting ever up towards the peak. He couldn't help noticing how straight the edges of the boulders were, how even and smooth were their sides. Some were almost perfectly rectangular, some square. Even more extraordinary, some seemed to show signs of having been carved into the elegant curves of arches and pediments.

Once he first noticed this, Benfro began to see evidence in every rock: the chip of hammer and chisel, the smoothed surface of a long-forgotten ornament. Strewn all around him were the remains of some magnificent great building, cast down long ago from the top of the hill he had spent all the day climbing. It must have commanded a spectacular view of the forest spreading into the hazy distance all around.

The closer to the summit he came, the thicker the

jumble of broken rocks. Whole columns lay in jagged lines where they had toppled, each interlocking block stretched just a little out of place by its fall. The path had straightened now, as if someone had gone to great trouble to clear it. Or maybe the destruction wrought around it had somehow been kept from its course. It was as clean as if it had been recently swept, and paved with flat, level slabs of stone, the joins so tight no sand was needed to grout them. Not a grain of dirt marked the surface, even though the ground to either side was dusty and barren. Low steps, each about twenty paces apart, made the climb to the summit easier. Shallow parallel grooves cut into them would allow a cart with the right width wheels to pass, but the rise was still such that Benfro could not yet make out the actual summit.

The first part of the great structure he saw was an arch. It put him in mind of the monastery of the warrior priests, only this was no brutal rock construction imposed upon the mountain but a magnificent carved stone edifice seeming to grow naturally from the ground. The wall surrounding the palace was mostly gone, crushed into the debris that lay in a thick carpet over the hilltop, but what remained was enough to keep all but the most determined raider out. It stood in places fifteen foot high, in others over thirty with the shapes of windows still dimpling its top edge, but where it met the road it climbed fifty feet or more to crown that massive arch.

Two great oak doors, as thick as Benfro's waist, lay smashed and splintered on either side of the opening. They were on the outside, he noticed, blown out by something within. Whatever it had been, it had exploded a long time ago. The wood was grey with age and weathering, riddled with holes from woodworm. When he reached out a hand to one of the doors it crumbled at his touch, the faintest odour of decay reaching his nostrils, dry and powdery.

The space beyond the gateway was open to the sky, but the walls obscured the view. Benfro stood for what seemed a long time staring up at the arch. It channelled the wind, which was cool on his face with an aroma of something unplaceable but not unpleasant. It put him in mind of lazy summer afternoons, hot rocks and the promise of a good meal. The road carried on, arrow straight into the heart of the massive derelict building, and he was about to step through when the claws in his shoulder suddenly gripped tight.

'Where is this?' Malkin's squeaky voice said, an incredulous tremble in it. 'Malkin not like it.'

'There's no one here.' Benfro tried to reassure his companion when in truth it had just given voice to his own nagging fears.

'Where are trees?' Their absence was obviously a source of distress for the squirrel. Benfro looked around. Half of the view, that in front of them, was obscured by the building. Behind, the hill dropped away from them, leaving only the distant green swathe visible through the jumble of fallen rocks. A ring of mountains surrounded everything, impossibly far away and unclear in the thick hot afternoon air, with only the occasional white cap determining where ground stopped and sky began.

'It's all right, Malkin,' Benfro said, as much to comfort himself. 'We've climbed a bit above the forest, but it's still there. We have to follow the road.'

The squirrel made no reply, instead shuffled itself closer to Benfro's head as if that would afford some protection from whatever nastiness lurked in the silence. The sun was beginning to sink into the distant horizon, lengthening the shadows inside the remains of the building and casting the broken edges in sharp relief against what sky Benfro could see. Still he felt none of the foreboding that was obviously troubling his companion. Without so much as a backward glance he stepped over the threshold and into a different world.

He stood in a courtyard of glittering splendour. The stone slabs beneath Benfro's feet were painted in bright colours, red, green, gold and silver. They picked out a design of some kind, but from where he stood he couldn't see what it was. Turning, he saw the inside of the arch, a tunnel the thickness of the great wall, at least twenty paces deep if not more.

A walkway circled the courtyard, let into the wall forty feet above the ground. Below this the wall was fashioned from smooth stone slabs, joined with such skill that you could not get a talon into the gaps. The only exits from the quadrangle were the great arch, now closed, through which he had stepped and a much smaller door on the far side. Surprised but curiously not alarmed, Benfro took a stride forward, then another. The road was still marked out in plain stones running straight to the far exit. He had walked the path so far, he reasoned he might as well continue.

The door was a far smaller affair than its great cousin in the outside wall of the courtyard, yet still it was massive.

It was a different style of arch, flanked on both sides by intricately carved pillars whose stone details seemed to writhe and undulate as Benfro looked at them. There were branches and leaves in the pattern and hundreds of animals poking their heads through the stone foliage. They reminded him curiously of the great mother tree, although they looked nothing like her. And here there were two trees, their upper branches leaning over and linking to form the top of the archway. At its peak a face peered down from the vegetation, and Benfro gasped when he saw it, for it was a dragon.

Neither was it any dragon. Even carved in stone and weathered by time, he could distinguish those proud features. They might only have met in a dream, yet he could recognize at once the face of Magog, Son of the Summer Moon. It gazed down with curious indifference on the splendour all around. This must be the great dragon's home. Cenobus.

A pair of oak doors black with age and studded with huge iron pins stood closed in the archway. Three stone steps climbed from the courtyard up to the entrance, and Benfro took them in three powerful leaps. Something about the place filled him both with awe and with strength. All his upbringing, the constant preachings of his mother and the village elders, told him that no dragon had any right to live in such splendour. And yet here was evidence that once, long ago, a dragon had done just that. Dragons, he had been told, had small wings because they did not fly. Yet his wings were huge and growing; he had flown. This place, with its magical impossibility, lit a spark deep inside – the idea that he might so far have been living a lie.

He longed to find out more. Grabbing the great iron rings that hung from the locks, he twisted them and pushed.

They resisted at first. Those great weights, unmoved in countless years, were loath to shift. For a moment he thought they might be locked, or barred from the inside by some obstruction, but it was only time that fought against him. With a grinding of rust the hinges finally moved, pivoting counterweights that swung into recesses in the wall. Once they had decided to move, the doors gave way with good grace, gliding open with only a modicum of squealing.

Inside was a vast hall lit with burning torches mounted in iron sconces high on the walls. Tapestries hung over the rough stone and a huge fireplace crackled with blazing logs. Low benches were placed around this to catch the heat, and a series of small tables were laid with food. Benfro approached warily – he had learned at least that much from his recent experiences – but there seemed to be no one about, no obvious trap luring him in. He did not notice the marks on the floor, a thick stripe paler than the flagstones heavily spread with dark reeds, which veered away from the fireplace and headed for a door in the farthest, darkest corner of the room. Neither did he notice the insistent tugging at his ear, the shrill little voice that warned against straying from the path. He completely failed to notice when, suddenly, the voice stopped and the tugging ended in one final desperate pull.

There were freshly caught river fish, beautifully prepared vegetables and bowls of fruits and nuts placed on the tables by the fire. Benfro was hungry and chilled, so he took a place on the bench nearest the flames and helped himself to some food. It tasted good, very much like the last meal he had eaten. He looked around for something to drink, hoping for some wine. A goblet, curiously chipped and battered alongside everything else, held only brackish water, but it was cold and it was wet, so he drank it down. No sooner had he replaced it on the table than it magically began to refill.

Movement in the corner of his eye caught Benfro's attention. At first he thought it was just shadows cast by the flickering flames of the fire, but when he glanced across the great hall, he realized that the shade was constant, not moving. Even where the torches guttered on the walls their light was curiously motionless.

When he stared at the lights, the movement appeared again, once more in the corner of his eye. He whirled his head around to try and catch sight of what it was. For a moment he thought he saw something, but it disappeared into the shadows before he could get a clear view.

'Who's there?' he said, a sense of unease beginning to spread through him. 'Show yourself,' he added, trying to muster a tone of command in his voice. 'Don't try my patience.'

They shimmered into existence like nothing he could describe. One moment he was staring at empty space, the next the air took on a frosted, glass-like quality, bending and flexing until something unbelievable stood in front of him.

There were seven of them, all slightly different, each about seven feet tall. The one nearest him was perhaps the oldest; certainly it had the most pronounced stoop and the others seemed to defer to it. Quite what it was,

Benfro was not sure. It had six legs covered in coarse tufts of thick black hair. Its body was segmented, a bit like a wasp's but fleshy and pale, some more of that black pelt coating its back. Its head was a stubby thing with a misshapen hole for a mouth and the multi-faceted eyes of a spider. Its arms were spindly black chitinous things that moved constantly, the ungainly pincers it had for hands working back and forth.

'Forgive us, master,' the creature said. 'We have felt your presence approaching these past two days, but you chose not to call us. We feared you were angry with us.'

'Angry? Why? What are you? Who are you?' Benfro asked, taking an involuntary step backwards, away from the horrible sight.

'Have we changed so much that master does not recognize us?' the leader asked, bobbing up and down in some perverse genuflection, its claws snapping open and closed like a dying crayfish. 'It has been many years, I suppose. Too many to count. We are your loyal servants, master, your Gweinyddau. We have waited patiently for your return.'

'I'm not . . .' he started to say, but thought better of it. These creatures could all too easily turn on him, and who knew what subtle arts they could command. If they could appear and disappear at will then he had no way of fighting them should they decide to be hostile. Instead he sat himself back down on the bench by the fire, doing his best to feign nonchalance. They thought he was their master, Magog, so he had better do his best impression.

'It has been many years,' he said. 'Too many, true. So tell me what has happened in all those years.'

'Master teases us,' the elder Gweinydd said. 'You created us to serve only you. When you are not here, we are not here. We know only the passage of time, nothing else.'

'But surely travellers have come this way. Haven't you welcomed them? Is there no hospitality in this castle?'

The Gweinyddau shuffled together, almost as if having a group discussion, though Benfro heard no spoken words pass between them. Six of them disappeared, fluttering out of vision like morning mist under the rising sun. The elder remained. It hobbled closer to where Benfro sat, peering up at him with its crazy eyes. He wondered how well it really saw him, for surely no one who had met Magog could mistake him for that giant among dragons.

'Master, please do not be angry with us,' the creature said. Close up, Benfro could see that it shook, though whether this was with age or fear he could not be sure. Its skin was mottled and diseased-looking.

'Why should I be angry with you?'

'When you left, we left also,' the creature began. Its voice was frail, croaking and wheezing at the end of its utterances as if it found breathing difficult enough without having to punctuate its breaths with words. 'We went to the place where we always go, to await your return. We waited, counting the slow passage of time as has always been our way. But you did not return. Still we waited, the slow years passing from one to the next. And you did not return. The centuries passed; we waited. Waiting is what we do. But we grew restless in our wait. My brothers began to talk of leaving that place, of coming back here to wait. At first I condemned their whispering as heresy, for truly that is what it was, but as the centuries rolled on even my resolve was tested and found wanting.

'One by one my brothers deserted me, came back here until I was left alone. Without their whispering voices to calm me, the void became a terrible place. A loneliness fell upon me then, such as you cannot imagine. I bore it for as long as I could, but I longed to know what had happened to you. Had you returned, found some of your Gweiny-ddau already here to serve you and not thought to call me back? Perhaps some great misfortune had befallen you and you could not call. I had to know. So, after too many years of waiting, I finally slipped unbidden back to this great castle.

'Master, it was a terrible sight. Some great beast had lain waste to the walls, blown the great front doors out into the night. Most of the roof was gone, and the tapestries were turned to dust with age. The whole place was a ruin and I searched through the rubble for any sign of your return. One by one my brothers came back to me as I picked my way through once-splendid rooms. We searched the castle from the lowest basement to all that remained of the tallest tower, but there was no sign of you at all.

'We have stayed here since, doing what we can to keep the place from falling further into disrepair, waiting all the while for your return. Over the years a few travellers have come here, but we have not welcomed them. It is not right that they should enjoy your hospitality when you are not here. We drove them off as best we could. Those that would not leave we lured into the dungeons, there to wait as we have waited for your eventual return.'

'What manner of beasts were these visitors?' Benfro asked. 'Are they still here?'

'No, master,' the Gweinydd said. 'Or rather only their bones remain. They did not have the patience to wait as we do.'

'Were there dragons among them?'

'There were creatures that called themselves dragons, master, but they were not what they claimed to be. Wretched beasts, they were weak of spirit and had no wings worth mentioning. They all left when we asked them to.'

'So what lies in the dungeons?' Benfro asked, both sad he had not found his father and relieved he had not found his bones.

'Strange arrogant creatures they were, master,' the Gweinydd continued. 'Small, with squat legs and short bodies. They bore weapons of light and would not heed our warnings. Some even tried to do us harm, as if you would allow harm to befall us in your own home.'

'Men,' Benfro guessed.

'Surely not men, master,' the Gweinydd said, incredulous. 'Men are simple-minded shuffling growers of grain with no spark in them. These were powerful mages all, despite their puny outward appearance. It took all the wit of my brothers and I to trap them, for they would not leave when we asked them to.'

'When was this?' Benfro asked, his astonished curiosity getting the better of him.

'They have been coming for hundreds of years now,' the Gweinydd replied. 'Every century it seems another band makes its way here. Each is the same as before, arrogantly claiming the castle as its own, or in the name of some king. They stamp around the courtyard, shit in the great hall and break down walls with their swords of fire. Always they think themselves the masters of everything they touch, so always we are able to lure them down to the dungeons. Once there, no creature alive or dead can escape, as well you know, master. These men, if men they be, do not last long without food and water.'

Benfro was suddenly taken with an image of the inquisitor, Melyn, trapped in a dark dungeon, unable to escape, with nothing to sustain him but the condensation on the cold stone walls, slowly starving to death despite all his magics. It quite cheered him up.

'So how long have I been gone?' he asked innocently, falling into the role that had been given him. The look on the Gweinydd's face was difficult to read, but it seemed a mixture of concern and surprise.

'Master, you do not know?'

'I've not been . . . Well, let's just say I haven't been in a position to count,' Benfro said, wishing he had kept his mouth shut. The ugly creature seemed to be thinking, for it fell silent a while before answering.

'Fully two thousand years have passed since you flew from the high tower,' it finally said. 'Master, please forgive me, please forgive all of us, but there were times when we thought you might never come back.'

'There were times when I thought I might not be able to,' Benfro said, recalling the fading jewel on the riverbed, the jewel that had grown steadily in power since he had retrieved it, feeding on the memories of the villagers and his mother. Without thinking, he reached for the bags slung over his shoulder. Neither was there. And then he realized. The food laid out on the tables was his own: fruit and vegetables gifted him by the mother tree, fish caught in the river that very morning. Only the brackish water in the ancient pewter tankard had come from this place.

'Where are my bags?' he asked in what he hoped was a nonchalant voice.

'Master, your bags have been taken to the kitchens. The food we laid out for you as you like. The fresh viand you trapped in the forest on your journey is being prepared even now, a feast to celebrate your return.'

Fresh viand? Benfro was not sure what the Gweinydd was talking about. He had brought fish, true, but that was already prepared. And the elderly servant had said trapped. The penny dropped and with it a terrible chill shivered down his spine to the tip of his tail.

'Malkin.' Benfro leaped to his feet, his tankard of water tumbling to the dusty floor. 'Where is he? Take me to him. Now.'

10

The Gweinyddau were perhaps Magog's greatest creation. They were certainly his most terrible. Bound to the palace of Cenobus, they were said to have been created from the spirits of his enemies stripped from their bodies at the moment of their deaths. Their punishment for having opposed his will was to be bound for all time to serve it. They existed only for his amusement, appearing at his command then returning to some unnamed place when he no longer required them. No one else would they serve unless that was their master's wish.

Sir Frynwy, *Tales of the Ffrydd*

Errol froze, unable to move for fear. The knife at his throat was sharp, stinging his skin; the guard's hold was unbreakable.

'Please, please. Forgive him.' Dondal hastily tucked the key into his pocket. 'He was raised in the mountains. There's much he has still to learn.'

The guard grunted, a cruel sound that did little to assure Errol he was being forgiven. For long moments the guard simply kept him held, as if deciding whether or not to accept the duke's explanation. Then, finally, he withdrew the knife and shoved Errol away. He hadn't said a word since they had arrived, Errol realized. He wondered if the guard was mute but was distracted from the thought by Dondal finally heaving the door open. They both stepped through and he locked it behind him.

'Only dukes are allowed to touch the keys to the palace,' Dondal said to Errol as they walked down a narrow alley almost identical to the one they had just left, stopping finally at an imposing wooden door set into a faceless stone building. 'Most ordinary folk aren't even allowed to see them. You'll have to be careful, Errol; the guise of a mountain-bred simpleton will only carry you so far.'

'I . . .' Errol began, but the duke held up a hand to silence him.

'No more talk. Speak only if you are addressed directly. In here you are a page, and pages must be seen but not heard. Now hurry. We're late.'

Errol wondered how they could be late when the king had not set a time for them to present themselves, but he kept this to himself and followed the duke as the stout old man trotted through corridors of ever-increasing size and splendour.

After the cold austerity of Emmass Fawr, the run-down dilapidation of Duke Dondal's residences and the rustic simplicity of Pwllpeiran, the palace was almost beyond belief. Errol wanted to stop, to stare, to marvel at the fabulously rich tapestries, the ornate mouldings inlaid with gilt, the enormous portraits of strangely familiar people, the carpet so deep his travel boots sank into it like spring grass, but he had to keep up with the duke. And besides there was just too much to take in.

They finally halted their near-run in a vast room with

wide floor-to-ceiling windows down one side. Through the glass Errol could see a huge formal garden dropping away in curved terraces towards a long castellated wall and beyond that the distant ramble of the city climbing the hills on the far side of the river. For the first time since stepping through the city gates, he could see the sky as more than a greying overhead strip of light.

'You're gawping again, Errol.' Duke Dondal wheezed slightly from his exertion. 'Try not to act like you've got a brain. It doesn't do to be noticed too much.'

Errol reached a pair of closed doors large enough to admit a coach and six. They were painted white, with intricate gold, red and green highlights on the carved panels. Two men, dressed in the same smart livery as the rude fellow who had summoned them to the palace, stood at silent attention on either side. At first Errol thought that the room was empty, but then he heard someone clearing his throat.

'Ah, Dondal, you've arrived.'

He looked around to see an old man, thin-faced and sporting a severe goatee beard, sitting behind a large desk at one side of the room. Errol tried to shrink into the shadows as he rose and walked slowly across the carpeted expanse towards them. The duke stood upright and stiff, giving no sign of deference whatsoever. The air bristled with an uncomfortable tension, made worse when the old man stopped a few paces away and stared straight at Errol.

'And what is this you've brought with you? A bit old for a catamite, wouldn't you say?'

'This is Errol, my nephew. I hope to present him to Prince Dafydd as a page.'

'And what makes you think the king would allow such a thing?' the old man asked, the sneer evident in his voice. Errol still had no idea who he was, nor whether to face the hostile stare or avert his eyes.

'He's Edgar's son,' Dondal said. The effect was instantaneous. The old man's whole bearing changed. His shoulders lost some of their stiffness and he turned to give Errol his full attention.

'Look at me, boy,' he said. Errol complied. The old man reached out and took his chin in his hand, not roughly. Moved his head from side to side as if inspecting a prize ram.

'Do you know who I am, boy?'

'No, sir,' Errol said, aware that this was the first time he had spoken Llanwennog to someone who needed to be fooled by his mastery of the language.

'I am Tordu, King Ballah's cousin, major domo of the palace and High Earl of Tynhelyg. Nothing happens in this city that I don't know of. Nothing happens without my approval. Do you understand?'

'Yes, sir.' Errol bowed his head as the old man finally released it. 'I wish only to serve my king in whatever capacity he sees fit for me.'

'Is that so, Errol?' the major domo asked. 'Well then, pray he doesn't decide he needs more soldiers for his army today.' And with that he swept past the both of them, nodding to the two guards, who pulled open the great doors.

Beyond was a room that made the hall they were standing in look like a peasant's tool shed. Errol couldn't conceive of such a space being enclosed: the ceiling was so high it could have been sky, the walls fifty paces away on each side, a hundred and fifty ahead of him.

Mindful of Dondal's warning, he tried not to stare too much as they hurried across the great hall towards the towering throne. But the closer he came, the more Errol was transfixed. At first he thought that the throne was unoccupied, then he felt a familiar but alien presence brush over his mind. It was like Melyn trying to divine his thoughts, but the timbre of the probing was completely different, more subtle. Errol let the flow of his recent experiences bubble to the top of his mind. It wasn't too difficult to fake innocent wonder and amazement at what he had seen since arriving at Dondal's run-down castle, and after a moment the tingling sense of being read faded away.

Tordu stopped twenty paces from the throne and dropped to one knee. Dondal did the same and Errol hastened to copy them.

'Your Majesty, I bring Dondal, Duke of Tynewydd, Marshall of the Southern Dividing Mountains,' he said, then stood and stepped to the side.

'Come forward, Dondal,' said a voice from the depths of the throne. Errol risked a quick glance up and saw a small broad man with shoulder-length white hair and a long beard that gave him the look of a mountain goat, leaning forward from the dark depths of the throne. One gnarled hand clasped a dark wooden arm like a claw.

Dondal rose, bowing his head once more, then motioned for Errol to come forward. With a terrible sense of dread Errol realized that something was wrong. Out of the corner of his eye he could see guards standing all around, silent and attentive, but there was no once else in the throne room.

'Your Majesty, I have come before you to make my pledge to the crown,' Dondal said in a clear proud voice, 'and to present you with Errol Ramsbottom, a spy for the Twin Kingdoms sent to infiltrate your royal house.'

Benfro rushed from door to door in the darkened castle. The elderly Gweinydd trailed slowly behind him, legs shuffling over the cold stone slabs, claws clacking in a nervous rhythm. Somewhere in the depths of this ruin the other creatures had Malkin, might even now be preparing the squirrel for the pot. And he had let it happen.

'Where are the damned kitchens?' he shouted.

'Master, surely you remember—' the Gweinydd began.

'Humour me,' Benfro countered. 'It's a big castle with a lot of rooms. You can't expect me to remember them all. Now hurry.'

'Master, I have already informed my brothers of your displeasure. Please understand, we only do as you have had us do in the past. We can do nothing else.'

'I need to find the kitchen,' Benfro said. 'I need to see my friend.'

'Then please follow me.' The strange creature shuffled round in the corridor before heading off the way they had come. Benfro followed, so slowly he hardly seemed to be moving at all.

'You call me master,' Benfro said after a few minutes' frustrated silence. 'How can you be sure I am Magog?'

'Master teases me again,' the Gweinydd said. 'My eyes maybe aren't as good as they used to be, but I can see a dragon's aura, read his sparkle as well as I ever did. True you have changed with the years, but then who has not? Yet I sensed your presence the moment you flew into the forest.'

'But what makes you so sure? I mean, I could be an impostor. I could be Gog.'

The Gweinydd stopped in mid-stride, a complex manoeuvre considering the number of legs it had. A shiver ran through it as if someone were dancing on its grave. It glanced back over its shoulder at Benfro, hundreds of tiny lights pinpricked in the reflection of its compound eyes.

'Master, did you just say what I thought you said?' it asked, a fear in its voice where before there had been an unctuous, toadying quality that promised much but delivered an obsequious nothing.

'Gog, my brother, yes.' Benfro felt the atmosphere thickening like milk and eggs brought to the boil. It was almost as if the whole great building were drawing in its breath. As if a primordial anger were heating the very stones that it was built of.

'Master would not speak that name for a hundred years before . . .' the Gweinydd said in a whisper that was almost lost in the electric silence. 'Master has burned lesser dragons for even thinking that name in his presence.'

'Well, perhaps that anger was what kept me away from here for so long,' Benfro said. 'But you still haven't answered my question.' They had reached a staircase now and were making slow progress up its treads. He wanted to pick the elderly creature up, carry it to the top, but he couldn't bring himself to touch that scaly skin.

'Master, I have never met . . .' The Gweinydd paused, millennia of conditioning not allowing him to continue.

'Oh, never mind,' Benfro said. 'As long as you're sure I am who you say I am, then we're both happy. But can we pick the pace up a little. I can assure you my wrath will be great if my companion has been hurt in any way.'

'The forest creature remains unharmed. I saw to it that my brothers knew of their mistake as soon as you told me, master. They await their punishment even as we speak. As do I.' The Gweinydd lowered its head in penance.

Ignoring it, Benfro rushed up the last few steps and across the room to where most of his possessions were spilled over a table. They had clearly been sorted through and deemed unsuitable to be sent to the dining hall. Sitting alongside the bags was a wicker cage with a small slotted window in the front and a cane handle in its lid.

'Malkin? Is that you in there?' Benfro grabbed the basket, fumbled with the fiddly catch mechanism and in the end resorted to peeling open the lid with one extended talon.

Two terrified beady black eyes stared up at him from the depths. The creature's fur was matted and ruffled, its tail a pale shadow of its former magnificent bushy self. It was trembling uncontrollably, and its tiny claws were clenched tight around the bars of its cage. It had soiled the inside of the basket in its terror, and the mess was all over its legs and smeared into its fur. A stench wafted up to Benfro as he stood over the tiny cage which reminded him in a strange way of the smell of the warrior priests. It brought a fury to him that was not directed at the pathetic little creature, rather at the architects of its misfortune. All the rage and frustration that had built up in him since he had tried to rid himself of Magog's jewel now broke through. He rounded on the elderly Gweinydd as it shuffled towards him.

'How dare you treat my companion in this manner?!' he shouted with such fury that the creature backed away from him and cowered even more.

'Master, you have always returned with provisions for your table,' it stammered towards the floor. 'We only thought—'

'You only thought!' Benfro puffed up with scarcely controlled fury. 'And who gave you permission to think? When did I tell you that you could return to this place? You have grown above yourself in my absence, Gweinydd. I will have to do something about that.'

He took a deep breath, rising towards the ceiling and feeling the heat inside him grow. It was a pure anger that filled him, an excitement of power he had not felt for millennia. This was how justice was meted out, how those who displeased him felt the true extent of his wrath.

'Appear before me. All of you. Now,' he bellowed. Almost instantly they were there, as sorry a collection of mismatched body parts and evil intent as ever you could find. He hated every facet of their being, everything about them. They reminded him of nothing so much as his failure. He knew his great castle was a ruin, even though it appeared whole. That magic was one he had worked a long time ago. He knew that pillagers and looters had taken their pick of his great treasures, his works of art and irreplaceable library. The knowledge of the ancient mages was lost, and all due to these pathetic wasted excuses for servants. He could stand their presence, their very existence, no more. It was time to correct the mistakes of the past and begin anew.

The power was upon him now, a great force built to a point where it could be contained no longer. The miserable creatures stood before him in a pathetic huddle, shifting listlessly from side to side, refusing to meet his gaze. So they would end as they had begun, afraid, bewildered, barely worthy of his attention.

'Benfro?' a voice asked – small, squeaky and laden with fear. He wanted to ignore it. It was an irrelevance, a distraction from the task in hand. He would deal with it just as soon as he had vented his wrath on the minions he had created to be his perfect servants, the minions who had so badly failed him. Yet something about the voice would not let him be.

'Benfro?' it asked again, and the short word slipped through the knot of his rage into a tiny silent corner of his mind. There it found a confused, frightened dragon kitling. He was Benfro, he knew. Yet this was his palace, the castle of Magog. These were his creatures, his Gweinyddau. But he had never seen them before this evening.

As if he were struggling in wet mud, his mind confused and tired, he looked round to the source of the voice. A squirrel, dishevelled and shrunk in upon itself, its tail matted in places, its fur a dull brown rather than the vibrant red it should have been, stood on the table by his side. It looked up at him with its black eyes full of concern. It had a name, he knew.

'Malkin?' Benfro said. And as he heard his voice, the

confusion ebbed away. The rage seeped out of him as if it had never been real. Slowly he slumped back towards the floor. His wings, he realized, were spread wide into the dark arches of the kitchen. With a glow of embarrassment, he folded them back to his sides. For a while the spirit of Magog had taken him over – he could see that now – but how long had it been in him?

'I'm not Magog,' he said to the Gweinyddau, who were still cowering in front of him. 'Magog died two thousand years ago.'

'Master jests with us,' the eldest of the creatures said, but he could see the seed of doubt germinating. Its face crumpled and creased in a parody of expression. 'Yet master is undoubtedly changed.'

'I'm not your master,' Benfro continued. 'My name is Sir Benfro, son of Sir Trefaldwyn of the Great Span. I came across the place where the last remains of your master lie. I rescued his jewel, his last remaining essence, from his watery grave.' He reached over for the bag of food, tipping the remaining contents out on to the table and sorting through it, looking for the jewel he had wrapped thickly in a bundle of leaves.

Malkin hopped across the table and helped with the search. The squirrel, no doubt adept at finding things, soon located the small package. Benfro couldn't help noticing that it still looked at him with a nervous stare as if any moment it expected him to explode. He knew that for a short moment he had stopped being Benfro, had become something more akin to the ferocious Magog of legend. It had changed how the squirrel viewed him, and the loss of their innocent friendship pained him more than anything else.

Taking the small package, Benfro opened it, unfolding layer after layer of thick green leaf until the minute gem lay like the centre of some bizarre flower on his outstretched palm. He held it up to the Gweinyddau.

'See,' he said. 'This is all that is left of your master.'

Errol stood perfectly still, not believing what Duke Dondal had just said.

Back home, in the forests around Pwllpeiran, he had perfected the art of disappearing. All you needed to do was stop moving, stop drawing attention to yourself, make your breathing so shallow as to be virtually inaudible and think yourself into the background. Many was the time he had avoided a taunting or worse from Trell and his cronies by simply acting like he wasn't there. Now he longed to be able to do the same thing.

But it wasn't going to work.

'Seize him.' King Ballah's command was almost lazy, but before Errol could do anything two guards had him by the arms.

'He poses no threat, Your Majesty,' Dondal said, bowing more deeply than before. 'I've seen to it that he has no weapons. In truth he's little more than a novitiate, and one taken from the peasantry by all accounts.'

'And how much did Melyn pay you to bring him here?' the king asked. Dondal reached into his travelling cloak, pulling out a heavy bag of coins. He stepped forward to the throne and handed it to the king.

'A tidy sum, Your Majesty,' he said. 'But I would sooner forfeit my title and lands than betray my king.'

'And yet you chose to keep this matter from His Majesty all this time? Or did you fear discovery and have a change of heart?' the major domo asked. 'How long have you planned this, Dondal? How long have you been in collusion with the enemy?'

'Is that how low my house has come in your estimation, Tordu? That you could believe we would sell out to the House of Balwen? My own brother died defending the crown.'

'And you tried to pass this impostor off as his son. How does that honour his memory?'

'But you fell for it, didn't you, Tordu?' Dondal said. 'So what's all this about nothing happening in this city without you knowing about it?'

'Gentlemen.' The voice was quiet but the effect was instant. Both the duke and the major domo fell silent, turning like chastised schoolboys to face their king. Errol felt the king's demand for attention like a compulsion in the base of his brain, as if there could be nothing he wanted to do more than listen to the old man. Only the guards' restraint stopped him from approaching the throne, but their tightening grips also served to shock him out of the spell. The old man's power was far more subtle than Melyn's.

'Bring the boy forward,' the king said. Errol didn't fight. He was still too stunned at the turn of events to begin to worry about what might happen to him. His mind was racing too fast to think straight.

'So you're one of Melyn's spies,' the king said as Errol

was forced to his knees in front of the throne. 'Well what have you got to say for yourself, boy?'

Errol stared up into the old face with its piercing black eyes. He was caught before he had even started. He would be put to death. He would never find Martha or see what had become of the dragon Benfro. But why? He owed no allegiance to the Order of the High Ffrydd or the House of Balwen. By the luck of the draw he had been born in the Twin Kingdoms, but his father had been a Llanwennog, one of King Ballah's subjects. Why should he die for a cause he so hated?

'I no more wish to serve Inquisitor Melyn or Queen Beulah than you do, Your Majesty,' Errol said. 'My father was Llanwennog. Melyn sought to use me simply because of my looks.'

'I see your father taught you our language. No doubt he also taught you our ways, so why did you decide to stay in the Twin Kingdoms and not return to your homeland?' the king asked.

'I never knew my father,' Errol said. 'My mother would never tell me about him. I never had a chance to leave the village where I was raised before the inquisitor came and took me away to Emmass Fawr. That's where I learned to speak Llanwennog.'

'Indeed?' The king made no attempt to hide his disbelief.

'It's true, Your Majesty,' Errol said, looking for any way he might possibly convince the king. A tiny window of opportunity had opened; if he could prove his loyalty to Ballah then he might be free of Melyn.

'Ah, but your loyalties lie elsewhere,' the king said,

'somewhere even I can't see. True, you've no love of Melyn. His sticky thoughts are all over you like a pox, but you've managed to fight them off. You're an enigma, Errol Ramsbottom, and I don't much like riddles.'

'I was sent to make contact with Princess Iolwen, to persuade her not to enter into marriage with any Llan-wennog prince,' Errol said. 'And failing that I was supposed to arrange an accident for Prince Dafydd. Those were my orders. I tell you this because I had no intention of carrying them out. As soon as the opportunity pre-sented itself I intended to abscond.'

'Yes, I can see that,' King Ballah said. 'But you're mis-taken if you think your candour will earn you any favour. You're supposed to be a soldier, boy. You obey orders. You carry them out to the death if necessary. It doesn't matter that you're on the other side; you should serve your country, your people in whatever role it sees fit. But you've decided you know better. You've decided to be selfish and follow your own heart. I'd see you executed before the end of the day.'

Errol bowed his head, defeated. This was it then – he was going to die. He hoped it would be quick and painless.

'But you're different, Errol Ramsbottom,' the king said. 'For one thing, you fooled me, and you must have fooled Melyn as well. That takes uncommon skill, not something I'd expect to see in a boy. And I'm also intrigued by your very nature. My eyesight may not be as good as it once was, but I can see an aura as well as I ever could, and there's something very familiar about yours. Guards, take him to the West Tower. See he is fed and watered.'

Errol felt the hands grip his arms once more, but when he went to stand, he found his knees too weak to support him. Roughly he was hauled to his feet and dragged away from the throne.

'Your Majesty,' Duke Dondal said, stepping between the guards and the long trek to the door, 'is it wise to keep an enemy so close?'

'Wiser, I think, than letting him plot and scheme on the borders of my kingdom, Dondal,' Ballah said. 'It's as well you gave me all the money Melyn paid you, otherwise I might suspect your motives. Now, please, my guest has travelled a long way and no doubt needs to rest. Let him pass.'

Reluctantly, Dondal stepped to one side. Errol's mind was still a-whirl with the rush of events, but he registered the look of dreadful rage and hatred on the duke's face as he was led past. Then he was heading for the huge doors and if not freedom then something closer to it than he had any reason to expect. As he moved away from the throne, the king's voice rang out clear for all to hear.

'And now, Duke Dondal, I believe you had come here to pay your tithes to the crown?'

Quite what response he had been expecting, Benfro was not sure. He was not prepared for what happened. First the eldest then the other Gweinyddau tipped their malformed heads back and uttered a strange ululation, a cry that reminded him of the howling of wolves on a moonlit night, except that it sounded nothing like that. It was a keening, but it was also the roaring of a storm wind through summer trees. It was a death scream, but it was also the last gasp of a dying stag, hunted to the edge of exhaustion and beyond, hope ended by a well placed talon. And as the noise rose, so the Gweinyddau seemed to fall apart. They didn't so much disappear as dissolve, mote by mote in front of his eyes. Dust spiralled from their limbs, dancing on invisible currents in the air. They melted together, a whirlwind of particles that swept up towards the ceiling.

But the ceiling was no longer there. The night sky opened out overhead, framed by the ruined walls of the castle. Stars shone sharp in the high cold air of the cloudless, moonless night, and the hazy remains of the Gweinyddau rose towards them like steam from a boiling pot, dissipating fast. For a moment Benfro thought he could make out a shape in the mass, a beautiful female dragon with her head bowed in sorrow, but it could have been his imagination. Did he imagine a voice, perfect like his mother's say, 'Thank you, Sir Benfro, for freeing us from our endless torment'? It was so faint it could have been the wind whistling between the ruined columns and collapsed arches. Certainly the cry faded until it merged with the breeze, dwindling to nothing.

Shuddering, he squeezed the gem tight in his fist.

'We go now,' Malkin said, its former chirpy self starting to reassert itself. The surface it stood upon was now rotted almost to nothing at the edges, brittle and dry with age, yet still it hopped about the table, picking up little handfuls of vegetables and placing them in a pile by the bag. Benfro could see its eagerness to be gone from this place, could understand it completely. He too longed to flee, but there was one thing that held him back. One thing his curiosity would not let go.

'A moment, Malkin,' he said as the squirrel started to throw provisions into the bag. 'There's something I have to try first.'

Lifting the little creature on to his shoulder, he walked out of the kitchen and into the great hall. As a ruin it was not quite as impressive as it had seemed before. A rickety old bench sat beside the empty fireplace and a small table was heaped with the remains of his last meal. Carefully he added what he could to the bag and, still clutching the gem in his palm, set out in search of something he knew must be nearby.

Deep inside the ruins of the castle, only broken scattered fragments of light pierced the gloom, yet somehow Benfro knew where he was going as if he had been here a thousand times before. When finally it was too dark to see, and he had already stubbed his claws on one fallen stone block too many, he unwrapped the jewel and held it in front of him. It glowed a tiny ruby light, just enough to see the smooth stone walls and arched ceiling, blackened with soot from the torches which had hung in the now empty rusted iron sconces.

With his guide to lead him, Benfro made swift progress to a great wooden door. Bones were piled at its base and at least one skull. He stared at this for a long time before recognizing its shape, the high forehead and wide nose cavity, the lower jaw still holding stumps of blackened teeth. A man, and an important one judging by the glittering gold torc that hung around his neck. He reached down and pulled the glittering bauble off the skeleton, breaking its neck and tumbling the skull to the stone floor as he did. Kicking the bones aside gave him a small thrill, as if that simple act of desecration and disrespect could go some way towards making up for the pain and suffering he had felt. The moment soon passed. Revenge would have to be far greater than that.

On his shoulder Malkin gripped tight with sharp little claws but remained silent. Steeling himself to the task, Benfro tried to remember everything that was himself. Strangely the dead man helped here. Seeing the skeleton made it all too easy to recall his mother's death and his silent walk through the burning village. He reached out and took the tiny red jewel between taloned finger and thumb, watching as the gem glowed brighter, tendrils like red mist twisting from it to wrap themselves around his hand. Immediately he could feel the assault on his mind, the rage building, but he was ready for it. He reached out for the door with his glowing hand and pushed.

II

Dragons' jewels are dangerous and wonderful things, and yet men cannot help themselves from seeking them out, for in the hands of skilled magicians they can be a source of great power, but to all but the most proficient they bring only sorrow and death.

As gems go, they are hardly remarkable. Duller than a ruby and rough-faceted as if cut by a novice, still they hold a terrible fascination that can tempt even the most fastidious soul. To hold such a jewel in one's hand is to live another, fantastic life, freed from everyday worries and concerns. It is a powerful illusion, intoxicating and addictive. Many have withered away to nothing, all thought of food, drink or any of life's pleasures overwhelmed by the single desire to be connected to that make-believe world.

It is said that a dragon's jewels are formed by the learning and experience of the beast as it goes through life. Certainly what little knowledge dissectors have gleaned over the years would suggest that dragon young have few or no jewels within their brains. Only fully grown beasts, and old ones at that, will yield more than a handful of gems. Even then, some promising-looking specimens, those considered by their own kind to be elders in what passes for their society, may have only one or two tiny jewels, as if they have long since stopped experiencing the world in which they live. Perhaps there is some kernel of truth in this observation, for many of the older Ffrydd dragons are sorry, pathetic creatures, quite resigned to a slow uneventful descent into senility and death.

Tradition has it that King Balwen slew the first dragon and claimed its jewels for himself and his heirs. To this day only the royal house of the Hendry may harvest the gems, although they have long since passed the actual task on to the inquisitors of the High Ffrydd. Dragon jewels are highly prized as gifts, perhaps the highest honour that the royal family can bestow upon favoured servants. Yet there was never a noble house to which this particular favour was extended that did not soon after suffer some tragedy in its line of succession. For if a dragon's jewels can be said to contain all their experiences and knowledge, it is true also that they will continue to gather experience and knowledge into themselves, taking them wantonly from whatever source of life they encounter.

The gift of a dragon's jewel is thus a double-edged sword. To possess one is to be favoured at court and to be trusted with a great and powerful secret. But it is also to be tempted beyond the ability of most to resist. There is a power to be drawn from them by the skilled magician, but for the weaker willed they can be a source of untold grief.

Father Charmoise, *Dragons' Tales*

The door resisted at first, but setting his shoulder to the task soon had it moving, slowly and with a terrible noise. Once there was enough room to squeeze through, he pushed past and into the space beyond.

Benfro was immediately aware that he could see without the aid of the ruby still clenched between his fingers. Light entered the room from somewhere, reflecting off an incredible hoard of treasure. He stepped lightly past plates of purest gold piled on the floor. His eyes were drawn to countless glittering white jewels, stacked neatly on deep shelves carved from the rock and rising from floor to ceiling. There were books and scrolls here too, filling wooden shelves surrounding the pillars holding up the ceiling. The wall farthest from the door was dominated by a huge fireplace, alongside which sat a comfortable-looking chair and a reading table with twin sconces for candles. Everything was clean and dust-free, as if it had been in constant use not hidden from sight for more years than it was easy to imagine. And it was all hauntingly familiar, as if he had been here before.

For a moment Benfro thought he had slipped back into the dream state, that this was once more Magog's memory of the place imprinted on his mind, but it felt different this time. He was aware of the jewel trying to inveigle itself into his thoughts. It was a constant itching at the base of his brain, a whispering voice too quiet to hear. But he knew what it was now, what it was trying to do. And so he could ignore it, even try to suppress it. He knew too that it wasn't affecting the way he saw this great room. Protected by whatever magics he could not begin to understand, the repository had stood in a time warp since its master last had left it.

With a great effort of will Benfro placed the glowing red jewel back into its wrapping of leaves, folded them tight around it and dropped the package into the bag with the food. He crossed the room to the fireplace, noting as he reached it that the rag-clothed skeletons of three more men lay on the hearth like logs set out for a fire. Scrapes in the blackened stone showed where they had scrabbled in their attempts to escape the place, but there was no sign that they had tried to take any booty with them.

A scroll was rolled out on the reading table, and he bent to make out its words. The faint illumination of the jewels was not enough light to read by, and he wished there were candles in the sconces. They appeared at his bidding, or so it seemed, twin wax spires, their wicks flickering with guttering yellow flames. Astonished, Benfro reached out a hand to feel the heat. It was real. He took one of the candles and carried it to the nearest shelf. Carved into the wall, it was more of an alcove and contained ten silver-white jewels. He picked up the nearest, feeling the weight of it in his palm, and was nearly floored by the memories.

He knew what it was to fly properly. Not the pale imitation he had managed by jumping off a cliff, nor the heady flights of his dreams. This was true mastery of the air. He could leap up with powerful legs, catch the wind with the great patterned sails of his wings and thrust himself higher and higher. He could see air currents spiralling up from the sun's heat, wind deflected by the massive ridges that rose from the forest fringes and the magnificent standing waves, born of the violent storms in the east, that would carry him higher and farther than anything else.

Stunned, he put the stone down and moved on to the next alcove. Here eight smaller jewels sat awaiting his touch. They were memories of a different kind, of hopeless love and a desperate need to be recognized. They spoke of rejection, despair and a deep longing for the final release of death. It shuddered Benfro to the core just brushing the edge of those memories. He quickly moved on.

Each alcove, he came to realize, was a different dragon. There were great warriors, wise mages, arrogant lords and beautiful, patient ladies. There were renegades, wastrels and ne'er-do-wells, memories of thoughts so simple Benfro could only assume they were those of hatchlings and ideas so complex they passed him by without even intersecting his plane of intelligence. There were images of great hunts, parties that lasted months, intellectual arguments that raged back and forth over hundreds of years, points never being conceded. There was love and there was hate and there was cold indifference. Above all else there was a certainty bordering on pride that these memories were the lasting legacy of the greatest creatures ever to walk Gwlad and soar through its skies. It was a breathtaking display of perfect superiority.

Benfro ran through the repository, sampling memories as if he were a child left alone and unsupervised in the kitchen when the cook has been called away on other business. It was an intoxicating mix of experiences that were so alien to him, so fantastic, and yet these things had been done by his own kind.

He lost count of the number of alcoves he visited, the lives he dipped into. Each was a perfect encapsulated moment, but each was also a unique life, unshared. It was as if the alcoves separated the jewels in a more fundamental way than he at first realized. The memories were separated, unable to interact even on the most basic level.

'Benfro, wake up now,' Malkin said. The little voice startled him; he had quite forgotten the creature sat on his shoulder.

'I wasn't asleep,' he said.

'Benfro sleepwalk,' Malkin insisted. 'Go from bauble to bauble in dream. Many hours pass.'

'Surely not,' Benfro said. 'I've only been looking for a few minutes. Half an hour at most.' But when he looked at the candle in his hand, it was half burned away, great gobbets of wax dripped down its length and over his hand. Judging by its thickness and weight, it should have taken at least half the night to get that far.

'These are dragons,' Benfro said, trying to explain his actions.

'Dragons,' the squirrel echoed, eyeing the rows of jewels. Then, with no further word, it scampered away into the semi-darkness of the vast room.

Benfro let it go, unsure what it was doing but too wrapped up in the treasures all around him to care much. He looked over the room from where he was standing. It was dominated by the alcoves, each glittering with its cargo of memories. They called to him with a silent voice, so hard to resist. He knew then that he could have lost himself in recollection, wasted away to nothing while he dipped into countless lives more pleasant than his own. Was this a hoard like the one his mother had looked after, in which Ystrad Fflur's jewels had been laid to rest after his reckoning? It felt different somehow but no less alluring. With an effort of will he dragged his eyes away from them, looked for something else.

The other candle, flickering in its sconce on the reading table, caught his attention. The scroll so carefully laid out for reading was faded with age, the runes picked out in ink turned brown over the years. The characters were archaic. When he peered more closely to read, he recognized, just barely, part of a story he had been told many times as a child: '... and it came to pass that Gog and Magog did battle over the love of Ammorgwm the fair, for neither could admit the other favour'.

Fierce was the fight, full fifty days,
The land lashed, wreaked by the wrath of their wings.
Grim Gog gouged his bloodkin, bright wisdom wasted.
Magnificent Magog, master of the air, mighty in all, yet
    could not best his brother.
Strange spells slung, scales scorched with their sending,
Lightning lit the sky, long lances of fire.
Thunder drummed a death dance through the realm.

Then came forth the fair one, fresh and fey,
Curious to contend what creatures caused such calamity.
Unbidden by the brothers, she breached their barriers.
Wild wizards both their castings combined, caught her
    by surprise, shield slipped.
Power so potent pierced her through, life left

And there it ended. Yet this was a telling Benfro had not heard before. True, Gog and Magog had fought over Ammorgwm, but she had refused both of their suits and gone to live a life of contemplation in a high eyrie. Or at least that was how it had always been told to him. There was never any suggestion that their warring had caused her death. He knew he was no great judge of poetry, but he recognized this verse as the work of an untalented amateur. The parchment showed signs of repeated scratching where runes had been removed; in places the sheet was worn almost to nothing. Some of the lines had just been crudely scored out with a quill, words replaced inappropriately just for the sake of alliteration. And what possible reason could Magog himself have for keeping such a piece in his repository?

Unless it were his own writing.

The idea thrilled Benfro with its sheer audacity. Until he stumbled across the remains of the great mage he had considered the tale of warring brothers just that, a tale. Sir Frynwy had called it allegory, a cautionary fable to teach the true value of keeping family and friends close. But now he could see a story anchored in fact. He had seen the ghost of Magog and now carried his last jewel. He had felt unnatural rage build at the very mention of the name Gog. He had met the mother tree, and she had appeared to him as the most beautiful dragon ever to have walked the earth, Ammorgwm. These were not mythical creatures but real dragons who had lived and breathed over two thousand years ago.

The fable spoke of how the brothers had split the world so that they wouldn't have to breathe the same air.

And yet that part of the tale had never rung true. Even as a fable it was too severe a reaction to them being spurned. If Ammorgwm had merely gone off and left them, they might have hated each other, but it would have been enough just to stop speaking. They would have parted, gone as far from each other as possible, but it would never have been necessary to do something as drastic as splitting the world, whatever that might mean.

But it made all too terrible sense if their bickering had killed the only thing they both truly loved. And if that were the case then somewhere out there were descendants of Gog, dragons who might yet be alive and well, dragons who might think freely and were not cowed by the power of men.

Dragons who might help him gain his revenge.

Benfro searched around for more parchments in the same formal and archaic hand, but the drawers and tubes close to the reading table contained mostly dust. What few scripts had survived the passage of the years were magical texts so obscure that he could make no sense of them at all: bestiaries with pictures of strange creatures, a series of maps of places he had only ever heard of in stories, with names like Fo Afron, Llanwennog and Mawddwy, the Twin Spires of Idris and the Sea of Tegid. There were other writings archived in the great repository, but he could have spent a lifetime going through the collected scrolls and ancient leather-bound books. The more he looked for things, the more he found. There seemed to be no end to the room.

'Benfro come. Malkin find friends. Come.' The squirrel appeared beside the writing table, hopping from foot to foot in excitement and pointing to a dark corner of the room. Not waiting to see whether it was followed, Malkin turned and scurried off back to whatever it had found. What could it mean – friends? As far as Benfro was aware he no longer had any friends except Malkin, and that was a strange friendship indeed. Confused, he followed into the mysterious depths of the room.

The little creature scampered away down a corridor formed from the seemingly endless pillars that held up the arched ceiling of the repository. More books and maps, gold and other priceless treasures were neatly stacked, catalogued and separated in their little niches all the way along. When they finally reached the wall, cut from the solid mountain rock, it was carved with hundreds, maybe thousands, of the same alcoves that lined the walls nearer the reading table. Only here most were empty, awaiting memories.

'What is it?' Benfro asked.

'Benfro friends,' Malkin replied, hopping from foot to foot and pointing at the filled alcoves. Hesitantly Benfro reached into one and picked out a single white jewel. The feeling enveloped him instantly, a sense of relief and joy that was intoxicating. But it was not the feeling that made him gasp so much as the identity behind it. For there was no denying that the dragon whose jewel he held was Sir Frynwy.

Errol had begun to wonder whether he would ever see the outside world again. He was in a comfortably furnished suite of rooms, bigger by far than any of the houses in Pwllpeiran. Meals were brought to him three times a day by silent servants; no matter how he tried to engage them in conversation they would say nothing. Even the guards outside his door refused to talk to him. His windows overlooked a courtyard which seemed always to be empty. He had considered trying to escape, but a thorough exploration of the options brought him no joy. So he lived from day to day, with minimal human contact and no idea of what the future held in store for him. Were it not for the books, he would probably have gone quietly mad.

There was a small library in the West Tower to which he had unlimited access. It was nothing compared to the great archives at Emmass Fawr, but it contained a wonderful collection of travel journals, including maps of places he had never even heard of. He lost track of the hours and days he spent poring over spidery handwriting, his grasp of the Llanwennog language becoming ever greater as he traced its development through hundreds of years. He found parchment, ink and quills, and for want of anything better to do started compiling a detailed list of the common roots between the language of his captors and the Saesneg he had grown up speaking.

It was while he was at this task one afternoon that he felt the brush of air on the back of his neck that meant someone had opened the door.

'Just put it on the table there,' he said without looking round, assuming it was time for his evening meal.

'Put what where?' a voice asked. Startled, Errol dropped his quill and looked up.

She had to be Princess Iolwen, there was no one else she could have been. Her face was light, her hair so blonde as to be almost white. Her cheeks and nose were not marked as much as her sister's, but she was freckled nonetheless. Only where Queen Beulah's expression was hard and uncompromising, Iolwen's was sad and wistful. She had been holding a book in her hand, but when she saw Errol she let it fall to the floor.

'Balch,' she said, her hand going to her mouth. Errol leaped to his feet, stepping forward to retrieve the fallen book. He dusted it off, straightening a folded page before handing it back.

'I'm sorry.' The princess took the book with hesitant fingers. 'For a moment there I thought you were . . . But he's . . . I mean . . .' She trailed off as if unsure what to say, still staring intently at Errol's face.

'Your Highness, my name is Errol Ramsbottom,' Errol said, bowing. 'Am I right in assuming I'm addressing Princess Iolwen?'

It took a moment for the princess to realize that he had addressed her in her native tongue, and Errol wondered if he had given her one shock too many.

'I haven't heard anyone speak Saesneg in so long,' the princess said. 'Where did you learn it? You speak it so well.'

'I grew up in a little village about two days' ride from Ystumtuen,' Errol said.

'What are you doing here?'

'I was sent here by Inquisitor Melyn to spy for him,' Errol said. 'Duke Dondal handed me straight over to King Ballah – having taken Melyn's money, I might add.'

A look of understanding dawned on Iolwen's face. 'I'd heard snippets of the story,' she said. 'But it never occurred to me the spy was still alive. I assumed he'd been executed like all the others. Why would they spare you?'

'I don't know, Your Highness. You're the first person who's spoken to me since I met the king. He said something about my aura being unusual and ordered me to be kept here. So here I am.'

'No doubt he has some scheme in mind,' the princess said. 'That's all he ever does – scheme and plot and manipulate people. But what about you? You seem very young to be a spy?'

Errol told her his story: of how he had been chosen against his will; how the inquisitor had tried to rewrite his memories and succeeded for a while; how he had learned to hide his true self from the probing of adepts; and finally why he had been sent. At this last revelation the princess scowled.

'Do you know how long I've been here?' she asked. 'I was made hostage when I was five. I'm nineteen now. Fourteen years of my life have been spent here. These are my people far more than anyone from Candlehall or Ystumtuen can ever be. They've raised me, educated me. They're my friends. Why shouldn't I love them in return? Why shouldn't I marry Dafydd if I want to? By the Shepherd, I don't even know why our two nations hate each other so.'

'If it makes things any better,' Errol said, 'I never intended to carry out my orders. I just wanted to get away from Melyn and the Order of the High Ffrydd. Perhaps if I can persuade King Ballah that I'm no threat he'll . . .' But he didn't finish his sentence. Partly because he realized then that his best possible future was one in which he spent the rest of his days in the West Tower, the worst in which the rest of his days could be counted on the fingers of one hand, and partly because two uniformed guards had stepped into the room. Confusion flickered across their faces when they saw the princess seated at the reading table.

'Princess Iolwen,' one of the guards said. 'Your Highness, you should not be here.'

Iolwen sighed deeply, then stood.

'Well, it's been nice talking to you,' she said to Errol. 'Perhaps we can do it again some time, if the king will permit it. I'd like to hear more about the Twin Kingdoms, even if I can't really think of them as home any more.'

'I'd like that.' Errol looked nervously at the guards. 'If the king permits it.'

Iolwen left the room, and Errol expected the guards to follow her. Instead they stayed, waiting in silence while the echoes of the princess's footsteps died away.

'I presume you want me to come with you.' He addressed the guard who had spoken. 'And I assume I'm not about to be set free.'

I 2

The power of flight is a dragon's birthright. Not for the dragon the tyranny of the ground, the dull trudging from place to place on feet worn sore by stony roads. The air is his home, and it is his duty to gain mastery over it. A young hatchling, even before his wings have begun to set, should be put to studying the manner of birds, much as he studies his runecraft and histories. For it is through such early observation that he will begin to understand the invisible currents that eddy and flow.

Particular attention should be paid to raptors, those masters of the aerial hunt. A diligent kit with patience and fortitude will learn much from their twisting and gyring, so that when he first takes to the air he will know instinctively how to soar and dive. If he lives near to the sea, then the youngling must observe the ways of the gulls and the giant albatross, for only then will he understand how to make the wind work for him, rather than battle against its unassailable power.

There are many who scoff at the notion that a dragon might need to learn to fly, let alone that anything as humble as a mere bird might be able to teach him. But there is no room for such

arrogance in one who would truly be a king of
the skies.

Aderyn, *Educational Notes for the Young*

Benfro rolled the memory of Sir Frynwy around in his
hand. It was a partial thing, like hearing a laugh down a
corridor and knowing that a welcome guest was arriving.
It sent a thrill through him to know that the old dragon
was here. But how had he come to this place?

'Malkin find Benfro friends,' the squirrel said, a note of
pride in its voice. 'All here.'

And they were, all neatly ordered and separated by
inches of cold stone. Benfro counted enough filled
alcoves for each and every one of the dead villagers. And
they were all white. Reckoned. Not red and raw. After
the agony of witnessing their deaths in his dream, knowing that they lay unreckoned and lost for ever in the
burned-out remains of the village, it was an untold joy to
see them here. But how had they come to this place? And
who had performed their reckoning?

Benfro put Sir Frynwy's single jewel back with its companions, sensing a momentary trepidation bordering on
fear as he released his hold. How had they got here, these
final remains of the old dragons? The great hall of the
village, which should have been their resting place, was far
distant, on the other side of the mountains. It made no
sense to him at all.

He reached out with shaking fingers to take one of the
jewels from a different alcove. With a touch he recognized
Meirionydd. It was almost as if she stood behind him,

talked to him. At once a hundred sweet memories of her filled his mind, the practical joker who had delighted him with her magical tricks and had taught him the best way to steal food from the communal kitchens. It was Meirionydd who had encouraged him into trouble, and she who had stood up for him when others, particularly Frecknock, sought to make his life a misery. She had always been the cheerful one, the first with a joke to ease a difficult situation. Yet now she seemed to be alarmed, alone, frightened. Something bad had happened, something terrible that the other villagers needed to know about, but try as she might she could not find them anywhere. Only their lonely cries echoed to her in the darkness. He tried to speak to her, called to her, but she was consumed with panic and could not hear. Or maybe the imprint of memories went only one way? That couldn't be right, surely. Ystrad Fflur had talked to him; Magog had controlled him. But touching only one of Meirionydd's jewels he could only sense a part of her.

Benfro plunged his hands into the alcove, piling all of the jewels into his cupped hands. Almost instantly he heard the voice in his head, a voice that he knew from a childhood that seemed years distant although in truth it was only days.

'Benfro, is that you?' Meirionydd asked. 'You've changed so much. Your aura is magnificent.'

'You can see me?'

'Of course I can, silly,' she chided. 'You're standing here right in front of me. And where is this place? Why did you bring us here? Where are the others? I can hear them calling out, but I can't reach them.'

'This is the repository in Magog's castle,' Benfro said.

'Ah, Benfro, you always were one for joking and mischief,' Meirionydd said. 'But it's unkind to play tricks on the dead. Everyone knows the stories of Gog and Magog are just tales.'

'But they're real,' Benfro insisted. 'I met Magog himself. In a dream, true, but I saved his last remaining jewel. I have it with me. I can show you.' His enthusiasm was unstoppable. He had always been this way with Meirionydd, desperate to please her. He would do anything for her praise.

'Dear me, Benfro. You're so like your father, you know. Always chasing after myths and legends. Never content to live in the now.'

'But it's true,' Benfro insisted. 'Look around you.'

There was a moment's pause which he could only assume was the old dragon taking his advice, then her voice came back, affronted.

'This is a collection of memories and other treasure,' Meirionydd said, 'but it's no dragon hoard. No wonder I can't reach the others; they're separated by dead stone. This is no repository. This is hell.'

'I don't understand.' Benfro stared at the neatly stacked shelves and the endless palely gleaming alcoves.

'Think, Benfro. You've seen the place where Ystrad Fflur was taken after his reckoning. You know how we are meant to go on. But a dragon's jewels shouldn't be kept apart. We're gregarious creatures, Benfro. In death even more so. We should be mingled together, sharing our memories like we did before you brought us here. This stone is like a grave: it cuts us off from each other. Worse, it cuts us off from everything.'

Benfro wondered what she was talking about, but something Meirionydd had said brought him up short.

'I brought you here?' Benfro protested. 'I didn't bring you here. I didn't sort you all out into these boxes.'

'Then who did?' Meirionydd's voice asked. It was a question to which he could find no satisfactory answer. And the more he asked it, the more an image came to him of sitting trance-like in front of this very wall, sorting through the muddled collection in his bag and placing each protesting memory in its own lonely place. He had no idea how he had got here before, but it made a horrible kind of sense. He had been here, and he had brought the last memories of the villagers to this prison.

'What should I do?' he asked finally.

'Take us all out of these horrible cells,' Meirionydd said. 'Pile us all together. Heap us at the junction of the Llinellau, where we can watch over the world.'

'I can't see the Llinellau,' Benfro said. 'Where are they?'

'Forgive me, Benfro,' Meirionydd said. 'I should have more sympathy, I know. I remember the difficulty you had with your lessons. But I thought we were lost, our memories leaching away. Then you came back to us, conjured the Fflam Gwir, the reckoning flame. It was a magical moment, Benfro. Whoever's been training you all these months must be a genius. Surely he can't have taught you all this without first showing you how to see the lines?'

'Months?' Benfro said. 'It's been only days since the men burned the village. Two weeks at most.'

'Not days, dear,' Meirionydd said, her voice carrying that serious tone that Benfro knew well. 'It's been more than seven months since I died in that fire. Seven months of slowly fading away, of knowing all my friends are close but being unable to talk to them. Trust me, little dragon. That's not something I'd forget.'

'But I . . .' Benfro began. He had no clear idea of how long he had tramped through the forest, but it was not much more than a couple of weeks, surely. He had no memory of months passing by.

'Still, they have,' Meirionydd continued as if she could read his thoughts. 'There are things in the forest that can rob a dragon of much more than that. And you've changed far more than a few days could account for.'

'How could I not remember?' Benfro asked. 'Where did the time go?'

'I don't know,' Meirionydd said. 'But it's been only a day since you reckoned us all and brought us to this place. Even so, a day is too long cooped up like this. Better to have faded away entirely. You must find the Llinellau. Put us all at a nexus. This place reeks of power – it must lie on a major source of the Grym. You can find it, Benfro. I know you can.'

'But I never could before,' Benfro protested.

'You never had such a magnificent aura before,' Meirionydd said. 'Goodness me, Benfro, you never had wings. I've never seen a dragon with such wings. Think about them and the strength they give you. Open your eyes and see.'

Benfro looked around the room, searching out anything that might be a source of great power. In most directions he could see only a few yards, the walls blurring into a jewel-lined mess like the moon shining through thick cloud. Only in one direction could he see any distance, back towards the reading table and its twin candles. They burned bright and clear, sharply focused even though they were distant. That had to be it. There was nowhere else.

Slowly he began to spread his wings, feeling the sense of power in them. He remembered the thrill of flight, the perfect control over air currents and the feeling that he was somehow connected to it all. And as he rode a long-dead dragon's memories, the Llinellau shimmered into view.

Great thick cables of light speared along the corridors formed by the pillars, criss-crossing in a luminous grid. They were not so much lines of light as an imprint on the fabric of reality. Thin streaks ran across most of the floor in a tight pattern, building as they crossed, larger and larger, until one great trunk speared straight from the wall behind where he stood and on towards the reading table. Somehow he knew that a line of similar magnitude would intersect at that very point.

'I see them,' he said breathlessly. 'I see the Llinellau Grym! They cross the floor. They're everywhere.'

'I knew you would, Benfro,' Meirionydd said. 'You just needed to find the right focus. Now you must take us from these prisons. Build a pile of our memories where the biggest lines meet.'

'What about the others?'

'Others?'

'The other dragons. There are thousands here, all sorted into little boxes like you were.'

There was silence. Benfro looked down at the softly glowing Llinellau and noticed Malkin staring up at him.

The squirrel had a quizzical look on its face but had remained silent all the while he had been talking to the jewels. No doubt it had come to accept the strange behaviour of this wayward dragon it had decided to befriend. Only there was something about it that wasn't quite right. Benfro could see that it was standing astride one of the Llinellau, almost as if it had chosen its place deliberately. The strange luminescence surrounded the creature totally, as if the squirrel were made of the same Grym as the lines. And behind it, almost a shadow of light, was the silhouette of the great mother tree, at once very small and impossibly big.

'You must free them all, Benfro,' Meirionydd said. He could hear the edge to her words, a seeping panic of claustrophobia.

'No dragon should be held like this.'

The dining hall was empty at this late hour, which was why Melyn liked to come for his meals now. Apart from important ceremonial feasts, he rarely ate with the novitiates, quaisters and warrior priests. Few dared talk while he was in the room. At times he was glad that his power was still such that it kept all around him in fearful awe, but lately he had begun to wonder if there was anyone who might show a bit of backbone, answer back.

He looked out across the hall from his seat at the top table. The food in front of him was half-eaten and unappetizing; his goblet of wine was barely touched. These days it seemed he needed less and less food, less and less sleep. It was just as well. Planning Beulah's campaign against Llanwennog was taking most of his time, and there was still the matter of a dragon out there in the forest of the Ffrydd somewhere. Perhaps he would send a troop or two of his best warrior priests out. If they could make it through the Rim mountains and into north Llanwennog, they could draw half of Ballah's army away from the border just by razing a few towns.

'Your Grace?'

Melyn looked up from his plate. He had been so wrapped up in his musings he'd not noticed anyone come into the dining hall. It was an unforgivable lapse, but whoever was there had managed to close their mind almost completely to him.

'Who is it?' he asked the darkness. A tall figure stepped forward, slightly stooped and with hair as white as the frost that rimed the morning grass outside the monastery even in the summer.

'Ah, Andro, I should have guessed,' Melyn said. 'It's been a long time since you managed to creep up on me unawares.'

'Longer still since I did it without trying,' the librarian said. 'You must have a great deal on your mind to let it wander so.'

Melyn heard the words of his teacher, taking him back to his earliest years in the order. There was no chastisement this time, but he could do without Andro's sympathy.

'The queen's war won't plan itself,' Melyn said, 'and there's the small matter of a dragon running loose in the forest.'

'Can one dragon harm you so much?' Andro stepped up to the table and settled himself into a seat. He had a roll of parchment in one gnarled hand. Melyn poured a goblet of wine from his jug and pushed it across the table.

'Probably not. But it's a bad omen nonetheless. And it wasn't like any dragon I've seen before. It flew.'

'I know,' Andro said. 'I saw it too. It was more like some of the beasts in their myths.'

'But you didn't come here to talk about dragons, did you, old friend? And I don't suppose you're all that interested in how I intend to invade Llanwennog.'

'Interested, yes,' Andro said. 'But I came to give you this scroll. It was brought here by a coenobite. He's in a bit of a bad way so I sent him down to see Usel.'

'A Ram? Here?' Melyn asked, noting the bloodstains on the parchment.

'An old friend, actually,' Andro said. 'Father Gideon. He was pretty much dead on his feet when he arrived. His horse will be lucky if it lives, and he's got a nasty arrow wound that'll take some healing. It would seem even Rams aren't welcome in Tynhelyg any more.'

'Why did he come here?' Melyn asked. 'Why not report back to Candlehall?'

'I suspect the reason lies in that scroll,' Andro said. 'And if he was trying to avoid the main passes, this is the first major stop on his route.'

Melyn opened the scroll, reading the news it brought him with a rising sense of anger and frustration.

'King Ballah has the boy,' he said finally. 'Dondal handed him over almost as soon as they arrived.'

'Errol?' Andro asked, his face dropping. 'Is he –'

'Dead? No.' Melyn pushed the scroll across the table so that the librarian could read it himself. 'At least he wasn't when this was written. Damn, but this throws all our plans out. Half the army was meant to go through the pass at Tynewydd. Dondal will be waiting for us to march into his trap. And now he'll have the bulk of Ballah's forces with him.'

'So, how can you use that to your advantage?' Andro asked, and once more Melyn was transported back to the classroom.

'Diversion,' the inquisitor said. 'We'll mass our peasant levies on the border, keep them guessing when we're going to strike. Make him think we still trust him. But I'll send all my warrior priests north through the Ffrydd. We'll cut back over the Rim and descend on Tynhelyg from the opposite direction.'

'We? You're intending going with them?'

'I can't fight this war from here,' Melyn said. 'Besides, I've unfinished dragon business in the forest.'

Benfro emptied his few possessions on to the floor and then filled his bag with the jewels of the villagers, sweeping them from their niches into a big pile. He could feel their relief as a silent sigh, a release of tension that he had not realized was there until it went. He carried the weight back up the corridor to the writing table, then lifted the candles from their sconces and placed them beside the skeletons in the fireplace. The table was heavy, carved from some solid dark wood. He couldn't lift it, but managed with much sweat and a great deal of squealing and scraping to move it away from the nexus.

The glow intensified as he carefully tipped the last memories of the village on to the floor exactly where the two great Llinellau met. They made a small pile and took on the same ethereal light. Mist-like tendrils rose in a spiral from the heap and for a moment Benfro feared the gems were alight, would burn away to nothing. But the mist only grew more solid, coalescing into a familiar form until a ghost image of Meirionydd stood before him. Not the old dowager dragon of his recent memory but the figure of youthful grace and beauty he had seen on his hatchday, when she had entered his thoughts to lift Frecknock's clumsy spell.

'O Benfro, this is truly a wonderful place you've brought us to,' she said. 'But you must free the others quickly. I feel their frustration and fear all around me. They've been alone for so very long. I fear some may be beyond rescue. Hurry, please.'

Unable to disobey, Benfro picked up his bag and, watched over by the luminous vision of beauty, he worked his way along the nearest wall, scooping jewels from their alcoves into his bag. When it was full he added them to the pile before heading off for more.

'Malkin help,' the squirrel said when it realized what he was attempting to do. It scampered back and forth, collecting gems as if they were acorns to hide away for the winter. Slowly the pile grew, spilling out from the central point in a heap that cast ever more light over the scene. With each touch of hand to stone, Benfro would catch a fleeting memory, an image perhaps or more often a feeling. Names sprang into his head, unbidden and unknown. Places too, and how to get to them, but only from other places he had never heard of. And all the while the pile grew and grew and the walls with their endless little carved pockets became emptier and emptier.

The hours passed, coalescing into each other in a seamless rush of activity. With each added essence, the pile seemed to radiate an ever greater urgency, demanding that he finish the task. His muscles ached, his belly rumbled and he felt a weariness that should surely have floored him, yet somehow Benfro took strength from the task, took encouragement from those he freed. And so he toiled, unthinking and uncomplaining in a manner he would not have thought possible.

Finally it was done. He swept the last stones from the last alcove, carried them over to the enormous pile and tipped them as best he could on to the top, though he could scarcely reach it now without clambering up the stack, and that seemed to him oddly disrespectful. Malkin had stopped some time earlier, when the lower tiers of alcoves had been emptied, and the squirrel now stood, motionless and staring up at their handiwork. A general aura of excitement filled the room, a soundless hubbub of voices in conversation. The smoke image of Meirionydd faded away, melding in and out of a hundred different shapes until it reformed into one solid image. She was the most magnificent dragon Benfro had ever seen, rising over the pile of stones like a mother protecting her eggs. Her long neck curved with the ceiling and dropped back down towards him, its head staring at him with intense glowing eyes.

'We thank you, Sir Benfro, for freeing us from the tyrant Magog,' the vision said. Its voice was mighty like a storm in the treetops. 'Our wisdom and our folly belong to the earth now, as it should have been aeons ago. Your fallen comrades tell me you seek the one known as Corwen. His place is to the north of here, only half a day's flying. Now we must go. There is much bitterness and resentment to be eased, much madness to be soothed. Some of us have been imprisoned here for thousands of years.'

Benfro was about to ask the image who it was, but it disappeared, the mist sucking back into the heap like the smoke from the after-dinner pipe he had watched Sir Frynwy take a thousand times. He stood for long moments just staring at the great pile, waiting for someone else to appear, but nothing came. His work here was done, he realized. It was time to go. And yet just as he was turning to leave a voice came to him, gruff and familiar. Ynys Môn.

'I always thought you'd come to something, young Benfro,' the old dragon said. 'But this astonishes even me. Still, you've a lot more surprises ahead of you, of that I'm sure. You're going to be heading out into the real world and there's something here you might want to take with you. Go through this treasure and see if you can find coins. You'll need money once you travel beyond the Ffrydd. A map would be a good idea too, if you can find one.'

'Beyond the Ffrydd?' Benfro echoed. It had never really occurred to him that there was anything beyond the Ffrydd. Even the maps he had seen earlier that night had been meaningless. But the old dragon did not reply. The pile of gems hummed with activity but it was voiceless, expectant and drawn in upon itself, a great melting pot of emotions and ideas kept locked away for far too long.

Finding coins was not difficult. There were chests of them neatly stacked around the pillars. Benfro had no concept of money but he had always taken Ynys Môn's advice so he filled his leather bag with as many as its strap would hold, adding a few other shiny trinkets, including the torc he had ripped from the skeleton at the door. There were so many maps he didn't know where to begin. But one was folded rather than rolled and drawn on some thin, lightweight fabric he couldn't name. It claimed to be *A Reckoning of the Northern Land Mass of Gwlad*, and he recognized the familiar shape of the Ffrydd on it, ringed by the Rim mountains. It went in the bag with the gold. Then, slinging the weight over his shoulder to go with the food, he shouted for his companion, who had disappeared into the shadows again.

'Malkin, it's time we left.' For a moment there was no reply, then the squirrel came running round a pillar, clearly excited.

'The sun,' it said, scampering up to Benfro's feet. It ran this way and that, jumping about with infectious glee. Then it set off behind one of the pillars. 'The forest. Come. Benfro look.'

How he had missed it during the night was difficult to say, except that the whole room did not seem to conform to any normal sense of dimensions. It was a window, hewn through the rock wall and opening on to a large balcony. A stone balustrade edged its two sides, but straight ahead there was nothing to stop a nasty fall. Malkin was peering over the edge in a manner that made

Benfro's hearts jump. He could see the forest spread out away from him, picked out in the dawn light, shadowed by the great mountain of Magog's lair. It was a very long way down.

'Careful, Malkin,' he said. 'You don't want to fall.'

'Malkin fall lots,' the squirrel said, turning as nonchalantly as if there were no drop at all. 'Malkin fall out of tree, land on head. Not hurt Malkin.'

'Still. I'd be happier if you moved a bit nearer the room.' Benfro realized that the squirrel was so small, so light, that it most likely could tumble a hundred feet without coming to any harm. But as he inched carefully closer to the edge, he could see that this was more like a thousand feet down, with sharp rocks to shatter anyone who fell. The cliff face was sheer and smooth, curving away from the opening where he stood on both sides and continuing its upward climb for many hundreds of feet to the castle ruin high above. Even so it struck him as odd that a room whose contents were so obviously valued and which was so well protected from the inside of the castle should be open to the elements like this. Turning, he made to re-enter the repository only to find that it wasn't there.

In a panic, Benfro looked back and forth for the entrance to the repository. A cold breeze whipped up the cliff face around him, appearing as if from nowhere and pushing him this way and that. Maybe it was his imagination, but the ledge which he had thought of as a balcony seemed to be getting smaller. Malkin scrambled up his tail, over his back and on to his shoulder, tiny claws clinging to his neck in alarm.

'Where room?' it asked, all its earlier cockiness gone as

it began to realize the predicament they were in. 'Where ledge?'

There was no doubting that the ledge was disappearing fast. Benfro could not see any movement, even if he stared at the edge, yet somehow, as if he were growing, it came ever nearer. His back was against the rock face now, cold stone digging into him as he hugged it ever closer. He curled his tail around his feet, its tip dropping away into oblivion, forced ever more upright as the ledge turned into a sill, the solid knot of muscle in his back pressed hard against the cliff. His wings creased and furled.

His wings! How could he have forgotten them? And he had the memories of flight in his head. True they were jumbled up with a thousand other experiences, but they had been so visceral, so laden with pure, simple pleasure they were never far from the front of his mind.

'Malkin,' he said, trying to look around at the tiny creature and realizing it was wrapped too tight to his neck for that, 'hold on tight. I'm going to fly.' The words filled him with a thrill of excited anticipation like the way he had always felt before carrying out some mischievous prank on the villagers. He poised himself, beginning to unfurl his wings, trying to think how best to launch himself upon the air.

In the end the decision was taken from him. There was simply not enough ledge to stand on any more. One moment he was balanced precariously halfway between leaping and dropping, the next he was tipping forward, his balance gone.

13

The union of two dragons is not something to be entered into lightly. To join is no mere physical thing, but a mixing of the souls and a sharing of spirits. A pact between friends may be no more than a formula of words, but to wed is to mingle two essences so tightly together that no power on Gwlad can ever take them apart. No power, that is, save death. And even in that finality, as a dragon's remains are consumed by the Fflam Gwir, so the spirit of the bereaved will be drawn to the ceremony whatever base physical barriers strive to keep them apart.

Sir Rhudian, Marriage of Gwynhyfyr

Reflexively, Benfro stretched his wings wide to the morning air, catching the rough upward current, smoothing it with wing edges that seemed to know instinctively what to do. Instead of falling he rose on the wind, swept up and around so that he could see the cliff wall, smooth as glass, jutting up from the forest like some great wound. The long slow rise of the hill he had climbed the day before dropped away on its western flank as if some enormous hand had chopped it with a blade so sharp it could cut thoughts. Sitting atop this vast rock, the ruins of the castle were picked out by the low sun in a series of jagged shadows, like teeth rotten with age. Only the front arch, the focus for the dark magic that protected the place, stood proud and tall in its decaying wall.

He circled the palace, high above it, for some minutes, savouring the feel of the cold air on his scales, the thrill of hanging in the air. He had never known vertigo, the irrational fear of falling that so many of the older dragons professed. Now he knew why. He had been born to fly. It was his birthright. The wind in his ears was a whistling wailing thing that sung a terrified song of joy as it welcomed this new creature to its embrace.

Then he remembered Malkin.

The squirrel sat almost on the back of his neck, gripping on for dear life with tiny claws that dug into his flesh where they could find purchase, scraped on his scales where they could not. The noise he was hearing, singing below the wind, was its screeching alarm as it was buffeted and bounced with each sweep of his massive wings. He had become so wrapped up in the joy of flying, the sheer pleasure of turning this way and that, of riding the currents and then climbing by sheer brute strength that he had completely forgotten his companion.

'Are you all right, Malkin?' Benfro shouted, his voice almost lost to the rushing air. He dared not look round at the creature, dared not turn his head lest it lose what little grip it had. Yet instinctively he knew it would be safe if it sat in the hollow of his shoulders. Or was that one of the thousand memories and feelings he had sampled that night, a skill from a long-dead dragon?

'Benfro fly. Malkin fly!' came the reply. It was not fear

the squirrel was feeling but exhilaration. It screamed with the excitement of it all, heedless to the danger of a fall. Benfro could feel the movement of its claws now, not as a frenzied scrabbling for grip but a constant moving, this way and that, to get the best view.

'Where Benfro fly?' Malkin asked, its voice barely discernible above the roar of the wind. It was a good question. Benfro banked in a slow circle, searching the distance for anything that might look like the clearing where Corwen was supposed to live. All he could see, even from his considerable altitude, was the vast forest stretching in all directions, undulating in long, slow hills and valleys as it went, like lazy ripples on a pond. Mountains ringed the landscape, some jagged and white-tipped, others brown ridges and mounds, hazy in the warming air. Only one gap appeared in this fortress wall, countless miles distant. It was as if some cataclysm, aeons ago, had carved a chunk out of the mountains, exposing the hidden depths of the forest to whatever lay beyond. The midday sun sat high overhead, though Benfro was no longer certain which day it was. Still he knew that Cenobus lay due north of the Graith Fawr, if the maps in the repository were to be believed.

Now high above the fortress, he could see the march of the Rim mountains rising to their highest point, a sharp peak, palely distant. That was the direction he needed to follow. It almost called to him. He fixed his sight on it, locked it in his memory and set off.

His back felt unbreakable as he soared over the forest. This was a far cry from the panic-fuelled glide he had used to escape from the warrior priests and their purloined monastery. Then he had been both terrified and in considerable pain as his muscles were asked to do something far more strenuous than they had ever done before. He had not flown since, and it felt to him like only a couple of days had passed, yet here he was, flying as if he had done it all his life, his back as relaxed as if he were just going for a walk. Was there truth then in what Meirionydd had said? Had he really slept for months in the shade of the great mother tree? Had she nurtured him, strengthened him while he slept? And if so why?

The tiny creature that sat on his back, face to the wind in contagious glee, might be able to tell him. The squirrel was her emissary. Benfro knew it had said it had come with him for the adventure, but he couldn't help remembering its aura, the way it had stood astride the Llinellau Grym as if it knew they were there, as if drawing sustenance from them. It was a creature of the tree, and while the squirrel seemed childlike and simple in many ways, he was beginning to learn from his experiences that outward appearances were more often deceiving than not.

For now it was enough just to exult in the sheer pleasure of flight, to sweep his wings up and down through the air in a steady rhythm that inch by inch pulled the far-flung mountains closer. Slowly the afternoon passed as the sun tracked its journey across the sky. There was not a cloud in sight, and the warm rays massaged him as he flew. Every so often he would hit a patch of thermal activity, where a darker canopy of leaves absorbed more heat, warming the air and forcing it up. There were rocky ridges too, poking their occasional sharp faces through the trees and deflecting the breeze. Whenever he felt a rising draught, he would pause a while, wheel slowly round as he had seen the buzzards do countless times, climbing higher and higher until the force could no longer lift his weight even with his wings unfurled to their full magnificent length. Then he could set off again for the pointed mountain in another long slow glide.

At some point in the afternoon he began to tire. It was a subtle thing at first. He would drift off course a bit, suddenly find he was flying towards some interesting-looking tree, larger than the forest surrounding it, or wheeling in a thermal without realizing he had come to it, unsure how long he had been circling, just maintaining his altitude. His wings were still strong, but it became increasingly difficult to focus on the task of flying.

And still the trees went on.

A half-day's flying was what the magnificent image of a dragon had told him, yet Benfro was certain he had flown longer than that and there was still no sign of a clearing, nor even the thicker vegetation that might have marked the passage through the forest of a river. His thoughts were becoming cluttered now, the memories of the stolen jewels rising in his mind and threatening to swamp the part that was him. He would find himself fondly remembering a stolen kiss, the summer that the rains never came, the joy of a perfect temba, its symmetry and alliteration pleasing both to the eye and the ear, its message as pertinent as the act of composition. Yet he didn't know what a temba was, had never known a drought and had only ever kissed his mother, whose affection was freely given and limitless.

The sun sank further and further, dropping steadily

towards the serrated teeth of the Rim mountains. As Benfro flew on, he found it increasingly difficult to remember what it was he was supposed to be doing. Only the tall lonely peak mattered. He had to get to it while the sun still painted its flank in shades of pink and orange. If that flame went out, then the world would be condemned to an eternity of evening, long shadows and the reign of the dark creatures of the night. The men were at his back, riding after him on great birds broken to their will. At their head, the inquisitor spurred on his steed with a malicious glint in his ruby eyes. A sword of flame sprang from his outstretched hand, guttering in the wind.

'Benfro, wake up. Fly too low.' The tiny voice broke through his stupor. The trees were reaching up to grab him, so close he could see their top branches as a thousand thousand groping hands. With a start, he swept his wings down reflexively, pulling himself back into the air. A cold flood of realization pulsed through him. He had fallen asleep in mid-air and been gliding slowly downwards in blissful ignorance. Only his companion passenger had saved him from a messy perhaps fatal crash.

Steadying his mind against the crushing weariness, Benfro tried to get his bearings. He could no longer see the mountain, so close was he to the treetops. They spread around him in a bowl, rising towards the glowing orb of the setting sun, now dipping itself into the forest. With a final effort of will, he pushed himself on towards that last rise, hoping against hope that there might be something over it, a thinning of the trees, perhaps, or a bald ridge where he could land.

But he didn't know how to land.

He had been flying on someone else's memories, reading the currents in the way a master would, but he had no recollection of landing. Panic gripped him as he remembered the shock and helpless danger of his previous return to earth. And this time he had the added responsibility of Malkin perched on his shoulders.

It was getting hard to keep aloft now, each sweep of his wings heavier than the last. He could feel that knot growing in the middle of his back as the muscles began to cramp and protest against their treatment. And still the rise was ahead of him, now higher than him.

The sun sank further into the trees, an orb that seemed to swell as it was devoured. Where the forest rose to meet its feeder, the branches of the trees turned flame red, as if a fire tore uncontrolled through the wood. The warm evening air rippled and burned, distorting everything, as Benfro ploughed on, desperately trying to keep above the trees. Closer and closer, the rise climbed in front of him, eating the sun as it came, sucking the life out of it, the red fading to yellow, blue, purple and black.

He felt the topmost branches tickle his belly scales with their leaves, feared for an instant his tail would snag. It smacked into wood, a numbing pain running up his spine, but it bounced and jumped free. The sun was almost gone now, the last wisps of light spreading through the trees as it trickled away. And then with a final burst of energy he soared over the ridge.

It was a large clearing. It was *the* clearing, he knew as soon as he saw it. A small river ran through the middle of it, deep and still for the most part, but tumbling over steep rocks where it entered on the far side until it levelled out near the middle. A little-used track of hard-packed earth crossed the clearing by the rocks, and where the rocks formed a small cliff there was a cave mouth.

With the last of his strength failing him, Benfro tried to wheel, to slow down, to get a better look at the place. The flat half of the clearing was covered in small shrubs and dry brown grass, with the occasional large boulder that had rolled down from the foothills that rose steeply some distance away. A crash-landing there would be fraught with danger. Only the path was clear of obstacles for any length. And the river.

'Can you swim?' he shouted over his shoulder to the squirrel.

'Swim?' the answer came back, a touch of anxiety in the voice now that they were so close to the ground.

'In the river,' Benfro added. 'I have a problem with landing.'

'Malkin hang on,' it said, claws gripping the soft skin of Benfro's upper neck.

It was too late to make any other arrangements. Benfro banked hard, trying desperately to lose some speed. Then he remembered the bags slung around his neck, one full of food and the other gold. One would spoil and the other drag him to the bottom. With a muscle-spasming wrench he clapped his wings down as far as he could, lifting himself higher into the air for long enough to haul the straps over his weary head. The bags dropped, hitting the thick grass by the track and tumbling towards the river. Over and over they went, spending their momentum with a gambler's recklessness. For a moment he feared they would clear the bank and bounce into the water, but they finally came to a halt, first the food bag and then the heavier leather sack with its coins.

Sweeping around for one final time, Benfro could feel the strain in his back, knew that at any moment he would not be able to hold himself aloft.

'Hold on tight,' he shouted to the squirrel at his neck. 'And leap free as soon as you think it's safe.'

'Malkin hold on,' came the reply. 'Malkin not know how to swim.'

Benfro's hearts sank at this. He had been counting on the little creature leaping clear when he hit the water, being able to save itself. Still, it was too late now. He was on his final approach, dropping with considerable inelegance towards the dark, still and hopefully deep water. His wings were like two great boulder-filled sacks that he somehow had to keep held out as far from his body as possible. Or did he need to fold them up before he hit? Suddenly racked with indecision, he pulled back from the onrushing river. Or at least that was his intention. But as he pulled up, so his head reared and his legs pushed forward. With a last heroic spasm of flapping, he slowed to an almost acceptable speed. And then he hit.

Water exploded in every direction. The slap of his impact jarred through his feet, up his legs and into his body, driving the wind out of his lungs. Unable to fold his wings, they flopped forward, slammed into the water and pulled him head first into a dive. There wasn't time to get his arms out of the way, to take a breath, to even think, before he had plunged into the depths.

*

Beulah travelled the Calling Road at the speed of thought. Her aethereal form sparkled with the power she drew from the Obsidian Throne. Where it clashed with the glamours of the road, strange colours rippled and eddied the scenery, as if it were painted on great canvasses blowing in an unseen wind. She could see that the road had been strengthened recently, no doubt in an attempt to attract the wayward dragon. Its pull was insidious, almost undeniable, but she shrugged it off. She was heading where it wanted her to go anyway.

In scarcely a dozen heartbeats she was upon the great building, more fortress than monastery. Its protective wards welled up at her presence, but she knew how to deal with them and slipped easily inside. She found the inquisitor in his private chapel, his aethereal form swathed in ruby light, his attention almost completely absorbed. Only as she stood directly behind him, within touching distance if such a concept was meaningful in the dream state, did he stiffen a little, sense her presence and then relax.

'I meant to contact you later this evening, Your Majesty. You've saved me the effort.' He shrugged off the red glow, turned to face her. 'What brings you here?'

'I was speaking to Clun this afternoon,' Beulah said. 'His wounds are almost healed, by the way. But we got to talking about his life. Believe me, it's like drawing teeth trying to get him to speak to me. He's so shy.'

'It's a wonder you even try,' Melyn said, and Beulah was sure there was a hint of bitterness in his voice. 'What would you want with the likes of him, a merchant's son from the back country?'

'He took an assassin's bolt meant for me,' Beulah said.

'And besides, he's young and strong, handsome too. He's not stupid, and he's not scheming like all the nobles, who spend their lives stabbing each other in the back. I like him.'

'Of course,' Melyn said. 'But you don't need to nurse him yourself. It's demeaning.'

'Far from it,' Beulah said. 'You of all people should understand that. He's a commoner, yes. But by tending him myself I show everyone how much I value my people. All of my people, not just the rich or the powerful.'

'So what was it you and he talked about?' Melyn asked.

'About his home, Pwllpeiran,' Beulah said. 'And about his stepbrother, Errol. I must confess that I'd quite forgotten him and all that nonsense with Lleyn's body. Tell me it was all nonsense, Melyn.'

'I always thought it was, otherwise I'd have mentioned him earlier,' Melyn said. 'The post-mortem confirmed the unborn child died with its mother. Either Prince Balch fathered the boy on another woman or Errol just happens to look a lot like him.'

'The Balch I remember wouldn't even look at another woman once he met Lleyn. He mooched over her like a lovesick puppy. So the boy's likely a bastard of his retinue. There were a number of royal cousins, I seem to recall. Perhaps we should nurture him; he might make a good puppet king in Tynhelyg. So what were you going to talk to me about?'

'Strangely enough, the boy Errol,' Melyn said. 'I sent him off to Tynhelyg as a spy to find out what Iolwen's doing. He should be there still, but our insider turned him over to the king.'

'Poor boy. It will crush Clun to know his stepbrother's dead.'

'He's not dead,' Melyn said. 'At least not yet. King Ballah's got him locked up in the palace, apparently. But that's not the worst of it. Your sister Iolwen is to marry Prince Dafydd within the month, and she already carries his child.'

'Iolwen? How could she? How could she sell out her own family?'

'We're as much to blame, I fear, Your Majesty,' Melyn said. 'We sent her to live with the enemy when she was scarce six years old. Is it surprising that she's come to regard her captors as more family than those who gave her away in the first place?'

'But a child, Melyn. King Ballah must be aware how much that would upset the balance of power.'

'Would that be the balance you're so keen on tipping in your favour?'

'We must hasten preparations for war.' Beulah ignored the taunt. 'Ballah won't be slow in launching an offensive as soon as he has a great grandson with a claim to my throne.'

'My warrior priests are on full alert, Your Majesty. And the noble houses have been building up their armouries since your coronation. But the battle plan needs to be changed. We can't hope to break through the pass at Tynewydd any more.'

'I take it you have an alternative?'

'I do, but I'll have to come to Candlehall to discuss it with the noble generals,' Melyn said. 'I'm leaving at first light.'

'Good,' Beulah said. 'And it's perhaps time I thought

about doing my duty. Goodnight, Melyn. Safe journey. We'll speak more of this when you get here.'

Beulah snapped back into her body in an instant, such was the power and pull of the great throne. It took her a moment to compose herself, then she stood and walked out of the hall, leaving the prone, sleeping form of Frecknock the dragon. The creature was completely spineless but was also very sensitive to fluxes in the aethereal. Beulah couldn't say why, but she felt safer travelling through the dreamscape when the dragon was beside her physical self. Keeping it nearby also helped to unsettle all those who came to the Neuadd to petition her with their petty grievances.

Two guards, both warrior priests, she noted with quiet satisfaction, followed her across the courtyard and through the corridors to her private rooms. She told them to guard the entrance and stepped into the darkened hall.

It was late, and what few servants she found she dismissed. Beulah was in no mood for an audience; there would be time for palace gossip later. In her chamber she bathed herself and dressed in a simple silk wrap. But she didn't climb into her bed, instead letting herself quietly out of the room like she had as a young child sneaking out after hours.

The room she was looking for was not far from her own; she had insisted on this. Its door was not locked and she let herself in silently, stopping on the threshold to listen. Soft breathing came from the bed across the room; he was asleep.

Clun's dreams were a tumble of confused images, much the same as any she had brushed with her mind. But there was a central theme to them which satisfied her ego. Beulah tending him, an association with caring and the first green shoots of a powerful selfless love for her were all in the mix of his unconscious thoughts. Unlike Merrl, there was no subterfuge, no artifice in him. He was plain-speaking, straightforward, dependable. And his wound was almost completely healed now, his strength beginning to return after long months fighting the poison that had been meant for her.

Letting her wrap drop to the floor, Beulah climbed into the bed, feeling the warmth radiating from Clun's sleeping body. She gently withdrew from his mind, reached out and stroked the side of his face, listening to the change in his breathing as he slowly began to wake. And then before he was truly aware, she leaned close to him, whispering in his ear as her hands wandered over his chest, felt the shiny smooth scar tissue of his wound.

He woke slowly, almost groggily, rolling over on to his side and opening languid eyes. Perhaps he thought he was still dreaming, that in his dreams he might truly have won the heart of the queen, so impossibly high above him. Whatever the reason, he did not panic to find her in his bed. He managed only to say 'My lady' in a hushed whisper before she kissed him deeply and wrapped herself about his sleepy body.

14

It has long been the custom among dragonkind to lay the reckoned jewels of their dead to rest in great collections. Wanderers and alone in life, it is the wish of every dragon to spend eternity in the company of his ancestors, mingling thoughts and experiences. It is the final duty of the healer to bring fire to the body of a recently dead dragon, reckoning its jewels. But it is the duty of the mage to take those jewels, that precious essence, and to place them in the sacred spot. And here the departed will be welcomed to the fold, one in many and many in one, adding themselves to the repository of knowledge and wisdom.

The mage is the guardian of the jewels and they are the focus of his power. He alone can know the location of the hoard, and it is his magics that protect and nurture it. Yet when the time comes for a mage to die, he will head off into the wilds and in a final act of self-immolation allow the world to take him to its cold embrace. The wise mage will choose the location of his death with great care. For only by laying himself to rest at a point where the Grym flows strongest through the earth can he hope to maintain a connection with his hoard. Even after death he will remain its protector, alone and vigilant for all time.

Healer Trefnog, *The Apothecarium*

Noise clamoured at Benfro's ears, the rushing bubbling cacophony of the waves as they crashed over him on their return from the banks, the river refilling the hole he had punched in its surface. For confusing moments he didn't know which way was up and which was down. He had no breath in his lungs and water filled his nose, his mouth. He wanted to cough and retch, but he could only breathe liquid.

And then his feet hit the riverbed. A thin layer of soft silt covered hard rock. It was a solid anchor that snapped the spinning world back into place. Balance returned, and Benfro pushed himself upright in a great heave, broke the surface like a fountain bursting forth. He expected to sink back, to have to tread water while he tried to clear his airways, but he was still on the rock. Standing upright, he discovered the surface of the river came only to his chest.

Coughing and spluttering, water dripping from his nose and mouth, he felt over his shoulder for Malkin. There was no sign of the little creature. He cast this way and that, splashing the surface in his search. The river had healed already from the wound of his landing, no ripples betraying a drowning squirrel. Long thin fronds of grass overhung the banks on both sides, hiding anything that might have lodged there. He wanted to call out, but he was still gasping and retching up the water he had breathed, so he could only manage a hoarse whisper.

'Malkin?' he croaked, but expected no reply. From where he stood, waist deep in the slow flow, he could not see over the slight rise of the riverbank. Perhaps the squirrel had been thrown clear of the water and had landed in the springy grass. He waded upstream, heading for the point a hundred feet or so away where the track dipped into a shallow ford as it crossed the stream. The water grew progressively shallower, the surface beginning to break over stones and small boulders. He scanned the clearing as best he could, but the last light was fading from the sky, red painted over the strips of cloud so high overhead.

'Malkin?' Benfro called out again, more strongly this time, though his throat burned with the forced swallowing of too much water. Still there was no reply. With mounting concern he pulled himself from the river and picked out a path back downstream to the point where he had hit. He could see nothing. Slowly he searched along the river, through the whole clearing and on into the woods where the water once more became shallow. He crossed, peering under the overhanging banks and feeling about in the black pools between rocks where a floating body would surely have come to rest. A body. There could be little hope that he might find Malkin alive now.

Miserable, Benfro waded back up the river towards the track and the cave, hoping he might spot something from there. His hearts leaped whenever he heard a noise, but it was always some bird chirping a greeting to its mate or a startled frog croaking into the grass. By the time he reached the bags, lying in the thick grass, he had given up all hope, a well of grief opening up as great as that he had felt at the death of the villagers and the cruel murder of his mother. Perhaps it was all part of the same thing. It was so terribly unfair. Everyone around him died and yet he survived. Why?

There were no answers as the night crept over the glade. His only company was the endless song of the wind in the trees and the occasional cries of nocturnal animals about their dark business. The stars shone bright overhead, clearer than he remembered ever having seen them, but there was no joy in their majesty. With a heavy heart, he opened the food bag and pulled its contents out, checking for damage. The fruit and vegetables were mostly well preserved, cushioned by the grass. He felt no hunger, only sadness and a deep fatigue that would not go away. More out of habit than anything else, he ate the last slivers of fish and swallowed a few leaves. A collection of nuts lay at the bottom of the bag, surrounding the leaf-wrapped jewel that had brought him so much trouble. They should have been Malkin's, he realized. They were not dragon food but provisions for the small creature. Once more he raised himself from the ground and cried out to the darkness, 'Malkin, where are you?' Once more the trees whispered a faint echo then returned to their endless gossip.

Benfro slumped down into the grass, desolate. Tears welled up in his eyes and he let them flow. There was no shame in his sorrow, and even if there had been he was too far gone to care. The night passed slowly by and a thin sliver of moon rose into the sky, casting a silvery light over the clearing. Whether he slept or not, he could not be sure. The weariness that crept over him as he flew had been blown away by the excitement of his landing and the desperate futility of his later search. Now, as he lay swaddled only in his grief, it returned, numbing him for timeless moments before being swept away by the pinprick realization of what had happened. It grew cold and ever colder as the night progressed and yet he just lay where he was, paralysed by grief.

She came to him before the dawn, walking a few inches above the grass as if that was the most natural thing in the world. She glowed with the light of the moon, her skin as pale as her hair, her eyes twin dark orbs that could swallow anyone who dared to stare into them too long. Her form was the same as she had appeared to him before – elegant, thin and tall, with that sharply angled slender face and long pointed ears. On her shoulder, looking as if nothing had happened, sat Malkin.

'Don't despair, Benfro; your friend has come to no harm,' she said. 'I asked him to join you on your journey as a guide. Now you've reached your destination he has returned to me.'

Benfro wanted to reply, wanted to ask a thousand questions. He needed to thank the lady for her help, but he was immobile, speechless. All he could do was watch as she stood before him.

'Tell Corwen he owes me one now,' she said with a wry smile. 'And as for you, little dragon, I've no doubt we'll meet again.'

The moon was behind her, a thin slip of silver light against the speckled black of the sky. It set into the trees, and Benfro watched in awe as the figure faded away into its light, an image of her smile lingering in his memory long after she was gone. He lay perfectly still, at peace for the first time in far too long. His grief was still a real feeling, but the blind panic at losing his guide was gone now, replaced with a joy at knowing it was back where it belonged. It was only as the rising sun began to pick out the treetops that he realized he had slept the night through in a kind of waking dream.

Picking himself up from his resting place, Benfro stretched away the kinks in his spine, resolving to find himself somewhere more comfortable to spend the next night. He surveyed the clearing, noting the steep slope that broke down from the north side towards him, the low cliff with its waterfall and cave mouth. It was exactly as he had imagined it. He knew this was where he was supposed to come. Even the mother tree had confirmed that for him.

Now all he had to do was find Corwen.

The clearing was perhaps five hundred paces from side to side across the slope, a little more from the topmost corner where the river emerged to the spot where it plunged once more into the trees. Benfro spent the whole day quartering it, this way and that, searching for any clue as to the whereabouts of Corwen.

The first place he looked was the cave. It would make a good place to sleep, he decided, warm and dry despite the rush of the waterfall a few feet from its mouth. This was only just big enough for him to squeeze through, but the cavern widened out beyond, arching up and back to a point where a shaft of light speared down from a hole in the forest above. Directly beneath this, placed with a great deal of care, a circle of flat stones had been built into a hearth. There was a stack of firewood against the rock wall near the fireplace, dry and cracked with age. Only the faintest cover of ash dusted the hearth. It was the only sign that anyone had ever been in this place – but not for a very long time.

The floor was a silty earth, dark and with a faint spicy aroma he couldn't identify. Still it was pleasant enough, scenting the air as he explored. It didn't take long to measure the full extent of the place, and it seemed to him that no dragon had ever lived there. He set about collecting as much dry grass and heather as he could from the clearing, piling it up in a corner close but not too close to the hearth so that he might make a more comfortable night of it. The satchel of gold coins he placed at the head of this makeshift bed, his food bag on a ledge in the stone wall.

Outside, Benfro tried shouting for Corwen, but quite apart from feeling he was being terribly rude, he was fairly certain that yelling would not get him any response. For a moment he was worried that he had come to the wrong place, but the dream of the mother tree, Malkin perched happily on her shoulder, reassured him. She had said he had succeeded in his quest, so this must be the place. Equally he was sure that the dragon was here, somewhere. His friends would not have sent him to the other side of the world for nothing.

The nagging worry set in at about midday, when it occurred to him that men might have found this place before him. Had he not lost months in the keeping of the mother tree and under Magog's malign influence? There was a certain implacable inevitability about Melyn, the inquisitor. Benfro could remember all too well the wave of incandescent fury that had grasped at him as he jumped from the cliff top and made good his escape. There was no way the old warrior would leave things at that. Benfro knew that somewhere out there a troop at least was scouring the forest in search of him. Perhaps they had come to this place months ago and carted off the old dragon. The thought filled him with a terrible sense of guilty dread. If he hadn't done whatever it was he had done to offend the men, they would never have come this far.

He searched the whole clearing, wading through the long grass at the bottom end, trying to convince himself that the scattered rocks might be the remains of some kind of dwelling. But there was no way the great boulders had ever been walls. What cataclysm had wrenched them from the mountain and thrown them into the clearing like a child's discarded toys, he couldn't even begin to guess. From near where he had searched in vain for Malkin's drowned body the night before, he could see the pointed tip of the great peak rising out of the treeline as it climbed away from him. Even though he was hundreds of leagues closer to it than he had been while circling Magog's castle, it still looked so distant as to be almost unreachable, its features undefined and misty. Yet it dominated the view as if it were beside the next valley, casting a shadow over the glade that chilled him inside even while the sun warmed his bones. He stared at it nevertheless, lost in the sheer grandeur of the spectacle. He knew, deep down, that he would have to get closer to that great mountain, to scale its snowy peak, to conquer it. Yet he didn't even know its name. Didn't even know if it had a name.

The morning was a memory, afternoon half spent when Benfro decided that his search was fruitless. Eventually hunger got the better of him. It was almost a wrench to stop checking for signs of a concealed path leading to a hidden cottage nearby. He was astonished to see how far the day had progressed, in marked contrast to his own endeavours. Still, there was the stream, and it had a series of deep brown pools. It was only to be expected that he would find some fish.

Retreating to the cave with his gutted and cleaned catch wrapped in broadleaves for baking, Benfro set about starting a fire on the hearth. The wood on the stack was brittle with age, tinder dry. With some dried grass he soon had a merry blaze going. To his delight, what little smoke the wood gave off rose straight up, pooling only slightly under the high ceiling before escaping through the crack and into the forest. Soon he had a glowing bed of embers and the hearthstone was too hot to touch. He laid the slabs of wrapped fish on the coals to cook and went to fetch his bag of vegetables.

It wasn't there.

He rushed around the cavern, hearts hammering in his chest. Lit by the flickering light of the fire he could see it much more clearly now. Yet there was only one ledge that he could have put his bag on, only one ledge in the whole cave, as it turned out. It was empty. He looked at the head of the makeshift bed he had prepared. His leather satchel filled with gold still sat there, unmoved. He paced once more around the cavern, but there was nowhere that could hide even one of the vegetables it carried, let alone the whole bag. The bag containing Magog's jewel.

Benfro stood up uncertainly. He had not tried to get rid of the gem, but it was gone. He did not know where it was. He remembered all too well the debilitating pain and dizziness that had struck him when he had flung the thing from him, yet for now at least he could still function. Had it lost its power over him? After all he had completely forgotten about it for the whole of the day, and had wandered over a mile from the cave. Perhaps his time at the castle had somehow severed the link, freed him from the curse. Or maybe he was far enough away from the centre of the monster's power that it could no longer control him the way it had done.

Benfro went to the cave mouth and looked out across the clearing. The evening sky had faded to night, but the moon was not yet risen. In the pale starlight the waving grass was a luminescing white mass, the rocks black enemies creeping slowly towards him. He shook his head to get rid of the image. They were just stones that had rolled down from the mountain long ago. He stepped out into the cool air and sniffed, trying to catch an aroma on the breeze, of what he was not sure. There were many smells: the clinging woodsmoke of his fire, the tarry dampness of the leaves, curling and blackening around the fish, the strange spicy tang of the soil and the sweet fragrance of the pines that struggled to grow on the rocky cliff face above him. The roar of the waterfall and the constant whispering of water on stone blanked out most of the sounds of the forest, but he could hear the occasional bark of a fox and the elegant songs of night birds.

Apart from the stars, the only light came from the cave mouth, yet it was enough to see the track, scuffed and marked by his day's restless searching. Perhaps some bold creature from the forest, attracted by the smell of the food in the bag, had come down into the cave and carried it off. That would certainly account for its disappearance. There was no way he could follow such an animal in the dark, and even if it were daylight he doubted he could make out any tracks from the mess of his own comings and goings. Further from the cave entrance there might be clearer signs, but any search would have to wait until the morning.

Benfro stepped back into the cave and returned to the fire. There was, he realized, nothing he could do about the jewel. All he could hope was that, wherever it was, it was near enough and secure enough to let him function. Tomorrow he could search more thoroughly; now he had to eat.

The fish was perfectly cooked, moist and pink as he peeled back the blackened leaves. All too soon it was finished. He banked up the fire, thinking as he did so that he would have to find more firewood before long. Then, tired from his long day's searching, he lay down on his bed to sleep.

It wouldn't come. For long, slow, timeless moments he stared at the flames, pondering the day. After the terrible events that had set him on his path and the rigours of his journey, actually arriving at his destination seemed like a terrible letdown. It was as if he had climbed to the top of some great mountain only to discover that all he could do now was go down again. Was this what Sir Frynwy,

Meirionydd and all the others had intended all along – that he should just get so far away from the warrior priests that they would never find him? Then what? Was he to live out his life as a lonely creature in a cave in the woods? No, his mother had told him to find Corwen. Meirionydd had told him too, and the mother tree had helped him to get here, although he couldn't be sure that was not a dream.

Benfro's mind churned over and over the same few thoughts. He couldn't sleep for them writhing around in his mind. It seemed unfair. He was here now, so where was Corwen? Who was Corwen, for that matter, and why was he so important that his mother had trusted Benfro's life to him? Then there was Magog's jewel. Just thinking of it brought a scowl to his face. He could see its dark ruby malevolence glowing somewhere not too distant. A chain of red, so thin it was invisible, yet unbreakable still, linked him to it, anchored him to wherever it lay. And all the while it was feeding on him, growing ever fatter while that spark which was Benfro faded away.

'And is it so bad to become Magog, Son of the Summer Moon?'

Benfro shot into the air as if he had been stung. His musings had lulled him into a gentle slumber, but now he was awake, hearts pounding. The fire was still glowing red, banked up in a neat circle for the night, and sitting directly opposite him was another dragon.

Melyn was angry at himself, but that didn't mean that anyone he came across would feel his wrath any the less. His talk with Beulah, for all that it had been brief, had reminded him of many things he should never have forgotten. Usel's post-mortem on Lleyn, for instance. The surgeon had delivered his report just before Melyn had been due to instruct the senior warriors, which meant he had not had time to question him about it. It had been satisfactory enough, detailed and thorough like the man who had written it, but a suspicious mind might have concluded that Usel had deliberately avoided him. And someone had to have helped with the procedure, yet no one was mentioned by name. Melyn had reread the report, and now the omission glared at him like a beacon on a far-distant hill.

This late at night there were few people around for him to bully, so all Melyn had to accompany him on his journey were his angry thoughts. It worried him that Beulah might be prompted into foolish action by his news of her sister, and her infatuation with young Clun was a potentially destabilizing factor at precisely a time when the crown needed to be secure. On the other hand, injecting a bit of common blood into the Balwen line might be no bad thing, and the novitiate certainly had talent enough to be chosen. Perhaps the queen had thought through her actions after all; he'd never known her to act out of simple love or compassion before.

Still, any such marriage would have to be very carefully managed, and Melyn cursed loudly to the empty corridors that this would be a job more suited to Padraig's skills than his own. He would rather walk unarmed into Tynhelyg than cede anything to the seneschal. It was as well he was leaving for Candlehall just as soon as there was enough light for the horses to see. There would be much delicate negotiation and manoeuvring, but yes, in the end a warrior priest would be consort. His control over the House of Balwen would be strengthened.

It was a long ride to Candlehall, and not one he looked forward to. Melyn much preferred to control things from Emmass Fawr, like a great spider at the centre of a web that spread halfway around Gwlad. In any other situation he would have spoken directly to the queen. There were few enough adept at communicating through the aethereal; it made no sense to have more than one at the Neuadd with the skill. But he could hardly ask Beulah to pass on a message to Padraig about how best to deal with the diplomatic ripples caused by her choice of consort.

At least that meant there were two reasons for going to Candlehall. Not that he took much comfort from the thought. It would still hurt his old bones just as much to make the journey.

Melyn's ill humour carried him all the way to the infirmary. Inside a low light glowed on a desk at the far wall and behind it, poring over a long manuscript, sat Usel.

'Inquisitor,' the medic said, half rising from his chair but not offering any kind of salute. 'What can I do for you at this late hour? Have you need of some medication?'

'I'm in rude health, Usel,' the inquisitor said, trying not to let his anger rise. 'But something has been bothering me lately and it's possible you might be able to help.'

'In that case, could I help outside?' Usel asked. 'Only there are patients in here who need all the rest they can get.'

Fuming, Melyn allowed himself to be led into the corridor. Everything about Usel's manner screamed lack of due respect, though nothing the medic actually did could be taken as offensive. It was more his manner.

'You carried out the post-mortem on Lleyn,' Melyn said.

Usel nodded.

'You found the remains of her unborn child?' Usel nodded again and Melyn stared deep into the man's eyes, trying to see the lie if it was there.

'I did,' Usel said. 'As you asked. She was near to term so the baby had formed some rudimentary bones. There wasn't much left, but something in the casket had preserved both mother and unborn child quite remarkably.'

Melyn could almost see the autopsy room: quick flashes of surgical instruments, the coffin on a wheeled trolley, jars full of pickling fluid, a young man dressed in too-large medic's robes.

'Who helped you?' Melyn knew the answer even before the image coalesced in the surgeon's mind.

'It was young Ramsbottom, actually,' Usel said. 'I hijacked him in a corridor. He said he'd been called to your office and then dismissed for the afternoon. That was the first time I met him. Remarkable lad. Very bright. Very quick. I'm just annoyed Andro got to him first. I could make a great surgeon out of him. Except that you've got him as your latest spy now, haven't you.'

'He saw the body?' Melyn asked, storing up the jibe for a time when the medic was no longer quite so useful to the order.

'Of course,' Usel said, and the images flickered uncertainly in his mind. 'He helped me take her out of the coffin, passed me instruments when I asked for them, weighed bits. Took notes.'

'And did he ask questions?'

'Of course. Like I said, he's very inquisitive and very bright. Most boys his age would be put off by the thought of cutting up a dead body, but he was fascinated. Then again, his mother's a healer, by all accounts.'

'He told you his mother was a healer?' Melyn said, and he could see the conversation play itself in Usel's memory.

'I told him that the order was all the mother and father he would ever know or need,' Usel said. 'I'm sure novitiates have been forgiven greater errors in the past.'

Melyn glowered at the medic. There was something he was missing, but he wasn't going to find out about it from Usel. The man was infuriating. Even if, technically, Errol should have been expelled for speaking of his past life, it was true that the law was more of a tradition and more honoured in the breach than in the observance. But there was nothing in the incident to indicate anything unusual. No spark of recognition. No magic

'Have I put your mind at ease, Inquisitor,' Usel asked, 'or is there something else you'd like to know?'

'No,' he said. 'On either score. Get back to your patients, Usel. At least you're of some use to them.'

15

Perhaps the most difficult skill to master is that of dreamwalking. Many mages adept at manipulating the Llinellau Grym never attain this ability; many more never even attempt it.

In its dreaming state the mind is much more attuned to the subtle nuances of the Grym, much better able to filter out the onslaught of unnecessary information and focus on the task at hand. And yet at the same time the mind at rest is at its least disciplined, allowing all the hopes and worries, desires and frustrations of life to come to the fore. Without the restraints of discipline to keep these in check, an inexperienced mage might find himself wandering endlessly through the ethereal realms in search of an idea. Or waiting endlessly for a loved one to arrive in a place that only exists in his imagination for an assignation that was never arranged.

The true dreamwalker is unaffected by these distractions. That is not to say that he does not have them, for to be without such concerns is to be devoid of all that makes a dragon intelligent, all that separates him from the base beasts of the forest. No, a dreamwalker knows all these things but also has control of his dreams, so that even asleep he can see with a clear focus, even asleep he can direct his actions. And so he can use the stillness of sleep to increase his reach or go to places that might otherwise be closed to him, cut off from the Grym by the manipulations of others. In his dreams he can go back to the source without losing his mind.

Corwen teul Maddau, *On the Application of the Subtle Arts*

The dragon was impossibly old. His face was sunken, one chipped fang protruding from his mouth where an ancient scar had puckered his lip. His ears were gnarled and bitten like a tomcat's, and what few scales still stuck to his cheeks were chipped and cracked, their sheen long faded to matt. In the gaps his skin was leathery and brittle. Only his eyes were bright, twin spots of life glowing in the reflected red of the firelight. Benfro shivered as he looked at them. It was as if his mind were an open book to be read.

'Who are you?'

'He was a great dragon, Magog, if the tales are to be believed. Some would say he was the greatest mage that ever walked this earth. Would it be so terrible to become him, to let him reign once more? He could destroy the men that killed your mother. He could destroy all mankind.'

'Who are you?' Benfro asked again, not daring to hope that he knew the answer, not understanding how this ancient dragon could have appeared in front of him.

'But there would be no you any more.' The withered creature ignored his question. 'No, Magog could only rise again if you were prepared to surrender yourself completely to him. There'd be nothing left of your mind once you did that, nothing left of your self. And what good is revenge if you're not around to savour it.'

'Corwen?' Benfro asked. 'Are you Corwen? Only, if you are, I've been looking for you. My mother —'

'Morgwm the Green. I knew her as a hatchling,' the dragon said. 'She was a promising student, a powerful dragon in her own right. But she was afraid. In the end her fear was her undoing. Now only a fraction of what she was – what she could have been – remains. Tied there, sitting in your bag.' His finger bony and long, its talon black and grimy, blunt at the end, he pointed at the leather satchel that still sat at the end of Benfro's bed. 'She feared the warrior priests, perhaps wisely since she had foreseen her death at their hands. And yet she helped the people. I always thought her kindness would be her undoing.'

Unthinkingly Benfro reached towards the bag, stroked the pocket on its side. Touching it brought memories of his mother flooding back: the smell of her skin after she had been preparing herbs, her indulgent smile when he correctly recited a recipe, the lilt of her voice when she was singing him a lullaby. All these memories and more washed over him like a warm blanket. And behind them all was a sense of pride in his achievements tempered with a maternal worry that longed to protect, could never quite give up.

'Stop that at once!' the dragon snapped, and where before its voice had been neutral, perhaps even nostalgic in its reminiscences, now it was harsh, commanding and carried with it a force that could not be denied. Chastised,

Benfro whipped his hand away from the bag, still snatching at the feelings of home as they slipped away like eels through his fingers.

'You can't afford to cling to the past, Benfro,' the old dragon said. 'Those memories you carry with you are not your mother. They're not even a pale imitation of what your mother once was. But they'll suck you in just as surely as Magog. Even now you long for that touch, but be warned. A dragon's jewels are not to be trifled with. Remove one from its fellows and only ill can come of it.'

'But I thought it was safe now,' Benfro said, beginning to reach for the pocket again. He stopped himself when he saw the scowl appear on the old dragon's face. 'I performed the rite of reckoning. I burned her remains.'

'And that was a noble thing to do indeed. But it is not enough just to sear the memories. They must be placed at rest, at a nexus. And they must be complete. All but one of your mother's jewels were taken by Inquisitor Melyn and his band of warrior priests. Until they're reunited, none will know any peace.'

'I will find them,' Benfro said. 'I'll find every single one and I will destroy those that took them.'

'Be careful what you promise, young Benfro. A dragon's word is his bond.'

They sat in silence for a while then. Benfro's mind raced at the things he had heard. A few of the pieces of the great jigsaw were beginning to fall into place, but there was so much more that he didn't know, couldn't understand.

'You are Corwen,' he said eventually.

'Corwen is long dead,' the dragon said, a cold evenness

in its voice. 'Dragons live a very long time, some say they can live for ever. But if that great mage is reduced to a single jewel, then what chance has Corwen of still surviving, eh?'

'Then who are you?' Benfro asked. 'And how do you know so much about me?'

'Your deeds are already spoken of in all of Gwlad. Yet you've a great deal to learn, young Benfro of the Borrowed Wings.' The old dragon smiled as he said the words, laughing at some inner joke. 'Some of it you know already, yet you stubbornly refuse to admit it. Open your eyes, kitling, and see.'

'But my eyes are open,' Benfro said, bemused.

'Are they? Then tell me what you see.'

'I see a dragon, wizened with age, sitting on the other side of this fire. I see cave walls, smoothed by time and glowing as if they were lit from within. I'm guessing the rock contains tiny crystals that reflect the firelight. Through the cave mouth I see the moon rising over the far trees across the clearing. Here beside me I see my leather bag, filled with purloined gold, and on that ledge over there I see nothing where Magog's jewel should be.' Benfro fell silent. He wasn't sure why he felt so smug, nor why he had rattled off such a list of things. It had been, he realized as he closed his mouth, a rhetorical question. Nevertheless, he felt he had held his own with this annoyingly cryptic old dragon.

'And is that all?'

'No, of course not,' Benfro replied, his spirits neatly deflated by a simple question. 'Would you like me to go on?'

'By all means,' the dragon said, his smile calculated to cause maximum offence.

'What would you like me to describe first?' Benfro asked, reverting to the childhood games he had played with Ynys Môn and Sir Frynwy. Answer a question with another question, and if all else fails just say, 'Why?'

'Describe my face,' the dragon said, patient amusement hanging from every word.

'Which part?' Benfro asked.

'Which part do you like best?'

'Which part are you most proud of?'

'Ah, now, pride. There's a useless emotion if ever I knew one. But tell me about my nose.'

'Your nose?' Benfro began, but there was no fun in the game any more. It was nice to have someone to speak to, but he had hoped for a slightly less banal conversation and perhaps a less senile companion.

'You think me senile? Well, in many ways you may be right. I haven't spoken to a living soul since last your mother passed this way. And that was many years before you were hatched. But I don't need that kind of company to stay sharp. I can see everything, if I wish. I can go any-where. Yet I choose to remain here, so perhaps I am just a sentimental old dragon.

'You, on the other hand, are a stupid and arrogant little kitling who has strayed into something far bigger and far more dangerous than he can ever hope to understand. Your very existence has tipped the balance of this sphere, and your actions since fleeing your persecutors have been one blunder after another. If it weren't for a few very powerful allies your mother made in her all-too-short life, you would have died within hours of her. As it is, I can't help feeling it would have been a blessing if the inquisitor had found you. Taken you off to the royal court to be a plaything for the queen. She might not have tired of you for a year or two before adding your jewels to her pile. So, yes, Benfro, I may be a little senile. But you're much worse. You are blind.'

Silence filled the room after this tirade. Benfro felt the life flood out of him as if he had been scolded by his mother. No one else had ever been able to make him feel so small, not even Frecknock with her barbed taunts and cruel pranks. There was truth in the old dragon's words. Benfro had to admit that he had seen more strange and impossible things since leaving the village than he had ever imagined. His life had been sheltered and insular. He had been protected, and his mother's kindness had left him completely unprepared for what the world might throw at him.

He had been sent here by the spirit of his mother to learn from Corwen. Even if Corwen was dead, he still had much to learn. This dragon had known his mother, knew Corwen, seemed to know much more than he did. Perhaps it would be wise to listen to what he had to say, to try and learn enough to survive in the world. Benfro swallowed his pride, what little of it he still had, and turned to the old dragon.

'What should I be seeing?' he asked. But the dragon was gone.

Errol was growing used to his encounters with King Ballah. They usually played out the same way. First he would be offered some fine food, engaged in casual conversation. The king was always polite, and Errol tried to answer his questions truthfully, but he knew that all the while Ballah was trying to get inside his head.

King Ballah was far more skilled at magic than Inquisitor Melyn, Errol thought. Melyn's approach to breaking him down had been first to get him incoherently drunk, then to simply force a completely new set of memories into him. Errol was still trying to pick out what was real from what had been implanted by Melyn, and the king's subtle diggings didn't help. Every so often he would ask a seemingly simple question, and Errol would find that he had two contradictory answers presenting themselves to him.

As the weeks passed, Errol came to realize that this mixture of false and real memories was what kept him alive. King Ballah viewed him as a weapon crafted by his enemy, and he was determined to learn as much as possible about that weapon before disposing of it. In order to stay alive Errol had to remain an enigma, but not one that there was no hope of solving.

'Tell me about your girlfriend, Errol,' Ballah asked him as they walked through the ornamental gardens in front of the palace. It was warm in the summer afternoon, and the air was full of heady orchid scents that only helped to fuddle Errol's mind. Behind the words the king was probing his memories for images, and as usual two sprang up. The first was Maggs Clusster, dressed in red. Errol felt no great emotion as he remembered her. If he felt anything at all it was pity rather than love, mixed with a heavy dose of disgust and contempt for the rest of the girl's family.

'And yet your mind says you love her,' the king said.

'It must have suited Melyn to make me think I loved her,' Errol said. It was his stock answer.

'What about the other one? She's unclear.' Errol felt the king's subtle touch on his mind again, only this time no clear face swam into view. He was left with a sense of green, a smell of the forest, a feeling of perfect happiness and with it a gut-wrenching sorrow. There was no name to go with the feeling even though he knew that he had remembered it once. But here, with Ballah pushing ever further into his memories, it had retreated. As if he had to protect her, whoever she was, even from himself.

'Ah now, this is more like it,' Ballah said. 'This is closer to the real you. Melyn worked hard to suppress this memory, but it won't stay down, will it?'

'I don't know,' Errol said. 'It feels different somehow.' He wanted to savour the memory, to pore over it and try to tease out its meaning, but he also wanted to keep it to himself. This wasn't something King Ballah needed to know about, surely. Still the king's mind pulled at his thoughts and, reflexively, he pushed it away.

'Still fighting,' Ballah said. 'Good, I like a challenge. But you won't win.'

They continued walking through the gardens, closely trailed by two silent guards. If the king was still riding his mind, Errol couldn't feel him. Instead he thought about the images the green girl had conjured: the forest back home and the stories he had heard. There were tales of great heroes battling evil, brave explorers travelling to the far corners of Gwlad, tragic lovers doomed to be apart: epic, sweeping tales of such grandeur they made even the royal palace and the city of Tynhelyg seem somehow paltry. And yet he couldn't grasp any of the details.

'Your Majesty, Prince Dafydd has returned.'

Errol looked up, startled by the new voice. The palace major domo, Tordu, stood in the path ahead of them.

'Good. I'll see him in the throne room.'

'He's already there, sir. Shall I have the boy escorted back to his quarters?' Tordu said.

'No, no,' Ballah said. 'I think he should meet the man he was sent to kill. Lead on, Tordu.'

They cut across the gardens and in through one of the full-height windows that led directly into the throne room. A young man was waiting by the throne. As Errol drew closer to him he felt like he was looking in a mirror, only one which reflected an older self. Judging by the look on Dafydd's face, the prince was having similarly unsettling feelings.

'Your Majesty,' Dafydd said, bowing slightly to the king. 'Who's this?'

'This is Errol Ramsbottom,' Ballah said. 'Melyn sent him here to spy on us and kill you.'

Errol felt the touch of Dafydd's mind like a shove in the chest. His knees buckled and he would have fallen had not one of the guards grabbed him, perhaps interpreting his movement as hostile. Unlike Ballah's soft almost mesmeric touch, Dafydd's grasp of magic was brutal and coarse.

Angry at the sudden onslaught, Errol retaliated. With a little gasp of surprise Dafydd rocked backwards, stumbled and fell to the floor. For a moment there was a tense silence in the room, then Ballah burst into loud, braying laughter.

'You weren't expecting that, were you, Dafydd.' Ballah chortled.

'What's he doing here? Why haven't you executed him?'

'Never mind that,' Ballah said. 'What's the situation in the Twin Kingdoms?'

'The noble houses are preparing for war,' Dafydd said. 'The normal crossings are closed and anyone looking even remotely Llanwennog is being treated with great suspicion. The lucky ones are being rounded up and escorted to Dina. The unlucky ones will be filling unmarked graves.'

'And what of the troops: how are they being deployed? What's Melyn's plan?'

Dafydd looked from King Ballah across to Errol, who was still held by a guard.

'Should I be telling you this in front of him?'

'Do you think me a fool, Dafydd?' The king's voice was suddenly hard.

'No . . . No, sir.'

'Then don't question my authority. Especially not in the presence of others.' Errol felt a rushing sensation and Dafydd fell to the floor once more. He seemed to accept his punishment with good grace, but Errol could see by the look the prince flashed in his direction that he had made another enemy.

'The warrior priests are largely still cooped up in Emmass Fawr, sir,' Dafydd said quietly. 'The peasant armies are making camps in the foothills of the Dinas Dwyrain mountains, close to the Tynewydd pass and near Dina itself. I suspect Melyn thinks he can come through Dondal's lands unopposed. The duke's always been flexible in his allegiances.'

All the while the prince was talking Errol could feel the delicate touch of the king's mind skimming over his own thoughts. Ballah was looking to see whether any of the report rang true. Errol suddenly recalled Captain Osgal scouting the hillside as they approached Dondal's fortified town. And he saw the gold being handed over – too much surely just to have him presented at court.

'Duke Dondal has chosen his side in this conflict,' Ballah said. 'This young lad here's proof enough of that. If Melyn tries to send forces through the pass, we'll cut them down before they even reach Tynewydd.'

'And are we going to sit tight, just let them attack us?' Dafydd asked.

'Queen Beulah's hold on the throne's not as strong as she'd like to think,' Ballah said. 'As yet she has no heir. I'm quite happy for her to waste as many lives as she feels appropriate on her foolish adventures. Each death will weaken her a little more. Meanwhile, your beloved Iolwen already carries your child. And is it not written that only a son of both houses can ever hope to bring peace to our two nations?'

Dafydd bowed his head, saying nothing, but Errol could see that his demeanour had lightened at the mention of Iolwen. It didn't take a mind-reader to see how much in love Prince Dafydd was.

'What of the boy?' the prince said finally, nodding towards Errol, who dropped his gaze hurriedly.

'He's a puzzle,' Ballah said. 'I'd really like to believe him when he says he means us no harm. But he's proving surprisingly resistant to my interrogation. And who knows what trigger Melyn's left in that addled brain of his. No,

I've kept him this long simply because he reminds me of Balch. But that's a sentimental old man's reason. I can't really afford to have him around, not when there's a war in the offing.'

Errol looked up at the king who moments earlier had been joking with him. He thought about the weeks he'd spent in captivity, well cared for but a prisoner nonetheless. He'd always known there would come a time when he was more of a hindrance than a useful pawn in this terrible game. He'd just hoped it would come a lot later than now.

'Take him to the dungeons.' Ballah did not meet Errol's eye as he spoke. 'I'll decide what to do with him later.'

Benfro slept badly that night, and in the morning he searched high and wide for the old dragon, but with no success. Neither could he find any sign of the food bag and Magog's jewel. But as the day progressed and he felt none of the debilitation that had hit him before, so he began to relax and explore his new surroundings. The forest around the clearing was rich with wildlife and he spent the afternoon hunting. Come the evening, full of food, he settled himself down by the fire and waited to see if anything happened. Slowly the warmth, his full belly and the gentle rushing of water outside lulled him to sleep.

The next day was the same, and the next. A week passed and he was still alone. He ranged far and wide, sometimes camping out for a night or two as he explored the area, but always returning to the cave. He began to wonder whether he had imagined the whole incident, but something told him it had been real. It was as if he had been set a task and the old dragon would return just as soon as he had completed it. If only he could work out what that task was supposed to be.

So it was that he once again sat on his bed of dried grass, listening to the constant noise of the waterfall and watching the dancing flames. And then all of a sudden he was overwhelmed with a great melancholy. He was alone in the world, imprisoned in a solitude he had never known before. His family were all gone, even his mother. There was no one and no reason to exist at all.

Wrapped up in his misery, Benfro didn't notice when the cave darkened. He had been staring sightlessly at the flames, but then the fire just went out. Only the cave walls glowed as if they were alive, pulsing with a steady rhythm like the beating of the world's heart. It was hypnotic, a slow tune that took his growing despondency and soothed it away. He felt light-headed and incorporeal, as if he were floating in warm water. A quiet murmuring noise distracted him from the strangeness. There were voices just outside the cave. He couldn't make out the words, but he knew the cadences and tones of the villagers. They were in discussion. It was a sound he remembered from his earliest days, huddled in a swaddling bed close to the fire in the great hall. There was the booming bass of Sir Frynwy, the coarse gravelly croak of Ynys Môn. A trill of happy laughter was Meirionydd, her jokes echoing around the other voices like waves breaking on a beach.

Without thinking, Benfro moved towards the voices, stepping through the cave mouth. But as he reached where he thought they were, so the voices quietened, faded away. He took another step forward, out into the clearing, and a wave of fear swept over him, trembling up his spine and making his loosely folded wings shiver. The night was cold and dark, cloud covering the stars and swathing everything in black. Suddenly afraid, he turned to go back into the cave. The entrance was no longer there.

Scrabbling and beating mindlessly at the rough stone, it was some moments before he realized that what he was pounding was not the sheer rock wall in the clearing but dressed blocks placed one upon another with tight mortar gaps in between. A wall.

He stood in a courtyard of immense size. The wall he had been hammering formed the outer edge of a roofed cloister that ran around the whole yard. Elegant pillars supported arches on the opposite side. They opened out into a great space, in the middle of which sat a huge stone building. It had tall windows of coloured glass that caught the sunlight on the other side of the yard, shining straight through the building and painting the grass in myriad hues. With dread pulling his hearts down, Benfro realized he had been to this place before.

'Do you think the queen will see us today?'

The voice cut through Benfro's dreaming like a talon. He looked round to see who had spoken and froze in terror.

Two men were walking up the cloister towards him.

'I don't know. I hope so. But you know what she's like with a new toy,' one of them said.

'It disgusts me the way she consorts with this

commoner. I've heard she nursed him back to health herself. The Shepherd alone knows what they get up to.'

It occurred to Benfro that these two men were not warriors. They were slight, even by the standards of men, and dressed in long dark cloaks. Their heads were uncovered, and what little hair they had was white, like the tufts that sprouted from Sir Frynwy's ears. No paralysing fear emanated from them; in fact he could feel little of their presence, which explained how they had come so close without him sensing them. He understood then that they had not seen him and that he could kill them easily. All he had to do was to wait until they came past where he stood, obscured by shadow, and grab them.

And then what? It was almost a voice in his head asking the question, a small nugget of reason trying to make itself heard. Benfro had no idea how he had come to be in this cloister. He had not flown, had not even left the cave as far as he was aware. And yet here he was.

'I've heard a rumour she's thinking of making him Duke of Abervenn,' one of the men was saying. 'Then she's going to take him as her consort.'

'Nonsense, Verrid. Queen Beulah wouldn't do anything so reckless. She's just rewarding the man who saved her life.'

'Boy, more like. I understand he's not seen twenty summers yet.'

Benfro only half-understood the words. He was aware that the men were coming ever closer, and looking around he could see that only the lie of the shadows was keeping him from view. There was nothing to hide behind and no exit from the cloister nearby save for into the courtyard through the arches. Could he cross the cloister and make it over the low stone wall before they saw him? It was unlikely. Indecision had him paralysed, and before he knew it the two men were alongside him.

With a desperate lunge, Benfro tried to knock them both to the ground. He had no plan, only to kill them both before the alarm was raised. Instead, his hand and outstretched talons passed right through them as if they weren't there.

'Did you feel that?' the man called Verrid asked.

'Feel what?'

'I don't know. It was like . . . well, like someone had just walked over my grave.'

'Honestly, Verrid, I don't know where you get these notions.' His companion shook his head. 'Now come on, we don't want to be late.'

Benfro watched, astonished, as the two elderly men trotted off up the cloister, disappearing through a doorway at the far end. He held out one hand in front of him, bringing the other up to it and touching them together. They felt as he would have expected them to. He reached out for the wall, patted it lightly. It didn't yield.

Bemused, he walked quickly up the cloister towards the doorway through which the men had left, his feet making no sound on the ground. He kept to the solid wall and its shadow, senses straining for any feeling that there might be other people about. Two large wooden doors stood open, and sounds of activity spilled out from beyond them. There were voices raised in the high-pitched shouts of urgent business, the clattering of metal on wood, the stomach-gurgling smell of fresh-baked bread and roast-ing meat. Benfro felt the presence of dozens of men. He wasn't prepared to take the chance that none of them could see him.

Turning from the doors, Benfro saw that opposite them the cloister opened up, a wide stone path leading across the exposed ground to the great building at its centre. There was something about the structure that both repelled and intrigued him. He knew he shouldn't be here, knew that he should be getting as far away as pos-sible, as quickly as possible, before he was found out. But at the same time the building called to him. It was utterly unlike the cloister surrounding it. Majestic, it was built on a completely different scale, with intricate carvings wrought into the stone as if it were soft butter.

The carvings were as crisp as if they had been newly sculpted. Benfro saw epic battles, great hunts and scenes from a mythology he knew all too well. This was a dragon palace. There was Rasalene himself, wooing proud Arhe-lion. There surely was Palisander at the Deepening Pools. Other stories were depicted in intricate detail, and he strained to make everything out in the evening shadows. With a start he realized he was standing quite close to the building. He had crossed the open courtyard somehow and now stood in front of the great wooden doors that barred entry.

Then, with a deep creaking groan that he felt through his feet, the doors swung inward. He could see nothing in the darkness of the great hall until a man, tiny in the enor-mous space, walked, backwards, out of the shadows and down the uncomfortably large steps. His head was bowed, and he passed Benfro without a glance before finally turning and heading off across the courtyard towards the refectory.

Curiosity was ever Benfro's undoing. He knew it always got him into trouble and yet he couldn't resist the invitation of the open doors. Treading lightly, he stepped up and into the gloom.

16

Gwlad is a big place, and those you might be seeking could be anywhere in it. So why set out in search of your foe when you can have him come to you?

The first step in achieving your goal is to know your enemy. This is as true in employing magic against him as it is in any other strategy of war. For the weak-willed it is enough simply to plant the command 'Come!' into their mind and they will. For others it may be necessary to take a more subtle approach. Use the mental discipline you have learned to study your opponent, to find out his needs and desires. Then play to these feelings, suggesting they may be fulfilled if he but come to a certain place or agree to do a certain thing. With practice you can influence even the most iron-willed of enemies until he stands, alone and unarmed, at your door.

A note of caution should be added here, although it applies to all practical applications of magic. Be aware that while you are seeking to manipulate others, they may very well be seeking to manipulate you. In a battle of wills it is for you to recognize the foreignness of thoughts placed in your mind even as you plant suggestions in the minds of others. Rid yourself of base desires, idle fancies and loose emotions, and your enemy will have much less with which to tempt you.

Father Castlemilk, *An Introduction to the Order of the High Ffrydd*

Candlehall was not Melyn's favourite place in Gwlad. There were too many people ill disciplined in their daily habits, ill disciplined in their thinking. Stray thoughts and emotions battered him like a blizzard so that he had to tune down his sensitivity. It made him uncomfortable knowing that there was so much out there he could not sense, so much swamped by the bland banality of daily existence.

It hadn't always been so. When he'd first risen to the position of inquisitor, the capital city had been a place of infinite possibilities. The babbling of emotions, passions and intrigue had been a murmur then, something to be dipped into like a well-written reference book. He had used his gift to weed out dissent among the ranks of the nobles, to vet the endless stream of merchants who begged the crown for favourable trading agreements, even to gently manipulate both the king and the other orders.

But as the years had passed, so the city had swollen ever larger, the cumulative thoughts growing from a whisper to a shout. Or was it that he'd grown more sensitive to it all, cooped up in his mountaintop retreat? It was of no matter. He was here now and he'd just have to put up with it.

It was a relief to get off his horse once they had finally

made it through the city and into the palace courtyard. Melyn's joints ached and creaked as he flexed his legs. The rest of the troop sat on their horses awaiting his command. He could sense their weariness too, but they showed no outward sign.

'Billet the men, get some food and rest,' Melyn said to Captain Osgal, handing him the reins of his horse as he did so. The captain saluted but said nothing. With a nod, the whole troop turned as one and trotted off towards the palace stables. Trying not to be jealous of the rest they would have, the inquisitor climbed the stone steps to the palace entrance.

'Inquisitor Melyn, what a pleasure.' Seneschal Padraig stood in the doorway, his smile not reaching his eyes.

'Padraig.' Melyn nodded the most minimal of greetings. Inside the hall was dark, torches not yet lit despite the encroaching evening.

'I have to admit it was a masterstroke,' Padraig said as they headed into the depths of the palace. 'Not even I saw it coming. You must have schooled the boy excellently.'

'What are you talking about? What boy?' For a moment Melyn thought there must be more news about Errol, but he knew that any such information would have reached him first.

'Why, Clun, of course,' Padraig said. 'And hiding him behind the gift of the dragon. If I hadn't sound intelligence to the contrary, I'd suspect you'd even set up the assassination attempt.'

'Ah Padraig, you see your own level of sophistication in every scheme,' Melyn said. 'I sent the young man to escort the dragon. It was his idea to give it to the queen as a gift in the first place. Anything that occurred after that is the Shepherd's doing.'

'Well, he certainly moves in mysterious ways,' the seneschal said. 'The whole palace is abuzz with rumours about the queen and the commoner.'

'All of them true, I've no doubt. You know Beulah as well as I do. Once she's made her mind up about a thing, there's no changing her. And I for one don't think we should try.'

'You would say that. He's one of yours after all,' Padraig said.

'It's true he's a novitiate of the High Ffrydd,' Melyn said. 'But I'd hardly say he's one of mine. He's only been in the order a year. He's not even a warrior priest.'

'She can't marry him,' the seneschal said. 'He's a merchant's son from some backwater village no one's ever heard of. The noble houses are close to revolt.'

'I think you're exaggerating a little, Padraig. Besides, she could always make him Duke of Abervenn. I believe that title's going begging at the moment.'

'You're as bad as she is,' Padraig said. 'You've no idea the work I have to do just keeping this place together. Quite apart from finding the gold for your war. It's a wonder we haven't had more unrest. Beulah's not as popular as her father was, you know. There's a limit to how much you can raise taxes. And how many sons you can conscript.'

'So what the Twin Kingdoms need is a reason to celebrate, something to bring the people together. Something to make them love their queen. Something like a royal wedding.'

'You've thought it all through, haven't you, Melyn,' Padraig said

'I've been on a horse for the last two weeks with no one to talk to except Captain Osgal.' Melyn laughed. 'Of course I've thought it through. And how we're going to overthrow the House of Ballah.'

'I'm all ears,' Padraig said, the old contempt scarcely hidden in his voice. They had passed through the great hall and were approaching the administrative wing, the seneschal's own little kingdom. 'I just can't wait to hear this great plan.'

'So you can pass it on to Ballah's spies?' Melyn said. 'I don't think so.'

'What are you saying?' The seneschal stopped in his tracks. 'How could you even imply—'

'Go back to running the palace, Padraig. Start organizing a royal wedding. Do what you're good at. Leave the war making to us old warriors.' Melyn sent a quick rough mental command to the seneschal, noting with a mixture of satisfaction and sadness how slow the man was to react. Padraig stiffened, then marshalled his reflexes enough to push Melyn away, though not before the inquisitor had seen past his outrage to the calculating schemes never far behind.

'One of these days you'll go too far, Melyn,' Padraig said, but he sank into a chair nearby and Melyn could see that he no longer intended following him to the Neuadd. He said nothing, simply taking his leave and heading out across the palace.

It was a long walk to the great hall, but Melyn had plenty to think about. He had seen from that briefest of glimpses that Padraig was already resigned to Clun becoming consort; he was just making as much noise about it as he could while he manipulated public opinion. No doubt several noble houses were being offered all manner of favours in return for welcoming the queen's choice. In a month or two everyone would be saying how wise and generous Beulah was to pick the lowliest of her subjects for the highest of offices. It would be a modern-day fairy tale.

Benfro felt like he was in a different world. Over the threshold was light and warm as if the collected sunlight of a thousand years were trapped by something even more impenetrable than those great oak doors. The entire interior of the building was one great hall, its ceiling high overhead supported by massive stone beams carved into a huge vault. The tall windows he had seen from outside seemed even bigger from within. They were intricately glazed with coloured panes, cut and fitted to show scenes from legend. The whole hall was a great story book just waiting to be read, but for now it was all he could manage to keep his mouth shut as he stared at the ever shifting light that played through the epic pictures and on to the floor.

And what a floor. It was stone as white as bleached bones and polished to a mirror-smooth surface. The individual blocks were as big as his mother's house, and he could only just make out the narrowest of joints. It took him a while to realize what was wrong as he looked down, so overpowering was the perfection of the craftsmanship. He could see the arched ceiling reflected overhead, and the great windows too. But he could see no reflection of himself. It was as if he wasn't really there.

His hearts stuttered in his chest like trapped rats, and a rushing sense of vertigo threatened to topple him. Snapping his eyes away from his non-image, Benfro froze, wondering why he hadn't noticed it before. As soon as he had entered the building.

The hall was dominated by a massive throne. It sat upon a dais at the far end, a heavy affair carved from rock as black as the night and yet glistening as if it were wet. Although it had been altered for a smaller occupant, it was plainly the throne of a dragon, and one of great size at that. But the only live dragon in the place lay curled up on the dais at the foot of the great chair. She was a miserable thing, no spirit left in her at all. A fetid aura clung to her skin like a coat of greyish-black slime. A halter of leather was around her neck and a thin silver chain led up from this to the dark recesses of the throne. Stepping forward, Benfro approached the dais and climbed the huge stone steps until he stood before the throne. Sensing his approach, the miserable dragon lifted a heavy head but looked straight through him. For a moment Benfro didn't recognize his old foe, so changed was she since last they had sparred. Frecknock had not fared well at the hands of her captors. Once proud of her appearance to the point of dandiness, now she was a shrivelled, pathetic figure, her scales limp and lifeless, her wings ragged and torn.

'What is it disturbs you, my little pet?' A voice spoke from the dark recesses of the throne. The silver chain pulled at Frecknock's neck, and the enslaved dragon looked around, a mixture of fear and hatred on her face.

'I thought I felt a presence, my queen.' Her voice was so obsequious, for a moment Benfro doubted it truly was Frecknock speaking. Gone was the haughty indifference and arrogant self-confidence. Here was a creature now completely subjugated, a broken, pathetic thing. He took no satisfaction from knowing she suffered so.

'A presence, indeed.' Something moved in the darkness, leaning forward from the great throne. A young woman appeared, dwarfed by the size of the seat she claimed for her own.

Benfro had seen her once before, but not this close. Queen Beulah of the Speckled Face was small even for one of her kind. Her face was not ruddy and bearded, like the warrior priests she commanded, but rather pale pink and speckled with random spots of brown as if some terrible disease had struck her in childhood. She was studying the area where he stood, cold black eyes glinting as she turned her head slightly as if to catch an image in the corner of her vision.

'Why, yes.' She tugged the silver leash with a thought. Benfro could see its end hanging in the air by her head, no heavier than a mote of dust. Her hands were clasped together over her stomach, as if she could not bear to touch the leash. 'Clever little dragon. There is someone here, and well hidden. Is it a suitor, come to try his luck? Don't be shy now, warrior. You obviously have great skill to come so to this place. Show yourself that I might appraise your physical worth.'

Frozen by the growing sense of fear that filled the great hall like ice, Benfro could do nothing but stand and stare, transfixed by the vision of the tiny woman and her tame dragon. It began to dawn on him that power was not necessarily reflected by size. Queen Beulah was small, true, but she radiated an evil more terrible even than that of Inquisitor Melyn.

'No?' the queen asked. 'Perhaps you're too shy? Or maybe you lack the skill. Did you come here by accident and don't know how to get home?' She peered almost myopically in his direction, again turning her head as if doing so might make him clear. Then she stopped, lifted her head in a sniffing motion, opened her mouth and almost tasted the air in front of her.

'This is no suitor come to give himself to his queen,' she snorted, anger flushing her speckled face. 'No wonder you sensed him first, my pretty little Frecknock. I smell dragon!' She backed away from the flickering lights into the darker recesses of the throne, shouting, 'Melyn! Inquisitor! Are you asleep? There is a dragon in our midst, an infiltrator!'

Benfro felt something hot on his back. He looked around and saw a figure that at once struck terror into his hearts and filled them to bursting with rage. Melyn strode across the hall towards the throne, his eyes blazing red as he scanned back and forth. Those twin points of loathing did not have his focus yet, could not seem to see him even though he stood in the open. He turned away from the throne, intending to flee the way he had come, but the great doors, much further away than he recalled, swung shut with an earth-shaking crash.

'Find him! Find him now!' the queen screeched from the safety of her stolen throne. Her voice was an angry bleating thing, demanding, not used to being thwarted.

Benfro leaped down the steps, running over the polished floor with all the speed he could muster. Somewhere there was a cave in a clearing where he felt safe. He had to find his way back there. Straining his ears, Benfro listened for the conversation of the villagers. Somehow he knew they were the key to his safe return.

'Sir Frynwy! Ynys Môn! Meirionydd!' he shouted as if they were nearby. 'Help me, please.'

'Your dead friends can't help you now, hatchling.' The inquisitor's voice speared through Benfro like a hot blade, like the sword of fire he had used on Morgwm the Green. The young dragon stopped in his tracks, unsure whether he had done so himself or some outside force had compelled him to. He whirled around, ready to face his enemy, seeing the terrible form of the inquisitor bearing down on him. Melyn's eyes blazed fiery red and he held that fateful burning blade in his hands.

'I have you now, abomination,' Melyn screamed, and Benfro could see the flecks of saliva around the edges of his mouth. 'I will kill your wandering spirit and leave your body to rot wherever it might be.'

Benfro backed away from the approaching inquisitor, his hearts pounding in his chest and panic stripping all sense from him. He was caught; he was going to die. Why had he come to this place? How had he come to this place? The floor was cold under his feet and he felt the rough stone wall press first his tail and then his back as he retreated.

The inquisitor lifted his sword high, ready to swing down and finish the job he had begun on Benfro's mother. Benfro was transfixed by the blade, but then something beyond it caught his eye – at the top of the throne, where the twin spires of stone that formed its back speared up to the ceiling. There was something in the air, flickering and twisting like some wind-blown rag. But it was a rag of stars, a clear night seen through a rent in the fabric of nothing. Something in him surged at the sight. It was at once meaningless to him and deeply moving, as if he saw a face he had not seen in a thousand lifetimes, a great love lost. And this annoying little creature with its trick magic stood in his way.

A terrible anger filled him, a familiar feeling that mixed despair and rage in equal measure. His stomach lurched, his throat glowed with inner heat and then with a ferocious roar he spat out a wall of flame. He wanted to see the inquisitor burn, wanted that terrible man to writhe in agony as the fire consumed him slowly. But the old warrior merely dropped his sword in an arc, deflecting the blast as he stepped back.

'I'm impressed, dragon,' Melyn said. 'But you'll still die.' He raised his hands and the magical fire was swept into a ball in front of him, trapped like its creator. Benfro readied himself for the attack. He could feel more fire building up in him. But then, in that instant before the inquisitor used his own weapon to destroy him, he felt a hand on his shoulder and heard a voice in his ear.

'Not now, Sir Benfro. You've much yet to learn.' It was quiet, reasoned and measured, but it was unmistakably Magog.

Benfro turned to face the great mage and felt himself pulled forward at great speed. Behind him the inquisitor roared, and it felt like hot claws were tearing at his brain.

But Benfro was moving rapidly now, faster than the wind over endless green forest. Familiar places flashed past in the twinkling of an eye, then he saw the clearing, surrounded by undulating foothills covered in dark green woodland, the river running through it like a scar. Faster and faster he hurtled towards the open cave mouth, the howling of the wind in his ears like a scream of frustration as the claws in his brain finally gave way, the inquisitor gone from his mind.

Benfro woke on his bed of dried grass. He couldn't remember going to sleep, just the incredible rush of relief when he had found himself back in the clearing. His head ached as if someone had pelted it with rocks in the night. His whole body was sore, and his throat felt like he had been shouting for hours. He could remember vividly the details of what he hoped had been a dream, but where had those images come from? And to see Frecknock so badly treated, such a shadow of her former venomous self, saddened him even as he knew it was all just a figment of his imagination.

The fire had burned down, leaving only the blackened stumps of the larger sticks arranged in a neat circle around the middle. Groaning at the discomfort, Benfro hauled himself out of his makeshift bed and limped over to the hearth. Poking about in the ashes revealed a few small lumps of charcoal still with an inner glow. With much blowing and handfuls of grass ripped from his bed, he soon had a fire flickering into life. He fed it with the remaining wood from the pile, building up a small compact blaze that would hopefully keep burning for the bulk of the day. Better by far to keep a fire going than have to go through the rigmarole of trying to kindle one from scratch. That was one of the many wise things his mother had taught him.

Outside the cave, the day was much further progressed than he had realized. The sun was already past the first quarter of its arc through the sky and well on the way towards its zenith. It was unlike him to sleep past the dawn and he felt disoriented coming into the day so late. He yawned and stretched, first his arms and then his wings, letting them soak up the morning rays. To his delight they unfurled like huge sheets, taking the breeze and battering it into submission. There was a reassuring strength in his back, despite the aches and pains, a feeling that he could leap into the air and fly anywhere he wanted. The freedom was intoxicating, a healing draught, and for the first time since he could remember Benfro tipped his head back and laughed.

The river yielded fat fish for his breakfast. As he sat and ate them, he felt a chill in the air. The sky was clear, only a few wispy clouds high up, not thick enough to shade the sun, and yet its glow was weaker than he would have expected. Looking around the clearing he could see the leaves on the trees turning brown, preparing to fall. Spring had not come to the forest when he had fled the village, which seemed like only a few weeks ago, but in truth many months had passed. Winter was on its way, and it promised to be cold. He would need to gather supplies of wood for his fire. And he might have to start thinking about smoking some of the food he caught, though he would need to find somewhere to store it.

It was nice to have a simple task to perform, and he set about it with gusto. The aches in his body soon disappeared as he broke dead branches from the trees all around the clearing and carried or dragged them back to the cave mouth. Working, he didn't have to think. It was sufficient just to do. Once he had gathered enough to last a month, piled outside on the track, he set about sorting it into sizes, breaking everything but the thickest into pieces that would fit on the hearth. Stacking as much as he could in the cave, he piled the rest carefully around its mouth, forming a narrow corridor from the track.

By the time he was finished, the sun was dipping towards the horizon and he was sticky with sweat and dust. As a kitling Benfro had hated stacking logs. To be fair he had hated any kind of strenuous manual labour, from preparing unguents for his mother to setting the table and washing the cooking pots. Yet now, with no one ordering him about or criticizing him, he looked upon his work with a sense of pride. He had set out to do something and had achieved it. With a lightness of heart he had not felt in an age, he plunged once more into the cool waters of the river to wash himself off and catch some supper.

Later, clean, full of fish and with the fire crackling away merrily with its new supply of wood, Benfro lay back on his bed and considered the day. He ached still, but it was the soreness of hard labour rather than the tired pain that had greeted him on waking. Stiffly, he got up from his bed and walked to the other side of the hearth. There was considerably less room in the cave now, with his supplies of firewood piled around the walls, but the space where his mysterious visitor had sat was still clear. As it had been every night since that first visit. He was beginning to wonder whether he hadn't dreamed the whole episode. Maybe everything that had happened to him since the men arrived had been a dream. It was a comforting thought, but cold. If this was a dream then he seemed powerless to wake.

'And who's to say what's real and what's a dream anyway?'

Benfro whirled round, searching for the source of the voice. Through the low flickering flames he could see a familiar figure sitting on his bed. The old dragon was back. Yet there was no way he could have crept into the cave unnoticed. Outside was silent save for the constant quiet rumble of the waterfall. Benfro was certain he would have heard even the softest footfall on the crumbly earth, smelt the sweet spicy perfume that pervaded the cave whenever it was disturbed. He should have sensed the presence of another dragon. Even the warrior priests he could sense at a distance by the hate and anger they radiated. Yet he couldn't even sense his visitor now, when he could see him not five yards from where he was standing.

'How—'

'Tell me what you see,' the old dragon interrupted in his annoyingly cryptic manner. Benfro sighed. Nothing, it seemed, was ever straightforward.

'What do I see?' He settled himself down on the floor, which, he noticed, was a great deal less comfortable than his bed. 'I see the same cave I was in yesterday. It's well stocked with wood now so the fire shouldn't go out. I can see out through the entrance to darkness beyond. I can see a haze of smoke rising from the flames. It dulls the glow of the rock walls, but they still sparkle with a life of their own. I can see the bed I made from dried grass and at its head there's my old leather bag, filled with gold coins. And I can see a dragon sitting in front of me whose name I don't know.'

'Is that all you see?' the dragon asked. There was no judgement in its voice, no sarcasm or humour. It was a simple question.

'Would you have me describe the shape of the embers glowing in the fire?' Benfro countered, a note of weary impatience in his voice. 'Or perhaps I could describe the aroma of this dry soil.' He picked up a handful and let it trickle through his fingers. 'I could count and measure all of the logs I collected today, but I'd rather know more about you. Who are you? Where did you go?'

'It's a shame that you see so little,' the old dragon said. 'As to where I went, well I didn't go anywhere. I was here. I'm always here. I was watching you, waiting for you to be ready.'

'Who are you?' Benfro asked again.

'I think you know who I am.'

'Are you Corwen?' Benfro asked.

'Corwen is dead,' the dragon replied.

'That's not an answer,' Benfro countered. 'Are you Corwen?'

'So you can accept that a dead dragon might appear before you, speak to you, teach you. Is that not mad?'

'I spoke to Ystrad Fflur after he died, and I saw Meiri-onydd in Magog's palace. She appeared to me as a young dragon, as she was in her prime. Yet I watched her die, burned to death by men. And I saw another dragon, the most beautiful and magnificent lady I have ever seen. She rose from the jewels I had piled up. Magog's collection. He had them all separated, alone. They were his collection. That was mad, evil even.'

'You saw the spirit of Gwynhyfyr.' A slight dreamy quality came to the old dragon's voice, as if he were drifting away in a reverie of his own. 'They say she was the fairest dragon to live in this realm. If you don't count Ammorgwm, that is.'

'She thanked me for freeing them. Then Ynys Môn told me to take the gold coins. He said I would need it when I left the Ffrydd.'

'Tell me, Benfro: where did you place all those jewels, those countless memories?'

'At the nexus,' Benfro replied. 'Where the Llinellau crossed.'

'Llinellau?'

'The Llinellau Grym. They criss-crossed the room like a net, but there was a point where they all met. That's where Meirionydd told me to pile the stones.'

'And had you seen these lines before?'

'I've tried,' Benfro said. 'Meirionydd was teaching me . . .' He trailed off, not wanting to think about her death.

'But you couldn't see them before,' the old dragon said. 'How did you see them in Magog's palace?'

'I don't know. They were just there. The power in that place was just so obvious.'

'And it isn't here? Look around you, Sir Benfro of the Borrowed Wings. Tell me what you see.'

The old dragon's voice was gentle, soothing, as if he knew hurt, had felt it himself many times before. Benfro looked around at the cave, marvelling at the way its walls glowed with the firelight. Or was it the firelight? The flames were low, little more than yellow-blue sprites dancing over the glowing embers. Yet the walls sparkled with a far brighter fire. Perhaps this was a place of power too.

Benfro concentrated, squinting at the stone. Was it his imagination or could he make out a grid, the faintest of white lines covering the walls like the web of some vast spider? The floor too was a mesh of ghostly strokes like the ones he had seen in Magog's repository. They were thin as gossamer, insubstantial as the air.

'I can see Llinellau everywhere,' he said with mounting excitement. The old dragon smiled at him from his seat. For some reason this was important to him.

'You see them. Good. What else?'

Benfro reached out for the nearest line, where it curved around his feet and folded tail. It was just out of reach, and when he leaned forward, he could have sworn it inched away from his grasp.

'I can't touch them. They move away from me.'

'The Llinellau Grym never move, Benfro,' the old dragon said, quiet earnestness in his voice. 'They're the one constant thing in the whole of Gwlad. Men live and die; dragons live and die; even the ancient trees will meet their end some day, but the Grym is the power of life. It's constant. It flows through every living thing, every point of this world. It's not the lines that move, Benfro, but you.'

That made slightly less sense than some of his mother's

more obscure lessons on herb lore. He could see the Llinellau move as he reached for them. Frustrated, he lunged, trying to grab with speed what avoided him when he was slow. Tripping over his feet as he tried to stand too quickly, he pitched head first into the fire.

'That dragon's beginning to annoy me.'

Beulah sat on the Obsidian Throne, toying with the silver chain that hung from Frecknock's collar. Melyn watched her from his own seat, set a little lower than the throne and to the front.

'It's the same one you saw before?'

'Oh yes,' Beulah said. 'There can't be more than one like that, surely.'

'You, Frecknock,' Melyn said, staring at the ragged creature he had gifted the queen. It was a pathetic beast, cowering behind one massive leg of the throne like a mouse that has escaped from a cat but knows it's still doomed. Looking at it and remembering the vast spread wings of the dragon that had leaped from Ruthin's Grove, he found it hard to believe they were from the same species.

'Your Grace?' the dragon answered. Even its voice was feeble.

'You said you knew the dragon,' Melyn said.

'I thought I did,' Frecknock said. 'I thought it was Benfro, Morgwm's kitling. But he's smaller even than me, only fifteen years old. A dragon will appear in the dream state as it sees itself, but not even Benfro would think himself so grand. I've never seen a dragon so magnificent. And Benfro could never hope to master the subtle arts in so short a time. He can't even see the Llinellau Grym. What you call the lines of power.'

'Then why did you think it was this Benfro?' Beulah asked.

'Because it felt like him. Only it felt like someone else as well. I'm sorry, Your Majesty, this visitation has confused me.'

'The dragon that escaped from Ruthin's Grove was easily as big as you,' Melyn said to Frecknock. 'It had wings large enough for it to glide. Who could that have been?'

'Sir Trefaldwyn had large wings,' Frecknock said. 'He was Benfro's father, but he disappeared years ago. Before Benfro was even hatched.'

'Where did he go?' Melyn asked.

'I don't know,' Frecknock said. 'Morgwm would never say. She didn't like to talk about it. But before he went he was always asking Sir Frynwy about the old times. I remember he used to discuss our stories at great length, as if he believed they'd really happened.'

'And you don't believe that?'

'Our legends and myths are just lessons, that's all,' Frecknock said. 'We dress them up as if we were once great mages and bards, but we're nothing special.'

Melyn wasn't completely convinced by Frecknock's words, nor by her apparent resignation to her fate. He recalled all too easily the vain creature who had sent her call out to the world in search of a mate. It was possible that another dragon had come searching for her, maybe even Benfro's father returning home. If that was the case then it was likely there were two of the beasts roaming the

Ffrydd. He had tried to follow their uninvited guest as it had fled, but he had never known anything move so fast. He had only managed the most fleeting of glimpses of its destination. He needed more to be able to pinpoint it.

'Where would Benfro go?' Melyn asked. 'We've quartered the forest around your old village, and he's disappeared. If he were aimless we'd have caught him by now. He must have been heading somewhere.'

'I don't know where any other dragons live,' Frecknock said. 'If there are any left at all. But Morgwm used to go north into the forest, sometimes for months at a time. She stopped when Benfro was hatched.'

'North, through the forest,' Melyn said. He tried to picture it from the times he had travelled in his youth. The north of the great forest of the Ffrydd was largely unmapped, a wilderness, but there were paths that ran through it, and passes other than the Graith Fawr that cut through the Rim mountains, or so he had heard.

'Have you ever been that way?' he asked the dragon.

'Not since I was a kitling. When we fled from the north we came through the pass just below Mount Arnahi. I remember the snow and the bitter cold. And an old, old dragon who lived in a clearing, all alone. He told me some funny stories, but I can't remember his name.'

It was enough. Melyn knew the great mountain, the highest peak on the Rim. He had only seen it from a great distance, but its distinctive shape brought an image to his mind. He tried to recall all that he had seen the night before. It had been a clearing in the forest, with a small river cascading over rocks. That had been the focus for the fleeing beast, but now Melyn could put it in context.

He could pull back and try to guess its location, if he could just see a little more.

The ground was undulating, climbing away from him into foothills, the Rim mountains. Eyes tight closed, Melyn tried to see more and more of the view; tried to concentrate only on what he could recall; tried to build up the exact shape of the distant ridge.

And there, rising over it all like a silent sentinel, that distinctive mountain peak. Closer than he had ever seen it.

'I know where he is,' he said finally. 'It's a long way from here, but we can track him down.'

'Who will you send,' Beulah asked.

'Send? Why I shall go myself,' Melyn said. 'But there's no point in leaving until the spring. I don't think our errant dragon will leave his little bolt-hole before then, and I need time to pick out five hundred of my best warrior priests.'

'Five hundred?' Beulah asked. 'Isn't that a bit much for one, maybe two dragons? And what about the campaign. I need your warriors at the front.'

'Your Majesty, they will be going to the front.' The faintest whisper of a smile played across Melyn's face as the plan he had been hatching finally came together. 'But I will need to beg a favour of you.'

'What favour?'

'Your dragon.' Melyn smiled. 'It knows the way through the Rim mountains. I'll want to take it with me.'

17

When taking on a new apprentice, a mage must consider many things. First is the candidate strong enough in the magics to be worth nurturing? There is little point in sharpening a soft blade. It is a waste of time trying to teach a pupil who is already set in his ways of thinking; any new apprentice should be young enough to be open to new ideas and yet old enough to understand the burden of responsibility which he takes upon himself. Before agreeing to teach one who has presented himself for that purpose, a mage should satisfy himself as to the motives of his would-be charge. Many a young hothead takes it into his mind to be a powerful mage, believing all the stories of Rasalene, Arhelion, Palisander of the Spreading Span, Gog and Magog. Such hatchlings as live in the realms of myth and legend should be guided into the noble calling of bard. Theirs is a creative mind unsuited to the rigours of the Grym.

The ideal apprentice should be young, but not still picking shell from his scales. He should be mindful of the energies that flow around him and naturally aware of the Llinellau Grym. He should be sensible of mind, fixed in the here and now, not dreaming constantly of the past or the future. He should be motivated by the most honourable of aims – to serve the memory of his ancestors and ensure the safekeeping of all dragonkind. He should be brave, for he will experience terror such as none should ever know, and yet he should not be impetuous; there is no room for the headstrong among the order of mages. He should be possessed of a good memory and an eye for even the tiniest of details.

Above all else, he should know patience and humility. The life of a mage is a solitary one, and the journey to that life both long and arduous. Of the many who step out on that path, very few will reach so far along it as to be able to call themselves mages. None will ever reach its end, for it is a journey of endless lifetimes.

Aderyn, *Educational Notes for the Young*

'Stop!' the old dragon commanded. There was something else in his voice this time, something that Benfro found impossible not to obey. The flames too seemed caught by the steely determination of the order, for they ceased their flickering, freezing in position as if an instant had been taken from time and held up for Benfro to see. He hung, ungainly and graceless, over a cold fireplace, unbalanced and yet unable to fall.

'Just what are you trying to do?'

'I was reaching for one of the lines. I thought I could get it if I moved quickly enough.'

'Reaching? Lunging more like. Now sit down again before you hurt yourself.'

Benfro tried, but he was rooted to the spot as if he were a tree. He could not move a muscle. He fought against the restraint, felt like he was thrashing around in a frenzy, even though he could see that his arms, legs, wings and body remained motionless.

'I can't move.'

'Nonsense.' The dragon pulled himself to his elderly feet with considerable difficulty and much painful popping of joints. He shuffled around the fire, and Benfro, from his awkward and unlikely position, almost bowing in obeisance, got his first proper look at the wizened creature.

He was older than any dragon Benfro had ever met. Older than Sir Frynwy, who he had thought the oldest creature alive. And he was small for a dragon, no bigger than Benfro had been before he had gained his new wings and the curse that came with them. He stooped low, supporting his upper body with a short shaft of wood that was taper-thin at its base, fattening up into a polished smooth ball at the top. The hand that rested on this was all sinew and bone, skin stretched taut like a corpse left to dry in the sun. Three of the fingers on this hand had talons that twisted and coiled and were cracked and blunt. The other three had lost their claws altogether, scar tissue marking their violent passing. The thumb was missing.

The old dragon shuffled slowly around the hearth, and Benfro noticed that his tail was half missing too, its point lost in some ancient battle that had left a shiny red stump.

His wings had once been magnificent, but now they hung like tattered curtains from a skeleton frame that hunched into a great arthritic crook in the middle of his back. His neck was long and thin, and around it there hung a silver chain with a small round pendant. Benfro could see this twist and turn in the frozen firelight, revealing an image of the dragon in the moon on one side and something he couldn't quite make out on the other.

'You really can't move?' The old dragon bent to look him in the eye. Close up, the elderly face was even worse than Benfro remembered from the night before. Each missing scale had in its place a pucker of scar tissue as if it had been plucked out in some terrible torture. One of the eyes that stared into his was clouded, yet still shone with the same bright intelligence as the other, as if, denied sight of the physical plane, it had instead developed the ability to look deep into the magical realm. He peered myopically at Benfro and then down at the floor.

'Strange.' The dragon scratched at his face with a hand as gnarled and broken as the one that seemed welded to his stick. 'Sit!'

Feeling a bit like a performing dog, Benfro couldn't help but obey the command. Without any message from his brain, his legs took the strain of his position and pulled him back. As he felt his backside come into contact with the floor, so everything switched. For an instant it was dark and then the fire started to flicker again. He could feel its heat on his face even though the old dragon stood between him and the flames.

'You're a puzzle, Benfro of the Borrowed Wings.' The old dragon settled himself down in the dirt beside him, and

Benfro noticed that he sat at the point where two of the thicker Llinellau crossed. They glowed brighter at his touch, pulses of light spreading from him, branching and branching at each point until they radiated through the walls of the cave like a quiet flash of lightning reaching out to cover the sky. Or did the light come from without, from a thousand different points, joining and joining until it met in the place where the dragon sat? It made Benfro's head spin.

'Who are you?' he asked the old creature when he had managed to focus on his face properly.

'Who do you think I am?'

'I think you're Corwen, but you say he's dead.'

'Death is not the end of a dragon, Benfro. You of anyone should know that.'

'So you are Corwen.'

'Corwen is dead. I am the collected memories of his life. His wisdom, if you will.'

'His jewels.' Benfro suddenly understood, and felt all the more foolish that it had taken him so long to get there. 'The jewels lie somewhere near here, at a nexus.' He stared hard, squinting to make out some pattern to the gentle surges of light that might point him in the right direction.

'You should have seen that the instant you arrived in this clearing. It is plain for any with the sight to see. Yet you spent a whole day wandering back and forth calling the name of a dragon who died over a thousand years ago. I followed you round but you refused to see me. I could only come to you as you drifted off to sleep, and then you disappeared into your dreams so thoroughly I couldn't find a trace of where you were.'

'You were in my dream?' Benfro asked, confused.

'No, Benfro. I was not. That's the whole point. You travelled the Llinellau somewhere – I watched you go – but I couldn't keep up with you. I was worried. You cannot see them awake and yet asleep you walk the Llinellau like no other dragon I have ever seen.'

'Am I asleep now?'

'Are you? I don't think so. Try getting up, pinching yourself. Dip your face in the waterfall outside. If this is just a dream then none of these things will happen.'

Benfro was loath to leave the cave. He had found Corwen, or at least the memories of him. Now he just wanted to keep hold of the moment, not let it go.

'What am I to do?' he asked eventually, when the silent thoughts that filled his mind had boiled down to that one salient point.

'That, my young dragon, is a very good question.'

Benfro looked up at the memories of Corwen. The dragon seemed solid enough, and yet he could feel the heat of the fire coming through the apparition as if he was not there at all. He wanted to reach out, to touch his companion, but he was afraid his hand would pass through him, that he would be as insubstantial as a ghost. It would have been disrespectful at the least and might even have caused great offence. The last thing he wanted to do was annoy the old mage. He had been sent here to learn as much as for his own safety. He didn't want to be driven away.

'Will you teach me?' Benfro asked. 'Teach me about the Llinellau Grym, about magic?'

'Oh, I'll teach you a great deal more than that, Benfro of the Borrowed Wings,' Corwen said. 'If you'll learn.'

'Why do you call me that?' Benfro asked.

'Benfro of the Borrowed Wings? I call you what I see. You weren't born with the ability to fly, were you.'

'No, none of the villagers could fly,' Benfro said. 'Sir Frynwy said our wings were a useless appendage, a throwback to a time when dragons were feral and wild, little better than beasts.'

'Sir Frynwy was a fool,' Corwen said with such abrupt bitterness that Benfro felt a stab of anger slice through him.

'Sir Frynwy was a wise dragon,' he protested. 'He was a good friend.'

'No doubt he was, but he was still a fool. A dragon's place is on the move, travelling. Pursuit of knowledge is what drives us, what keeps us alive even after we are dead. Your good friend Sir Frynwy, Ynys Môn, Meirionydd and all the others, they denied their heritage when they settled. They abandoned the old ways. If the men hadn't killed them, they'd eventually have dwindled away to nothing.'

'But Sir Frynwy was a great bard,' Benfro said.

'Yes, he trained as a bard,' Corwen said. 'He was apprenticed to old Hafren, who was himself Albarn's best pupil. I'm sure he told you everything as legend. No doubt he recounted the exploits of Palisander and the trials of Ammorgwm the Fair. Did he tell you of Queen Maddau the Wise? I know he did. And he told you of the endless battle between Gog and Magog. You thought it a splendid tale of fabulous beasts, powerful beyond kenning. It never occurred to you that it might have been true. But then you met Magog – he gave you your wings. So where does that leave the myths? Are they true or are they false?'

'I don't know,' Benfro admitted.

'And I suppose your mother told you all about men, about how they rule over creatures ten times their own size, about the cruel subjugation of the dragon races that has led to our near-extinction? Do you know why men hate us so?'

'They covet our jewels,' Benfro said. 'And yet they fear them too.'

'That's one of their rationalizations,' Corwen said. 'That's what they've persuaded themselves to believe over many, many generations. But if they truly feared our jewels then they wouldn't covet them so. They wouldn't track us down, torture and kill us. They would leave us in peace to live out our lives in solitary travel, exploration and adventure. Had they left us in peace, we might even have been able to share our knowledge and wisdom with them, allied ourselves to whatever causes they sought to pursue.'

'So why *do* they hate us?'

'They hate us because we made them that way,' Corwen said, a glint of triumph in his eyes, as if the death and destruction waged on dragonkind was something to be proud of.

'We?'

'Well, I say we,' Corwen said. 'It wasn't us, not me or you. But it was certainly a dragon. I can't remember it myself, but there was a time when men were simple creatures, living in rude huts and raising cattle and sheep. Then all of a sudden they had intelligence. They could reason, build, fight. Above all they could use magic. And they were consumed with a hatred for dragonkind that was breathtaking in its simple ferocity. This wasn't something that came to them over a thousand years. This was something that happened overnight. Only a mage, and a powerful one at that, could perform such a spell.'

'Who?' Benfro was appalled.

'I don't know.' A look of sadness passed over Corwen's face. 'It was before I was hatched, over two thousand years ago. But the legends tell of it happening around the same time that Gog and his followers disappeared. Not long before Magog himself vanished. That was when the life went out of most dragons, abandoned by their greatest mages and faced with a terrible new enemy.'

'I found out what happened to Magog,' Benfro said. 'I saw him die.'

'Hah! There are those who say he never really existed,' Corwen said. 'But I learned at the feet of Albarn the Bard, and he was apprenticed as a kitling to Rheidol, who was Magog's favourite. When I was young, dragons still hoped that their warrior chief would one day return, but I accepted his death around about the same time I encountered my first inquisitor. Still, I've always wondered how one so great and powerful met his end. Tell me, Benfro. Tell me what you saw.'

So Benfro told him his tale, starting at his mother's death and finishing with the crash-landing in the clearing. As he spoke, the old dragon seemed to shrink in on his already diminutive self, becoming older and more bent with each passing word. He said nothing to interrupt, save for a sharp intake of breath at the point where the great bird smashed in the skull of the greatest dragon ever to live, killing him like prey while he slept. When Benfro had finished, he looked up at Corwen, surprised to see his eyes wet with tears for something that had happened so long ago.

'The bird you describe is a lammergeyer.' He shrugged his shoulders and pulled himself back together. 'While I lived and travelled – and I lived for a very long time, travelled a very great distance – I saw one, maybe two. They're cowardly creatures, eaters of carrion. I've never heard of one coming anywhere near the Ffrydd. Their home's on the other side of the world, the far side of the Sea of Tegid. They don't do the killing, rather clean up after someone else has done the work. For one to come that far and act as you say, it would have to be possessed. And to possess a mindless creature like that would take a mage of such power as I have never encountered. I doubt if even Magog himself could have done it.'

'Then who?' Benfro asked.

'That I don't know,' Corwen said, and Benfro could hear the despair behind the words. 'But it tells me how you won your wings, and that they're as much a curse as a blessing.'

'A curse?' Benfro asked, flexing slightly and feeling their reassuring weight at his sides. 'They're magnificent. How could they possibly harm me?'

'A dragon's gift is also his bond, Benfro,' Corwen said. 'You're linked to Magog's unreckoned jewel by the most powerful of magics. He survives through his connection with you, taking you over little by little. Had you left the jewel where you found it, that process would have been subtle, undetected until you were too far gone to notice. There would be no more Benfro, only Magog, risen again. As it was, you're a kind-hearted soul and you sought to bring final rest to the great warrior mage. You took his jewel with you. I suspect he didn't think you'd do that.'

'How does that change things?'

'Have you learned nothing from Sir Frynwy's tales? Magog was greed and jealousy in dragon form,' Corwen said. 'Do you think that after many thousands of years dead he would be any different? So close to you, for so long, he can't help himself from digging his claws deep into your psyche. That's how you managed to get into his repository. No other dragon alive has ever entered that sanctum. And who do you think put your friends' jewels in there?'

Benfro thought of the great room with its seemingly endless ranks of dragon jewels all cut off from any contact with others. It was a singular act of cruelty beyond his comprehension. What possible crime could those condemned souls have committed to warrant such torture, over so many centuries? Then he remembered the pain he had felt when he had tried to rid himself of the tiny red ruby. He remembered the voice trying to find his name, tempting him into the watery grave, a companion for long-dead bones.

'I . . .' he began, but could think of nothing to say.

'You've been completely in his thrall at least once, Benfro,' Corwen said. 'He's made you do things that you'd never consciously do. But he doesn't control you now. So there's hope.'

'What should I do?' Benfro's voice sounded very loud in the cave.

'You must sleep now, young Benfro,' Corwen said. 'I'll watch you don't wander off in your dreams tonight.'

'But there's so much I don't understand, so much I need to know.'

'And you think you can learn it all in one night?' Cowen scoffed, a little bit of humour returning to his voice. 'I doubt a dragon's lifetime's long enough to even begin. It won't kill you to rest a while. There's much to do in the morning.'

'What about Magog's jewel? Do you know where it is?'

'It's somewhere safe, somewhere you can't touch it, but neither can you be rid of it. That will be a more difficult task.'

'And my borrowed wings? Benfro asked, aware that he was tired, yet still desperate to know more.

'Ah yes, your wings,' Corwen said. 'They were a gift you should not have taken, for they came with a high price attached. At the moment you have not the knowledge or experience to fly, yet you flew here. Every time you use your wings Magog is flying, not you. Every time you fly he takes a little more of your soul. You must take control of your wings, Benfro, learn to use them yourself. Tomorrow, when the sun rises, you will have to begin to earn them.'

He flew above the trees like some improbably vast raptor in search of prey. Overhead the sun sat in a cloudless sky of perfect blue. The air was so still and clear it was as if it wasn't there. Beneath him the trees marched off in all directions like waves of green. In the distance the great mountain rose from its bed of foothills, straining and stretching ever higher into the sky. It called him, its snow-capped peak an arrow point in his mind. He could fly to the top, easily. And from there he could conquer the world.

'That's Magog talking, Benfro. Mount Arnahi holds nothing for you. Come back down now.' The voice was Corwen's, but it brought to his mind an image of the tiny pink gem sitting in its wrap of browning leaves some-where dark and mysterious. He banked without a thought, casting his gaze over the endless trees and seeking out his destination. He saw the line of the river first, a subtle change in the shade and tone of the canopy etching a zig-zag route down from the mountains. Following it, he finally saw the clearing in the distance. It astonished him to think he had flown so far. Surely only a few moments had passed since he finally made that successful launch.

Taking off had been difficult, to put it mildly. He hadn't a clue how to go about it, and Corwen's suggestions had seemed ludicrous. First he had simply unfolded his wings and flapped them like a pair of giant hands, pushing the air down. This was a partial success in that it took his weight off the ground, but when he had tried to convert this into forward motion, the world had turned upside down, and the next thing he knew he was lying on his back in the long grass beside the track. The old dragon's cackling laughter in his head had not improved his mood. Neither had Corwen's endless supply of useless sugges-tions, like 'Stop thinking about it; just do it,' and 'It's as natural as the sun and the moon; let it happen.' More con-crete advice would have been helpful. In the end, after running like a scared deer along the track, flapping his wings and trying to leap into the air had ended in numer-ous bruises and scratches but no success, he had climbed around the back of the cliff, to where the waterfall plunged forty feet into the river below, and launched himself into the air. It had been a close call, his tail sweeping through the grass and clanging off a few rocks, but he had managed, somehow, to claw his way up and away. And now he was returning.

'Where will you land this time?' Again the voice in his head was Corwen's, but the image it conjured up was all Magog. 'I don't think the river's a very good option.'

Benfro banked and turned as he arrived over the clearing. The sun's high angle picked out the rocks strewn through the grass and emphasized the hard-packed, unyielding surface of the track. Only the water was soft, and only relatively so. Still he knew this was something he had to do, a basic ability he had to master, like walking. But as he slowed and the ground came ever closer, his wings felt less like splendid blades that cut the air at his command and more like two great useless flaps of skin, weighing him down and making it impossible to manoeuvre.

'Slower, Benfro. You're coming in too fast.' Corwen's advice was little help as the ground rushed up to meet him. 'Elegance is the key to everything. Try to be true to your nature.'

Benfro thrust his wings forward in a great spasm that drove the wind in front of him, flattening the grass around his intended landing site and revealing a dozen or more rocks that he hadn't realized were there. Miraculously, the move seemed to slow him, but as soon as he drew them back for another beat, his speed built up again.

Once more he slammed his wings down, lifting his

head up and away from the rapidly approaching ground. As if by magic, his body rotated around the fulcrum in the middle of his back, that hard knot of muscle and sinew that he was only just beginning to grow accustomed to. His feet shot forward and down, ready to accept the hard embrace of the ground, still twenty feet away, but it was the tips of his wings, almost touching on their downward stroke, that were closest. He could feel the ends of the tall grass stems with them and instinctively whipped them back for one final beat to settle him slowly.

Instead he accelerated, covering the last few feet far too quickly to be able to sweep them forward once more. Wings still halfway up their backward stroke, he hit the ground with an almighty crash, driving the wind out of his lungs. Momentum carried him forward, tipping him head first towards the rocks. Instinct took over then, the life-saving gut reaction of a thousand childhood falls from trees and banks. He let his legs crumple and tucked his head in close to his chest, turning the fall into a roll. He tumbled over and over, crushing the grass and flattening small bushes. Finally, battered and bruised, he came to a rest upside down against a large boulder a hundred feet away from his chosen landing place.

For some moments he just lay there, gazing at the upturned trees and the sun, curiously low for the hour. Dazed, it was a while before he realized he couldn't breathe, a while longer before he realized that, yes, he could breathe, he had just forgotten to do so. Coughing and spluttering he took great gulps of air, clearing the fuddle in his mind before setting about the task of pulling himself together. This took longer than anticipated as he had somehow managed to wrap his arms around his knees and his wings were twisted awkwardly behind his back.

'Splendid,' the voice of Corwen said, and then the old dragon himself appeared in his view. 'You almost had it there. Just a matter of timing. You want to get the last downstroke to stop you dead just as your feet tickle the ground. It'll come with practice, I'm sure.'

'What is that mountain?' Benfro asked, recalling the way it had called to him, beckoned him to fly towards it.

'That is Mount Arnahi,' Corwen said. 'The mightiest of the mountains of the Rim. Some say it's the tallest mountain in the whole of Gwlad. It held a certain fascination for Magog, if the tales are to be believed.'

'Why would he want me to go there?' Benfro asked, debating with himself whether he had the energy to get up or not. The ground wasn't that uncomfortable, really. Groaning, he managed to roll himself the right way up. He sat with his back against the rock, checking for bruises, breaks and any cuts, but apart from a few chipped scales he was remarkably undamaged. Even his wings, which could so easily have been ripped and torn, were intact. He stretched them wide from his sitting position, catching the sun and letting its warmth soothe the aches away.

'I suspect it was your wings that called you to that place,' Corwen said. 'I'll say this much for Magog: when he makes someone a gift, he doesn't do it one-heartedly. You'll have to work very hard to earn those, young Benfro. Very hard indeed. So I suggest you stop lazing about in the sun and get back up in the air.'

'What, now?' Benfro asked incredulously.

'Straight away now,' Corwen insisted. 'While the

memory is strong in your mind. If you must leap from a cliff to take off, so be it for now. We shall concentrate on learning to land, which I think you will agree is by far the most important skill to master. Come on now, up!'

Weary and aching, Benfro pulled himself to his feet and started out across the clearing in the direction of the cave. He was covered from head to toe in fine dust from his crash landing, and his throat was dry from the cold clean air and the hot sun. So, instead of climbing through the trees and making his way around the back to the top of the cliff, he strode past the cave mouth and its pile of logs and on into the river, wading upstream from the ford and into the deep pool where the waterfall cascaded down. It was cold and refreshing, and he dunked his head under the water, drinking great draughts. He swam against the current until he could feel the cascade above him washing away all the grime and sweat of his exertions. Setting his feet on the slimy bottom, he stood upright, pushing his head and neck above the surface and into the cataract itself. The water bubbled and frothed over his head, making it hard to breathe, so he took a step back and opened his eyes.

He wasn't in the clearing.

Errol preferred his suite of rooms in the west wing.

He wasn't sure why King Ballah had suddenly decided he was dangerous. Perhaps it was the return of Prince Dafydd. Melyn had always intended Errol to kill the prince and maybe there was something planted deep in his brain that would make him try. There was enough other rubbish in there that the inquisitor had used to smother his true memories, after all.

At least he now had time to try and sort some of those memories out. He lay on a hard pallet fixed to the cold stone wall of a dungeon cell somewhere far beneath the oldest part of the palace. Without any windows, it was difficult to gauge the passing of time, but judging by the meagre meals brought to him at intervals, several days had passed. It would have been nice if someone had told him what was happening, but he had seen no one since being dragged from the throne room. His food appeared through a small hole in the door, which also provided the only light for the cell. Whoever brought it said nothing, and the only noise was the scuttling of rats.

Shivering, he looked for the lines, trying to draw some warmth into himself. But they were nowhere to be seen, or he had forgotten how to find them. It was too long since he had used any of that magic; now, like a door with rusty hinges, he couldn't seem to get his head to move in the right way. Miserable, Errol curled up into a ball to try and conserve some heat.

A key scraping in the lock of the dungeon door woke him from an uncomfortable sleep. Before he had time to gather his wits, two guards had grabbed him and hauled him to his feet. He was dragged out of the door and down a long dark corridor lit intermittently by smoky torches that gave the air a burned-tar reek. He didn't fight, couldn't see the point, even when they brought him into a large room and dumped him on a high-backed wooden chair with arms.

It was a round room, bare stone walls hung with chains and shackles. The chair was not quite in the centre, and overhead Errol could see a round skylight with grey clouds beyond. It was more comfortable than his pallet bed, at least at first, but rough hands grabbed his arms and legs, strapping them down with wide leather belts. Too late the stupor that had smothered his reason leached away, a rising fear taking its place.

'You're an interesting diversion, Errol Ramsbottom. That much I'll give you. But then maybe that's all you are – a diversion to keep me occupied while Melyn moves his other pieces about the board.'

Errol tried to look round, but the chair held him fast, high boards at his neck restricting the movement of his head. He knew the voice well enough: King Ballah.

'But I can't quite believe that Melyn would let you go if he wasn't confident he had you under his complete control,' the king continued. 'Oh, I've no doubt that you reckon you've outsmarted him, but think about it. You, a fifteen-year-old boy, pitting his wits against the most powerful mage the Twin Kingdoms has ever produced.'

'I don't work for Melyn,' Errol said quietly. With a sudden violent motion the chair pivoted, and he was facing the king. For all his great age, Ballah was an imposing figure and strong. He was flanked by the two guards who had brought Errol from the west wing, and behind them stood the major domo, Tordu. None of them was smiling.

'So you say,' the king said. 'And it's possible that you don't even know what his plans for you are. But they're in your head somewhere and I mean to get them out.'

Errol felt the king's mind invade his own, digging down into his memories, rifling through them like a pig rooting out truffles in the autumn woods. It was far heavier-handed than his earlier subtle probing, a bit like Dafydd's crude attempt. But where the prince had been unskilled, Ballah was simply ruthless, digging through his memories in a thorough search.

Without quite knowing how he did it, Errol gathered the foreign tendrils of thought together and pushed them away from him, hard. The king rocked back on his heels, blanching as if he had just been punched in the gut.

'Still the fighter, eh? Well, we'll soon put a stop to that.' He motioned to one of the guards, who went to the wall and came back with a heavy hammer.

'Ankle, I think,' the king said. 'That way he won't be able to run away.'

The guard nodded silently, then raised the hammer and brought it down sharply on Errol's left ankle. Pain smashed through him the like of which he had never known. He heard bones break, and all the air seemed to disappear from his lungs. Somewhere he could hear someone screaming. For a moment he wished they would stop; the noise just seemed to make the pain worse. Then he realized that it was coming from his own mouth. Strapped into the chair, all he could do was gulp back his sobs and bite his lip until it bled.

Then the tendrils were back, softer this time, as if the king had regained some of his patience. They were like gossamer webs blowing through the wind of his thoughts. Every so often they would alight somewhere, examine the memory they found, then fly off again. Errol screwed up his eyes, focused on the agony swelling up his entire leg and threw it back at the king.

This time the guards had to pick Ballah up off the floor.

Errol saw them helping him to his feet as he opened his eyes once more. He knew he shouldn't anger the king, knew he should just let the old man rummage around in his head until he found what he was looking for, if it was there at all. But he couldn't help himself: he wanted to keep his memories private.

But Ballah wasn't angry. He was smiling.

'Do you know, that's the first time anyone's done that to me since I was a boy,' he said. 'It's a pity you let yourself get caught. With a few more years' training you could have been a great warrior. But I will break you, Errol Ramsbottom. And then I'll find what it is your precious inquisitor has hidden behind your defences. The other ankle, Milo.'

Errol knew what to expect now, which only made the pain worse. This time though he could feel himself slipping into unconsciousness before the king managed to get a grip on his thoughts. He let oblivion cover him like a warm, comforting blanket, thinking of the times his mother had nursed him through sickness and injury.

'Oh no, you don't.' The words were accompanied by a sharp blow to the side of his head that crazed Errol's mind while knocking him back to his senses. He opened his eyes but couldn't focus enough to stop the king from swaying round and round in his vision. He suddenly remembered Trell Clusster pushing him to the ground, and the time he had lashed out and broken his nose, earning Clun's respect. He could see the whole scene playing out in front of him. First the melee of bodies, kicking and punching him; then the book lying torn and broken-backed on the ground; then the surge of anger and grabbing someone, Trell's face and the sound his nose had made as it broke. And, riding it all, viewing it as an outsider, that same strange feeling that he knew must be King Ballah.

Struggling against his restraints, Errol thrashed his head from side to side, trying to throw the king out of his mind. But the guards were working him over now, punching him in the ribs and stomach, twisting his ruined ankles. The pain was everywhere, and through it all ran the stream of his memories.

And then he was seeing things that hadn't happened, the memories Melyn had implanted in his mind. He danced with Maggs Clusster, drank too much, pledged his allegiance to a bored-looking Princess Beulah and promised he would some day become inquisitor. He ran like a mad thing through stubble fields playing games of war with the other village boys. He practised magic, swordcraft and archery in the halls and courtyards of Emmass Fawr. He sat in Melyn's study listening intently as the old man told him how he might infiltrate the palace at Tynhelyg, how Duke Dondal would almost certainly turn him over as soon as he had the chance. The talk of stopping Iolwen from marrying Dafydd was just a cover to get him in. Once there he should spin a tale of coercion, do whatever was necessary to get Ballah to accept him. It shouldn't be too hard, since he had the looks of Llanwennog royalty already. It might take months or even years. He should be patient, bide his time, learn as much as he could and be ready for when the call came.

It was everything Ballah wanted to see, all the king's worst fears confirmed, and watching from a distant corner of his mind Errol wondered whether this was the final truth or just another layer of lies.

Barely conscious, Errol scarcely registered that the beating had stopped. The pain surrounding him was warm and friendly now, something to be embraced; the sound of the king's words an irritant to be swatted away like flies on a summer evening. But somewhere deep in his mind he registered being unstrapped from the chair, lifted between the two guards, dragged away back to his cell and thrown on to the straw-strewn floor. He couldn't have moved if he'd wanted to, so he just lay shivering and somewhere else, the final words of the king whirling around in his head in search of some sense.

'I've got from him all I need. Take him away. Prepare the block. We'll execute him in the morning.'

18

Build up a picture in your mind of the place you wish to go. Try to see it as clearly as if you were there already. No, see it more clearly than that. Sense all the tiny details that go to make up a place: the shape of a doorway and the detailing of its architrave, the smell of the floor as you walk across it, the sound of the room when it is empty, the feel of its air playing across your face and body. You must remember the way the light falls on the walls, the pattern of shadows. You must remember every detail.

It may be easier, when starting this exercise, to imagine a place you know well. Keep it small, a room perhaps, and stand yourself in the middle of it. Turn slowly, noting all the objects that you can recall, their position, their condition, everything about them. Once you have them fixed in your mind, turn slowly again, filling in those things you have forgotten. Perhaps that wardrobe has a broken leg or a drawer. Maybe the fireplace is smaller and darker. Turn once more, adding yet more layers of detail to what you see. Do not forget the floor beneath your feet and the ceiling above your head. If you do not know the place as intimately as if you are actually there, then you will not be able to find it.

Once you are satisfied that you have your place perfectly represented in your mind, consider the Llinellau Grym. See how they fill the room as they fill every part of the world. See the force that flows along them, into and out of that place, never ceasing, always on the move. Now consider this. Those same Llinellau in that room are connected to the place where you are. In truth there is no distance between you and that room. All you need to do is step once and you will be there. But be warned, for while the Llinellau connect all places to your special room, they also connect your special room to all places. Step with hesitancy, unsure of your destination, and you could end up anywhere. Or worse, everywhere.

Corwen teul Maddau, *On the Application of the Subtle Arts*

It was a dark place, lit only by what little sunlight could make it through the curtain of wetness splashing down. Dappled shadows flickered over the rippling surface of the pool, and beyond that, as his eyes adjusted, Benfro could make out a cave. He waded forward through the water to the pool's edge and hauled himself out. The walls were green and slimy with algae, the floor slick and wet, but a few paces further on the rock was dry. Even the air lost its dampness, as if something protected the cave from the passage of time.

It was a far bigger space than the cave in which he had slept the previous two nights. He could feel an enormity to it even though he couldn't see how far it went back into the hill. What he could make out in the gloom were signs of occupation, but from long ago. There were a few rough pieces of furniture: a table, its surface clear but covered in a layer of dust through which his fingers left thick tracks, one large chair and a couple of low benches, a dresser leaning forward precariously under its load of tarnished metal plates. Tucked into a recess off to one side was a huge bed and at its foot a massive chest, iron straps holding the old split wood together, a stout lock denying access.

Benfro wandered around the cave, touching and staring. It was obvious that this had been the dwelling of a dragon, and that meant it had to have been where Corwen had spent his last years. With a shudder of embarrassed guilt he realized that he was delving into his personal effects.

The far end of the cavern was black. No light penetrated there, and even his acute sight, fast adapting to the conditions, could see nothing. Yet it called to him, that blackness, like a siren in his mind. Without thinking, he found himself walking in the direction of that voice, unconcerned that he could see nothing. He could feel the faintest of breaths on is face, and the dry soil under his feet had that same strange spiced aroma as in the other, smaller cave, only here it was stronger. It got into his head, filling his brain with exotic befuddlement.

'That's Magog calling. I've placed his jewel back there, where it can do least harm,' a calm voice said at his side. It shattered his trance, bringing Benfro back to himself with a bump almost as abrupt as his crash-landing. He was suddenly aware of how cold it was in the cavern with his skin wet and shivery. Looking over his shoulder, he saw the image of Corwen. The old dragon glowed with the same gentle light as the Llinellau Grym, and without him thinking or even squinting the lines swam into Benfro's sight. Their soft glow showed the shape of the place as well as any candle or torch, and he could see how the various pieces of furniture had been placed where the thicker lines intersected. Only the bed was not placed directly on a nexus, its alcove curiously blank.

'Sleep is not the best time to travel the magical pathways.' Corwen once more saw right into Benfro's mind. 'I think you would agree after your experience the night before last?'

Benfro nodded but said nothing. The cave was simply breathtaking, its shape seemingly perfect, the undulations and alcoves, shelves and levels all placed exactly as he would have wanted them were it his home. He had to stay and explore, the kitling in him never far from the surface, but there was important work to do. He had to learn to fly. Turning, he headed back towards the wall of water, noticing again how its noise was strangely muted, the air of the cave unnaturally dry.

'Where are you going?' Corwen asked.

'Back outside.'

'Do you want to get wet again?'

'I don't mind. It's sunny outside. I'll soon dry off.'

'But there's no need,' Corwen said. 'Tell me, in what direction does the other cave lie?'

Benfro considered this for a moment. He knew the angle of the river to the track, could easily picture the scene as he had seen it from the air. So if the waterfall was in that direction it meant that the other cave would be . . .

'Over there.' He pointed.

'And you can see the Llinellau running to that wall?' The old dragon's voice was quiet and patient. Benfro looked and noticed for the first time the pattern behind the grid. There were seemingly countless gossamer-thin threads, spreading over everything like a web. This network stretched between thicker lines, which formed a larger grid of their own, and this in turn was the filling for an even larger grid. The intersection of two of the thickest lines lay beneath the one chair at the head of the table. One of the lines came from outside, through the pool and the waterfall, and continued on down the dark tunnel, not so much disappearing into the dark as becoming impossible to see, as if it were obscured by something intangible. The other line speared right through the wall he had just pointed at.

'Now remember last night,' Corwen said. 'Remember what you saw in the cave.'

Benfro closed his eyes and tried to picture the scene. He had a good head for that sort of thing and he was confident that the image he conjured up in his mind was an accurate replica of the previous night's revelation. He could see the Llinellau forming the same intricate pattern of nodes, small growing to large. If he concentrated on the small grid, then the large faded away to nothing. Focusing on the large blurred the small until it was no more than a haze. For a moment his head spun as he tried to see it all at the same time, then, with a mental shrug, he gave up and concentrated only on the largest grid.

Like the cavern in which he stood, there was only one intersection. It met under the hearth, with one line coming straight through the entrance. The other met it at a right angle, spearing away through his bed of dried grass and towards him through the solid rock of the mountainside. He could see it then, as a continuous unbroken whole, as if there were nothing between the point where he stood, astride it, and the small pile of glowing embers banked up for the day. It was as if he could just take a single step forward and . . .

'Ouch!' he shouted as his feet started to burn. He opened his eyes and looked down. He was standing on the hearth. There was no way he could be where his eyes were telling him he was. Then instinct took over and he ran from the cave, hopping from scaly foot to scaly foot before jumping into the river. Steam hissed and sizzled as the water cooled his burned scales.

'Maybe you wanted to get wet anyway.' Corwen appeared by his side, laughter in his voice and his eyes.

'How? What? Where?' Benfro looked up and saw the sun, still high but beginning to drop towards the evening. The clearing was as he remembered it, the river too. Glancing to his side he could see the waterfall still crashing down from the cliff top, obscuring the entrance he knew he had not come back out of.

'Young Benfro, you're a natural,' Corwen said, scarcely able to contain his glee. 'It took me years of training to do what you just did.'

'What did I just do?'

'You travelled the Llinellau Grym, young mage. Stepped from the physical plane for an instant.'

'I just . . . The lines . . .' Benfro searched for words to describe what he had felt. 'I could see where I wanted to be and where I was. They were joined by the light. It was just a step forward.'

'Ah, if only every pupil found it so easy,' Corwen began, then a thoughtful look clouded his eyes and furrowed his brow. 'And yet it was almost too easy. Are you sure Magog was not helping you?'

'I don't know,' Benfro said. 'How would I know?'

'Were you aware of what you were doing?' the old dragon asked. 'Describe it to me in detail.'

Benfro said what he had done, how he had built the picture in his mind, seen the connection between the two caves.

'That's a great talent you have. To accurately remember a place down to such detail is usually the hardest thing for a student of the magic arts to master. And yet you did it without thinking. Have you always had this talent? Think, young Benfro, for it is very important.'

'It's something my mother taught me to do.' He tried without success to stifle the tremor that came into his voice, dam the tears that welled up in his eyes. 'I had to learn where all the different herbs and potions lived even before I learned to read. I used to fetch them with my eyes closed.'

'There's no shame in grieving for loved ones lost. Your mother may have had her faults, but she is worthy of your tears. And if she taught you this one thing then I can rejoice that she learned something of importance from her time with me.'

'I will reunite her memories.' Benfro walked slowly

back to the cave. 'I don't know how I'll do it, or when, but I won't rest until she's at peace, joined with the ones she loved.' He picked up the leather bag of purloined gold and looked once more at the lone white jewel. He didn't touch it, but he could feel its presence. He placed the bag on the narrow stone shelf, and as he released his hold, he felt a change in his mind. It was not the lonely feeling that had been with him since he had left the village, not the dull aching loss that had seeped into him as the shock and trauma of his mother's death slowly morphed into a permanent dull pain. Instead it was the excitement-tinged sadness of leaving home on his own terms. He was off to search for fame and fortune like all the great heroes of legend, but he would be back some day to prove he was worthy.

Stepping back out of the cave, he could see the figure of Corwen waiting patiently by the ford as if he had known what Benfro was doing and understood his need for solitude at that moment. The old dragon seemed even smaller now than when first they had met, yet Benfro could see power emanating from him, a heat like the sun but warming his mind rather than tired muscles and aching joints.

'That's a brave and wise thing you've done,' Corwen said. 'Memories should be held dear but not carried around like a great burden. Your mother would have been proud.'

'She is proud,' Benfro said. 'And I'll make her even prouder when I add all her memories to the great gathering at Magog's castle.'

Corwen released a deep resigned sigh. 'Your promise is

admirable, young Benfro,' he said. 'But I warned you before not to make such undertakings lightly. A dragon's word is his bond, and a mage's word even more so. No dragon has ever been able to overcome the inquisitors. I fear you may become just another of their victims.'

'You yourself told me that the warrior priests have their power from us,' Benfro said, an almost drunken bravado sweeping over him. He had tasted a tiny fraction of the power that coursed through the veins of the world. Everything was possible now. 'I will find a way to take that power back.'

'So be it.' Corwen's mood lightened as if he too had made an important decision, and the choice now taken had lifted the weight of uncertainty from his shoulders. 'But you're not ready to begin your task, my young pupil. Not by a long way. So get back up that cliff. You have to learn to fly.'

Errol lost track of time, lying in the damp straw on the floor of his cell. There was only pain to keep him company; even the rats had deserted the place, as if they knew his fate and wanted no part of it. He seemed to have lost control of his limbs. All he could do was lie and wait. And hurt.

When they finally came for him he had no idea whether it was a day or a year or a lifetime later. It was almost as if he were detached from his body, floating overhead and watching as the curiously nondescript guards hauled him up by his arms and dragged him away. It should have been painful, he thought, wincing at the the angles his feet made with his legs. But he felt nothing at all.

A part of him wanted to stay where it was, numb and unfeeling, floating somewhere in the cell, but his body was being dragged away and he was curious to know what would become of it. So he followed the faceless guards through the maze of corridors, up flights of stairs, along back corridors less opulent than those he had seen earlier, and finally into a familiar courtyard, now filled with noisy people. In the centre of this stood a scaffold standing clear above the heads of the tallest spectators. As his body was half carried, half dragged across the courtyard, the crowd moved aside to let it through before coming together again, like water parting around a rock in a stream. Their noise was indistinct, raucous; he couldn't make out what they were saying. And when he tried to focus on any individual, they seemed to fade away. Only the mass made any sense.

There were three people awaiting him on the scaffold. Tordu, the major domo, stood shivering in the chill. Duke Dondal stood to one side, his distaste at being in the same place as Tordu evident in his every movement. Finally there was a brawny man with a black hood pulled over his head leaning on the haft of a huge double-edged axe. Errol found himself disappointed that King Ballah could not be bothered to turn up to the execution he had ordered, but it was an abstract disappointment, a feeling removed from its source. The whole scenario felt unreal. He was going to die, his head parted from his body, and somehow he couldn't bring himself to care.

Time seemed to come in chunks. One moment he was floating over the crowd, the next he was kneeling at the block, staring intently at the myriad nicks and chunks hewn out of it over many years of use. Tordu was saying something, but for all his mastery of the Llanwennog tongue, Errol couldn't understand a word of it. He knew he should be utterly terrified, but he felt nothing. Then he glanced up at the windows of the West Tower, to the suite that had been his first prison. Two faces peered down from the window. Princess Iolwen's pale face was aghast, and as she met Errol's eyes she turned away. But the other figure stayed, and with a surge of astonishment he recognized her. Martha.

How could he have forgotten her? A huge wave of emotion engulfed him at the sight of her face. She was looking at him with that same half-smile, half-frown that she always had when she was trying to understand why he couldn't see what was so obvious to her. She wasn't concerned at his plight beyond wondering why he had allowed himself to get into it. Getting out was simple. He knew what to do.

The shock of seeing her slammed him back into his body. Suddenly he was kneeling at the block, listening to the major domo read out a long list of crimes – too many by far for him to have committed in his short life – and his whole body was a blinding mess of pain. He looked up towards the tower through eyelids swollen and bruised, but it was too far away over the heads of the baying crowd for him to make out any detail. How could he possibly have seen anyone there?

But he had seen her, hadn't he? Or was his mind playing last-minute wishful-thinking games with him? No. He had felt her with him, like she had been with him in the forest back home, standing at his side and helping him to master the lines.

The lines. He could walk the lines. He could escape even from here. But to where? And how? Beside him Errol could hear Tordu come to the end of his litany of evils perpetrated against the House of Ballah. Then rough hands shoved his head down onto the block. His thin neck felt cold against the wood as a rope was wound around it to stop him moving. Trying to suppress his panic, he searched out for the lines. They were everywhere, went everywhere. He didn't know what to do, where to go.

The last thing he heard was the swish of the axe as it cut through the air.

Benfro lost track of the days he spent in the clearing. They melted into one endless round of work. There was flying every day, and with time he began if not to master the intricacies of taking off and landing, then at least to limit the damage he caused in his attempts.

Corwen pushed him hard, making him perform endless physical tasks that seemed pointless. He had cleared vast areas of the forest of dead wood, piling it around the feet of the larger conifers. He had rebuilt the weir that crossed the stream just upstream of the ford, making the crossing easier even when the rains came, although since his arrival he had seen no one other than himself and the old dragon who might benefit.

For a month he collected all the rocks from the clearing that were bigger than his fist yet small enough for him to move and piled them on the side of the track opposite the mouth of his cave. Following Corwen's instructions, he then used them to build a small low-walled enclosure with a single entrance, though he couldn't begin to guess what it was for. At least there were large stretches of the clearing that were stone free now, though the impact of his variable landings meant they were pretty much grass free as well, the ground battered and churned into a fine dusty dirt that got between his scales and itched like he was crawling with tiny bugs.

The woods around the clearing were rich with game; the deer were so tame it was almost a shame to trap and kill them. The river salmon were becoming more wary, however, keeping to the wispy fronds of waterweed or hiding under the overhanging banks whenever he swam. He had slowly increased the length of time he could hold his breath to the point where he could sit motionless on the riverbed for upwards of half an hour. Usually one, sometimes two fish were curious enough to approach, but they were jittery, and there were evenings he had to dine only on the vegetation he could scavenge from the under the trees.

Flying, food and sleep were the only things on his mind for most of the time. He lived for the thrill of soaring through the air in the early morning. It had become almost a ritual, to rise with the dawn and climb straight to the top of the cliff. If the weather was clear, he would wait until the sun began to poke its head above the trees, then throw himself towards it like some living sacrifice. He was growing stronger by the day, able to soar higher, further and longer. He could manoeuvre in the air as lithely as any bird and took great delight in chasing crows, buzzards, pigeons or anything else that flew too near. In many ways it was like swimming, something he had done so much as a kitling that it was second nature. He only had to think about what he wanted to do, not be concerned with how it could be done.

Taking off was not so natural. He had managed it only once, and that had nearly ended in disaster as rapidly approaching treetops threatened to knock him out of the sky. Only a last-minute inelegant sharp banking turn had saved him from serious injury, and he had rather lost his nerve after that. The cliff was a safer option.

Landing was coming along slightly better, possibly because once he was in the air there was no option but to come down some time. He could slow himself to the point where final impact only hurt a little and did no lasting damage, especially if he hit one of the soft patches of brown dirt he had worn with his repeated attempts. But he still could not keep his balance on landing, so he had developed a technique for minimizing the damage, dropping forward into a roll as soon as he felt his feet touch the earth. It was not elegant, but it got him down without breaking anything.

Corwen did not come to him every day. Sometimes the dragon spirit would not show up for a week or more. He would set a task and then depart, not returning until it was completed. How he knew, Benfro couldn't tell, but the old dragon was always there for the last few minutes of the job and always seemed to know exactly what he had been doing.

And so it was, as he packed the last of the small stones into his wall, placing them carefully to fill the gaps and tie everything together, he sensed the presence of a watchful eye behind him.

'You're nearly done with the corral. Good.' The old dragon spoke as if he were continuing a conversation from a few moments earlier rather than uttering the first words Benfro had heard in eight days.

'It's finished. Yes, master.' Benfro turned to see the wizened old figure. He seemed so small, yet today there was a straightness in his back, a change in his demeanour that Benfro took to be a good sign. Either that or he had been alone for so long he was seeing things that weren't there. 'But I still don't know what or who it's for.'

'As I said, it's a corral, Benfro.' Corwen stepped off the track and through the narrow opening into the middle of the enclosure. 'It's a safe place for farmed animals when the nights get long and predators come down from the mountain in search of a meal.'

'Farmed animals?' Benfro asked. 'I don't understand. What is farmed?'

'Ah yes,' Corwen said. 'I'd forgotten how lush the forests of the lower Ffrydd are, and how temperate the clime. Up here in the foothills winter is an altogether harsher mistress. Haven't you noticed how the sun takes longer each morning to raise itself above the trees? How it cuts a lower arc through the sky and is gone earlier each evening?'

Benfro had to admit that he had. It had concerned him a little that this was happening much faster than it did back home. Back where his home used to be. He had noticed a chill in the morning air too, and the frequency of the rainstorms was growing steadily. Not the warm, washing rain he was used to, but a harsh, cold, wind-blown wetness that got between his scales and chilled him so it could send him scurrying back to the cave and the fire.

'Ynys Môn taught you to hunt and to fish,' Corwen

said. It was not a question, Benfro noted; more a statement of fact. As if his master had been in conversation with the villager recently. 'He taught you well too. But he taught you nothing of the seasons. And why should he? They hardly exist down there, save for a greater dampness in the springtime. Here there will soon be snow. There'll be months when you'll not be able to find the leaves and herbs you've been eating. I've even known the river to freeze, though only occasionally.'

'But what of these farmed animals?' Benfro had learned the hard way that Corwen was prone to wandering from the subject of any lesson. Usually the digressions were important in their own right, but just as often they merely left him more confused than before.

'Where there's plenty you can take what you need when you need it,' Corwen said. 'But this isn't such a place. In the past, when dragons lived all over the land, we charged men with breeding animals that were docile, stupid, easily led. Some say that great Rasalene himself created mankind to do this service for us. That may be legend or it may be truth. It's not important. But the men kept their animals in vast flocks, fattening them up on the lush hill grass all the summer long, so that when the winter came there would be food to eat. Corrals such as this one you have built were for the animals to shelter in when the nights grew long. They'd huddle together for warmth, and the walls would protect them from wolves and lions. During the day they'd roam the clearings, foraging for what food they could find, watched over by men. Or they'd be fed on grass cut and dried in the summer and stored in caves.

'We dragons were wanderers then, and men respected us for the wisdom we brought and the magic we used to make their miserable lives more bearable. So they bred far more than they needed and gave willingly whenever we asked.'

Benfro cast his eyes over the structure he had spent the last ten days creating. It wasn't very big. Its only entrance was just wide enough for him to get through if he squeezed, and once inside he could do little more than turn round. The walls were not high, coming up to his chest. He couldn't help thinking they would provide scant protection.

'It doesn't seem all that secure,' he said.

'For a start you'd guard the entrance, both to keep your stock in and anything else out,' Corwen said. 'And it's true, this is a very small structure. But I'm not trying to teach you to be a farmer, Benfro. You'll not starve here, with your hunting skills. Though you may find your diet becoming quite monotonous.'

'Then why have I built this?'

'Because I always meant to build one myself and never managed to get it done.' A faint smile played across the old dragon's face.

'You mean it's for no purpose?' Benfro looked at the blisters on his hands, felt the ache of his arm and leg muscles from endless lifting and carrying. Above all else he remembered the long hot hours of toiling away to carry out what he thought was an important task, a vital step along his path to becoming a mage. He had undertaken the job without a question because he knew that Corwen was teaching him all he needed to know to take on the warrior priests and beat them.

'And that's one of the first lessons you need to learn.' The old dragon cut into his thoughts as if they were words painted in the air above his head. 'You must always question everything. Maybe not aloud – I've no doubt your mother taught you manners – but never, ever assume that anything is so just because someone tells you it is.'

Benfro looked from the solid structure to the not quite physical image of the old dragon and back. He put a hand out to the wall, patting its reassuring bulk. Then, with a degree of trepidation, he reached out for his tutor, meaning to touch him gently on the shoulder but fully expecting his fingers to pass right through. He closed his eyes as his hand fell on the spot where it should have made contact, not wanting to trust his sight. He could feel the air, cold and damp with the promise of rain. A light wind played about his talons – and then Corwen was there.

He could feel him.

He snapped his eyes open to see his hand resting on a shoulder that still looked insubstantial but which did not yield to the slight pressure he put on it.

'I thought you were a ghost,' Benfro said.

'Not a ghost, a memory,' Corwen corrected him. 'Look carefully and tell me what you really see.'

Benfro paused a moment. Normally when Corwen asked him to look, he meant he wanted Benfro to look for the Llinellau Grym. But he was outside in the daylight. How could he possibly see their vague glow against the glare of the sun?

'Forget the sun,' Corwen said. 'Ignore the light. See with your inner eye.'

It was the kind of cryptic advice Benfro was used to

receiving. He had no idea what the old dragon meant, but he knew that he had to try. Screwing up his eyes against the glare, he concentrated on the cave mouth. The piles of wood on either side shadowed it, and he knew that one of the thick Llinellau passed inside. Yet he could see nothing.

'Why do you cling so hard to the physical?' Corwen asked. 'Close your eyes, picture the scene as you've seen it a hundred times before. Use that wonderful memory your mother gifted you with.'

Benfro did as he was told, letting his lids drop lightly down and relaxing his forehead muscles out of their habitual puzzled frown. He built up a picture of the clearing as he remembered it, starting with the cave and working outwards. It was not a place he had studied hard, just somewhere he lived in from day to day. So it came to him as something of a surprise how easily he could recall details he had never noticed before: the position and shape of the bushes, the patches of worn earth, the kink in the track as it skirted a boulder as big as he was and too large to move; all these and more slotted into place as he cast his imaginary gaze over the landscape.

But there were no Llinellau.

He considered the space behind him, recalling with greater difficulty the shape and form of the corral he had just completed. It appeared bigger in his imagination, the walls closer and higher than they should have been. The part he had just finished was clear, each stone an individual, considered and placed with deliberation. But away from his immediate gaze it was indistinct, a sandy brown blur as if his eyes were filled with tears. Concentrating, he tried to recall the work he had done the day before, moving back along the wall as if he were inspecting it close up. Individual stones whose shapes had stuck in his mind leaped out of the blur, more and more building up to a mental picture of the whole as he slowly paced himself back to where he had started. The corral shrank to its normal size, its detail set solid in his mind.

And still there were no Llinellau.

He turned his attention to the river. There was no way he could remember the exact state of the water at any given time, but the arrangement of rocks in the weir and the patterns of wet and dry as the track undulated through the ford seemed clear enough. He could see up to the waterfall, its falling plume crashing into the pool with a familiar roar. Was that the real waterfall or his memory of it? In his mind he had moved in close, somehow hovering above the water. The noise had risen to match his distance, filling his ears and blotting out all else. He turned to view the clearing from his new perspective and everything was changed.

It was glowing with a golden light that pulsed gently in time to some unimaginable rhythm. The sky was not the pale autumn blue that he remembered, but a shifting mix of purples and oranges spread over a background of black. Light speared from the distant treetops, piercing the heavens with innumerable pinprick stars. The sun hung heavily over the trees, a great swollen orb that sizzled and spat in its own heat haze. The grass was a sea of silver, reflecting an inner light that waved and twisted in the breeze. Shrubs and bushes were multicoloured explosions in the waves, green and blue and yellow like fire. But it was the trees ringing the clearing that were most magnificent. They shone like beacons, every conceivable colour swirling around their trunks and through their outstretched boughs to their leaves.

And the Grym was everywhere.

'You see it now, don't you?' a voice said in his ear. Benfro felt a touch on his hand, as if someone had placed their own over it. Eyes still closed, he looked over at his master. But this wasn't the old dragon he had come to know. This was a creature only slightly less splendid than Magog himself. He was huge, towering above the cliff, and his scales glistened with an iridescence that was painful to look at. He had wings so large that, even folded, their joints rose above his head, held high and proud. He was suffused with a glow every bit as golden as that which filled the whole clearing, save for a dull redness that spread around his magnificent head – an alien thing, out of place and jarring. But what caught Benfro's attention more was the way the redness spread like a canker down one side of the dragon's neck, to his shoulder and the hand, his own hand, clasped there.

An idea began to grow in the back of his mind then, a dawning realization that scared him even though it was only half formed. But before he could complete the thought, something hit him like a punch to the gut, driving wind and sense out of him like pulp from a squashed fruit. He pitched forward, knees buckling beneath him, and crumpled to the ground.

19

Quite where the myths surrounding dragons come from, nobody knows. It is believed that dragons are fire-breathing creatures with great powerful wings capable of bearing them over vast distances; that they can swoop down on the unwary and carry off whole cattle in their talons; that when cornered they can belch forth a magical flame which consumes only flesh, leaving a victim's bones and even his clothes untouched. All these and more myths about dragons abound, no doubt the invention of some or other parent anxious to instil a little discipline in the family. All are untrue.

Many believe that dragons do not exist at all. That too is untrue. I have encountered numerous dragons on my travels and found them in the main to be unexceptionable beasts, humble to the point of obeisance and quite unprepossessing. It is true that a dragon is bigger than a man, but then so are many creatures that walk this earth. If you do not fear the gently lowing dairy cow on her way to the farmyard for milking then neither need you fear a dragon.

A dragon's wings, for they are indeed possessed of such appendages, are a sorry thing to behold. Anyone who has read the works of Barrod

Sheepshead will be most disappointed at the pathetic flappings of skin that hang from the backs of these creatures. Never could they have been used for flight, and it is the opinion of many dissectors that they in fact serve to cool the beast's body in hot weather, it being unable to sweat.

Dragons possess a rudimentary intelligence that sets them perhaps a little higher than the other base beasts of the forest. They congregate in small communities and affect an almost human lifestyle, perhaps in imitation of their betters. By some freak of nature they breed only seldom and live to a great age. In all my travels I met just one creature who claimed to be less than a hundred years old, but since they measure such things by counting the seasons and seem to have no writing at all, time perhaps has different meaning to them. Of one thing there can be no doubt: there are few dragons left in this world and their numbers are dwindling.

Father Charmoise, *Dragons' Tales*

The sight of Emmass Fawr rising from the mountain ridge always raised Melyn's spirits. It had been his home for many decades now, the seat of his power. Its vast size at once made him feel all-powerful and yet humbled him. And more important than anything else, it was here that his god chose to speak to him. Weary from weeks on the road, he wanted nothing more than to spend some time in contemplation and prayer, to feel the warmth of the Shepherd wash away his aches and pains.

Smoke was pouring from the chimneys of the rude houses clustered around the great arch. Melyn scarcely felt the cold, warmed as he was by the Grym, but he recognized the onset of winter. Another year almost gone. It was too late now to begin the campaign against Llanwennog, even if he had wanted to. His warrior priests could survive the bitter cold, but their horses would suffer in the mountain passes, their supply wagons would get bogged down in the snow. Better to wait until the year had turned. By the time they had made their way across the forest and taken care of the dragon, the passes would be clearing.

The troop rode through the arch and on up to the monastery complex with Melyn at its head. Groups of novitiates were drilling in the main courtyard; warrior priests went about their daily routines; quaisters bustled novitiates between lectures; and the monastery staff went about their unseen business of maintaining what was as much a small city as the headquarters of a religious order.

All seemed normal, calm and as it should be when Melyn handed his horse over to a stable boy. He hauled himself up the stairs to his personal quarters, noticing not for the first time how much more his joints creaked and moaned at the climb. A visit to the bathhouse for a soak and steam would soon sort that out, but first he needed to go over the reports from his time away.

Andro was waiting for him at the top of the stairs.

'Your Grace, it's good to see you returned safely,' the old librarian said.

'And you, Andro,' Melyn said. 'But you didn't come up here just to welcome me home. What's the bad news?'

'It concerns Errol,' Andro said, and Melyn saw that the

old man was unusually agitated. He wrung his hands constantly. Melyn was aware that the librarian had taken a liking to the boy, but the death of a novitiate serving the order and the queen should be seen as a fine example to his fellows.

'I'll miss him too, Andro,' Melyn said. 'But he'll graduate to the priesthood posthumously. He died honourably.'

'You don't understand,' the librarian said. 'He's not dead; he's here.'

Benfro heaved the contents of his stomach, mostly semi-digested fish and wood sorrel leaves, on to the hard-packed stones and dirt of the track. His head was reeling as if someone had hit him with a tree and his lungs didn't seem to want to work.

'What ... what happened?' he managed to whisper after some minutes of wheezing had passed.

'You tell me,' Corwen said. 'You were fine for a moment, and then I lost all contact with you. Tell me what you saw.'

'I couldn't see anything.' Benfro latched on to the first solid memory that he could. 'The sun was too bright, even in the shadows.'

'But you closed your eyes.' Corwen's voice probed the mess of thoughts in Benfro's head. 'What happened then?'

'I still couldn't see any lines. I couldn't see you, either. But I moved across to the waterfall. Then it all changed.'

'I think we'd better go inside,' Corwen said. 'It's getting late.' And it was true. Benfro had not noticed before – he had been too busy vomiting on the road, too preoccupied with the war going on in his head – but the sun had dipped below the treeline, painting only the canopy top on the distant ridges in orange and green.

'A drink first,' he said, hauling himself to his feet. The world spun alarmingly around him and he sat back on his tail for steadiness. It was a struggle to cover the few short steps to the water's edge. He knelt by the weir, grateful that it raised the water level by a few feet, not so far for him to bend down. The surface was mirror-smooth, reflecting back an image he could not believe.

He was staring at another dragon, so close their noses were almost touching. Instinctively he flinched away, and the other dragon did the same thing. It was a ferocious-looking beast, fully twice his size. Its face was a mask of shiny scales, each catching the light and refracting it in an endless variation of colours. Its upper fangs pierced its lips like two knives, curving down to sharp points as white as silver. Its lower fangs, shorter but no less menacing, locked with their cousins in an uncompromising grimace. Its ears were long and thin, scooped back at their feathery tips in an enquiring, almost quizzical fashion, and its eyes burned with a fiery red malevolence that was both intimidating and strangely exhilarating.

But it was something else that struck him most. Flickering in and out like a shadow in colour, a shape cast by firelight, was a pattern of colourful lights. They danced and writhed in time to his thoughts and the *thumpity-thump* rhythm of his hearts.

Benfro moved his head the better to see the swirling colours at their cat-and-mouse game. The other dragon moved in time with him, and he suddenly understood. He lifted a hand, marvelling at how much bigger and stronger it was than he remembered, and waved it between him and the image. His alter ego lifted the opposite hand and waved it too. When they met, the surface of the water split and the image was destroyed.

The colours faded away in a series of ripples that circled out of his view before returning as echoes and forming intricate patterns on the surface of the pool. For a moment he was transfixed by the simple complexity of it, but the chaos soon reverted to a mirror-smooth surface. Once more he could peer in fascination at what he now realized was his own reflection.

Benfro had never been one for looking at himself overmuch. He had seen the way Frecknock would spend hours in front of a glass or gazing into a still pool. She would pout and preen and sing little songs to herself, generally flying into a rage as soon as she realized that she was being watched. Still, he was generally aware of what he looked like. Even with the addition of his wayward wings, he had bulked out only a little. Or so he had thought. But the face that stared back at him from the water was a complete stranger.

Weariness tugged at him, but it was no match for the fascination he felt as he explored his new face, feeling those fangs with sharp-taloned fingers, stroking those scales and marvelling at the way the light played on their smooth hard surface. His forearms were as thick as stout tree trunks, his shoulders bulging and squared where once they had drooped. Indeed his whole upper body had filled out so that his wings no longer looked like artlessly tacked-on appendages, but rather as if they belonged where they were. He would have opened them out, flexed their vastness against the approaching night, but he was too drained.

With an enormous effort of will, he pulled himself to his feet. Only when he turned did he see the stooped figure of Corwen, standing by the cave mouth and watching him, intently.

'I grew so big,' Benfro said. 'When?'

'Ah, Benfro, it's good to have you back,' the old dragon said. 'Please, step inside. I no longer feel the cold, but I can see that you do, far more than you'll admit.'

Slowly, almost limping with the effort, Benfro dragged himself into the cave. The fire was nearly out, dull embers piled up neatly in the middle of an ocean of white ash. For a moment he just stood, surveying the distance between fire and bed, weighing the weariness that he felt now against the effort that would be needed to get a new fire started in the morning if he let this one go out. In the end a lifetime of conditioning took over. He could hear his mother's voice chiding him for letting the fire get so low. He dropped to his knees once more, picking a few small dry strips of kindling from the pile he had laboriously prepared and cracking them into place over the coals. Taking a short breath in, he blew gently on the fire to get it going. He did all this with a weary acceptance that the job would take time and that it would be some hours before the cave was truly warm, so it was with some surprise that he saw a tiny jet of flame gush from his mouth and devour the twigs.

'Oh!' Corwen exclaimed. 'How splendid.'

'Is it?' Benfro asked, too tired to be amazed any more.

All he could see was his fire reduced instantly to ashes, his hopes of warmth dashed by a cruel trick. And on top of it all, the embarrassment at what he had done in front of another dragon.

'But of course,' Corwen said. 'This is the real you now. I'm sure of it. The great Magog, Son of the Summer Moon, would never stoop to breathing fire. Not even if he was freezing. But this is a skill only a dragon true to his nature can hope to master. Many spend all their lives at it and never manage anything.'

'I did it before, in my dreams,' Benfro said. 'Or at least I thought it must have been a dream. But the villagers' bodies were reckoned by the flame and their jewels ended up in Magog's repository.' Absentmindedly he reached for some more substantial logs, piling them up like a miniature funeral pyre on the hearth. 'I was so ashamed. I didn't want to say.'

'Ashamed?' Corwen asked. 'Why should you be ashamed?'

'Breathing fire is a throwback to a time when dragons were no better than beasts, feral and wild,' Benfro said.

'Now that's Sir Frynwy talking, if ever I heard him,' Corwen said.

'He told me, yes,' Benfro said. 'But my mother taught me too. When she was showing me the herbs and oils to use for the reckoning ceremony.'

'Herbs and oils,' Corwen scoffed. 'Nonsense. And your mother knew it. True, the right mix will produce the flame, but it's a pale shadow of a true reckoning. What you gave to the villagers was only your birthright as a dragon. There's no shame in it. But this –' the old dragon pointed at the smoking logs '– is a mark of true greatness. What you've just done is far more skilful than producing the reckoning fire. You've breathed a true flame.'

'I only blew on the embers,' Benfro said. 'I never meant for anything to happen.' He leaned forward and blew on the pile again. This time a great gout of flame spewed forth, catching on the dry wood and setting it instantly alight. It blazed with a merry warmth and he huddled close to it, too exhausted to be in awe. Too tired even to sleep.

'Ah, Benfro, cherish this memory,' Corwen said. 'Remember yourself now. This is you.'

'What do you mean?'

'You carry with you the essence of Magog. It's hard for me to tell where he ends and you begin. When you see the Llinellau Grym, when you disappear in your dreams, I don't know whether it's him doing it or you. Most likely it's a combination of both. But this –' he pointed at the flames '– is you and only you. Magog is nowhere in this magic.'

'How do you know?'

'Magog was great. He was a brilliant mage,' Corwen answered. 'But he was also arrogant and vain. Even Albarn the Bard agreed on that, though he left much out of his great telling. Magog despised all dragons for the limitations of their bodies. It was probably him who started this nonsense about fire-breathing that Sir Frynwy and your mother clung to. He'd never have sullied himself by doing it.'

'Does it really matter?' Benfro asked. He wanted desperately to lie down on his bed and go to sleep, but he wanted to sit in front of the fire and soak up its warmth even more.

'Matter?' Corwen said. 'Young Benfro, nothing matters more. Every day Magog takes a little more of you away. I've tried to teach you what I can. Physical labour has earned you the strength that previously you borrowed without knowing it. Now at least when you fly or fight or just walk endless miles it will be your own effort, not his. He won't be able to sink himself deeper into you that way.'

'Is that why you made me fetch all that wood, build that what-do-you-call-it? Corral? Just so I'd be less scrawny?'

Corwen sighed. 'Benfro, when you arrived at the mother tree, you were barely alive. Yet all you felt was a bit tired. You'd walked for days without food, flown for hundreds of miles on wings you could scarcely lift, survived a fall from the topmost branches of a truly vast tree. You simply don't have the stamina to do these things. No Ffrydd dragon has had that kind of power for thousands of years.'

'So it was Magog keeping me going,' Benfro said, his voice barely a whisper.

'Exactly so,' Corwen said. 'But he couldn't keep you going for ever. And he wanted you to survive. That's why he sent you to the mother tree. She's always had a soft spot for our kind. She took you in and gave you the rest you needed. It took half a year for you to recover.'

'But it was only one night,' he protested weakly.

'The mother tree exists in her own time and place,' Corwen said. 'To her time is just another illusion to be manipulated. You remember only one night, but she will have entertained you, nursed you back to health over many more.'

Benfro stared into the flames, soaking up their warmth. He was still dog-tired, as if he had built the corral in a day, not the weeks the task had taken him.

'What happened back there? When I collapsed?'

'You should know better than me,' Corwen replied. 'It happened to you, after all.'

'I . . . It felt like someone had punched me. But there was no one there. I was looking at the Grym, then you spoke. And then there was just pain.'

'Sometimes it happens that way, if you push too hard too soon. Still, you're feeling better now,' Corwen said. It was not a question. 'That's good. I'd hoped the exhaustion would wear off. And it hasn't taken as long as I'd feared. You're progressing well.'

'I need to eat something,' Benfro said, stooping for the door. 'There's a side of venison in the other cave that'll cook nicely on this fire.'

'So why get wet?' Corwen asked.

'What?'

'You intend to fetch your meal by swimming through the waterfall,' the old dragon said. 'Why?'

'Because . . .' Benfro started to say, then stopped. It was as plain as the day what he should really do, what he could do. The realization made him tingle with excitement as much as it made him curse the endless times he had swum to his makeshift larder, especially on rainy days when getting dry again had been all but impossible and he had slept damp. He quickly closed his eyes, anticipation chasing away the last of the weariness. The Llinellau were there in an instant, his memory of them as sharp as his rising hunger. He focused on the one that he straddled, standing in the doorway, and followed it to the point where it intersected at the hearth, under the flickering flames. He could follow the path, turning and disappearing through the rock wall to the cave beyond. Already he could see the familiar room with its ancient furniture. And there, in the last evening light still flickering through the waterfall from the darkening sky outside, hung his food. He could step from where he was to there with just a thought.

But he didn't.

It was the memory of the flames that caught his attention first. Or at least he thought of it as a memory of the flames, but it didn't behave like a memory should. The flames were motionless, as if caught in a bubble of time, and they were a myriad different hues, blue and purple and silver-white, none of the colours a flame should be. The logs on which they fed were unburned, just as they had been when he piled them up, before he breathed the fire.

His mind straying from the meat hanging in the other cave, Benfro found himself focusing on the intoxicating Grym that ran from where he stood, through the bizarre flames and on into the hillside. He had never really thought about the other Llinellau, but now he realized that they must all lead somewhere. And something about this one pulled him in, beckoned him to explore. Curious, as he ever had been, he took a step forward, realizing too late the other strange thing about his memory of the cave.

Corwen was nowhere to be seen.

*

Blackness enveloped Benfro and with it an incredible cold. He couldn't breathe; some great weight was clamping him like an iron fist. It smothered his face, clasped his hands to his sides, flattened his wings against his back. Motionless and helpless, he wondered if he had materialized deep in the rock. Would he die here, buried under the mountains? Would his unreckoned jewels fester and burn in the darkness?

He tried to remember what he had done, but his mind was a rushing of jumbled thoughts, red dots whirling around in his sight. He tried to shake his head to clear it, an instinctive reaction that struck him immediately as futile. How could he possibly move his head if he was stuck in solid rock? Yet something gave way, and a tiny space opened in front of his mouth. He tried to breathe in and realized that his lungs were already full. He must have taken a deep breath before stepping into . . . Where?

Red-hot stabs of pain grabbed at his chest as if there were needles in his lungs. He thrashed his head from side to side, back and forth as much as he could to make a space, hoping against hope that it would somehow fill with air. And then he could hold his breath no longer.

The flame billowed out in the darkness, too close to his eyes and face. It hit whatever surface bound him and carried on through as if it were no more substantial than mist. Benfro felt the grip around him loosen, first his upper body, arms and wings, then his abdomen and legs. For a brief moment he could see something resembling the inside of a dome painted in orange and white. Then the flames died away, leaving him blind.

At least he could move now, and breathe. He took a

great lungful of air, tasting a sharp moistness in it. Still he was out of breath, as if someone had stolen half of what he had just taken in. He gulped more, trying to get rid of the spots that were the only thing he could see. Unsupported by whatever it was that had held him up, it was easier to sink to the floor on his all-too-weak knees. It was wet there, little pools of ice-cold water on what felt like stone, as if it had just rained in his little prison.

Slowly, hesitantly, Benfro reached out for the nearest wall. His hand came into contact with a surface but it was not rock. Whatever the material was, it was as cold as ice, but it was not hard. Soft and powdery, it crumbled under his fingers, robbing them of warmth as it melted to form great drops that fell to the floor, adding to the growing puddles. He could hear a constant *drip, drip, dripping* now as the roaring in his ears died away with each successive breath. And behind the noise of the water, far off or muffled by this strange wall, the wind wailed a storm like none he had ever known.

Struggling into a seated position, Benfro tried to gather his wits about him. The air in his little cage was turning sour – he could feel each lungful doing less good, smell the taint of his own odour. It was also getting warmer, as if his body heat were trapped. He didn't know if he could breathe more fire but he had to make more space for himself somehow.

He sat perfectly still for a moment, listening to the moan of the wind. Was it louder in one direction? It seemed so. Carefully he shuffled that way until he could feel the cold press of the strange surface. He leaned down to the floor, listening hard, and lifted his head slowly until he reached the point where he was sure the sound was greatest. Reaching in the darkness, he took a great handful of the powdery substance and scooped it aside. The exertion brought the spots back before his eyes. He had to pause and take deep but unsatisfying breaths before he felt strong enough to continue. His head ached and his arms felt like lead, but he pressed on, scraping away at the wall until it became more of a tunnel, its material dumped in the space behind him. There was no turning back.

It seemed to take hours. Each tiny handful was the effort of a lifetime, but slowly he inched forward to his goal. The wind roared at him, so close but impossibly distant. Sometimes it dipped and he was convinced he had gone the wrong way, was busily tunnelling away from his salvation. Then it would speak to him again, sing that violent song that convinced him he was right. Shifting the soft material seemed to free up more breathing space, banishing the taint of his own smell, though each inhalation left him wanting, light-headed as if there were something missing.

Benfro was colder than he had ever known. As he dug, sensation left his fingers first, freezing them in a scoop-like claw that he could not unclench. Then his hands and forearms went dead. On the floor his knees and legs were stiff and heavy, but still he pushed on, relentless. He would not give in, could not give in, until with a lunge he was through.

The wind immediately blew powder into his face, stinging his eyes. The darkness had been so total, he had forgotten they were open. Now he quickly snapped them shut against the storm. Feeling as best he could with his frozen hands, he made out a rough opening about twice the size of his head and filled with the same material he had tunnelled through. At the edges of this aperture he met with hard resistance – stone. It was all so confusing, so alien. He had to breathe fire, clear more of a space, see. But he needed a good fill of air. Desperate, he shoved his whole head through the aperture and opened his mouth.

It was as if someone were trying to inflate him. The wind rammed down his throat, cold as ice and laced with tiny flakes of powder. He could feel the gusts and eddies ripping at his ears, trying to pull his head from his shoulders. He braced himself against the stone edges and exhaled hard before letting the wind fill him once more. The chill spread through his chest, threatening to dampen any flame he might have been able to produce. Doubt flickered through his mind then. True, he had made flame before, but he was still not quite sure how. It had come to him because he had wanted it to, but that couldn't be all there was to the trick, could it? Unsure, he turned from the wind, thought of warmth and blew out hard.

Nothing happened.

He turned once more into the maelstrom, filling himself with cold clean air. There had to be something, some state of mind. How had he done it before? He didn't really know. Back in the cave he had been too tired to care what was happening. He just wanted to be warm and to sleep. Well, he was tired now, the cold sapping his energy as effectively as a rain cloud in front of the sun. He had not been thinking about what he was doing, but that was a difficult trick to carry off, if that was what he had to do.

The wind dipped for a moment, the constant slash of cold powder against his face halting as abruptly as if it had never been. Tentatively, he opened his eyes, slits only at first, ready to clamp them shut should the storm try to blind him again. What he saw made him forget the cold and difficulty he had breathing.

He was surrounded by stars.

They filled his vision, above and below and to the sides. There were so many of them it was like a dream. There surely couldn't be that many in the sky, and yet he was seeing them. He thought he recognized a few of the constellations, but they were accompanied by so many other bright points he could not be sure of the Carw Hela or the Blaidd yn Rhedeg. Neither could he understand how he could see them without looking up. Here there was nothing but sky all around. Scudding clouds blustered around the nightscape, obscuring much of the view, but most alarming was the fact that he couldn't see the ground.

A gust of wind kicked up again, peppering his face with icy shards of powder. Open-mouthed with awe, he swallowed a faceful, spluttering and gagging as he turned away from the incredible view. The powder turned to water, fresh and cold in his mouth, chilling all the way down to his stomach, which clenched convulsively as the liquid hit its void. For the first time since his strange journey began, Benfro remembered the hunger he had felt, the terrible emptiness as if the fire had consumed everything inside him. A few mouthfuls of water were not much to keep him going, but they were something. He swallowed again, belching to try and clear what had gone down his airway, and a thin, weedy flame billowed out from his nostrils.

He understood then. He needed something in his belly

to create the flame. But there was nothing to eat, only this endless white powder swirling in through the opening. It was, he realized, frozen water. Sir Frynwy had told him about ice and hail and snow, but he had never seen any of them before. And Corwen had mentioned that snow would come in the winter, but he had been too preoccupied with other thoughts to give this information much heed. The only place he knew where snow was found was at the top of the tallest mountains. And the higher you went, the thinner the air – that was something Ynys Môn had told him. Well, the air here was thin indeed. He was panting as if he had run a mile and still his lungs called for more.

The heat of his tiny flame had not helped clear the snow at all, but the warmth of its generation spread through his veins, bringing life back to his cold tired muscles. Pain lanced through his fingers and hands. It was the first thing he had felt from them for what seemed like ages. He flexed them, then winced in agony and wished he hadn't. More snow was blowing in through the opening behind him, but the light of the stars filtered through too, illuminating the scene.

White dominated. Benfro was standing in a tiny space not much bigger than his body, surrounded by packed snow. At his feet he could just about make out a stone floor. There were flagstones, which meant that someone had built the place he was in. The opening behind him was too regular a shape to have been natural anyway. He turned once more and felt around it with his newly sensitive and very painful hands. There was a smooth sill, several feet deep, and on one of the sides what appeared to be a metal latch. Feeling for the other side, Benfro discovered two hinges disappearing into the snow. He brushed it aside, scooping great chunks away to reveal a flat plate of glass set in a metal frame. He dug deeper, shifting great mounds of chilling white into the area around his feet. Finally he had cleared enough space. He grasped the window and swung it on its hinges. They protested at first, bending alarmingly under his fading strength, but finally gave in. The whole thing swung around to cover the opening, its latch clicking into place and holding it against the wind.

Instantly the noise died away to a quiet whistling. The storm that had been battering his face dropped to nothing, and the last of the swirling snow fell to the floor. Benfro was shivering uncontrollably now. He had never been so cold in his life as he slipped down into a crouch and then rolled over to sit on the snow-spattered floor. The hollow space in his stomach gnawed and groaned at him, reminding him of what he had to do now, though he was reluctant to even try.

Slowly, fearful that he might not be able to stay awake if he got any colder, he took a large handful of snow and shoved it into his mouth. It was difficult to swallow: he had to wait for it to melt so that he could gulp it down as water. A pathetic dribble that drained life from him made its way down into his gut. He needed more, so he took another mouthful, and another. His tongue went numb, his teeth ached and the endless white powder took longer and longer to melt. But slowly, oh so slowly, he could feel a frozen fullness coming upon him. True it was a water-bloated satiety, but it would have to do.

Finally he could swallow no more. His mouth was so cold that the snow would not melt. He was dimly aware that somewhere down below the numbness of his waist there were legs, feet, a tail, but he could no longer feel them. And if his plan didn't work, then he would not be able to stand up again. He would die here, surrounded by white.

At least breathing seemed to have become easier, he thought as he took a deep breath and concentrated on warm thoughts. The icy lump in his stomach gurgled and churned. Good. It was time. He pictured the hearth in his mind, piled up with logs in a neat pyre, a funeral for some tiny but important creature. Then, with the last of his fading energy, he exhaled.

'Honestly I've no idea how he got there. Someone must have beaten him up for the gold he was carrying, or something.'

Errol understood the words on a basic level, but they meant nothing to him. He was dead, surely. But if he was dead, then why did he hurt so much? His whole body ached with a dull intensity that couldn't be ignored. He tried to move, hoping to find a more comfortable position in which to be dead, but sparks of fire lanced through his ankles, forcing a gasp of pain through lips that felt swollen and cracked.

'I think he's waking up,' the voice said, and Errol thought that he recognized it. He tried to open his eyes but one of them seemed unwilling to cooperate. The other would only half work, and he looked out of a narrow slit at a white-haired old man. At first he thought it

346

was Andro, but he was wearing a different cloak to the librarian, the dull brown robes of a coenobite of the Ram.

'Where am I?' Errol tried to ask, but his throat was dry and the sound that came out was indistinct.

'Here, let me give him some water,' another voice said. Tilting his head, Errol managed to make out the face of Usel, the medic, before a wave of nausea washed everything in red. He felt his head tilted back by strong hands and then liquid sweeter than honey trickled through his lips.

'Not too much at once. We don't want him to choke.'

Even swallowing was painful, but slowly Errol managed to drink. And as the liquid washed the dust and dryness from his throat, so it seemed to wake him from the stupor of his dulled thoughts. By the time he felt strong enough to open his eye again, he realized that it had been nothing more than water.

'Someone's had some fun with you.' Usel peered closely at Errol, pulling open his eyelid with a gentle thumb. 'What did you do to upset them?'

'Duke Dondal handed me over to King Ballah.' Errol's words came out something like 'Dugdunnl hundev blah.' Then it began to dawn on him that he was in a bed, being tended to by Usel. He wasn't kneeling at the executioner's block in Tynhelyg.

'Where'm I?' he asked, trying hard not to slur the words.

'You're in the infirmary at Emmass Fawr,' the old coenobite said. 'We found you lying on the stone plinth down in Ruthin's Grove. You've been unconscious for three days. What happened, Errol? You were supposed to be in Tynhelyg.'

'Who?' Errol asked, his voice rasping in his throat as if he'd been shouting for days.

'Dear me, I'm forgetting my manners,' the coenobite said. 'My name is Gideon. I knew your mother. But we can speak of her later. Tell me how you got here.'

'I was in Tynhelyg.' Errol's words came a little more easily with each sip of water from the bowl Usel held to his lips. 'But Duke Dondal sold me out to the king. They were going to execute me. Then . . . I don't know.'

'That much I already know,' Gideon said. 'I was in Tynhelyg myself when you were captured. Usel here's been tending the injuries I sustained while escaping. Our kind aren't very welcome in Llanwennog any more. But how did you get to Ruthin's Grove, Errol? Who brought you and why?'

'I don't know. Honestly, the last thing I remember was seeing Princess Iolwen at the window. They tied my head down on the block. Then . . .'

'Rest, Errol,' Gideon said. 'You've been badly beaten; it's not surprising if you're confused and disorientated. You'll need time to heal. Use it to think hard about what happened.'

'But . . .' he started to say, but Gideon held up his hand, and Usel once more tipped the bowl to his lips. It tasted slightly different this time, a faint edge of bitterness that reminded him of some leaves his mother used to infuse in hot water. Applied to a wound, they would cleanse it of all foul humours; drunk as a tea, he recalled, it was a powerful sleeping draught. Too much of it could kill.

Errol tried to fight the poison, but Usel's hold was firm.

'You must sleep now, Errol. This will help.'

Errol drank a little, feeling unconsciousness creep up on him. And at the last moment, as he slipped under, he felt the familiar tendrils of thought in his mind and heard the hated voice of Inquisitor Melyn shout from the far end of the room, 'Is he awake yet? Damn the boy, I need answers.'

20

Apart from the palace of Cenobus and the Place of the Silent Stone, Magog had one other retreat, to which he would go when there was some great magic that needed to be wrought. None knew where this place was save Magog himself, though many speculated that it lay in the warm dry lands on the far side of the Sea of Tegid. Rumour had it that this was where he cast the spell that would split the world, and that here resided his secret library, the collected knowledge of the greatest mages that had ever lived, right back to the time of Rasalene himself.

When the years that passed had turned into centuries and still Magog did not return from his battle with the men, some of his followers feared for the worst and prepared themselves to fight. They knew that they could not hope to succeed, for who could possibly vanquish a foe that had defeated the most magnificent mage to have ever lived? And yet with the reach of men growing ever wider and ever stronger, it was only a matter of time before the palace itself was overrun. So it was that a small band set out in search of Magog's retreat, hoping to find the lost secrets of his great power.

There were four of them: wise Ceredig, who flew west, towards the setting sun; brave Ogwy, who headed south; noble Rhagfyr, who ventured into the far north; and fair Meinir, who searched ever east. Onwards and outwards they flew, further and further to the four corners of the world.

And to this day they fly still, become the four winds blowing in endless search of a name they can no longer recall.

Sir Frynwy, *Tales of the Ffrydd*

The flame was not what Benfro expected. He had hoped to produce a hot orange conflagration that would consume all it touched, belching thick black smoke into the air. This was a different thing altogether. It was blue and clean and burned with a heat so fierce he could feel it through his face scales. And it seemed to be selective. It billowed up against the wall of packed snow, cutting it away like a shovel, turning it instantly into steam. It swirled around his body, licking his scales with a thousand tiny tongues that cleaned him like he had never been cleaned before. It warmed him but it didn't burn.

With remarkable speed the room was cleared. A thick fog hung in the air, condensing on to the stone walls and dripping down to the flagged floor. As his eyes reaccustomed themselves to the near-darkness, Benfro was surprised to see furniture: a large comfortable-looking wooden chair, a vast reading table similar to the one he had found in Magog's repository, an elegantly carved glass-fronted bookshelf, lined with leather-bound tomes. Most gratifyingly, though the heat of his fire-breathing was beginning to work its way through his muscles and bones, there was a large open fireplace with a stack of logs piled beside it. And alongside this, positioned to receive the fire's warmth but not any sparks it might produce, lay a large camp bed. It was as if the room's previous occupier had merely stepped out for a moment, forgetting to close the window, and the room had filled up with snow. But how long ago that had happened, he could only guess.

Pulling himself to his feet, Benfro struggled across the room to the fireplace. It was heavy going, as if he were wading through thick mud. His legs were weary beyond compare and every little effort reduced him to breathlessness. Slowly he built a pile of logs in the hearth. They were damp on the outside from the recent thaw, but brittle and dry beneath. All he needed was a little flame to get the thing started and he would have light and heat. But his stomach was empty.

Once more he looked around. The snow was all gone and the water it had turned into was draining steadily away in the direction of a wooden door set into the wall on the far side of the room. He hadn't noticed this before, but it was the only way in or out. The window was far too small for his bulk. There was nothing to eat or drink in the room. He could have opened the window, scooped more snow from the sill – it was piling up against the glass nicely – but somehow he couldn't bring himself to eat more. He was hungry beyond belief and tired beyond reason. All he wanted to do was lie somewhere warm and sleep. He didn't much care about the damp. Breathing in, he tried to squeeze his stomach, to produce just a tiny flame. He broke some of the smaller logs up into dry kindling, splitting them down and down with his talons until they were little more than tapers. He blew on them, hope desperate to win out against reason.

Nothing.

Dispirited, he rolled over until his back was against the inglenook inside the fireplace and stared at the logs. All he wanted was a fire; was that so much to ask? He didn't care how he had got here, or even where here was. He couldn't even worry about how he was going to get back to Corwen's clearing, his home. He just wanted to see flames leaping from the wood, feel their true heat filling the room. He just wanted to sleep.

The crackling noise woke him. He had not dreamed and could not know how long he had been asleep. The light dancing in his eyes confused him at first. Daylight wasn't meant to shift and shimmer so. Slowly he opened his lids and focused on the fire blazing in the hearth. It had not consumed much of the wood he had placed there. Bemused but not ungrateful, he fed it some more and basked in the welcome heat.

The fire spread light through the room, turning the window pane into a slab of black slashed across at a strange angle with white. He could see now that the walls were hewn from rock. The skill of whoever had carved the stone was evident in the fireplace, which was large enough to sit in but whose chimney narrowed quickly, allowing the smoke easy escape but trapping the fire's heat. Overhead, the ceiling rose into a vault whose point, nestling in flickering shadow, was situated over the centre of the room. Directly beneath it, the chair and reading table were positioned to allow both a view out of the window and to receive warmth from the fire.

The bookcase was a huge piece of carved ornamentation, quite unlike anything Benfro had seen in his life. Black as the night, it shone where the firelight struck its ornate fretwork. The bottom half of it was split into three hinged doors with three thick drawers above them. On top of this were eight shelves, each filled with large leather-bound books. He wondered why they had not been damaged by the snow, or even by its recent melting, but a slight reflection gave the reason away. There were two doors, glazed with huge sheets of flawless glass and framed in the same dark carved wood, only so thinly as to be almost invisible.

Benfro stared at all this for a long time, concentrating on just breathing in and out. He still had no strength to explore, even though his curiosity was piqued. He would have done anything for some food. The warmth that had spread through him after breathing the fire had now faded, leaving only the pit of his stomach, abused and empty, for company. Stripped bare, it couldn't even gurgle and groan. At least the wood on the fire seemed to be burning steadily. Although the bed was only feet away, he had not the energy to clamber on to it. He was as comfortable as he would ever be, slumped in the inglenook. It was just a matter of waiting until his strength returned.

And then what? He had no idea where he was, except that it was high up. He wasn't sure how he had come here either, although there was something about the Llinellau he knew he should be remembering. He tried to see them, fully expecting there to be a major intersection at the point where the chair and table were arranged in the centre of the room. There was nothing, or at least there was nothing he could see.

He cast his eyes over the room once more. There was, he fancied, a nexus not far from the window. It was a pale glow, as if the sun were shining down through a tiny hole in the ceiling. But it was still night and there was no moon to make such a mark either. He blinked and the spot was gone. Perhaps it had been his imagination. Certainly it was difficult to think straight when every breath was an effort unrewarded.

He must have dozed off then, for the next thing Benfro knew the sun was shining through the half of the window not blocked by snow, painting a bright square higher up on the ceiling than seemed possible. He felt stronger now, though hungrier than ever, and struggled to uncertain feet. His head was light, and spots sprang into his vision as he fought with the thin air, What should have been a matter of seconds took minutes, but finally he made it, gasping, to the window.

The sill came up to his chest, and the snow against the closed pane reached his chin. With heavy arms he opened the window and pushed this away, trying his best to clear the opening so that he could see out properly. It took far longer than the simple task should have done, and when he was finished he had to lean against the cold stone and try not to retch. He was breathing as hard and fast as he could, and yet it was like there was a stout cotton bag over his head. Finally, when the spots began to clear from his vision, he lifted his head and stuck it out the window.

He could see the ground now, and its distance made his

head spin. The perspective was all wrong, everything too far away. The sun was low in a hazy sky, seeming almost to be below him. Flanking it, he could see a ridge of mountains spreading out like a wall and beneath them was a sea of green, unbroken for countless miles. There was only one place he could be. Mount Arnahi.

Benfro leaned as far as he could out of the window, trying to see where on the mountain he might be. But the walls were too thick and the snow reflected the sunlight with painful brightness. He would have climbed on to the sill, edged his way out and looked down, but the opening was too small and he had nothing like enough energy. Instead he slumped back down on to the floor, cherishing the memory of what he had seen but exhausted beyond the point where he cared if he saw it again or not.

Sitting there, he remembered the wooden door set into the wall just a few paces from him. The floor sloped slightly towards it, narrow channels between the flagstones channelling any water that way. As the wind gusted a little more snow over his head and let it settle on the floor, he realized why. But the door was big enough to let a dragon twice his size through, so there was more to it than just drainage. He crawled across to it on his hands and knees.

By the time he reached the door, he was so tired it was all he could do to lie on his side and stare at the handle, so far above him it seemed unreachable. He gasped for air, forcing the thin substitute that filled the cave into his lungs, fighting against the lightness in his head that threatened to send him back to sleep. Gritting his teeth, Benfro once more hauled himself to his feet, swaying dangerously until he caught hold of the door handle. It was a massive cast-iron loop, and he held on to it as if it were a lifeline. It was almost too heavy to turn, solid with cold and age and rust. He thought it wouldn't budge, and his vision dimmed with the effort. Then, with a final heave, it popped up.

Expecting the door to open into the room, Benfro spent several minutes leaning back, holding on to the latch and cursing his weakness. Only when he stopped for a moment did he realize his error. There was no latch on his side of the door. So he shifted his weight forward, ready for a hard push to get the hinges moving. The door gave easily, as if recently greased, and overbalancing, he pitched forward into the darkness beyond.

'When will he regain consciousness?'

Melyn looked down at the sleeping figure swathed in crisp white linen like a new-born babe. Errol's face was a mess of purple and yellow bruises, one eye swollen completely shut, the other puffy and weeping yellow from the side. His nose had been broken and blood still clotted his nostrils. His lips were split and twice their normal size.

'He's very badly injured,' Usel said. 'I've been keeping him unconscious to aid his recovery.'

'Damn you, man. I need him awake,' Melyn said. 'I need to know what happened to him. And how in the Shepherd's name he came to be in Ruthin's Grove. He's meant to be in Tynhelyg.'

'He'll be no use to you if he's dead,' Usel said, and Melyn wondered why it was he suffered the medic's insolence. He was used to being feared, avoided, respected.

Usel simply treated him as he treated everyone else. But then the man was perhaps the most skilled physician in the Twin Kingdoms. Damn him.

'Well I want to know the moment he's awake enough to talk. And I expect you to heal him, medic.'

'I'll do what I can, Inquisitor,' Usel said. 'But someone's taken a lot of trouble over breaking his ankles. I'm not sure he'll be comfortable walking any great distance again.'

'I don't care about his comfort,' Melyn snarled. 'I just want what's in his head.' He stalked out of the room, almost crashing into a novitiate who was hurrying along the corridor towards the infirmary.

'He's not awake, if you've come to see him,' Melyn said to the cowering boy. 'That fool Usel's got him drugged into a stupor so deep even I can't get anything from him.'

'Actually, Your Grace, it was you I was looking for.' The novitiate held out his trembling hand with a small roll of parchment in it. 'This just arrived by bird from Tynhelyg.'

Melyn snatched the message from the terrified boy, unrolled it and peered at the tiny writing. It was of course coded, and the light in the corridor was far too weak to decipher the scrawl. Frustrated, he limped back through the monastery complex and up into his tower rooms, cursing his age all the way. There, where the afternoon light shone in through the windows, he could spread the parchment out on his desk and begin the laborious task of translation.

Half an hour later he was back in the infirmary, four warrior priests behind him. Usel the medic still tended the boy, aided by the coenobite who had first brought him news of Errol's capture. Both of them looked up in surprise at the inquisitor's sudden return.

'What's he doing here?' Melyn demanded.

'Father Gideon knows more about healing bones than any man alive,' Usel said. 'He's already set Errol's ankles and he's helping me with his ribs. It's a delicate operation.'

Melyn stared at the old man, trying to see into his mind, but it was closed tight. He could tell by the way he stood that Gideon had travelled far and wide, learning many secrets along the way. Not the least of which was how to deflect a casual mind-sweep. Well, if he was a trained medic and could help to keep the boy alive, Melyn would tolerate his presence. At least for now.

'Very well. But I need him conscious.'

'He's not going to wake any time soon,' Usel said.

'Nevertheless, he will wake just as soon as your drugs wear off. You won't give him any more until I've had a chance to speak to him. And just in case your medical sensibilities come before your devotion to the order, these four warrior priests are going to sit and watch.'

Benfro couldn't tell how long he had been unconscious. His first returning awareness was of cold. His feet and hands stung with it. Then, when he tried to move them away from whatever was chilling them, the pain dragged him awake. Every muscle in his body was bruised, or at least that was how it felt when he tried to shift. His head pounded with waves of nausea and his arms felt like they were on back to front.

Slowly, agonizingly, he began to pull himself together.

He had ended up on his front with one arm twisted beneath him. The other was wedged between his body and a cold stone wall. At first he thought he was stuck: certainly any attempt at movement brought waves of agony and not much motion. He managed to extract his arm from underneath him; his weight had cut off the blood flow and he spent some minutes silently screaming as the feeling came back. And all the while his breathing was forced, the thin air still refusing to give him the support he was used to.

He lay against the wall of a small alcove that opened up into a larger cave. The stairs down which he had fallen climbed away with curiously broad low steps, curving in a gentle arc until he could see no further. Beyond him the cave was natural, not carved like the room above. The walls were rough and pitted, and the floor, uneven in the main, was covered in a thick layer of fine gravel. Larger rocks pierced this at random, like strange creatures drowning in a stony sea. The light filtered through from his left, its source hidden around a rocky outcrop that formed one side of the alcove.

A stiff cold breeze filled the cave, brushing past him and on up the stairs. Guiltily Benfro remembered that he had left the window open. The snow would fill the room with the next storm. He wondered how long it had taken to cram it completely.

Weak from hunger and the thin air, cold and bruised, he picked himself up and staggered into the light. Everything hurt, even the pads of his feet as he picked his way over the sharp gravel, but the pain seemed to sharpen his mind, fight off the light-headed weariness that had triggered his fall. The mouth of the cave was wide and tall, big enough to stretch out his wings and not touch the sides, had he the vigour and the inclination. But it was filled halfway up with snow. It flooded into the cave mouth like a mudslide in white, a soft but unyielding barrier to the outside. Through the gap he could see the sun high in a blue-black sky. The heap of snow between him and the outside might have been as big as the mountain itself; there was no way he would be able to climb it and certainly no way he could dig it away.

Dispirited, Benfro turned to look at the rest of the cave. It seemed to go on for ever, stretching into endless darkness. It was just possible that there might be another way out, he thought. So, ignoring the aches from his stomach and the protests from the rest of his battered body, he set off to explore.

He discovered that the more he walked, the easier it became. He still felt weak and breathless, but not with the incapacitating weariness that had been with him since he first arrived in this strange place. The cave carved its way back into the mountain, zigzagging as it went. He expected it to get darker as the snow-filtered light from the entrance was cut off by the endless twists and turns, but the walls gave off an eerie green light of their own. He could not be sure, but he thought the gravel floor might be sloping down very gently. He soon lost all sense of direction with nothing but the rough walls and their random sharp turns to guide him. At least there was only the one passageway, so he would be able to retrace his steps if it became really necessary.

No sooner had he thought this than he came across the

doors. There were three of them, all stout dark wood and of a similar size, material and construction to the one in the top room. Their latches were ornately wrought iron, blackened with age but rust free. One stood directly in front of him, at what was the end of the cave, the other two flanked it on either wall, twenty paces or more apart. Since that was the way he had been going, Benfro opened the central door first.

Beyond it lay a passage only slightly larger than the door itself. It was hewn out of the solid rock in a perfect rounded arch and it speared arrow-straight away from him to a point so far distant he couldn't be sure whether it was light he was seeing or just his imagination. Wind whistled past him, bringing a cold blast from the snow-filled entrance. It caught the door, whipping it from his grasp and slamming it shut. Taking the hint, he turned to his left.

This door opened on blackness. He could see nothing beyond the frame. Again the wind blew, but weaker this time as if the air was less keen to enter the space. It felt like there was a vast open nothingness beyond – something in the way the darkness swallowed the tiny noise that the hinges made. He kicked a little of the sharp gravel into the opening, expecting to hear it rattling down steps or clattering into a wall. Only silence met him. He waited, seconds turning into minutes, his breathing as shallow as he could manage, straining for a sound. When it came, it was very faint, but unmistakably the echoed *ploip* of stones hitting deep water from a great height. Carefully he closed the door.

The third door swung open almost before he reached

it, as if whatever lay beyond wanted to be discovered. Light poured through the opening, warm and welcoming. There was the faintest aroma of cooked food and scrubbed wood that drove all thoughts of caution from Benfro's head. Trying hard not to drool, he stepped into a large room dominated by a long solid table with low benches along either side and a massive carved chair at its head.

'Go and tell the inquisitor the boy's awake.'

Errol heard the words through a sea of numbness. He floated in his head, cocooned from the pain and suffering, which were just memories. Somewhere out there the real world was waiting for him with promises of misery, but for now he could pretend it didn't exist.

'Here, drink this,' a familiar voice said. 'You need to get some fluids back into you.'

Errol felt the touch of a bowl to his lips, and then sweet liquid filled his mouth. He tried to open his eyes, then realized that they were already open. The shapes he had thought random dream images coalesced into the friendly face of Usel.

'Welcome back,' the medic said. 'I thought you were going to sleep for a week.'

'How long?' Errol tried to say, but his throat was still too dry. He reached up and took the bowl, nearly dropping it as the agony returned. Usel caught it, spilling only a little on the white sheets.

'There's something in here for the pain,' the medic said, holding up the bowl once more. 'I'd far rather put you out completely, but Melyn won't allow it. He wants to speak to you. In fact he's wanted to speak to you for quite some time now.'

'I can't hide from him.' Every word brought with it a wince of pain. 'I can't think straight. I'm not even sure how I got here.'

'No one is, Errol. That's the problem,' Usel said. 'Word's going round that Ballah's men dumped you in Ruthin's Grove to show that they could move about here unnoticed. I'd stick to that if I were you.'

Usel stood, placing the empty bowl on a small table beside the bed. For the first time Errol noticed that three warrior priests were standing at the far end of the room, staring at him.

'I have to go now,' Usel said.

'Where?' A sudden terror surged through Errol at the thought of being left alone with the inquisitor. 'You'll be coming back?'

'Of course,' Usel said, and somehow Errol knew he was lying. 'And don't worry. Andro's about as well, He'll make sure you're given all the time you need to recover.'

Errol wanted to say more, but the medic had turned away. He watched him cross the room and say something quietly to the warrior priests. They stepped aside and he left. Then they once more formed up in front of the door.

'My ankles are both broken,' Errol said, unsure whether his weak words would carry across the infirmary. 'I'm not going anywhere.' He had meant it as a joke, but it rebounded on him. The painkilling draught was working its magic on him, but he knew that he was trapped in this bed as surely as he had been trapped in the torture chair in Ballah's dungeons.

How had he got to Ruthin's Grove? His mind cleared slightly as the pain dulled, but his thoughts were also slowing down, made sluggish by the potion. He remembered being dragged through the palace out into the courtyard. He remembered the people as a faceless, amorphous mass save for the major domo and the grinning axeman. And he remembered a pale worried face at the window in the West Tower. Iolwen turning away. Not Iolwen but Martha. Or was it Iolwen after all? And the lines going everywhere. Anywhere but where he was. It was simple to get away from trouble; he just had to remember how it was done.

A noise in the corridor snapped the warrior priests to attention. Errol could hear the hurried approach of many feet. He knew the inquisitor was coming, and he knew that the old man would see straight into his thoughts and memories. He hadn't the strength to build a world in his mind for Melyn to see, hadn't the clarity of thinking. His confusion would be his undoing. He had to escape. If he could just remember how.

As if coming to his aid, the lines swam into his vision. They criss-crossed the room, an intricate web of power and life, each one a link to limitless possibilities. He had to find a place to go, choose one only from the clamouring multitude. But the noise of approaching doom was louder now, and as he struggled with his task Errol watched one of his guards turn to open the door.

For the briefest of instants he thought he saw Melyn approaching along the corridor. Then something clicked in his head and everything turned upside down.

*

There were plates and cutlery made from the finest silver and wrought with the same delicate patterns as the candelabra that illuminated the scene. Two places were laid, one at the head of the table, the other to its right. The smell of cooking meat made his stomach gurgle in anticipation, but there was no food. Benfro slid himself on to the bench in front of the lesser place setting. It didn't seem right to assume he could take the head of the table.

Pain twisted in his stomach, an acid burning that felt like it was wearing its way out through his intestines and the leathery skin of his stomach. He belched a sour burp that etched his throat and spread fire out across his chest. Anything at that point would have been good, even water, and he reached greedily for the huge goblet just in front of his right hand.

To his surprise it was full not of water but of wine. Benfro had only ever drunk wine once before. Not even Meirionydd had dared to thwart his mother's edict that he was too young for it. When he had finally managed to steal a few dregs from the bottom of Sir Frynwy's barrel, it had been an unpleasant sour-tasting liquid full of bitter glass-hard shards. Just remembering the incident made him feel ill.

This wine was nothing like that.

Its flavour brought to mind those stolen gulps, but there was none of the sourness. Instead this wine was thick and rich, like crushed raspberries with an underlying tartness that was at once refreshing and stimulating. He sipped, resisting the urge to tip the whole cup down his throat. The liquid coated his mouth and slid down his gullet, soothing the burning as it exploded into his empty stomach. Try as hard as he could to exercise restraint, the goblet was soon empty, and he placed it down where he had found it with a tinge of disappointment.

Hunger still gnawed at him, and while wine was perhaps not the best thing he could take to assuage it, nothing else seemed available. There was another goblet, larger than the one he had emptied, at the place setting at the head of the table. Since to the best of his knowledge he was alone on the mountain, he slid up the bench and reached for it.

Something stopped his hand, and a burning sensation whipped through his fingers and up his arm. The candles flared, going from yellow-orange to blue before settling back again as he withdrew his hand. He tried again, and the same thing happened. On a whim, he slid off the end of the bench and approached the great chair. It would have been comfortable for a dragon twice his size. A deep velvet cushion covered the seat and the arms were carved from great chunks of hard black wood, topped with padded leather. The back of the chair reached up for the dark ceiling like some forbidding edifice, with twin spires that looked like they could wound the sky. There was no way that he could move such an enormous seat. Yet it sat far enough from the table to allow access. Expecting to be rebuffed, as his hand had been when he reached for the wine, Benfro carefully stepped up to the great throne and clambered into the seat.

It was very comfortable, almost soothing to his aching muscles. He had expected it to be too big, and yet it appeared to be just the right size. Somehow it, or the table, had moved, as his legs were now tucked under the boards, the place setting with its full goblet within easy reach. He stretched for the wine, fingers tentative as he tensed himself for the shock which didn't come.

If the wine that he had drunk before was a revelation, the blood-red liquid he sipped this time was even more exquisite. Maybe it was the combination of the comfortable chair and the alcohol, but with each swallowed mouthful his breathing became less laboured, the very air seeming to thicken. Too soon the goblet was empty, and he placed it back on the table with an aching regret that he had not eked it out more. To his surprise, by the flickering light of the candelabra he watched the empty vessel refill. The wine in it tasted just as good as it had the first time, but he wished there was some food to go with it.

No sooner was the thought in his head than the silver platter in front of him was heaped with roasted meats. Beside it a smaller plate held dumplings, batter puddings and root vegetables. A silver jug, which he could have sworn was not there moments before, steamed with the heady aroma of rich gravy. Not one to pass up a gift, however unlikely it might appear, he grabbed a fork and began shovelling the food into his face.

Benfro was unaware of the subtle flavours of the unfamiliar foods before him; neither did he care that he could not name most of what he ate. Such was his hunger that he just needed to get as much in as possible. Perhaps, in the back of his mind, he was aware that this meal was magical, impossible, and might disappear at any moment. Yet he could feel the weight in his stomach and the numbness crawling over his skin as the wine began to have an effect. He took another swig and felt his worries and cares slipping away.

Finally the meal was over. Benfro felt a passing sadness as the plates disappeared and the goblet no longer refilled itself. Still, he was more full of food than he could ever remember. The thought of moving filled him with dread, so he just sat there, lolling back in the great throne and enjoying the sensation of bloat. He was weary beyond compare and looked around the room for somewhere he might sleep. There was nowhere that recommended itself to him. The floor was packed dirt with the occasional sharp boulder poking up through it. The walls were jagged and uneven. Only the chair itself was comfortable, but not for sleeping.

He remembered the bed in the upper room. The fire might still be burning, he supposed. He tried to stand, thinking that after such a splendid meal he might have enough energy to climb the stairs down which he had earlier tumbled. The table seemed to edge away from him, shrinking rather than moving, but as he levered his suddenly heavy body off the seat, the world started to spin. His head was numb, uncomprehending, and it was all he could manage to do to push himself back into the chair, slumping against one of its massive arms. Perhaps sleeping here would not be such a bad thing after all.

Yet the bed still called to him. He could see it in his mind's eye, a soft flat cushion by the fire that was surely warm and dry and welcoming. In his stupor he glanced about the room and noticed, for the first time since he had arrived, the Llinellau Grym criss-crossing their way about him. In the centre of the room, under the table, though he could somehow see right through, a pair of thick white bands intersected, but the greatest lines crossed under his chair. He couldn't see them through his own body, but he could feel them. They hummed with a low sound, like the bees busying themselves in the laurel bushes where he used to hide when Frecknock was on the warpath. It was difficult to focus on anything – images kept slipping from his gaze, splitting in two and going off in opposite directions. He could see the dining table, but he could see the reading desk as well. By the wall there was a low dresser, but it was the bookcase too. The candles flickered and burned in their candelabra just where the fire was. His seat was a massive ornately carved chair, and yet it was the simple chair in the upper room.

Snapping his head up as if someone had poked him with a pointed stick, Benfro woozily looked from side to side. Something ice-cold played across the back of his neck and head. Turning and trying to rest his weight on the side of the throne, he fell sideways. Someone had removed the arm. And why was he lying in a pile of snow? Why was he staring up at a window, pulled open to reveal a small square of evening sky against a frozen white border.

Slowly it dawned on him what had happened. Drunk from the wine, he had ridden the Llinellau. For some reason he could not understand, Benfro found that incredibly funny. He started to chuckle, and the sound just made things worse. He gasped for breath, his head reeling from too much wine and the thin air, yet all he could do was lie in the snow and laugh. Not even the memory of his mother's death could stop him as the fear and frustration and anger boiled out of him in a hysteria far more potent than tears could ever be.

21

There is an old saying among the simple farmers of the Hendry: 'Never accept a dragon's gift.' In its most basic form it simply means be wary of unexpected generosity, which may come with strings attached. Quite why it is a dragon's gift that should be denied, rather than a Llanwennog's it is hard to say. Certainly the wars and enmity between King Balwen's people and our barbarian neighbours to the north-east have been a fact of life for so long that they are now a part of our language. Who has never heard their mother call out, 'Behave or you'll be sent to Llanwennog,' or cursed a travelling merchant for peddling shoddy goods with, 'Never was a Llanwennog so fair.'? And yet it is dragons who are seen as the epitome of untrustworthiness.

Father Charmoise, *Dragons' Tales*

Benfro woke with what felt like a thunderstorm raging inside his head. His mouth was full of sand and his tongue had swollen to twice its normal size overnight. He tried to move and the drumming increased tenfold. Pain lanced through him as if his brain had grown too big for his skull. Keeping still minimized the discomfort, so he kept still.

He could hear the fire's crackling and feel its heat on his side. For a long while he couldn't work out where he was. It was unlike his mother to rise early and stoke the fire. Normally she would have shooed him out of bed, chided him for sleeping when there was wood to be collected, water to fetch and herbs to be sorted. He waited for her footstep, the subtle change in the surroundings that meant she was near. He wanted to tell her of his headache, ask her for something to take the pain away. More than anything else he wanted just to see her, to hug her, to know she was there. And it was then that he remembered the inquisitor and the sword of flame appearing in the air. He remembered the fear that paralysed him and the dead, burned remains of the villagers. He remembered everything.

With a groan as much of weary self-pity as of the pain of his hangover Benfro rolled over on the bed until he could see the fire and the rest of the room. It was almost exactly as he had uncovered it the day before except that the chair was lying on its side. Had he knocked it over? He could remember only vague disjointed images from his meal the night before, and laughing uncontrollably, painfully, unable to stop.

He tried to sit up, but quickly decided that was a bad idea. Besides, he told himself, the bed was comfortable. Perhaps if he slept some more the pain would go away and he would be able to think straight.

It was much later when he woke for the second time. His head ached less, but the pain had been replaced with a terrible thirst that clenched his throat almost as tight as the thin air. Sitting up was less fraught this time, although his head still felt both like it was muffled in a pillow and at the same time edged with flame. He stood, crossed the room unsteadily to the window and opened it wide. Scoops of snow shovelled into his mouth brought blessed relief, and he stuck his head out of the window, cramming it as deep into the miniature snowdrift as he could manage. The cold bit at his ears and chilled the scales on his face, fighting the fire in his head. It was wonderful.

Closing the window, Benfro turned back to the warmth of the fire, noticing as he did so the writing table. He righted the large comfortable-looking chair, sat himself down and dropped his elbows on to the table. There was a single large sheet of parchment laid out on it, but he could not read it by the light from the fire.

As if he had wished for them, lighted candles appeared in the twin sconces fixed to either side of the table. The writing on the parchment was faded almost to nothing, but peering at it closely, his eyes squinting at the challenge, he could just about make out the words, written in the archaic script his mother had taught him for labelling herbs and potions.

Evening is here already and tomorrow I go to deal with my brother's spiteful legacy. The men are everywhere, multiplying as only their kind can. And now they are possessed of an intelligence and magical ability that puts them head to head with the most powerful of my warriors. I have felt Palisander's dying thoughts, heard the screams of Myfanwy and Geraint. It is as if these creatures knew all along what we did to them, how we kept them simple-minded to act as our unquestioning slaves. Only now they have the wherewithal to take their revenge.

I will track down their leader, this so-called king. The scrying window has already shown me where they mass. Like flies around a rotting carcass, they flock to my brother's most foul palace, his throne in its candled hall of pompous grandiosity. The very thought of that place brings a cold rage to my scales. Was it not enough that we split the world? Not enough for him to take his weak minions away from my sight but he had to put this abomination, this stain, on the land he left behind? How childish he proves himself, as ever he was, to destroy that which he cannot have, lest anyone else gain pleasure from it.

There was a space in the parchment then, as if a picture was intended. Perhaps the author had not found the time to complete his tale. Benfro peered hard at the smooth yellowing surface, searching for any sign that something had been written or drawn, but it was blank the width of his hand. When the words continued, the writing was not so neat, not so assured.

What has the fool done? How could he have given so much power to creatures that cannot know remorse, that have no guilt, no shame, no mercy? They tap the Grym like adepts, wield blades of fire that cut through stone and paralyse even the strongest-willed with irrational fear. Worse, he has given them an insatiable hunger – for power, for knowledge, for conquest. They covet our jewels yet lack the understanding of how to use them. They eschew the reckoning and take our memories raw. Would that I could take solace in the knowledge that this will be their undoing. Yet there are so many of them and multiplying every day. They breed so fast, grow to adulthood in the blinking of an eye. We are outnumbered a thousand to one. I fear they will destroy us all before we can overcome them.

At the bottom of the parchment the writing was spidery and blotched, as if by a different hand altogether. This part had been written at speed, Benfro could tell, for he had often been chastised by his mother for rushing his letter work, desperate to finish so he could get outside. This hand could almost have been his own, were it not for the obvious age of the ink.

Am I defeated? Is this what the world will become? I, who once proudly held sway over half a world, am reduced to fleeing from a man? And yet never have I met with such ferocity, such strength, such unrestrained joy in the wielding of absolute power for absolute cruelty.

They have a king now, these men. How quickly they organize themselves into a parody of civilization. I sought to negotiate with him, to put an end to our needless war. We are few and do not need to eat their meat if they do not wish to share. A wily creature King Balwen, he suggested we meet at my brother's palace. Only when I arrived at that hateful place, that dreadful town, did I realize this was where he had set up his court. The nerve of him, a creature scarce half again as big as my head, sitting on my brother's absurd throne in his ostentatious hall. I am always at my weakest in that place, and he must have known that. I could feel him testing me as we spoke, trying to probe my mind, but he is not as skilful as he would like to think. His pathetic fumblings left him wide open to my suggestion.

So the challenge is made. The day after tomorrow we will meet on the field at Cae Felin. He will send his most powerful inquisitor to do battle, and when I defeat him, another will take his place. I do not know how many he has, but even as ruthless and foolhardy a creature as this self-crowned king will think twice when twenty of his most powerful warriors lie dead at his feet.

But what if I should fail? These inquisitors are formidable foes who do not hold with the rules of etiquette and chivalry. They have slaughtered innocents in their sleep, bashed open their skulls for the dangerous treasure within. They have drunk the blood of my cousins and found a taste for it. As I sit here and contemplate their next move, I cannot help but wonder how they will try to cheat. If they all attack at once, can I withstand such an onslaught?

I must not dwell on such impossibilities. I will prevail as I have always done. But this retreat is not the place to rest and gather my strength. I will return to the Silent Stone, where it all began, where my foolhardy brother broke our pact and set this dreadful wheel in motion. Ammorgwm, I write these words for you, wherever you have gone. I fear that my brother has brought about the destruction of our kind even as he has built himself his own little world to rule. The door is open, though it should have been closed. Let us pray the men never find it.

Benfro stared at the parchment, blinking occasionally but otherwise motionless. He was reading words written by Magog more than two thousand years ago. The greatest dragon ever to live had left this mountain retreat and gone back to his first home to prepare for the fight which should have ended the war between dragons and men. But King Balwen had planted doubt in the mind of the greatest dragon ever to live. Was it not possible that he had also found out the secret location of the Silent Stone? And if a sentient creature could not enter the clearing without being invited, what was to stop a mindless beast, a lammergeyer enraged and guided by the king's meddling, from flying in and attacking the resting mage?

'Finally, you've worked it out.'

Benfro looked up from the table and parchment to see who had spoken. To his astonishment a great dragon stood between him and the fire. Had he been more observant, he would have noticed that he could still feel the heat of the flames, even though the image appeared solid. But it was impossible to notice anything else when confronted, in a small room, by the greatest dragon that had ever lived. Magog, Son of the Summer Moon.

'Now all you have to do is take my revenge.'

The floor was stone, hard and cold. Errol shivered in the feverish darkness, trying to work out where he was. He should have been in a bed in the infirmary. Or should he have been kneeling at a block in Tynhelyg, waiting for the executioner to chop off his head? He tried to look around, but the effort and pain of lifting himself off the ground was almost too much. Slowly he inched himself on to his side the better to take in his surroundings.

It was a small room with stone walls and thin windows, little more than arrow slits, which let in a whistling draught. Outside it was dark; inside the only light came from two fat tallow candles that flickered on a stone altar. Something else glowed there, reflecting the light in red, but from his position on the floor Errol couldn't see what it was. On the far side of the room a heavy oak door stood closed. It might as well have been a mile away for all that he could hope to reach it, but Errol gritted his teeth against the pain in his ankles and ribs and set about dragging himself over the threadbare rug towards it.

'Don't bother,' a voice said. 'You'll only find Captain Osgal on the other side.'

Errol looked around sharply, nearly passing out as his brain struggled to keep up with the motion. When he saw the face he knew he was going to see, he let himself collapse to the floor, defeated.

'I was going to have the warrior priests who were meant to be guarding you thrown into the Faaeren Chasm, but it seems they really weren't to blame,' Melyn said. He was sitting in a simple wooden chair in the shadows at the back of the room. 'Now perhaps you'd like to explain to me how a boy with two broken ankles can get from the infirmary to my private chapel in the blinking of an eye?'

'I don't know,' Errol said.

'Oh, but I think you do.' Melyn stood, opened the door and called in the captain. 'And you're going to tell me all about it.'

Errol could taste Osgal's nervousness at being summoned into the private chapel. This was a place only for inquisitors. His astonishment at seeing Errol lying on the floor was even more apparent, but like the professional soldier he was, he recovered quickly, hefting Errol over his shoulder like a dead ewe and following the inquisitor out.

They went up to Melyn's private chambers, which were at least warmer than the chapel. Errol winced as he was dumped into a hard wooden chair, almost cried out when Osgal produced some rope and tied his arms and legs. The captain then held his mouth open while Melyn poured wine straight from a pitcher down his throat. He choked on the sharp liquid, but swallowed it gratefully. His throat was dry, his stomach empty, and he really didn't care what happened to him any more, just as long as the pain stopped soon.

It wasn't long before the wine began to take effect. Errol found it more difficult to keep his eyes focused. His thoughts were slippery like eels in a spring river and he found that the pain was something he could ignore, at least for now.

'Tell me what happened in Tynhelyg,' Melyn said after what seemed to be a very long time. Errol felt sleepy, but he managed to open his eyes enough to look at the inquisitor.

'Dondal turned me in.' He tried hard not to slur his words. 'Ballah locked me up inna Wes' Tower. I met Iolwen there. She's pretty but sad. Then he broke my ankles an' had my head chopped off. Or somethin' like that.' For some reason this seemed very funny to Errol, so he laughed, then stopped when he saw the look on the inquisitor's face. 'What happened to you?' he asked Melyn, wondering inside why he was behaving the way he was. 'Y' look like a dragon jus' belched in y' face.'

The shock in his brain was like a faceful of icy water. The inquisitor's fury was like a tempest, blowing through his memories, smashing open doors and overturning the furniture. Still fuddled by the mixture of pain-relieving draught and strong red wine, Errol could only wither under the onslaught. He had no time to construct a false memory and was too tired anyway to even begin.

Almost idly, a spectator to the plunder of his memories, Errol wondered why the inquisitor had suddenly flown into a rage. It had to have been what he'd said, and to be honest with himself he didn't know why he had said it. It sounded like a good little aphorism, but he couldn't recall having heard anyone use it before. But when he thought about it, the inquisitor had just recently been belched in the face by a dragon. He could see the incident and feel the horror and surprise as Melyn lost his grip on the aethereal dragon. On Benfro.

With a start Errol realized he was looking at Melyn's memories. Whatever magic the inquisitor used to get into his mind, it was obviously a two-way street. He wondered what else was going through his tormentor's mind, and an image of Queen Beulah appeared in front of him. No, not Queen Beulah. Though her face was similar, this was a different woman – older, naked and in the throes of passion.

'Get out of my head!' Errol heard the words an instant before something hard smashed into the side of his face, knocking him into temporary senselessness. When he came round, it was to the familiar pain as his bonds were roughly untied. Captain Osgal once more hauled him up and threw him over his shoulder.

'Take him away,' Errol heard the inquisitor say through the foggy blur of his drunken, drugged mind.

'What shall I do with him, Your Grace?' Osgal asked, his deep voice reverberating through Errol where his head lay against the captain's back. Melyn's answer came instantly, without time for hesitation or thought.

'Cast him into the chasm at first light.'

'Master Magog, how is it you create the flame for the fire and candles?' Benfro asked. They sat at the dining table in the room he had explored earlier. Once more there had been a feast, and the food had gone some way to damping down the raging headache he still felt. Full almost to bursting point with questions, this was the first that Benfro had managed to pluck from the confusion of his mind.

Magog looked up from his plate of steaming stew, swallowed and placed his fork back on the table. With deliberate, almost exaggerated slowness, he raised a napkin to his mouth and dabbed at his lips before placing it alongside his fork. When he was satisfied all was neat and tidy, the mage raised one bony taloned hand, palm upwards and fingers slightly bent.

'Like this?' he asked, and a perfect sphere of light appeared, hovering within his grasp without actually touching any part of his hand. It was flame, Benfro could tell, but not like anything he had ever seen before. It flickered within itself, faint patterns swirling around like creatures chasing their own tails.

'Here, you take it.' The dragon mage uncurled his fingers towards Benfro. The orb rolled out of his hand and floated, spinning slowly, towards him. Instinctively he reached for it, cupping his hand as he had seen Magog do to receive the gift. But instead of hovering above his hand, it settled into his palm. Pain seared through the leathery skin as an incredible heat burned him.

He yelped, pulling away from the orb as quickly as he could. 'That hurts.'

'It's fire,' Magog countered, an evil laugh in his voice. 'What do you expect?'

'But how . . . ?' Benfro said, shoving his burned hand into the jug of water that sat by his place.

'Observe.' The mage curled his hand into a fist and lifted it towards him. The glowing ball of fire rose and sped through the air. As it neared him, he opened his hand again, palm out towards the fiery orb. It slowed, then stopped an inch from his skin, and once more sat cupped but untouched in his outstretched hand.

'How did you do that?'

'Were you not watching?'

'I saw, but I don't know how you did it.' Benfro realized his mistake even as he uttered the words. Corwen always asked him to describe what he saw, not expecting him to use just his eyes. Magog was trying to encourage him to use his other senses, to see the Llinellau and possibly something more.

'Please, could you do it again. I'll try to be more observant.'

'Very well.' Magog went through the trick again. First he extinguished the existing flame, blowing it out with a theatrical puff. Then he conjured another into being and rolled it through the air towards his young apprentice. Benfro watched closely, but not the action itself. Rather he was looking to see if his master manipulated the Llinellau in any way. What he saw was not what he was expecting at all.

The image of Magog glowed all around, his aura a tight shadow of red light covering him like a well fitting coat. Benfro was not adept at reading auras. He knew that forest animals had a certain life force around them, as did the trees and other plants. He could see their glow, but it didn't extend out from them as was the case with sentient beings and was nothing at all like the magnificent swirl of colours he had seen in his own reflection. Magog looked more like a simple beast than the greatest mage that had ever lived.

Benfro looked down at his own arms and saw that they too were clothed in a thick layer of light. His was a rainbow of hues, pulsing and swirling as he bent his elbows and flexed his hands. Bringing his two index fingers together so that the talons almost touched, he could see the aura swell and distend, reaching out to make the connection long before any physical contact occurred. He pulled his hands apart and the light stretched, getting thinner and thinner like some strange goo, the colours fading into white before the bond was broken. He could actually feel the tension snap as he brushed his fingers past each other again and again without ever touching.

'Now take the orb,' Magog said, and Benfro looked up. The ball of fire was stationary, floating in the air just below his head height. It was a blaze of brilliant light in his enhanced vision, awash with whites and yellows and oranges, all undercut with that same angry red that surrounded its creator. And, stretching through the dark air between mage and ball, the thinnest of glowing strings connected the two together.

Benfro reached up, not touching the flame but feeling its heat. It was hard to tell where the fire ended and the aura began, but as he studied it and as his eyes grew accustomed to the glare, so he began to make out the boundary. Closer, he brought one cupped hand up until his own aura just began to caress the fringes of the orb. And then something clicked in his head.

It was as if he had always known how to do it. He couldn't imagine a time when he had not. It was simplicity in itself to guide the ball with his own aura. He passed it from hand to hand, marvelling at the way it tingled but didn't burn.

'Now send it back to me,' the dragon mage said, startling Benfro into nearly dropping the ball. He had become so wrapped up in it that he had forgotten where he was and what he was doing. Benfro opened his hand to roll the ball away, as he had seen his master do, but nothing happened. It didn't roll, didn't drop, just sat there, stuck to his palm by the thickness of its aura.

He tried to push it away with his other hand, which worked, but instead of floating through the air, the orb simply rolled off and fell on to the tabletop, where it started to burn through the wood. Swiftly Benfro scooped it up again and dashed water from his jug over the charred mark. He was doing something wrong, but what?

Looking up at Magog, he could see that the thin cord connecting him with the fire was gone. Had that been the key? Did he have to extend his aura around the flame, use that to both hold it aloft and push it along? He tried to imagine what that would feel like, tried to imagine the thick multicoloured coating around his hands and arms swelling. To his surprise, it did, forcing the orb up from his hand. He opened his fingers and extended the field out from them. The fire rolled slowly along the colourful trail. Further and further he extended his reach towards his master, feeling the flow around him. The room was forgotten, his meal and the burn on the table distant memories. All his concentration was focused on the fire and the fading lines of his aura stretching away from his hand.

He was aware that his arm was heavy, almost shaking with the effort even though earlier the ball had felt almost weightless. It rolled so slowly and his master was sitting so far away, not even stretching to take back his conjured fire. Still he would not fail now. He was determined to succeed.

It was as if time had stopped. Magog was smiling slightly with that enigmatic expression that Benfro could never quite read. Was it encouragement or a sneer at his clumsiness? He was so motionless as to be almost a statue; only the thin pulsing red light around him signified that there was sentience there at all, and not very much at that. It was as if he wasn't really there at all.

Benfro's eyes scanned the image, seeing for the first time how his master tapped into the Grym. Red spilled down the normally pristine whiteness where he connected with the Llinellau. In most directions the lines faded back to their normal white within a few paces of the great dragon, but one line stayed deepest crimson, spearing out through the door. And fainter than the lines themselves, barely visible at all, a thin rose cord snaked through the air from Magog, straight towards him.

Dawn wasn't far off. The blackness of light was fading to reveal the distant details of jagged peak and scrubby tree-strewn gorge. Stars peeping through gaps in the clouds seemed pale, as if a night of twinkling had worn them out and they needed a day to recuperate. This was the quiet hour, when the wind died away to nothing and the only noise was the occasional screech of an owl hurrying home.

Errol wanted nothing more than to rest his head, to lie somewhere still and warm and let the trouble of the past weeks, months, years roll away from him. He wanted to surrender himself to oblivion, but even that was denied him. Slung over Captain Osgal's shoulder, he felt every step as a jarring, agonizing pain in his shattered ankles. Each breath was a trial, and his encounter with the inquisitor and his wine had left his head feeling like a battleground picked over by carrion birds.

They were going to throw him into the Faaeren Chasm. Eight hundred feet straight down on to jagged rocks. And after all he had been through, he couldn't care less. If it meant the pain would end, he welcomed it.

But that was just the melancholy talking, the after-effects of the potion. He didn't really want to die, just to rest a while. He longed to be free of these people who wanted only to use him. He would happily have walked away from the Twin Kingdoms and Llanwennog, gone so far away that no one need ever worry about him coming back. But for some reason he couldn't begin to understand, they didn't want that. They didn't want him to be happy. They didn't want him to find Martha. They wanted rid of him completely, and the best way they knew of doing that was to throw him off a cliff.

The Faaeren Chasm was reserved for the worst traitors, the wilful failures and those who broke the most sacred laws of the Order of the High Ffrydd. Setting foot inside the inquisitor's chapel without an invitation was enough to have him executed, but Errol knew what had pushed

Melyn over the edge. He'd felt it just before the old man hit him with the empty wine pitcher. Melyn had been afraid of him because Errol had turned his magic back on himself. He had waded into the inquisitor's mind and seen dreadful things. Melyn couldn't allow anyone with that kind of ability to stay alive. And so he was to be executed.

They were going to throw him into the Faaeren Chasm. Osgal was making his way up narrow steps hewn into the rock face. Up ahead the plateau looking out over the gorge was shiny with morning dew. Technically the other side of the chasm was Llanwennog land, though nobody lived in the mountains. Neither could you cross anywhere for two days' ride in either direction. The cliffs plunged into the earth as if some giant had hit the mountains with a hammer the size of the moon, splitting them apart in a jagged line. And here, at Emmass Fawr, was the highest point.

Errol didn't struggle as they reached the plateau; there was no point. Even if he had managed to escape Osgal, he couldn't walk. Ballah's torturer had seen to that quite effectively. But he would have liked there to have been a little ceremony at his death, a pause perhaps and maybe a few words. As it was he scarcely had time to register the change in the captain's pace before he was pitched forward and over the edge, like a basket of night soil thrown from a window into the street without so much as a gardyloo.

22

An apt pupil should always be encouraged. Those who show talent for magic must not be held back waiting for others of their age to catch up, lest they become bored and attempt dangerous conjurings. Even so it may be that some pupils are blessed with skill beyond their understanding. This is a perilous situation and must be handled with care. If you suspect you have a student with such ability, test him with magics he should not be able to perform. Explain to him the more esoteric and complicated procedures then have him attempt them while you supervise closely. Failure at this point will likely fuel the pupil's ambition to succeed and give to him a focus for his energies that will keep him from exploring further unsupervised.

If he should succeed at the task you set him, then it may become necessary to dampen his magics with your own. Such a pupil will be a great and powerful mage if he can be protected from the fatal follies into which his youth and inexperience must inevitably lead him. Go carefully into his dreams and build a wall around the memories of his success. But be careful. The dreams of those powerful in the Grym are a strange and unsettling place.

Aderyn, *Educational Notes for the Young*

Melyn sat in his study, a full goblet of wine in his hand. He had been holding it for at least an hour, watching the light seeping through the windows and wondering whether he had done the right thing. Such self-doubt was a new feeling for him, but he had never come across such a dangerous enigma as Errol before. The boy had walked into his mind like it was open house. And the image he had plucked out – Queen Ellyn in her prime. When both of them had been young and foolish. Melyn had thought he had erased the memory. So how had the boy stumbled upon it so readily?

No, he was better off dead. It wasn't as if he was any use as a spy any more. Not now every nobleman in Tynhelyg knew what he looked like. And if that meant Usel lost a potential apprentice, well that was what the medic got for being so disrespectful.

Melyn called in his guard, putting the goblet down as the man entered. He was one of Osgal's troop, but for the life of him the inquisitor couldn't remember his name.

'Go and find Usel,' he said. The guard nodded his assent and disappeared. A moment later Melyn got up and followed him out. It would take at least half an hour for the message to get down to the infirmary, another for the man to return. Meanwhile he would go to the chapel and pray to the Shepherd for Errol's soul.

The chapel was cold in the pre-dawn, the candles still burning on the altar. Melyn took Brynceri's ringed finger from the reliquary and placed it between the two flames, then knelt down. He could feel the stiffness in his joints, but he pushed the discomfort aside and tried to open his mind to his god.

It wasn't long before he felt a presence in the room. His heart soared with joy at the thought of being once more blessed. To talk with the Shepherd was to gain his youth and vigour again. But this was somehow different. He could still feel the aches and pains, still sense the chill of the draught from window to door, and yet undeniably a presence had entered the room.

Melyn tried to relax, remembering the teachings of his old quaister so many years ago. There was no point trying to force the Shepherd to come. If he wanted to, he would and in whatever form he saw fit.

Then he heard a low moan behind him.

The inquisitor's anger mounted inside him again as he rose, made the sign of the crook and turned to face whoever had dared to break one of the sacred laws of the order.

Lying sprawled on the floor, blood leaking from his nose and pooling on the stone, unconscious and pale as a freshly laundered sheet, was Errol Ramsbottom.

Melyn looked at the boy, knelt down and shook him. He looked like he'd hit his face with some force, almost as if he'd been thrown to the stone floor. His breathing was shallow and ragged, his skin flaccid and cold. Quickly Melyn hauled him up, marvelling at how slight he was, and carried him from the chapel. Earlier he had wanted Errol dead, had just wanted to be rid of him, but now he realized that the boy was too much of a mystery to discard so lightly. He had an ability unique in all of Gwlad, and Melyn would not rest until he had uncovered the secret of how it was done. He thanked the Shepherd for showing him the foolishness of his earlier rash actions. Here potentially was power and magic such as he had never dreamed of.

As he carried the unconscious Errol along the corridor towards his private chambers, Melyn met the guard running towards him.

'I hope the medic's just behind you,' he growled at the anonymous man, ignoring the way he stared goggle-eyed at the boy in his arms. 'This lad needs attention and fast.'

'Your Grace, I came as quickly as I could,' the guard said. 'I've searched the infirmary and his rooms. Usel is gone.'

The crash of the fireball landing in Magog's dinner brought Benfro back to himself. He was suddenly breathless again and very weary. Little beads of sweat pricked out around his scales and the glands beside his eyes. He was filled with confusion as one half of his brain tried to process what he had seen and the other tried desperately to pigeonhole it away before anyone else knew what he was thinking about.

'So close, young Benfro.' Magog extinguished the flame with a wave of his hand. 'But not perfect yet. Still an admirable attempt. It's just a pity you let your mind wander. You must learn to be more disciplined about your work, learn to focus.'

Benfro reached for his goblet, wishing that there was something a little stronger than water in it this time. He should not have been shocked when the liquid he gulped down was wine, but he still managed to choke on it. He wiped the dribbles from his face before taking a more measured drink, feeling the magic liquid warm him all the way down to his stomach. It dulled the worry in his mind as well, quelling some of his confusion while adding a different bewilderment of its own, a pleasant befuddlement.

The distraction was complete as pudding appeared in the form of a vast bowl of fruit and berries, most of which he could name only from pictures he had seen in books. Despite having eaten well, Benfro found that he was incredibly hungry still. He fell upon the fruit, shovelling it into his mouth as quickly as he could manage, barely tasting anything in his haste. It was only when his plate was nearly empty that he realized he had been eating summer produce.

'How can you get these things?' he asked, picking a melon seed from between his fangs with a talon. 'Surely they won't grow in winter.'

'It's not winter everywhere, Benfro,' Magog explained in his long-suffering teacher's tone.

'I don't understand,' Benfro said. 'It's winter outside.'

'And on the other side of Gwlad it's summer,' Magog said. 'And in the middle of the world it's always summer, always hot. At either end of the world it's cold. This is the way the world works.'

'Oh' was all he could think of to reply. Then something occurred to him. 'Is this place near the end of the world then?'

Magog put down his melon rind. 'Not particularly, no,' he said. 'Mount Arnahi is at about the same latitude as Tynhelyg in Llanwennog, but much, much higher. That's why the air's so thin and why it's so cold in winter. I'm surprised Sir Frynwy taught you nothing of this. He came from a family of renowned travellers and adventurers.'

'He never said anything of having travelled,' Benfro said. 'He seemed, I don't know, too old to go very far. My mother used to make poultices for him, to help soothe his aching joints.'

'Your youth narrows your mind, Benfro,' Magog said. 'Sir Frynwy had lived more than a thousand years before you were born, yet you see him only in terms of the time you knew him. Is that how you look at everything?'

'I . . . I don't know.' Benfro had been aware of the age of the villagers, but only in the same way as he had been aware of his feet. They were old – that was all that mattered. He had never really considered that they had had lives before he was around.

'It's not something over which you need concern yourself.' Magog cut into his thoughts in much the same way that Corwen had done, as if he could see them like runes on a parchment. 'Only something of which you must be aware. Don't judge things solely by what you can see of them. But I digress. You asked me a question, and I was showing you the answer.'

Benfro was confused for a moment, his mind muddled by the wine and the tiredness he felt from having held the ball of flame. Then he remembered.

'The fire,' he said. 'You showed me how to handle it, but how do you make it?'

'Good,' Magog said. 'You're learning a little discipline. Try not to be drawn from the subject of your enquiry until you have an answer that satisfies you.'

'So how's it done?'

'Think, young apprentice. You know already how it's done, although you've not yet shown the inclination to do it.'

Benfro stared at the candelabra with its multiple points of flame. He could picture the fire and the twin sconces ablaze somewhere above him. How could he possibly know how it was done? All he had ever done was wish for a flame and it had appeared. Was that all there was to it?

He held up his hand, cupped as it had been when he had held the flaming orb. Nothing happened. He screwed his eyes up, trying to make out the aura that had swirled about him. It was difficult with the dulling effect of the wine pulling his senses apart, but eventually he managed it. He wished the flame would appear.

Still nothing happened.

'I don't understand,' he said, dejected, after some minutes of determined hopefulness had ended in a complete lack of success.

'Wishing for something won't make it so. If that were the case then my brother wouldn't have had to gift the men their magical skills,' Magog said.

Benfro slumped on his bench and stared at the table in front of him, searching for inspiration. There was nothing but his pudding plate, a few sorry fruits still heaped to one side, along with the hard skin of the melon he had consumed. And then it hit him. The food had come from all over the world. Why not bring fire that way as well? And for that matter, why not bring candles, firewood, furniture – anything? But how was it done? It was to do with the Llinellau, that much he knew, but how did it work?

He stared at the candelabra again. Where it sat in the middle of the table two fine Llinellau intersected. Neither of them passed where he was sitting, but other lines, finer still, branched and forked their way to him. He studied one route, then another, looking for something in them but not quite sure what. For a moment the task absorbed him completely and it felt as if he were travelling down each track, stopping, backing up and starting again. He had read of mazes grown from vast hedges and designed for amusement, although, having himself been hopelessly lost, he was unsure of what fun there was in getting so on purpose. This was a bit like he imagined a maze to be, but the task was strangely compelling, almost addictive.

A candle flame was his centre of attention now. It was a goal that needed to be reached. He knew there was a correct way to get there; it was just a matter of seeking it out. But what would he do when he got there? The question came too late as he finally found the path.

It was difficult to describe. He was sitting on the bench, staring at the nearest candle on the candelabra, but he was also in the flame, surrounded by its fire and heat, yet untouched by either. For a moment he could feel the panic rising in him, but he fought it down. There was no cause for alarm. Surely he could not be hurt by a candle.

He reached out, at once aware that he lifted his hand above the table and that he grasped for the flame that surrounded him. The flame had the same tingly quality as the orb that Magog had made, brushing his aura as he tried to get a grip on it. Like runny mud, it slipped and slithered through his fingers, defying his grasp. Frustrated, he tried to encase it in a ball, which he extended from his hand. To his surprise this seemed to work. Now all he had to do was get the flame back to his real hand.

Even though he had managed to find the route to the candle flame, it was just as difficult, if not more so, to retrace that strange path. The route back to his self was not as obvious as he had assumed it would be. The criss-cross pattern was a confusion of light. The Grym was intoxicating, pulling him this way and that like a fallen leaf in an autumn storm. He began to panic again as he became lost in the maze. It was frustrating too, as all the while he was sitting on the bench and staring at the candelabra.

It felt like he could go anywhere, but everywhere clamoured for his attention. He could hear the sounds of laughter and screaming, waves crashing on a shore and the moan of wind in the trees. He could smell flowers and honey, the stench of blood and the reek of burning flesh. There were places of perfect quiet and scenes of such breathtaking beauty he had to close his eyes to stop being drawn to them. Even then he could still feel their pull. And all the while he had to concentrate on the thin web of aura restraining the fire and keeping it from burning him.

There had to be some way of identifying his self in the roaring growing tumult of everything that battered his senses. He knew himself like he knew nobody else; if only he could latch on to that uniqueness that made up Benfro. Fighting to suppress the fear that lapped at the edges of his reasoning, he tried to think of a memory that was uniquely his. It came straight to him – a lifeline that he would rather drown than take – his mother, subservient, prostrated; cruel malevolence personified in those burning red eyes; a blade of fire conjured from nowhere like the flame he now held but shaped into something far more deadly; a death as brutal as it was pointless.

With a snap he was back in his body, and in his hand burned a tiny orb of flame. He should have been proud, but the visceral memory poured cold grief on any other emotion he might have felt.

'Thirty minutes,' Magog said, his voice flat, uncomplimentary but at least not sneering. 'I'm impressed. Most novices your age can't stay in the stream for more than ten. I fully expected to have to come in and get you out. Using such a visceral memory as an anchor was inspired, if a little unorthodox. And you even managed to bring back the flame. You'd better put it out though, because any minute now you're going to faint.'

Melyn strode with angry haste, his palms itching to do someone harm. His personal guards followed him along the endless corridors of Emmass Fawr at a short distance, none of them anxious to get too close, he presumed. Their cowardice only fed his rage. Then, as they turned a corner, Captain Osgal came into view, his face red, his breath short.

'Despite or perhaps because of your inability to carry out the most simple of tasks,' Melyn said, 'I have the boy. He's under guard in my personal chambers. Perhaps you'd like to explain how he turned up in the inquisitor's chapel? Didn't I tell you to take him from there and cast him into the Faaeren Chasm?'

'He disappeared, Your Grace,' the captain gasped. 'I

threw him off the edge, and he just vanished. He hadn't fallen more than a few feet. I searched around the cliff, but there's nowhere to hide and he wasn't even conscious when I—'

'And you expect me to believe you? You expect me to believe that some force more powerful even than me rescued a condemned traitor from his just punishment.'

'Your Grace, that's what happened. I swear by the Shepherd.' Osgal dropped to his knee, bowing his head in supplication.

Melyn was about to strike the captain for blasphemy but checked himself. He knew well enough that Osgal had carried out his task; the man didn't have the imagination to do anything else. There was no point wasting his anger on those loyal to him.

'We'll talk of this later,' he said. 'Right now we've a medic to track down. Take some of the guard and sweep the whole monastery. I'm going to check the mortuary.'

Osgal departed with half of the guards and the air of a man reprieved. Melyn watched him go then led the remainder of his men down the long steps into the depths of the mountain and the halls of the dead.

It had been many years since last he had come to the mortuary. He had forgotten how cold it was, cut off from the Grym by so much solid lifeless rock. And he had forgotten that smell of dead flesh; not rotten like a battlefield after the fray, but just as disturbing.

The long vaulted room was lit by torches, their black smoke disappearing through holes in the ceiling. Mostly they cast more shadow than light, but at the far end a number of lamps had been rigged up with glass lenses to illuminate a small working area. There was a desk cluttered with papers, jars, medical instruments and several heavy books. There were a number of wooden scroll boxes shoved against one wall beside a deep sink stained with centuries of strange chemicals and blood. An arched doorway led through to the storage room, where cadavers lay in narrow alcoves carved from the rock.

Melyn grabbed a torch from its sconce and went through. There was no sign of the medic, but something else had been bothering him, and now that he was down here he realized what it was. It didn't take him long to find what he was looking for, and he directed two guards to carry the covered stretcher back into the autopsy room.

Melyn pulled back the sheet and looked at the well preserved corpse. 'Princess Lleyn, it's been a while.' Behind him one of his warrior priests made retching sounds but Melyn ignored him, concentrating on the body. It was very well preserved, but that was to be expected of gallweed poisoning. Under her leathery skin the princess had dried almost to nothing, her limbs tight in agonized contortion. Usel had made some effort to lessen this, cutting open joints and slicing tendons, but the princess was not a beautiful sight. Her head was tipped back as if she were screaming; her stiff belly was still round with the shape of the child she had carried. She looked like a corpse giving birth.

But where was the child? Melyn bent close, looking carefully at the cuts. He was not trained in medicine, but even he could tell the difference between Usel's work and the incision that had been made before the princess had been buried.

'Bring that light closer,' he barked at one of the guards, cursing his inability to conjure up light in this lifeless place. The guard was hesitant and stepped back again as Melyn put his hand through the incision in the corpse's abdomen, feeling for the dead heir that should have been inside.

'By the Shepherd, man, she's been dead for fifteen years,' he shouted. 'Now stand there, still, or I'll suck the life out of you to make a light for me to see by.'

It was hard work, but slowly he managed to inveigle the egg-shaped form out of Lleyn's dry womb. Finally he held it out to the light, turning it over in his hands, inspecting the detail of its construction as his rage grew ever greater.

'Find Usel. Put every warrior priest on to it. Post his name around the whole country. A reward of a year's salary to the man who brings me his head.' Melyn weighed the object in his hand, observing the perfection of its form. He had not seen magic of this skill performed in many a decade. 'No, make that ten years' salary.'

He almost ran out of the mortuary in his haste to get back to his chambers. He needed to contact Beulah with utmost urgency, but even more importantly he needed to see Errol, to make sure that the boy couldn't escape him again. And such was his preoccupation that he forgot completely the homunculus clutched in his angry grip.

Beulah lay on her back and stared at the dark ceiling. She was exhausted, but it was a deeply satisfying exhaustion that made her arms and legs feel weak and burned in her belly like a warming fire. Beside her Clun slept, his breathing so light he could almost have been dead. She worried that she might have been pushing him too far, not that he was an unwilling partner in their lovemaking. But he was still not fully recovered from his wound.

Or maybe he was. Maybe she simply wouldn't let herself accept the truth because she wanted to keep him close by, to tend him and care for him the way she had never been cared for. She liked him being dependent on her as much as she liked his naivety and inexperience. And there was no real reason to worry about him leaving; despite their ongoing physical relationship, outside the bedroom Clun still treated her with the deference due to his queen. He was still awkwardly coming to grips with the nuances of royal protocol and finding out the hard way that not everyone was prepared to think the best of people until shown otherwise.

It was amusing to watch the various reactions to rumours of the affair. Some noble families acted as if nothing were happening at all, still pressing their suits and jockeying for position to provide a consort to the queen, a father to the royal heir. Others had melted away from Candlehall, returning to their provincial seats to nurse bruised egos and plot how to make the most of the new situation. Within the palace itself there was a buzz of disbelieving excitement, as if the servants were all living in a daft fairy tale. Even now Padraig was laying the foundations of a story that would make Clun appear an eminently suitable consort. Favours would be called in, old skeletons aired and a hundred and one other ways found to exert pressure on the noble houses until they all agreed. Beulah didn't much like the seneschal, but even she could see he was a master of the art of politics.

'Your Majesty.' The voice was a tiny whisper, almost an idea rather than something she had heard. Beulah knew the voice, and with little effort she slipped into the aethereal. Melyn's figure materialized at the side of her bed.

'Melyn,' she said. 'What perfect timing.'

The inquisitor looked around the room, saw the sleeping Clun. 'I see you've ignored all the advice Padraig and the others have been giving you.'

'Clun is sweet and innocent and heroic, and I thank you again for sending him to me as a gift,' Beulah said.

'It pains me to say this, but you'd do well to take Padraig's advice,' Melyn said. 'And if you must marry Clun, it'd be better if your belly wasn't swelling at the time.'

'I wasn't born yesterday, Melyn,' Beulah said. 'It's bad enough that I've got to produce an heir; I'll not do anything to cast doubt on his legitimacy. But I'm guessing that's not what you came looking for me to talk about.'

'Perceptive as ever, Your Majesty,' Melyn said, and for the first time since his appearance Beulah realized that he was talking to her while riding a horse. In the darkened aethereal bedroom his legs were hidden by the bed, and he was gently rocking back and forth as if playing with himself. It was both funny and curiously unsettling.

'I'm on my way to Candlehall as we speak,' Melyn continued. 'I have the boy Errol with me. Or should I say your nephew Errol.'

'What!' Beulah dipped back into her conscious body for a moment, losing the image of the inquisitor. Cursing, she let herself sink back down into the mattress and willed herself to relax. Melyn rippled back into view as she slowly tuned her mind back.

'You shouldn't rely so much on the throne to help you, Beulah,' the old man said. 'It makes you feel powerful, but you'll end up like your father if you let it get too deep a grip on you. Soon you won't be able to perform even the simplest of spells without it to help you.'

'Yes, yes,' Beulah said. 'You can lecture me on the uses and abuses of power any time. Tell me about the boy.'

She listened intently as the story unfolded, not interrupting the inquisitor with all the questions that flooded her mind. Only when he had finished did she speak.

'You're right to bring him here,' she said. 'Together we should be able to break down whatever natural defences he has. I've no doubt we can uncover his little secret. But you mustn't let anyone know his true parentage.'

'Don't worry yourself on that account, Your Majesty,' the inquisitor said. 'We'll find Usel; he can't have got far. And I'll soon root out any traitors at Emmass Fawr.'

'I was thinking of Errol's mother,' Beulah said, glancing over at the sleeping Clun beside her. His aethereal form was, if anything, even more perfect than his physical body. 'It's a pity, really. But you'd better deal with her husband as well. You never know what she might have told him on their pillows.'

'It will be done,' the inquisitor said. 'I'll send Captain Osgal. He's dependable. Terrible, what bandits in the western woods can do to a merchant's caravan. We should be with you by the end of the week. I expect Clun will receive the bad news about his father a few days later.'

'Make it quick and painless,' Beulah said, not quite knowing why she cared.

'Your Majesty.' Melyn nodded his acceptance of her

order and faded from sight. Beulah stayed in the aethereal for a few moments, letting her mind slip through the palace nearby. There were few souls awake, guards mostly, though further away the city bubbled with life. Her people, her subjects, and she intended to keep it that way.

23

Perhaps the most difficult magic a dragon can perform is that which is focused on himself. History is littered with tales of hopeless young lads desperate to win favour with their beloveds attempting to improve the hand that fate and heredity have dealt them. In the more harmless examples, such as that of Sir Blinedig, the result was no worse than that every animal for a ten-mile radius became besotted with him and could not leave him alone. Myfanwy of the Crimson Scales was so disgusted by the constant trail of beasts that she left the valley where he lived and fled to a faraway land. For the rest of his long life Sir Blinedig had only the animals as his companions.

More salutary, perhaps, is the tale of Godrwys teul Gwynhyfyr, who tired of the taunts of his peers that he was weak both in body and in the ways of the Grym. In attempting to prove them wrong he succeeded only in turning himself into stone. To this day his statue resides at Cenobus, its unreckoned jewels unreachable and slowly fading away into nothing, his memories lost for ever to dragonkind.

Yet the most remarkable and daring magic turned upon the self concerns the great mage Magog, and none knows if the story be truth or yet another of the myriad legends that have grown around his mysterious disappearance. For it is said that he found a way to take some of his own jewels, the sum of his being, and hide them in a place of great power. Here, it is said, they watch over the world, experiencing everything, influencing everyone and waiting for one to rise who might act as a vessel for the great mage's return. It is to be hoped that this is mere myth, for if true it is the most monstrous of all magics.

Corwen teul Maddau, *On the Application of the Subtle Arts*

Errol remembered almost nothing of his journey to the Neuadd. Laid on a straw pallet in the back of a wagon, he slept as much as he could, and whenever he woke enough to talk, someone would force a sleeping draught down his throat. He didn't really mind; asleep he could forget about the pain, escape from his endless cycle of woes. In his dreams he flew with dragons and walked the forests with Martha by his side.

At Candlehall they had the decency to wash him and give him fresh clothes. Someone even replaced the bloody bandages around his ankles. His hair was still wet when a pair of guards carried him through the courtyards and into the great hall of the Neuadd. Melyn walked in front of them as they approached the huge throne, and in any other circumstances Errol would have been fascinated by the place. Now, however, his mind was dull with days of drugged sleep. He couldn't stand unaided, so when the guards stopped at the edge of the dais leading up to the throne, he crumpled to the ground in an untidy heap.

'This is the boy?' a female voice asked.

'Errol Ramsbottom, Your Majesty,' the inquisitor said.

'Stand, Ramsbottom.' Errol felt a command behind the voice, but he was used to such manipulation and shrugged it off. Looking up, he stared at the face he had first seen on his mother's wedding day. She looked older, though not much more than a year had passed since then.

'I said stand, Errol.' Again he felt the compulsion behind the words. Shaking his head he noticed for the first time a dragon sitting at the side of the throne, her head bowed as if in deep shame. She was bedraggled, thin and totally pathetic, tethered to the throne by a silver chain. It was such an incongruous sight that he thought he was dreaming it. Then the beast looked up and caught his eye. He recognized the dragon who had appeared to him in that strange trance outside the inquisitor's study so many months ago.

'Frecknock,' he said, and the dragon's eyes widened in surprise.

'How dare you ignore your queen,' Beulah said. 'Stand. I command you.'

Errol dragged his gaze away from the dragon and addressed the queen.

'Your Majesty, I can't stand. Both my ankles are broken.'

'Bring him here,' the queen commanded the guards. Errol winced as he was once more lifted and then carried up the steps, closer to Beulah and her pet dragon.

'Why can't you be like your brother?' the queen asked.

'I don't have a brother . . . Oh, you mean Clun?'

'Yes, Clun. Honourable, brave and handsome Clun. He took a crossbow bolt that was meant for me. Did you know that?'

'I . . . No . . . Is he all right?' Errol was confused. One moment the queen was anger personified, the next she seemed sweetly innocent.

'He is now,' she said. 'After I nursed him back to health. Now I'm minded to reward him for his selflessness by making him a duke and taking him as my consort.'

Errol's head reeled. Without knowing quite why, he turned once more to the dragon and asked, 'Is this true? Is Clun here?' For her part, Frecknock seemed to shrink at his words, burying her head under her arm.

'What did you say?' Beulah snapped, not friendly any more.

'He asked if what you said was true.' The inquisitor stepped forward and grasped Errol's chin, dragging his head round so he could stare into his eyes. 'Where did you learn Draigiaith, boy?'

'I don't know,' Errol said. 'It just seemed the right thing to say. To a dragon.'

'And how many dragons have you met in your life?'

'None. Well, unless you count the one that escaped from Ruthin's Grove. I only saw him.'

'You're a poor liar, Errol,' Melyn said. 'Yet somehow you manage to keep the truth from me. Well that ends here. Your Majesty?'

Errol felt a surge of fear as Beulah fixed him with a sneer. 'Go,' she said to the guards. Unsupported, Errol fell to his knees. 'All of you, leave,' the queen said. 'Except you, Melyn. I might need your help with this.'

One by one the guards and other servants left the great hall. Errol heard their footsteps echoing on the shiny floor, fainter and fainter until only he, the queen, Melyn and the dragon remained. He felt the tendrils of thought in his mind long before anyone said anything. They were different to Melyn's as much as they were different to King Ballah's. They were gentle, almost subtle and soothing, reminding him of his mother looking after him when he had a cold. But they were also insidious and powerful, picking open memories he had forgotten himself.

'Sir Radnor,' Beulah said after a long silence. 'These dragons do like to give themselves honorifics. But surely to be a knight you must have a king. Where's the king of the dragons now?'

'It's a sign of recognition and respect. it means you're recognized as the head of your family.' Errol remembered everything now. It was as if the queen had unpicked a seam, and now all the stuffing of his past life was tumbling out. A confused mass of images that had been locked away. It swept up the false past that Melyn had created for him, the past he had been trying to unravel and separate from what he remembered as true. He couldn't think, had no control over the cascade of images that whirled about inside him. He could feel the tendrils of Beulah's mind whipping about inside his head, trying to get a grip on the maelstrom with little success. The more she failed, the more frantic she became and the more power she thrust into him. It was discomfiting at the start, but soon the sensation began to burn. He could feel his fingers twitching, out of control. Then his arms began to

409

spasm, his torso and legs. And still the queen pushed harder into his mind.

The queen.

Beulah.

An image flashed through Errol's mind, and with the last of his will he latched on to it, held it like he had never held anything before. A young body, fit and curved and naked. Sweat sheening toned healthy skin, freckled face flushed, lip bitten with concentration, eyes savagely triumphant.

The queen.

She gave a little shriek of angry surprise. Shouted, 'Why you . . .' And then the tendrils in his mind turned out the lights.

'You can't begin to understand the subtle arts until you've learned what it means to be a dragon,' Magog said as Benfro tried hard not to complain about having to memorize passages from an archaic leather-bound tome called *Educational Notes for the Young* written by some dragon called Aderyn. Along with several history books it was all he had read in days. The great mage had taught him no more tricks since he had conjured the flame, insisting instead that he learn about his heritage.

'But I am a dragon,' he said.

'Are you?' Magog asked. 'Were you a true dragon before I gifted you your wings? Even now you don't know how to fly properly. And what if I was to ask you to fetch me a borguril, would you know where to find it? Do you even know what it is?'

Benfro didn't answer. As ever Magog was right, but it wasn't easy to admit it.

'I know it's hard, Benfro,' the mage said. 'I may be old, but I remember when I was your age. I wanted everything to happen now. And I was certain I knew better than my elders.'

'I don't think that,' Benfro said. 'I just want . . .' He stopped as the great mage froze. Magog held himself perfectly still, and something seemed to go from the room for a moment. Then he shuddered and dissolved into nothing.

'I must attend to a small matter.' His voice echoed in Benfro's mind. 'Keep studying that book. Learn what it means to be a true dragon. I will return soon.'

And he was gone.

It wasn't like the times when the mage had simply not been visible. Even then Benfro had been able to sense his presence. He hadn't realized it until now, but Magog had always been there in some indefinable manner. And now he was gone. Utterly. Benfro sat at his reading desk, staring at the space where the great dragon had been. Where the image of the great dragon had been, he reminded himself. Magog was dead; what he saw was a memory of him. Like Corwen.

But he couldn't be like Corwen, could he? Corwen's jewels had been reckoned and placed at a nexus of the Llinellau. Magog's one remaining jewel had lain at the bottom of a pool for thousands of years. How could the mage be here in this place at all?

Gazing down at his hands and arms, Benfro could see

his aura dancing with livid colours – yellows and greens and violets. And there, snaking away from him like some monstrous leash, the thinnest of tethers hung pale as a water-washed wound. It looped through the air as if it had been twirled and had not yet fallen back into shape. A rose cord tying him to Magog. He followed its progress across the room, but he didn't need to look to see where it went. The flickering slippery spot just behind the chair sucked at his very essence like a drain, making his head spin just to think about it.

Steadying himself, Benfro sat down and rested his head on his hands, elbows splayed over the tabletop. The book laid out in front of him was a history of the Ffrydd, but he no longer had any stomach for tales of Magog and Gog forging the world to their own warped way of living. The subtext he had not seen before was plain to him now. Those two all-powerful mages had taken a peaceful and harmonious place and ripped it apart out of sheer blink-ered arrogance. He couldn't even see how dragons had benefited from their excesses. And now one of them was trying to destroy his soul.

Slamming the book shut, he carried it over to the bookshelf and put it back where it belonged. Then he picked out another at random, taking it to the desk before even reading the title.

It was old, and felt heavier than it should have done, a bit like the *Llyfr Draconius* that Frecknock had stolen from Sir Frynwy. Benfro wondered what had become of the old dragon's library. Had it burned with his house, or had the men taken it away? And what terrible secrets would they glean from it if they had?

His momentary panic was cut short as he noticed the title of the book he had taken from the shelf. It was called *The Llyfr Cyfareddol*, as far as he could work out from the constantly shifting words and letters on its dark leather cover. There was apparently no author, just ancient runes packed so close on the pages they seemed to dance with each other. It was almost a foreign language. He knew the words, and if he thought hard, short phrases and even whole sentences made sense, but only until he moved on to the next line, when what had been evident to him before slipped away like a quiet thief. And yet he was fascinated by the book, unable to stop reading.

He lost track of time, sitting there and turning page after page. Sometimes he would flick through with great speed; at other times he stared blankly at one page of shifting runes for half an hour or more. It didn't occur to him that he had not eaten, nor that Magog was still nowhere to be seen. He was completely absorbed by the book.

And then, finally, he turned the last page and closed the leather cover. He couldn't recall any of the book's contents, was not even sure that he had read anything at all. But he felt a curious satisfaction at having completed something. Much like he had felt a lifetime ago when he had put the last stone in place and completed the animal pen. A pleasant weariness overcame him then and he leaned back in the chair, head tilting to gaze up at the ceiling.

The room was ablaze with power.

Melyn knelt in the austere chapel deep beneath the Neuadd. It wasn't quite right, this place of worship used by the royal family. He had been here before, but never felt as at ease as he did back at Emmass Fawr. Perhaps it was the weight of rock above him, or maybe it was the halls of jewels he had to pass through to get to it, the festering power of countless thousands of dragons slain down the generations for the glory of the House of Balwen. It was difficult to dismiss the thought that there were a thousand thousand conversations going on around him, just out of earshot. And in a way there were. The Neuadd was a place of great power, sitting at a perfect nexus of the lines. The jewels directed and refined that energy, making it possible for an adept such as himself or the queen to tap into the thoughts of anyone in Candlehall or even further away. So it shouldn't have surprised him that here, right at the centre of it all and surrounded by the crystal hoard, he should have had difficulty in shutting out the thoughts of an entire city.

But he had to shut them out. He had come here to meditate, to pray and perhaps to communicate with the Shepherd. And this chapel, for all that it unsettled him, was the most powerful place outside Emmass Fawr that he could use. If only he could understand the boy's secret. Then he could move between Candlehall and Emmass Fawr in the blinking of an eye. And if others could be trained to do it too, then they could infiltrate the enemy's castles, take out key people, overthrow King Ballah. But if the Llanwennogs uncovered the secret first . . .

Wrenching his mind back to his prayer, Melyn focused on Brynceri's ringed finger. He carried it with him all the time now, a little piece of the Shepherd's beneficence wherever he went. Here in the catacombs, surrounded by endless ranks of long-dead dragon jewels, its single ruby reminded him of the true path, the power and glory of the Shepherd. It glowed with an inner fire that filled him with joy to behold.

For perhaps the first time in his life Melyn felt that he truly needed to speak to his god. The work of a lifetime was starting to unravel at the edges. All this time he had been doing the Shepherd's bidding, purging the world of his enemies, guarding against the Wolf. And now, when it should all have been coming together, when the final reward should have been in sight, unexpected difficulties were popping up: the boy, the queen's sudden infatuation with a young commoner, the dragon.

'The dragon is of no concern to you.'

With the voice Melyn felt a surge of relief flood through him. The aches and pains of too many days in the saddle were nothing more than a distant memory.

'My lord.' Melyn basked in the radiant joy of his presence.

'And Queen Beulah's chosen will serve her well. But you are right to be worried about the boy.'

'What is he? How can he do what he does?'

'He is an abomination,' the Shepherd replied. 'A union of godless Llanwennog and Balwen's chosen. A servant of the Wolf, his soul is a dark thing, playing with the cubs in the Wolf's lair.'

'His thoughts are difficult to divine,' Melyn said. 'On the surface they seem normal, but beneath is turmoil. I've tried to see his plan, but it slips away from me. His thoughts hurt.'

'You are foolish even to try, my servant. Step too close

to the Wolf and he will devour your soul completely. No, the boy must be destroyed.'

'I have tried, lord,' Melyn said. 'I ordered him thrown into the Faaeren Chasm.'

'And I could have allowed him to die then, but such was not my will. It is important that Queen Beulah see the evil forces gathering against her. This coming war will not be easy for her. She will be assailed by doubts, tempted by the Wolf, brought low with grief and finally triumph over all adversity. The House of Balwen, the people of Balwen, will rise anew from her.'

Melyn felt the joy rise in him. The love for his lord was like first love, all powerful. Nothing would get in its way.

'My blessing be with you, Melyn son of Arall,' the Shepherd said. 'You know what must be done.' And then he was gone.

Melyn knelt in his ecstasy, tears coming unbidden from his old eyes. Slowly the room came back to him, and he realized that he had been somewhere else, somewhere perfect and undeniable. As the audience with his god faded to a cherished memory, so the floor under his knees grew harder and colder. And the whispering thoughts of the city crept up on him again. He found it harder and harder to hold the moment, though he clenched his hands together in prayer. The voices seemed to be goading him, telling him that the boy was more valuable alive. He held a secret, but was that secret so precious that he could forsake his god for it?

No. It was the Wolf tempting him. The boy must die.

But if he could give up his secret first . . .

Melyn struggled with his conscience for hours, praying

for enlightenment, hoping the Shepherd would return and tell him what to do. But his god stayed silent, and finally the inquisitor rose to leave. Only then did he realize that he clutched the king's ring tight in his hand. He had no memory of taking it out of the reliquary on the altar, let alone slipping it off Brynceri's desiccated finger.

It was like nothing Benfro had ever seen before. The Llinellau didn't cross the floor and walls; rather they formed a perfect replica of the room, following the curves of the furniture and fireplace, but hanging in the air like smoke. There were three major lines spearing up from the floor and anchoring the whole framework cage into the space. One of these came through the fire and disappeared up the chimney. One shot up into the vault of the ceiling. The third and biggest pulsed with a swirling light that hurt his head to look at and came from the shimmering spot in the middle of the floor. But this was not the most unusual thing about it, for unlike all the other Llinellau he had ever seen, this one was red and it ended in mid-air at about head height.

Colours bubbled out of it like water from a rising spring. They sprayed out around it, filling the cage formed by the rest of the lines with a sea of light that somehow dissipated into nothing before it reached the walls. Sitting on his chair, Benfro could only watch it for what seemed like an eternity. It was both beautiful and terrifying.

Finally, the image began to fade, replaced by a dull ache at the base of his brain like an echo of his hangover. He fancied he could still just see the Llinellau and the colourful fountain of Grym, but if he focused on any particular place they disappeared like playful ghosts. The point on the floor under the table still shone, as did the bigger spot, which shimmered unpleasantly and made his head ache more. He looked at the fire and realized he could see the source of its endless flame easily, nestling beneath the unburned wood and the flames. How he'd managed to miss it before, he couldn't imagine.

Benfro stood up on weary legs. Replacing the book in the bookcase, he noticed that he was hungry. He turned towards the door and then realized that he knew an easier way to the dining room. It was no more than a step away. Without even thinking, he was there. The dining room was dark, empty. Again without thinking, he imagined the fireplace in the room high above him, reaching out to it as he recalled the candelabra on the table. Almost too easily, the candles burst into light. His place, however, was unset, as was Magog's at the head of the table. He sat and wished for food, but none appeared, nor any water to drink. Relaxing, he tried to imagine what the dragon mage had told him, what Ynys Môn had told him years ago, he now remembered. The Llinellau connected everything, everywhere. With practice you could travel them, but you could also reach out along them and bring things to you. Food, wine – anything you wanted was there for the taking. You just had to know where to look. And how.

The Llinellau opened up to him. There was an endless array, an infinite number of possibilities. He could feel some tug at him, others fend him away. He wanted food, but he didn't know how to find it. There was no sense or logic to the impulses, no way to reason what he wanted into existence. Aware that instinct had served him well before, he cast out in a random direction, hoping to grab whatever came to hand. It appeared in front of him, dropping on to the table with a dull thud.

A turnip.

At least it was food. Benfro picked up the root and examined its white tip and purple skin. It had obviously not come direct from some field, as it was clean and the leaves had been removed from its crown. He put it back on the table and tried again. This time he managed to produce a melon, whole rather than prepared. At first he was not sure what it was, but slicing it open with a talon revealed its secrets. He marvelled at the skill Magog had gained, to be able to produce food, drink, cutlery and crockery all at once. It was an almost impossible task to contemplate, but he had seen it done. For now, though, he would have to be content with his melon.

Sticky but less hungry and thirsty than before, Benfro wondered what had become of his master. Surely many hours had passed since he had disappeared. In all the days he had been learning in the retreat he couldn't remember a time, apart from when he was asleep, when the mage had not been at his side. He had not always been visible, but he had always been there, an indefinable presence.

Perhaps this was a test. Had he been left to his own devices to see if he could manage? The link was still there, the thin red line attached to his aura. Was it his imagination or did it pulse as if it were a tube sucking tiny gobbets of life force away from him? And where did it go if the dragon wasn't in the room?

But the dragon had never been there. Magog was an image, a projection of his self in the same way that

Corwen could appear. And yet how could this be so if Magog had only one remaining jewel and that was many miles away? Benfro looked at the insubstantial leak from his aura into the Llinellau. It twisted away from him as if trying not to be seen, but he could just about follow its trail – under the great chair, across the room to the door and through to the hall beyond. Benfro followed it out. He expected the cavern to be dark, but Llinellau criss-crossed its walls and floor, showing him its shape even if lichen had not glowed on most of the surfaces. The red line shimmered across the floor to the room opposite, its colour deepening as he came closer to the doorway. He paused, knowing full well what lay on the other side, then pushed open the door.

It was still pitch black inside, but as he looked the line started to define the space, rolling out across the void like dawn painting a distant hillside. Others joined it from the sides, forming spokes that met in a hub like a blaze of crimson fire. Benfro stared at the far-off point, trying to make out some form to the darkness. All he could see was the angry red glow, pierced from all sides by slender rods of light. Feeling around the doorway, he thought there might be a ledge, but it was difficult to gauge how wide it was, and impossible to tell whether it was safe. He went back to the dining room and fetched the candelabra, but its candles went out as soon as he left the room. Putting it back, he cast his mind to the fire upstairs, endlessly burning, and wrapped a piece of his aura around it. Stepping back to himself was as easy as pulling on a leather jerkin, but he was still astonished to see the ball of flame appear in his hand. Somehow he felt it should have been more difficult, that it should have taken months of diligent study and practice to master the art. It was almost as if he was cheating, though he didn't know how. Nevertheless, he held the glowing ball aloft and stretched forward into the all-enveloping darkness beyond the door.

The light pushed back the blackness in slow motion, as if it were molasses, cold and sticky. The cavern was enormous, reaching up above him to a massive vaulted ceiling and stretching away in a circle so large he couldn't see the other side. And in the middle, rising from the emptiness as if it floated on air, a slender pillar of rock split the darkness in two. Its top was slightly higher than his vantage point and all the red lines converged on its tip.

From the doorway a rock ledge protruded forward perhaps five feet, then dropped away into nothing. Even holding the orb above his head and peering down, Benfro couldn't make out the water he knew was below him somewhere. To the right of the doorway the ledge became a series of steps hewn out of the wall and descending in a slow spiral. He felt he wanted to get across to the pillar, but this was the only route so he took it.

The treads were greasy and damp, exuding an oily substance that made every step treacherous. Counting his steps under his breath reassured him for a while in the overwhelming space, but soon the mounting numbers and lack of obvious progress conspired to daunt him. He fell silent. Looking up occasionally, he could see the top of the pillar receding, marked only by those livid ruby lines.

Finally the stairs ended in a broad stone shelf. A neat arch in the wall was blocked by a massive wooden door remarkably similar to the one in the repository. It resisted all attempts to open it but a chill breeze squeezed through the gap underneath.

Opposite the door the shelf stretched out into the darkness, narrowing and rising as it did so. Even with his globe of fire, Benfro could not tell if it went all the way across to the pillar, but it was substantial enough to encourage him on. He stepped as lightly as possible on to the bridge, legs tensed and senses tingling for any sign of collapse.

It held, carrying him in a gentle arc across the depths. At its centre the arch was so narrow he had to put one foot in front of the other as if he was on a tightrope. It was a skill he had learned long ago, as a kitling, running back and forth along the fallen tree trunks that spanned the river near the village. So it was no great challenge, though the gaping black depths on either side tugged at him.

The pillar was of the same dark stone as the cavern walls, smoothly carved and coated with slime. An even narrower set of steps wound around it like honeysuckle clinging to a dying tree. They were barely wide enough for him to climb, scraping his left shoulder and wing on the stone as he went. To make matters worse, they frequently sloped away from the pillar towards the void, their slippery coating doing its utmost to throw him off. There was nothing on the pillar to hold on to – no rope, no carved handholds, no iron pegs.

It was slow going, and the climb began to take its toll. Benfro had not noticed the thinness of the air for some time, but neither had he tried to do anything more strenuous than writing and occasionally wandering along the gently sloping passageways of the complex. He could feel his lungs aching with the effort of extracting air. His legs were growing heavier and less responsive exactly when he needed them to be supple and quick. He looked up and was dismayed to see that the top of the pillar was just as far away as before, or so it appeared. But he couldn't stop now other than to rest for a moment. The stairs were too narrow to turn and go back. So he pushed on.

It seemed to take a lifetime. Twice he slipped and fell, staying on the stairs more by luck than skill. Each time he felt it would be easier to lie there in the cold and slime, to sleep for a while. But he couldn't give up now, not after coming so far. And if he fell asleep he would surely tumble off the steps into oblivion. So he picked himself up and forced his weary legs on.

As he reached the top, so the stair narrowed, until he could only climb sideways, hugging the pillar like it was his dearest love. Looking over his shoulder, he thought he could make out the pale green luminescence of the door where he had come in, slightly below him and far off in the gloom. It raised his spirits to think that he had climbed further than he had gone down. But then the stairway stopped.

He was on a narrow ledge not much wider than the length of his feet. Above him, tantalizingly close but just out of reach, he could see the top of the pillar. From this close it burned with a fearsome light and radiated heat. At least this had dried the stone, making it impossible for the slime to thrive. Still he was effectively stuck. He looked at the orb of fire he had made, still floating just above his right hand. He no longer needed it, so he let it extinguish and then reached up, searching the rock for handholds. He found one just above his head. There was also a crack in the stone by his knee that he could get a toe into, if he could just lever himself up a little bit.

It took a long time and caused agonizing pain in his talons, but eventually he managed to wriggle his way to the top of the pillar. He hung there, clasping handholds that were big enough for only one talon at a time, and pulled his head over the ledge to see what lay there.

It was a pile of jewels.

Dragon jewels.

Red dragon jewels.

24

What can be said of the Grym that has not been said before? It is the very stuff of life itself, the force that fills every living thing, from the lowliest blade of grass to the most powerful of inquisitors. It is a power of such immensity that only the tiniest fraction of it, mishandled, can cause a man to burst into flames. Yet controlled, channelled and moulded to the will of a warrior priest, the Grym becomes a weapon of incredible power.

Most novitiates will have seen the blades of fire conjured by the inquisitors and lesser warriors. These are but the most obvious manifestation of control over the Grym. Remember that the power runs through every living thing, gives it form and meaning. Thus it is that one so skilled can use the Grym to manipulate the very core of another man's being. An enemy can be influenced so subtly and so completely that he is content to plunge a knife into himself or the body of his most cherished friend.

The Grym is thus a weapon, but it is much more than that. Not only does it inform every living thing, it also connects them by the most subtle of links. You do not need to be standing beside your target to influence him, nor even to be able to see him. It is enough to know that he exists to be linked to him.

The skill lies in finding that link among the uncountable number of connections in the web of life.

Father Castlemilk, *An Introduction to the Order of the High Ffrydd*

Beulah stared through the bars at the sleeping boy. He was lying in filthy straw, his legs positioned awkwardly so as to take the weight off his ankles. His very existence angered her; that someone could go to so much trouble to make her think he had never been born. After all she had done to right the wrong that was Lleyn's infatuation with the Llanwennog Balch, all the sacrifices she had made over the years, consolidating her power and rebuilding the status of the House of Balwen so that she could carry out her divine mission, for him to suddenly appear was like a slap in the face.

But she couldn't kill him.

It wasn't that she had a problem with eliminating family. Her rise to the throne had been on the dead backs of her less able relatives. She'd only kept her disgusting excuse of a father alive for as long as she had because of the laws of the Twin Kingdoms. And now that she was the ultimate power, she could and would change those laws to suit her needs. Any who protested would soon find out how much she valued the lives of those who opposed her. But that wasn't why she couldn't kill him.

It wasn't even because of the secret ability the boy had. True it would be a weapon beyond imagining, but if it were to fall into the hands of Ballah and his adepts carnage would ensue. And what if it was something to do with his half-breed nature, a side effect of the mingling of the blood of the two royal houses, a hybrid product of the two magical lines. If that were the case then Iolwen's child, already growing within her if intelligence reports were to be believed, could not be allowed to reach term. Better to kill them both, and as soon as possible. But even that wasn't why she couldn't bring herself to kill the boy.

Leaving him, she climbed from the dungeons and walked across the palace complex to her private rooms. She paused at the door to her bedchamber, then changed her mind and continued on to the room where Clun slept. She had asked him to move into her chambers, but he had protested. The first sign of resistance in him, she realized, but he was right nonetheless. It was one thing to visit him, talk with him, sleep with him when she chose; quite another to have him live with her before she had formally taken him as her consort. First he would have to be ennobled, introduced correctly to court society. And then he would become something belonging to everyone, the royal consort. In time she would let go of that much of him, but for now she wanted him all to herself.

And that was why she couldn't kill Errol. He was Clun's stepbrother. It puzzled Beulah why that should bother her. She had ordered the elimination of his father and stepmother after all. But Clun had spoken at such length about Errol and held him in such high regard. Beulah recognized something of the way she had felt about Iolwen. Until her sister had ruined it all by sleeping with the enemy.

Her mind was in such turmoil that at first Beulah didn't notice the different atmosphere in the bedchamber. But as she closed the door quietly behind her she felt an electric sensation, a cleansing that brushed away the concerns in her mind and filled her with energy. It was something she had felt only very occasionally before, and then only in the inquisitor's chapel at Emmass Fawr. The presence of her god.

Clun stood beside the bed, naked as the day he was born. His muscles were relaxed, his stance easy, but a red glow burned behind his eyes as he spoke in two voices: his own overlaid with something richer, deeper and more powerful, a voice that made her knees weak and sent flutters of anticipation through her belly.

'My lady, you worry over nothing,' he said. 'The boy you have locked up in the dungeons is not my brother. He sold his soul to the Wolf and now there is a demon where once Errol Ramsbottom stood.'

'Is this true?' Beulah asked, crossing the floor to where her lover waited. He radiated a fierce heat, and a sheen of sweat glossed his skin.

'He must die,' Clun said. 'And I will grieve for the brother I have lost. But he was lost to me a long time ago. Only now have I discovered the truth.'

Beulah turned towards the door, uncertain whether she should find a guard and order the deed done. But before she could take a step, Clun had reached out and clasped her arm. It wasn't a rough grip, but insistent nonetheless.

'My lady.' He pulled her close to him. His heat was intoxicating, the glow in his eyes seemed to burn into her brain, filling her not with pain but with joy. She could lose herself in him like she had never lost herself before. With a tiny whimper of pleasure she let herself be pulled down on to the bed and kissed the fiery mouth of her lover, her god.

They were like the jewel he had retrieved from the river, but ten times the size and blood-red rather than pale. Benfro could not count their number, but it was more than two dozen. They sat on a circle cut into the stone, which was smooth as marble and carved with strange runes he could not read from his awkward angle. The circle reminded him of a bird's nest, that of some great raptor, perched high on an inaccessible pinnacle. But if this was a nest, then where was its guardian?

Benfro lunged upwards, catching the top of the pillar. The space was small and he was tired, his arms barely strong enough to hold his bulk. With a sickening sense of having done something really stupid, he overbalanced and crashed into the gemstones. They scattered like marbles, cracking together and rolling around the circle. Several tumbled over the edge, falling with a series of horrific clatters as they bounced off the steps, then hitting the water far below. The echoes ripped through the great cavern like the screams of some mortally wounded animal.

And then the screaming merged into one great wail. Benfro looked up and saw a huge dragon flying towards him. Its legs were extended in attack, talons ready to kill. Its eyes blazed with such hatred and anger as he could not imagine. Even Inquisitor Melyn's eyes had not burned with such violence.

'What have you done?' The voice of Magog shook the whole cavern and loosened Benfro's already tenuous grip. The great beast, far more feral than he had appeared before, landed on the top of the pillar and tried to gather the stones back into the circle. But it was an insubstantial image, a pale shadow of its former self. Only the wind from its wings had any true substance, that and the shaking of the whole mountain. Several more of the jewels tumbled over the edge, leaving only six scattered haphazardly about the small area.

Incandescent with rage, the image of Magog, the memory of the greatest mage that had ever lived, turned on Benfro. Its red eyes were so dark they were almost black, sucking the life out of everything around them with an irresistible force. It crouched low until its nose was so close to his that he imagined he could feel its breath, hot and threatening.

'You will suffer for this, stripling.' All semblance of reason was gone from the beast now. Benfro recognized the madness that had tried to drown him at the Silent Stone. This was the true Magog, vengeful and bitter, driven by the need to live for ever at the expense of the souls of others.

'Four thousand years of toil went into this place,' he shrieked. 'The greatest work of magic ever undertaken. Even my foul hag of a brother couldn't conceive of such a spell. And you think to destroy it through idle curiosity?'

Benfro gripped the rock as hard as he could. He didn't know why, but he knew then he had to get rid of those last six stones. Perhaps he could lunge at them and sweep them all from the top, but to do that he needed a secure foothold. He was hanging on by the tips of his talons, and even in his terror and pain that still calm voice in the back of his head was counting the seconds until his arms gave up.

'You have no idea how long it's taken to get you here,' the image said. 'Dragonkind was almost wiped out by that scab of a brother of mine when he unleashed men on this world. I've sacrificed everything to keep your family alive. To keep my family alive. You can't conceive of the time I've waited for your mother, sweet Morgwm, finally to fulfil her duty. Daughter of Biel, who was daughter of Ymlaen, daughter of Eirwen, daughter of Galadrel, daughter of Myfanwy, who was fathered by me. You're the first male dragon to be born since my spiteful brother cast his curse upon my world. And what a disappointment you have turned out to be.

'Well, I've been patient enough.' Magog's image was almost translucent now. 'I cannot wait any longer for you to decide to learn what you should already know. Better for me to take you now. Goodbye, Benfro. It's time for Magog, Son of the Summer Moon, to live again.'

The image lunged forward. Benfro recoiled from the the long scaly fingers reaching towards him, but there was nowhere for him to go. Pain battered at his head like nothing he had ever felt before as Magog reached into his mind, peeling away layer upon layer of the experiences, memories and emotions that were his essence. It felt like his skull was going to explode, too small to contain the millennia of hatred, envy, greed and lust that made up the great mage.

Then it occurred to him what to do, as if a voice had spoken in his mind. Trying to ignore the probing of Magog's memories as they slid their evil fingers into his brain, he imagined his own aura stretching over his body like a second skin, soft and flowing but hard as steel and able to encase fire. With a thought he snapped it tight around his head, relishing the surprise on the mage's face.

'Finally, at the end, you fight,' the image said, astonishment turning into an almost childlike delight. 'And you've learned too, though it will do you no good. My hold on you is total. But struggle by all means. It makes victory all the sweeter.'

Benfro paid no heed to the words, glad only that the feeling of having his mind flayed had evaporated. He concentrated on extending his aura down from his dangling feet and tail to the ledge below. He could not see what he was doing, and dared not look round lest he betray his intention, but the image of Magog was too wrapped up in its monomaniacal glee to notice.

'The world will know fear when I rise again,' it said, bringing to Benfro's mind the oft-stated aphorism his mother had used about chickens and eggs. 'These pathetic wingless creatures that try to be dragons will be destroyed. I will create a new proud and ruthless race in its place. And we will hunt, oh how we'll hunt. What better prey than one that knows fear, one that can anticipate its doom? These men will be sport indeed for my new master race.'

Benfro could feel it now, not quite like he was actually standing on the ledge, but a lessening of the weight on his fingers, a relaxing in his arms that stilled the traitorous counting voice in the back of his head. It was enough to strengthen his resolve. Already he could feel the probing memories cracking the shell of protection he had so hastily thrown up around himself. Without a second thought he tensed his legs and threw himself forward, sweeping out with his arm.

'What?' was all the image of Magog could say before the last six jewels shot off the top of the pillar and arced away into the darkness. As they fell a terrible screaming rocked the whole cavern, loud enough to deafen Benfro and shake his grip loose from the stone. The image stood up, wings wide, screeching with rage, then it leaped from the pillar after the jewels. Benfro watched it go, fading away to nothing as its screams dwindled too. Silence amplified by the ringing in his ears, He tried once more to extend his aura down, hoping to lower himself that way. Too late. His fingers slipped and he crashed back to the narrow ledge, already knowing what was going to happen next. With a sickening crack the ledge broke away from the pillar and he plunged backwards into the abyss.

Errol heard the grating of the key in the lock and felt the squeal of rusty metal as his cell door opened. He didn't move. Even if he could have stood, he wouldn't have bothered. There was no point. They were clearly going to kill him. It was just a question of time. Then it would be all over and he could rest.

His head still hurt from whatever drug had kept him unconscious all the way from Emmass Fawr. His ankles had lost the edge of their initial pain and now just ached constantly. He wasn't sure whether he could feel his toes any more and was disinclined to try wiggling them. His broken ribs still grated with every breath, but their pain had become an old friend. Until he was picked up.

Two guards dragged him through corridors and up

stairs. He briefly saw the morning sky and wondered at the light reflecting off the glass windows of the vast Neuadd. But before he had time to collect his thoughts, he was being swallowed up by its open doorway, gulped down into the belly of the beast.

It was much as it had been before. There were few people in the vast hall. Guards stood to attention at all the doors; a thin-faced elderly man sat at a desk to one side of the dais, and in the huge black throne Queen Beulah lounged against one massive stone arm. Inquisitor Melyn sat upon a small wooden chair. The dragon was curled up as small as she could manage, trying to find a spot behind the throne where she wouldn't be noticed. Another man stood beside the queen, tall and strong, and as he was dragged closer, Errol recognized him.

'Clun.' His voice was little more than a hoarse whisper, but his stepbrother would not meet his eye, turning instead and gazing at the queen.

'Do you know this traitor?' she asked him.

'No, my lady.' It was unmistakably Clun's voice, and yet different too, as if someone else was operating him. Someone who didn't know how Clun spoke. 'I knew a boy once who looked like this one, but he died a long time ago.'

'What? Clun, it's me. Errol. Look.' He would have said more, but one of the guards cuffed him hard across the face.

'Don't speak unless ye're spoken to,' he hissed.

'Bring him here,' Beulah said, and once more Errol found himself being lugged up on to the dais.

'Hold him up.' The queen stepped down from her throne and walked towards him. She was dressed simply but elegantly, in clothes that were practical rather than the ornate frippery normally associated with royal courts. Errol couldn't read her face, and he really didn't want to feel her walking through his mind. Desperate, he cast his head sideways, taking in the details of the Neuadd he had missed before: the elegantly carved walls, their details smashed away; the massive stained-glass windows, all random pieces like a jigsaw puzzle hammered together by an impatient toddler. Even the floor slabs bore the marks of some great design, but they had been lifted and replaced so as to obliterate it almost completely.

'What happened to this place?' he asked. His reward was another fist to the face. Dazed by the blow, he looked down at the floor and spat out a bloody tooth. Then he noticed something that hadn't been there before. The pattern on the floor was a curling tail, and the slab next to it continued the motif. Looking up, he saw the windows made whole, their many-coloured panes depicting a scene that sparked memories of a tale he had been told of dragons ruling the world. Names came to him: Rasalene and Arhelion, Palisander of the Spreading Span, Maddau the Wise. They were here in glass, their tales unfolding from window to window. The carvings on the walls continued the telling so that the whole fabric of the Neuadd was one great story.

'Dragons.' He tried not to laugh because that only made his ribs hurt even more. With the words and the pain the reality of the vandalized hall reasserted itself. But he knew that what he had seen was the truth. 'Dragons built this place. Like they built Emmass Fawr. We're just rats scurrying around in their halls after they've gone.'

He sensed the blow coming and tensed for it, closing his eyes. There was a loud slapping noise, but he felt nothing, and when looked again it was to see Queen Beulah standing close to him, her hand clasped around the guard's gauntleted arm.

'Enough,' she said, then turned her attention to him. 'Are you really a rat, Errol Ramsbottom,' she asked, 'or are you just a traitor?'

'I'm no traitor, Your Majesty.'

'Just a rat then.' Beulah smiled a cold heart-stopping smile. 'Do you know why you're here?'

'No, ma'am,' Errol said.

'Well, let me enlighten you then,' the queen said. 'You're here because you have deceived your order. Normally a novitiate would be cast into the Faaeren Chasm for that, but I understand you already have been, and survived. How is that possible, Errol Ramsbottom?'

'I don't know, ma'am.' Errol wished that she would just get on with whatever it was she intended doing.

'Do you think the Shepherd saved you?'

'I wouldn't presume to know his will, ma'am.'

'Or have you sold out to King Ballah, given your soul to the Wolf?' The words hit Errol with brutal force. Queen Beulah wanted him to confess, here in front of witnesses. Then she could take him out into the city and have him ritually executed. It would be a long drawn-out process of excruciating pain. Suddenly he wanted to live, to escape. Anywhere had to be better than here. If he could just find a way.

He searched for the lines, casting out with his mind, ignoring all the distractions around him. They swam into his vision like great fat fish. Huge coils of unimaginable power radiated from all directions. And all of them converged on the great mass of the throne. It was a vast powerhouse, tapping the energy of the whole world, and he could use it to go anywhere. If he could just work out how to do it.

A red-hot fire blossomed in Errol's chest as he felt along the nearest line for escape. It suddenly became hard to breathe, and the fat lines of power faded from his sight. His eyes snapped into focus on the queen once more. She was shaking her head slightly, her eyes looking below his face towards his chest. The strength seemed to leach out of his neck, and his gaze dropped too, to where Beulah's outstretched arm stretched towards him.

'Can't let you run off like that.'

Her hand was wrapped around the hilt of a short silver dagger. The rest of it was buried in his chest. Errol could feel the life ebbing away from him, the room darkening. He wanted to say, 'Thank you,' but he lacked the strength even to mumble that much. The last words he heard were the queen's.

'Throw his body to the dogs,' she said.

Benfro plunged through the black, tumbling head over tail. Instinct had pushed him away from the pillar as he lost his balance, so at least he wasn't crashing into it as he plummeted. When he swept the last of the jewels away, the light had faded, the red spokes of the lines winking out as if they had never been. Now he fell in darkness with only the swirling colours of his aura for company.

He wondered why he did not spread his wings. He had

leaped off the cliff top in Corwen's clearing so many times he could now do it with his eyes closed. He tried to open them slightly, angling to catch the air enough to right himself, though in truth he could not be sure which way was up. The action took more effort than he expected and he had to extend his wings to their full reach just to slow himself. The air was not just thin to breathe, he realized, it was thin to hold him up as well.

Trying to build a picture of the cavern in his mind, he brought his wings together in a great sweep against the direction of his fall. Miraculously he didn't crash into a wall or the pillar, but he was flying blind. The effort of holding his wings open was almost too much for him to bear. He didn't know how far he had fallen or how much further there was to go. And while he knew there was water below, he didn't know how deep it was. Some instinct flickered in his mind then and he banked away. His tail clattered off stone, sending stabs of pain up his spine. It was hard to tell if his sight was working, because everything was black about him, but his head certainly felt like the life was being leached from it, and the knot of muscle in his back burned with a fierce agony.

At first he thought he was seeing spots in front of his eyes. Tiny pinpricks of red winked and shimmered below him, coming ever closer as he plummeted. Then he realized he was seeing the scattered jewels spread over the cavern floor. He tried to flap his wings to slow his descent now that he had some reference point. Nothing much happened and it was all he could do to keep them outstretched. At least the jewels gave him a general idea of where the pillar and walls were.

He remembered the water too late.

He hit belly first, and valuable seconds of stunned astonishment passed as he tried to understand what had happened. Cold as ice and crystal clear, he had not seen the perfectly still surface and had flown straight into it. Water crashed into his face, forcing its way down his throat and gullet as his impact drove all the air from his lungs. His outstretched wings, too tired to fold into his sides, took the force of his momentum and wrenched painfully in their sockets, but they kept him afloat.

Spluttering and gasping, Benfro thrashed around in the darkness. He couldn't think, and the water was so cold it was sapping his remaining strength. He could feel it dragging him down, and there was no fight left in him to oppose its relentless pull.

Then his feet hit the bottom.

The water was only chest deep. He stood in it while he coughed and retched and tried to get the rest of it out of his lungs. Once he could breathe properly, he waded through the dark to where he gauged the pillar to be, walking around it and feeling the stone for any sign of steps. There were none, and the surface was a smooth as glass, impossible to climb.

Standing still, with the last of the waves from his impact ebbing away, he finally noticed the noise that had been at the back of his mind all the while. It was the gentle roar of water running over rock. He tried to locate where it was coming from in the darkness, but the cavern was too large, the echoes bouncing off water and walls confusing and disorienting. He needed to see and he needed to get out of the freezing water, but try as he might he couldn't conjure up the Llinellau. If only he could find them, then he could reach out to the fire, so warm and welcoming far above. Or had it too gone out with Magog's passing?

In desperation, he reached out to it as he done before, using only his memory of the place. He didn't expect it to work, but he tried anyway, scooping up the flickering flame, shaping it into a ball with his aura and drawing it back to himself.

Light blazed in his outstretched hand, chasing the darkness away to hide in shadows. There was heat too. He could feel it burning through the inches of his aura. Bringing the orb closer to his chest, he shivered as he tried to warm himself by the captured flame, but it was too weak to make much difference.

Keep moving, he thought, and now that he had light to see by, he could seek out the source of the noise. Wading to the wall nearest him, he saw that it too was smooth, but little rivulets of water ran down its surface from cracks and crevices higher up. He reached for one just above him, but it was too far and his arms were too tired to pull him up anyway.

Something brushed past his leg and in his surprise he nearly dropped the ball of flame. Instead he lowered it to the surface and peered into the clear water. Fish surrounded him, attracted by the light. They were similar to salmon but completely white with opaque eyes. And they were huge, fully the length of his arm. They were quite unfrightened by his presence, swimming around his waist curiously, nibbling at his scales as if nothing interesting had happened to them for many, many years.

As he watched, one of the fish darted away in that

unpredictable manner of their kind. It swam swiftly to the cavern floor and prodded the nearest red jewel, nudging it with its nose until it floated a few inches above the stone. With a single almost vicious gulp, it swallowed the gem-down. Looking around him, Benfro saw a few of the other stones, shining red one moment, then gone the next as the fish gobbled them down. He smiled to himself, unsure whose jewels they had been but certain that a great deal of Magog's power had resided in them. If there were fish in here, there had to be a way out, and if those fish could be encouraged out then the jewels would swiftly be spread over a huge area. The idea warmed his soul, but his body still shivered.

Moving on, he traced his way around the outside of the cavern, one hand on the stone, the other holding aloft his light. He fancied the noise was getting louder, and finally he found its source.

A large arch had been carved in the cavern wall. From what he could see with his meagre illumination, it had stood forty, perhaps fifty spans high at its apex, and almost as wide at the base. Some time in the past it had collapsed, the rubble forming a solid dam which held back this icy lake. Water poured over the top of the barrier, cascading away into darkness, but it was a thin sheet, not deep enough for the salmon to escape.

Benfro climbed out of the water, hauling himself on to the rubble while the fish still clamoured around his light. The stones moved alarmingly under his weight and he could see how the water flowed through tiny cracks in the dam. Carefully he let himself down the other side and into a large tunnel. It wound down and away from him, the embryonic river swirling around its centre. It must, he thought, lead to the outside and escape.

He set off down the tunnel, light held aloft, then he had a thought. Turning back, he returned to the dam, climbed up it and inched across to its centre. There were several large blocks which had been loosened by the constant current. He was sure they would not take much effort to shift.

Benfro lowered the ball of flame to the water. He could see the fish shooting towards it, their fins rippling the surface. Without hesitating, he wedged himself as best he could and heaved against the first block with his feet. It gave way easily, opening a rift that let water pour through. The fish, caught by the sudden current, were swept through the gap to fall, slapping and jumping, on the tunnel floor before being washed away.

The weight of the water caught the next two stones, taking them after the first without any help. Too late he realized what he had set in motion as, one by one, the boulders were peeled off. He stumbled away until his back was pressed against the tunnel wall. Still the deluge ripped apart the weak structure, the gentle stream turning into a raging torrent.

And then the rock he was sitting on went. He fell into the maelstrom, and before he could even think his head was underwater. His attention gone, the aura surrounding his light snapped away and the fire went out. In the pitch black he was turned over and over, banging against wall and floor as he was swept down. But after the initial torrent the water calmed itself into a swift-running river. He tried to get his feet down and his head up, to both stand

and breathe, but the floor was slippery. Eventually he managed to break the surface, gasping for breath as he was borne down the tunnel.

He couldn't see where he was going or where the walls were. He could only feel them each time the current slammed him against the stone. And then he started to make out shapes. Gradually light seeped into the world, harsh and white. Benfro could see the stone around him and the surface of the water. Bubbles and eddies were fascinating things, so long was it since last he had seen natural light. Even his hands looked different as he held them up. Indeed he was so absorbed in the novelty of light that he didn't notice the opening galloping towards him from which the illumination came. At least not until it was upon him.

He shot out of the cliff face in a fountain of white water, and only after he had been in the air for a handful of seconds did he realize that he was far too far above the ground. He twisted and turned, instinctively flinging his wings wide to try and catch the air. But the water covering them froze in an instant, pulling them down and him along with them. Before he could even brace himself, the snow-covered ground slammed into him and the lights went out.

25

In dreams you have the power to take a person wherever you please. An unguarded mind is an easy thing to manipulate, an unguarded mind asleep even more so. Remember this each time you make your peace with the Shepherd and settle down for the night, for there are those around you who would slip into your dreams and do with them what they will.

Be wary for the signs. If you wake feeling unrested and you can remember little of the night, then it is likely you have been under attack. If you find yourself unsure whether or not something you know is true, chances are that you have been told it in a dream. Many a battle has been won before a single drop of blood has been shed, simply because a general has ridden away from the field, convinced the fight is already all over.

Father Castlemilk, *An Introduction to the Order of the High Ffrydd*

'Wake up now. It's time to go.'

Errol heard the words through a warm fuzzy darkness. He was floating in a sea of nothing, his body senseless, the pain gone. He wasn't sure how long he had been wherever he was, and he didn't really care. If this was death then he was happy to be dead, away from the cares of the world, the pain, the random cruelty and suffering. Time had no meaning in the comfortable darkness until the voice came along and ruined everything.

'Come on, Errol. You've got to wake up,' the voice said. It was a pretty voice, a young woman's voice. He knew it from somewhere but he didn't want to think about that. If he tried to remember who it was, then he would have to go back through memories he'd much rather ignore.

'Errol Ramsbottom, I know you're in there. You're not dead. You've got to come back to me now.'

Something fluttered on the edge of Errol's bubble of nothing. It was as if the lightest of breezes played around his fingers, tousled his hair. But it was a definite sensation nonetheless. He tried to fight it, tried to maintain the pretence that he was bodiless. If he had no arms and legs, then no one could hurt him by breaking them. If he had no heart it couldn't be pierced by the queen's silver blade.

The image of Beulah's face leered at him as he fought against the tide of being. She had distracted him with her inane talk, he realized now. Her plan had always been to kill him, but she couldn't let him know that was what was about to happen, or he might have disappeared on her. But why would she want to kill him? What had he ever done to her?

'Errol, come on!' The voice was insistent now. Not Beulah but another strong woman he had known. His mother? No, he didn't want to search his memory. He would much rather be dead. No one could hurt him when he was dead.

His body was getting heavier and it seemed he was lying on a cold stone floor. Something hard and unyielding pressed into his back. He wanted to move, but he couldn't remember how. A part of him flinched at the memory of the pain. His ankles throbbed, and he was suddenly aware of a grating noise in his chest. He was breathing, and his heart *thump, thump, thumped* away, roaring in his ears like a summer storm.

'Errol, wake up now.' He felt hands touch his face. The queen had touched his face, and now he saw her through eyes tight closed, bending over him. She had a dagger. How had he not noticed it before? She was pulling it out, palming it as expertly as a trained assassin. He wanted to stop her, but his arms were paralysed by her stare as slowly, oh so slowly, she reached forward and pushed the blade into his chest.

Errol screamed. White-hot pain filled him like fire exploding in his heart. He snapped forward, hands clutching at his chest, eyes wide open, dragging in a great lungful of air.

'You're alive.' The voice filled with a joy he had not expected. He tried to focus, shaking away the image of the smiling queen. A vision of perfect beauty swam before his watery eyes.

'Martha?'

Magog came to him in his dream.

Benfro knew it was a dream almost from the moment he found himself in it, though he couldn't remember going to sleep, couldn't remember anything. He wanted to leave, to wake up, but he was stuck. He didn't even have the luxury of reacting to events. All he could do was watch as they unfolded in front of his eyes.

At first it was nice. He was flying again, soaring above the trees and mountains with effortless ease despite the slight ache in his left wing, which niggled away at the back of his mind. From his vantage point he could see the whole world stretching away from him in a great dome. Mount Arnahi was directly below him. It reached up into the sky, surrounded by smaller mountains and hills that cut through the land like a crusted scar, puckering as it healed. Beyond the mountains to the east he could see endless blue, stretching away to the horizon. To the west and the south was green, ringed with a great ridge of rock but spilling out through a gaping hole opposite the great mountain. To the north the sky darkened and white snow covered the ground. If there were more to the world up there, he could not see it.

Benfro was fascinated. He was higher by far than he had ever flown, much higher even than the top of Mount Arnahi. He wanted to circle more, to commit what he could see to memory. And he yearned to explore the world. He needed to see all the places laid out beneath him like so many pieces in a game of shards. But he was not in control of his actions. He could only try to remember it all as he folded his wings and dived earthwards.

He plummeted towards the green, building speed so that the air buffeted his face, ripped at his scales and made it almost impossible to breathe. Closer and closer the trees loomed. He would surely crash, surely die. Then, at the last possible moment, he thrust open his wings and pulled back his head. The strain was enormous. It was as if he were trying to lift the weight of his mother's cottage. He felt like his back was going to snap in two, but slowly the dive turned into a swoop. Still falling, but more slowly now, his momentum carried him forward as much as down, and he finally levelled out at treetop height, whistling past the uppermost leaves with a wind that ripped them from their branches and sent them dancing through the air. His tail clipped twigs, and with one great downward sweep of his wings he rose again.

At once he saw where he was heading. A tor rose from the forest like the carcass of some impossibly huge beast, long dead and turned to stone. On its top a once-proud castle stood, its walls now fallen into ruin save for a massive arch marking the entrance. But he was not heading for the top. Instead he skimmed the trees, climbing abruptly towards a cave mouth halfway up the tor's smooth vertical side. A small flat ledge appeared to grow out of the cliff as he approached, and he landed on it with a dexterity he had never mastered before. A quick glance over his shoulder at the forest below and the great mass of the mountain so far distant as to be almost invisible, then he turned and walked into the dark recess of the repository.

It was exactly as he had left it, the great pile of gems heaped at the base of the reading table and spilling over the floor. The pillars marched off in all directions, holding up the low vaulted ceiling and supporting the endless bookcases, map stores, trophy cabinets. In the walls close to him the niches stood empty and waiting. He knew why he was here, knew what it was he was going to do even though he fought it with every fibre of his being.

He bent to the pile, taking a stone from it and feeling the resonance inside. It was like the sound of a question without the meaning behind it – a curious shrug. Unwilling, he picked up another, comparing it to the first. It was not the same so he put it back. He sifted through the piled stones until he had seven that were identical. They felt whole, even as they filled him with a sense of panic and fear. Screaming inside, he carried them over to the wall and placed them in an alcove.

The pile glowed with a livid green when he returned to it. Ghostly images flew from its top, circling in the air, peering at him. He couldn't hear what they were saying, but he could tell from their expressions that they were pleading with him, cursing him, abjuring him. He wanted to stop what he was doing, to apologize and put everything right, but he could only sit in the back of his mind and watch as he picked the jewels out, painstakingly matching them before restoring them, group by group, to their little prisons.

He could see the Llinellau too, spreading through the room, only instead of the pattern he was used to, here all were regimented and false. Tiny thin strands went to each of the alcoves, but none intersected. Individually, each alcove was connected to a single fat red line that began at the table and headed arrow-straight for the far distant Mount Arnahi and its broken retreat. As each alcove was filled, so the pale cord stretching from it turned pink and then red, pulses of something he could not begin to understand being sucked from the jewels. Not Grym for sure, but something more potent even than life itself. It sickened him to see it, especially knowing he was responsible.

'Don't weep for them,' the voice of Magog said. 'They have a great purpose still to fulfil.'

With these words Benfro gained some small control over his movements, the dream of the repository fading into the background. It was still there, if he chose to focus on it, but mostly there was just him, surrounded by an indistinct location, and the dragon mage.

Magog looked smaller than he had done before, but was no less terrifying for that. His eyes blazed with a fiery hatred, beyond insane and now simply evil. His wings were half folded, a pose that allowed their joints to rise higher than his head, twin bony spears of ebony black. His arms were folded over his scaly chest, claws extended to scrape at leathery skin. Benfro could feel himself shrinking under that glare, mesmerized by the thin strand of red that curved from Magog's forehead to his own. Other than that one connection, the dead dragon had no aura at all, whereas Benfro could see the light flickering around himself like a protective shield.

'Don't try to fight me,' Magog said. 'You'll only damage yourself, and you have an important task to complete.'

'Why are you doing this?' Benfro asked, though in his hearts he knew that the dead mage cared for nothing but himself and his own preservation.

'Because of you, young would-be usurper,' Magog answered. 'When you removed these jewels from their proper place, it was annoying. But I'd outgrown them. My knowledge and wisdom was preserved in the pillared hall. My power came from the earth itself. I only had to bring you there and make you ready. But I misjudged your curiosity. I won't do that again. There was just one small task

I had to do. I left you alone for not more than two days and you almost destroyed everything.

'So now, as you can no doubt see, I need to fall back on my old source of power. These jewels go back to the time of great Rasalene himself. They contain knowledge, strength, experience and wisdom. But above all they contain power. You will help me harness that power again. And when that task is complete, you will surrender to me completely.'

Benfro stared around him at the repository. He knew he was standing there, talking to Magog, but he also remembered his fall, realized that he must be lying at the foot of Mount Arnahi. This was a dream. It had to be. But he could feel the anguish and alarm billowing from the pile of gems. It had to be real. Confusion paralysed him, his mind flipping from impossibility to impossibility.

'Ah, young Benfro,' Magog said. 'If you'd just kept to your studies and not stuck your nose where it didn't belong, then you might have begun to understand. I really did mean to teach you all that I know. That way your body would be better able to withstand the strain of holding my consciousness. But you've denied me that luxury now. I'll possess you soon, and when I do it will be needlessly painful and restricting for me. You will feel such pain as you cannot imagine. And then you will cease to exist.'

An evil glint flickered in the dead dragon's eyes, and what might once have been a smile twitched his twisted mouth, thin and cold with wicked glee.

'Now, you've work to do. There is no escape, apprentice. We are joined in a way that cannot be broken. You are my tool and I will use you to rebuild my strength.'

Benfro fought hard against the implacable force that compelled him to sift the jewels and separate them in cruel isolation. His senses sharpened with time until he could hear the wails of anguish as he ripped apart friends, lovers, husbands and wives, parents and children, separating them to a life after death of torment and an inexorable draining away to nothing. He wept for them even as his hands worked away.

Then he found Meirionydd.

She didn't fight him as he lifted her soft-white gems. Instead she talked to him in that quiet calm voice that he remembered and loved second only to his mother's.

'He has a power over you, Benfro – that much you know. But it works both ways.'

'What do you mean?'

'The link between you is a powerful thing. With it he can control you in your dreams, make you do things which I know you don't want to do. But you can use that link to compel him too. Especially now that he's weak.'

'But he's so powerful. He knows so much and controls it all with such ease. How can I hope to compete with such a strong mind?'

'By being true to yourself, Benfro. Magog didn't create you; he only moulded you. He had nothing to do with the first fifteen years of your life. If anyone's responsible for that, then it's us; Sir Frynwy, Ynys Môn, your mother and I. Even Frecknock has had more influence on you than this insane remnant. Remember her, remember us all. That's the key to your redemption.'

Tears came to Benfro's dreaming eyes as he found the last of Meirionydd's jewels.

'I don't want to do this.'

'Then don't do it,' she replied.

He stood up, confusion surrounding him, his mind a flurry of images and memories. He could see his mother standing at the cottage door and calling his name. He sat in the corner of the great hall listening to the measured tones of Sir Frynwy as he told, once again, the legend of Gog and Magog and Ammorgwm the Fair. He dived into the dark brown waters of the river, hearing the advice shouted by Ynys Môn as he watched proudly from the bank. He ran home through the bushes and trees, along paths only he knew, eyes streaming tears and ears still burning at the taunts and abuse hurled at him by Frecknock.

'It's no use, apprentice,' came the voice of Magog. 'You can't escape me.'

'You won't have me. I swear it!' Benfro shouted, writhing against the force that held him. Twin pains hit him hard. One burned in his head, an unimaginable blossoming of white and red and orange. The other coursed through his left wing, stabbing up to the knot in his back and spreading to his shoulder. With the last of his remaining wits he focused on the damage to his wing. It was a real thing, a solid fact, an anchor. He could feel the ground digging into his back, a rock lodged painfully against a sprained joint. His head on fire, he rammed himself hard against it. Pain blossomed from his wing as something went *pop*, but it was a clean, honest pain. It dragged him from the repository, his last vision of the place white jewels tumbling from his grasp and back to the too-small pile at his feet. And then, screaming in agony, he woke up.

*

Errol stared at Martha's face, drinking in every last detail. She had changed in the year and more that had passed since his mother's wedding, that dreadful night when they had planned to run away together. She was older, seemed more mature. Her eyes reflected a depth of experience he couldn't begin to fathom. And there was something else about her.

'Your hair,' he said, his voice little more than a whisper. 'It's short.'

'It's nice to see you too, Errol Ramsbottom,' she said. And before he could be certain they were tears forming in the corners of her eyes, she swept him up into a great hug. His ribs creaked, and the point in his chest where the queen had stabbed him flared as if someone had poured boiling water on to his heart. He tried not to wince, wanting nothing more than for their embrace to last for ever, but something in his manner must have given him away. Martha released him, slowly lowering him back to the ground.

'I'm sorry,' she said. 'That was thoughtless of me. But why did you let them hurt you so?'

'I didn't seem to have much choice at the time,' Errol said. He had begun to take in his surroundings. They were in a stone-walled chamber, where he didn't know. The ceiling was vaulted, the apex of each arch hidden by an ornate carving. Following the arches down, he could see more decoration cut into the stone. And throughout the carvings were unmistakable signs of vandalism, the removal of all dragon imagery.

'We're still in the Neuadd,' he said, and his euphoria at

being alive turned instantly to terrible dread. He hadn't escaped after all.

'The soldiers dumped you here,' Martha said in a matter-of-fact voice. She was running her hands over his chest, feeling his ribs and the narrow slit of a wound over his heart. 'The queen told them to cut off your head and display it on the north gate. I persuaded them not to.'

Errol was going to ask how, but he was knocked back by a wave of sensation. It wasn't pain, far from it. He felt like he had been squatting down and had stood up too quickly. Everything faded yet somehow intensified at the same time. He was aware that he was looking at the room, but he couldn't register any of the details his eyes were seeing. And then slowly everything seeped back to normal. Except that now when he breathed his chest didn't creak and groan. He couldn't feel his cracked bones grinding against each other. And the wound in his chest felt like just a memory.

Amazed, he looked down. There was a neat short scar showing through the tear in his shirt. He touched it and it felt old.

'What did you do?'

Martha just smiled in that way he had always found so annoying. She was busy untying the messy bandages that had been wrapped around his ankles. As the wraps came off, so a sour rotting odour filled the small chamber. Errol tried not to gag even as he realized that it was his own flesh that was putrid. In all the pain of the last few days he had hardly noticed as the sensation had ebbed away from his lower legs. Now there was no feeling there at all.

'Maggots,' Martha said.

'Is it that bad?' Errol asked, wondering if he would ever walk again.

'No, Errol,' Martha said. 'We need to find some. They'll eat the rotten flesh away, clean out the wound so that I can help heal it. I can't do anything more for you here.'

'Then I'm lost,' Errol said. 'I can't walk. You can escape though, Martha. Go quickly before someone comes.'

'I can look after myself,' Martha said. 'And you don't need to walk, silly; just go home. Hennas will look after you.'

'Home?' Errol asked. 'How? Oh.' He blushed at how foolish he had been. So happy to see Martha, so amazed at the power she wielded with such confidence, he had completely forgotten about the lines. But even as he remembered them, so too he remembered his old doubts and uncertainties. He could feel for the lines, see something of the places they went, but he had never mastered their use in the way Martha had. She seemed to step from place to place with ease. He could only see the infinite possibilities, each one calling him with equal force. When his life had depended on it, he had walked the lines without a thought, but that was the problem: if he thought about it, he couldn't seem to do it.

'Remember Jagged Leap,' Martha said. 'Remember Sir Radnor. Call to him if it helps. He's sure to answer. But do it quickly; more guards are coming.'

Errol let the lines flood into his vision. They were everywhere in this place, as if the building had been designed to channel them towards the throne. For a long while he was drawn to its dark brooding presence, fascinated by its seemingly limitless power and the susurrus of uncountable voices that echoed around it. They didn't speak any language he could understand, or maybe they spoke all languages; their jabbering was relentless, numbing and yet strangely compelling.

'Not the throne, Errol,' Martha said. 'It was never meant for you.' And Errol realized that he had been seconds from travelling straight there, right into the lap of the queen.

'Look outwards,' Martha said. 'Look for Sir Radnor.'

Errol tried. He imagined the rock at Jagged Leap, building a picture in his mind. He remembered the sound of the water as it splashed over the rocks, the smell of the trees in the warm summer sun, the feel of the grass beneath him and the gentle breeze. Somewhere along the lines it was there. In a million million possibilities, one was the right place. The place he needed to be. Sir Radnor, he thought. Help me, please.

'Treachery! Guards, to me!' The voice shocked Errol out of his meditation. He looked up to see Inquisitor Melyn at the door to the chamber. His face was red with rage, and as he stepped forward he conjured up a blade of pure white energy in one hand, hurled a ball of flame with the other.

Martha stood between Errol and the inquisitor. She lifted her hand almost casually, and the flame exploded as if it had hit a glass wall.

'Go now, Errol,' she said. 'I'll follow. I found you twice already. Another time won't be hard.'

The inquisitor was almost upon her now, and Errol watched in paralysed terror as more guards appeared in the doorway and spread out along the walls to surround them.

'I can't leave you here,' he protested.

'You can't help me by being here,' Martha said. 'And I'm not leaving until you've gone. So go.'

There was such force in her words that Errol found himself reaching out for the lines without thinking. He knew where home was and how to get there. It was as easy as sliding from one room to the next. But as he faded out of the chamber in the Neuadd the last thing he saw was Martha face to face with the inquisitor and surrounded by a dozen warrior priests.

'Martha!' he screamed, but all around him was blackness. He felt weak and weary, as if the magic that had restored his ribs and healed his wounds in moments was now taking back the weeks from him. He could feel himself slipping into unconsciousness, but he had to make sure he arrived home. Lose control in the lines, and he would be dissipated all over Gwlad. With the last of his strength Errol re-formed the image of Jagged Leap in his mind and cast out towards it.

Something pushed him away.

'It's not safe.' Sir Radnor's voice boomed in his head. 'You must go somewhere else.' And with the dragon's last word Errol felt himself pushed in a direction he hadn't realized existed. It was like falling and standing still at the same time, a nauseating wrenching of his mind. The darkness spun and he felt like he was going to be sick. And then he was lying on dry grass and heather. There was a rich spicy aroma about the place, and a fire crackled warmly beside him.

'Ahh, there you are,' a voice said in Draigiaith. Errol tried to look, wanted to see who had spoken, but a wave of fatigue washed over him. He couldn't open his eyes, and he no longer had the strength to fight. Finally defeated, he surrendered himself to sleep.

26

The mother tree takes many guises, it is said. Some dragons claim to have travelled to the centre of the forest and seen it, standing in all its improbable grandiosity as tall as a mountain and home to all the beasts of the world. Others tell tales of a strange lonely creature, as beautiful as the full moon, coming to them in the hour of their greatest need. Yet more ascribe unusual behaviour by familiar forest animals to its presence, while there are those who swear that they have been touched by its magic even though they cannot recall seeing anything unusual at all.

Given the nature of dragon superstition and the lengths to which some of their kind will go in seeking the tree, it is hardly surprising that a wide range of hallucinations has come to be associated with its presence. Almost any event can be given undue meaning if it coincides with a random change in fortune.

Father Charmoise, *Dragons' Tales*

There was nothing but pain. It was the same overwhelming debilitation he had felt when he had tried to throw away the jewel, only multiplied a thousand times. His muscles twitched and spasmed and his head was so full it felt like it was going to explode. He could see only red, with the occasional flash of white. Noise roared in his ears as if every forest sound were magnified beyond belief. He could hear the desperate singing of morning birds as if they were inside him and clamouring to get out. The roar of the stream over rocks was like a thunderstorm trapped in a cellar. Even his hearts banged away like battering rams at a castle gate.

Everything hurt. His skin prickled and burned at the slightest touch. His muscles were cramped and filled with tiny hot knives. His joints ached and swelled, bursting with acid pus. His stomach churned and roiled as if it were gorged with real fire. And above everything, above the wrecking of his being, he could hear a strong strident voice laughing as it spoke. Magog.

'I will take you now, Sir Benfro of the Borrowed Wings. Here, in this desolate place, your soul is forfeit.'

Benfro tried to fight. He tried to find his aura, to grip the cord that joined him with the object of his destruction. But he was too weak and the pain was too great. He could feel himself slipping away towards the darkness. There was nothing he could do any more. He had used up all his strength just breaking free of the dream, and Magog had been waiting for him anyway. The dead dragon might use his body to destroy mankind, but it would not be Benfro who avenged the villagers for the atrocity inflicted upon them. A pit of despair opened beneath him, and he fell, all sense of self being stripped away.

And then something grabbed him, yanking him back. A voice he recognized but couldn't place rang clear through the fog of his pain.

'Fight him, Benfro. You must not let him win.'

Grabbing the voice like it was a hand extended to save him from drowning, something in his mind clicked. The pain subsided, fading away with a howl that died like a wolf call on the mountain wind. With a gasp he was awake. He could see again, sense his aura around him, ragged and weak but nonetheless intact. The rose cord stretched from his forehead, fading into the distance. He reached up for it, clasping it with his aura and squeezing hard. There was no point trying to pull it away. He knew it was fixed to him with something far more potent than his own magic, but there was no reason why he should let it leach the life out of him.

As he squeezed, so he could feel the strength returning to him, and with it the will to live. He couldn't understand how he had fallen into such misery now that his depression was lifted. It was as if that had been a different person, indistinct and alien to him. With a last effort he extruded a length of his aura and tied it, with one of the locking slip-knots that Ynys Môn had taught him, around the line that connected him to the diffuse spirit of Magog.

Melyn stared at the slight girl standing over Errol's prone body. He knew her from somewhere, he was sure. Perhaps she was a palace servant, but it was of no matter. He would deal with her just as soon as he had seen to the boy. How Errol had survived Beulah's knife he didn't know, but he wouldn't last long against a blade of light.

Shouting for his warrior priests to join him, the inquisitor stepped into the chamber. He called up his blade and for good measure conjured a ball of flame which he threw at the girl. She deflected it with a casual wave of her hand, and in that moment he recognized her – the girl of Errol's dreams, the one he had worked so hard to erase from the boy's memory, the one he had tried to read at the wedding party, who had intrigued him then with her innate ability.

'You can't hope to escape,' he said to both of them as a dozen warrior priests ran in through the door, fanning out to encircle the pair. Then, right in front of his eyes, Errol faded away. There was a flash in Melyn's inner vision as the lines flared out from the spot where the boy had lain. And then he was gone.

'It looks like he has.' A whimsical smile spread across the girl's face.

'Do you think yourself so superior that you dare mock the Inquisitor of the Order of the High Ffrydd?' He wanted to distract her, play for time to get his men close enough to grab her. He was certain that she shared Errol's secret, and he was beginning to understand something of how it might work, but he needed to break her down, to cut open her mind and find out just how she functioned.

'You worry so much over such a little thing,' the girl said. She was surrounded by warrior priests now but didn't seem overly concerned. Directly behind her, Sergeant Oenfach stepped forward, blade of light in one hand, the hilt of his heavy fighting sword raised in the other, ready to deal a concussing blow. Melyn expected to see her topple, but something else happened entirely. First the warrior stopped. His blade faltered, sputtering like a candle out of wax. Then he fell to his knees, light spilling from his mouth and eyes, sword clattering to the floor. He screamed, but no sound escaped from him, only light.

Melyn watched, equally horrified and astounded as the sergeant dissolved in an explosion of the Grym, his life radiating out along the lines in all directions until there was nothing left of him at all. The girl hadn't even looked round.

'What did you do to him?' Melyn asked.

'Me?' the girl said. 'Nothing. He was the one trying to bend the Grym to his will.'

'Oenfach was a skilled magician, a trained warrior priest,' Melyn said. 'What just happened to him? Where is he?'

'He took from the Grym; it took him back. He's everywhere, lighting up the whole of Gwlad.'

The inquisitor sized up the slight girl in front of him. She seemed completely immune to his mental probing, her mind as closed as the vaults deep beneath the Neuadd. Neither was she affected by the aura of fear with which he was filling the room. Any non-adept within a hundred paces of the hall should be quaking if not actually incapacitated by terror at the moment, yet she stood before him unafraid, unchallenged, mocking.

'Seize her,' Melyn shouted to the remaining warrior priests. To their credit they only hesitated a moment before leaping at the girl. But when they met at the point where she had been standing, she was no longer there. Melyn was almost too slow in reaching for the sight, but he thought he saw a flash of light pulse along a great trunk-like line that ran between his legs and out of the door into the great hall of the Neuadd. He shivered involuntarily, spinning on his heels in time to see the girl reappear close to the Obsidian Throne.

'Quickly, to me.' He ran across the hall, extinguishing his blade of light as he went, taking its power back into him. The queen stood before the throne, transfixed. Clun, who had been at her side, stepped into the space between the two young women. He held a short sword, but its point wavered as the inquisitor neared. He seemed torn between his duty to the queen and something deeper.

'Martha?' Clun said.

'You're under a glamour, Clun Defaid,' Melyn heard the girl say. 'But don't worry. I'm not here to do either of you harm. A child should have both its parents.' She looked around the hall, up at the ceiling and across to where Melyn was approaching at speed. It was as if she was looking for something. Then her eyes lit upon the throne.

'Ah yes, of course,' she said.

'Kill her, Clun!' the inquisitor yelled. 'Run her through, boy!'

But Clun seemed powerless, standing like a gently swaying statue between the motionless queen and the slight girl as she walked past him like she might a stranger in a busy street. She stood before the throne as Melyn leaped the steps on to the dais; climbed on to its massive seat as he ran across the short distance. He pulled another ball of fire out of the air, hurling it ahead of him as she stepped back into the dark recesses of the chair and disappeared. The flame erupted with the inquisitor's rage, illuminating the interior of the massive throne for all to see.

The girl was gone.

*

Benfro trudged downhill through the snow-silenced night woods, following the sound of the stream that rilled through the trees nearby. Away from Mount Arnahi and Magog's retreat. He couldn't fly; one wing was damaged from his fall, and little shocks of pain pulsed through his back and shoulder with each misplaced footfall. He had extended a loop of his aura to try and support it in a makeshift sling, but as he grew ever more tired, so it was harder and harder to concentrate.

He didn't dare sleep. Magog was waiting for him in his dreams, he was sure. He'd find himself back at Ceno-bus, sorting out jewels and putting them into their hideous little stone cells. Feeding Magog's power. Letting him grow. Sleep was not an option. He had to find the clearing. Corwen would be able to help him.

The Llinellau taunted him as he stumbled through larger and larger trees. They were everywhere, would take him in an instant wherever he wanted to go, but he was too tired to focus, his mind too full of confusing images and memories. There was nothing for it but to walk, thanking great Rasalene for the full moonlight that showed him the path.

The second night was even harder than the first. Sleep dragged at him, pleading with him to just sit a moment, catch his breath, lean his wounded wing against a mossy tree trunk. Despite his impromptu magic sling, the pain in his damaged joint grew slowly more persistent. He could see, just by looking, that his aura was fading as his strength ebbed away. All his effort of will went into keeping the sling tight and warding off the devil that wanted to evict his soul. Frequently he knelt by the stream and splashed

466

his face, hoping the cold wetness would shock him awake. Even then it was almost too much to stand again.

At one point he caught himself staring at his reflection in the water and couldn't remember how long he had been there. He could almost hear the whispers in his mind, calling him to sleep and delightful oblivion. The realization shocked him awake again and he staggered to his feet. Dawn was once more lighting the sky as he lumbered away, shaking and fearful.

At times he forgot who he was and what he was doing. All he knew was the stream. He had to follow it. That was all. And he must not sleep or stop for rest. Sometimes he would almost drift off as he strode, but each time his wing jarred him awake. It became a game of anticipation, waiting for the next wave of agony to come and drag him back to the real world.

Somehow it was night again, though he couldn't remember the transition from day. The moon rose, lighting the forest with an eerie white glow, as he walked ever on. He fancied he could see ethereal creatures hopping from tree to tree, keeping pace with him. They flew like fireflies, hovering over the Llinellau which criss-crossed the land, flashing in and out of existence. Fascinated, he watched them, trying to guess where they would appear next. He held out his hand, and one swooped through the air before landing on an outstretched finger like a tame bird.

But it was no tame bird; it was a dragon in miniature, a perfect simulacrum of pale, ghostly white. It hopped along his arm and on to his shoulder in a manner that reminded him instantly of the squirrel Malkin.

'Who are you?' he asked, but the creature made no reply. It simply sat beside his head, keeping him company. It was a reassuring presence, a friend when all else seemed dangerous and threatening. He was so happy just to have it on his shoulder it was a long time before he realized that he wasn't tired any more.

Around the dawn of the fourth day the tiny creature leaped into the air, circled his head once and then disappeared. Benfro wondered if he had lost his mind. If he had, it was a more pleasant way to go than Magog had offered. He stooped to the water, took a drink, then stood up again. He had grown so used to the stream that he had stopped looking at it properly. Now he saw a familiarity about it that brought joy to his hearts. He knew this place, had hunted in the woods around him and caught fat fish in the very waters from which he drank. Straining his ears against the dawn chorus, he could just make out the distant roar of a waterfall.

Were it not for the pain in his wing, he would have run. As it was, he jogged as quickly as he could. In minutes he had left the trees and was standing on his old launch pad high above Corwen's clearing. He was home.

He scrambled down the slope to the track, noting with pride how his stone pen had stood up to the winter. The logs still stood piled on either side of the cave mouth, and without a backward glance he hurried in.

The wizened old dragon sat beside the fire as if he had not moved since Benfro's sudden disappearance months earlier. He didn't look up to greet his charge, just poked at the burning logs with a stick.

'You took your time,' he said gruffly.

Benfro stopped. Corwen's tone was all wrong. Surely he should have been pleased to see him? Didn't he know what had happened, what trials and tribulations he had been put through? No, of course he didn't. And everything had changed. There was no way they would be able to go back to the simple cosy existence he had known before.

'I got lost,' Benfro said, which sounded like an understatement. Corwen put down his stick and looked up. There were tears in his eyes.

'I thought I'd lost you too, Benfro. I'm sorry. I underestimated Magog's power. I underestimated his malevolence'

There was a strange smell in the cave that Benfro couldn't quite identify. It made him uneasy and brought an undercurrent of anxiety, grief and helplessness to mind, a bit like he had felt under Magog's influence, but different, older.

'We tried to help you,' Corwen said. 'But you were so far away.'

'We?'

'He arrived here a few days ago. Says he has met you before,' Corwen said, and his eyes were looking past Benfro to the bed of dried grass. Slowly Benfro turned to see, though he knew already what was lying there. The smell said it all. Less pungent, less reeking of its own ordure, and overlain with the stench of festering wounds, nevertheless it was the same smell he would always associate with his mother's murder. A man.

He lay there on the bed, dwarfed by its size and souring the grass that Benfro had collected for himself. He was scarcely alive and so fast asleep as to be almost unconscious. His ragged appearance and terrible injuries were almost pitiable, except that Benfro had no place in his hearts for the people who had brought him so much grief. He wanted to lash out, to kill this pathetic scrap of skin and bone. He could feel the frustration and anger of the past year building in him. Even the emptiness of his stomach could not stop the flame he was conjuring. Hate alone, madder even than Magog, would bring about the start of his vengeance.

Then he felt a hand on his arm. He looked round to see the face of the old dragon tense with concern, and everything drained out of him as if he had been punctured by a kind knife.

'He saved your life, Benfro,' Corwen said. 'Don't give in to Magog after all you've been through.'

Benfro was suddenly very tired, as if the willpower that had kept him going had suddenly run out. He had struggled against all the odds to get back to this place of sanctuary, hoping that Corwen would know what to do. And now he was faced with something he just didn't have the energy to come to terms with.

'What is he? Who is he? Why is he here?'

'His name,' Corwen said, 'is Errol Ramsbottom. He's the true heir to Queen Beulah's throne, though he doesn't know it. As to why he's here, well, he was sent here by a dragon's memories, much as you were. And he's fleeing the persecution of the warrior priests of the High Ffrydd, much like you. I'd say the two of you have a great deal in common.'

Acknowledgements

This book may have burst forth, alien-like from my lone, feverished imagination – perhaps aided by too much late night cheese and a rush to complete my Welsh homework – but an army of people have helped take it from those first strange ideas to the finished product you hold in your hands (or the words on your electronic reading device of choice, I'm not fussy). Thanking everyone individually would be another 130,000 words, but one or two deserve singling out for special praise.

First off, my agent, the indescribable Juliet Mushens. Without her persistence I doubt Benfro would have flown beyond my self-published efforts. Thanks too to Alex Clarke, my editor at Penguin for these and the Inspector McLean books. He and the rest of the team have put a lot of effort into honing my words, and a lot of faith in my little dragon.

A big thank you to all the e-book readers who took the time to contact me when I self-published this book. Especially those who pointed out typos and other continuity errors. Since then the text has been professionally edited, so hopefully this edition is error-free. If any still remain they are entirely my fault.

Thanks too to Stuart MacBride, who persuaded me many years ago that sheep would not make believable villains, even in epic fantasy. I think he's probably right on that one.

And finally, the biggest thank you to Barbara, who first suggested that Sir Benfro would make a good name for a dragon.